Surrender to Me

"Full of steam, erotic love, and nonstop, page-turning action, this was one of those books you read in one sitting." —*Night Owl Reviews*

"Delicious and entertaining, the scenes are unforgettable, and the characters are to die for. Fabulous read!" —*Fresh Fiction*

Delicious

"Too *Delicious* to put down . . . a book to be savored over and over." —*Romance Junkies*

"This one is a scorcher." —*The Romance Readers Connection*

Decadent

"Wickedly seductive from start to finish." —Jaci Burton, *New York Times* bestselling author

"A lusty page turner from the get-go." —*TwoLips Reviews*

Wicked Ties

"A wicked, sensual thrill from first page to last. I loved it!" —Lora Leigh, #1 *New York Times* bestselling author

"Not a book to be missed." —*A Romance Review*

"Absolutely took my breath away . . . Full of passion and erotic love scenes." —*Romance Junkies*

Strip Search
(writing as Shelley Bradley)

"Packs a hell of a wallop . . . an exciting, steamy, and magnificent story . . . Twists, turns, titillating and explosive sexual chemistry."
—*The Road to Romance*

"Perfect for readers who enjoy their romance with a hint of suspense."
—*Curled Up with a Good Book*

"Blew me away . . . a great read."
—*Fallen Angel Reviews*

Bound and Determined
(writing as Shelley Bradley)

"Much sexy fun is had by all."
—Angela Knight, *New York Times* bestselling author

"Steamier than a Florida night, with characters who will keep you laughing and have you panting for more!"
—Susan Johnson, *New York Times* bestselling author

"A searing, frolicking adventure of suspense, love, and passion!"
—Lora Leigh, #1 *New York Times* bestselling author

Theirs to Cherish

SHAYLA BLACK

BERKLEY BOOKS, NEW YORK

THE BERKLEY PUBLISHING GROUP
Published by the Penguin Group
Penguin Group (USA) LLC
375 Hudson Street, New York, New York 10014

USA • Canada • UK • Ireland • Australia • New Zealand • India • South Africa • China

penguin.com

A Penguin Random House Company

This book is an original publication of The Berkley Publishing Group.

Library of Congress Cataloging-in-Publication Data

Black, Shayla.
Theirs to cherish / Shayla Black.—Berkley trade paperback edition.
pages cm
ISBN 978-0-425-25123-2 (pbk.)
1. Heiresses—Fiction.   2. Hiding places—Fiction.   3. Sexual dominance and submission—Fiction.
4. Sex-oriented businesses—Fiction.   I. Title.
PS3602.L325245T48   2014   2013038419
813'.6—dc23

PUBLISHING HISTORY
Berkley trade paperback edition / March 2014

PRINTED IN THE UNITED STATES OF AMERICA

10 9 8 7 6 5 4 3 2 1

For two incredible friends.
You both know why.
Thank you for helping me see this story
in a whole new light. Hugs!

Prologue

"I know this is awkward and that your pregnant wife is probably pissed you're here, so I'll make this quick. Will you help me disappear?"

Callie Ward stood with her arms crossed against the blustery November wind, just out of the beams of the mini-mart's lights flooding the parking lot. She stared at Logan Edgington, nervously tapping her toe. The former Navy SEAL had no reason to help her, given how bratty she'd once been to him, but he was the only person she knew who could make her vanish, this time for good.

He crossed his beefy arms over his wide chest and looked at her as if she'd lost her mind. She'd lost everything else, so why not?

"Disappear?" He glanced at his watch. "It's midnight, Callie, so yeah, Tara wasn't thrilled when you called. I left my warm house for this 'life or death' shit, and you're telling me now that you just want to get out of town? Didn't I hear that you're collared now?"

Automatically, Callie pressed her fingers to the bare hollow of her throat, missing the familiar wire of white gold with its delicate lock. "Yes, but—"

"You know how this works. Talk to your Dom."

"He's the one I'm running from." Her voice trembled.

The moment Callie had realized the extent of her "Sir's" betrayal, she'd run like hell. She'd gotten too comfortable. Complacent. Almost dangerously happy.

She sniffled, then sucked it back, refusing to cry. She would not think about the fact that she'd fallen in love with Sean Kirkpatrick— if that was even his name.

Logan's pissed-off-Dom glower gentled as he leaned in, now all protective male. "Did he threaten you? Hurt you?"

Not the way Logan meant. But what the hell could she tell him without giving everything away?

Crap. The cover story she'd planned on the three-hour drive from Dallas to Shreveport wasn't going to fly. Logan was too smart not to see the holes in her tale. Then again, sheer utter terror had a way of rattling a girl's train of thought.

She was going to have to trust Logan or he'd walk away. It wasn't as if he'd ever pursued her, so she couldn't accuse him of prying the story out of her because he had ulterior motives. He'd only ever had eyes for pretty redheaded Tara. And he didn't worship the almighty buck. Logan was one of the good guys, a straight shooter all the way. He couldn't be bought, nor would he ever willingly put her in danger. It made sense to choose the devil she knew over the one she apparently didn't at all.

If Logan was going to help her, he deserved the truth—but not here.

"Can we sit in your car? It's freezing." And she didn't trust that hers wasn't bugged.

Logan looked as if he didn't much like the question, but after a brief hesitation, he shrugged and led her to a big black truck. He unlocked it with his key fob and opened her door. A minute later, he settled himself in the driver's seat. "If this asshole hurt you, Thorpe won't stand for it, especially under his roof."

Mitchell Thorpe. She closed her eyes, picturing his familiar, stern face. So often, she could swear that his penetrating gray eyes saw right through her. He'd given her a job, a home, a circle of friends, a lifestyle she craved. He was the first man she'd truly loved. He'd always have a chunk of her heart.

It killed her to know that she'd never see him again.

"I can't drag Thorpe into this. It's too risky. Anyone who knows me would assume I'd go to him first." She wrung her hands. "I hate to put you in this position, but no one would suspect that I'd ask you for help. Everyone at Dominion knows I'm not your favorite person."

He frowned. "I like you a lot, Callie. I just think that, as a sub, you're bratty as hell. You don't bend much more than an inch and you don't trust worth a damn."

Callie drew in a breath and gave him a shaky nod. "I know. I have reasons."

"Every stubborn sub does. Look, you're not my problem anymore. I'm just laying it out there."

"I really can't afford to trust anyone, but you're my last hope. I feel terrible for involving you, but more than anyone I know, you can handle it. I have nowhere else to turn. I can't go back to Dominion. Ever." She rubbed her hands together and closed her eyes, praying like hell that she wasn't making the biggest mistake of her life. If she was, she could be dead by sunrise.

"What the hell have you gotten into?"

"My name isn't Callie Ward. Nothing that you—or anyone else—thinks you know about me is true."

He sat back in the shadows, looking somewhere between skeptical and tense. "Okay, then who are you?"

"My mother called me Callie when I was little. But I'm sure you know me by my full name." She swallowed. *Please, God, let this be the right choice* . . . "I'm Callindra Howe."

Logan's eyes nearly popped out. "*The* Callindra Howe, the missing heiress from Chicago?"

Of course he'd heard of her. Her name had been splashed all over the news for the last nine years. There were almost as many reported sightings of her as there were of Elvis or aliens. Poor little greedy orphan who'd killed her family for a buck, according to the press. Callie wrapped her arms around her middle. *If they only knew the truth . . .*

She nodded. "That one."

"Bullshit. You were a pain in my ass sometimes, but you're not the kind of woman to slaughter her loved ones."

"Thank you! I was framed. I don't even know by whom or why."

Logan's expression turned flat. "Why should I believe you're her?"

Good question. The only thing she had of her former life was her mother's Fabergé egg, but Logan had no clue it had been Cecilia Howe's pride and joy before ovarian cancer had quickly snuffed out the bright light of her smile. With no way to corroborate the egg's authenticity at the moment, Callie had left it in her backpack, shoved in the trunk of her car.

"I've got nothing but the truth. I'll tell you what really happened and hope that you'll believe me so that when I beg you to make me disappear for good, you will."

"I'm listening." He tossed his forearm over the steering wheel and stared, looking like an immovable mountain.

Callie swallowed nervously. "What you know is that nine years ago, my father and sister were shot in our house and that the gun was found in my room, wiped clean."

"Your boyfriend told everyone that you killed them for the money the night you ran off together."

Holden had been gorgeous, defiant, wild, and full of grand ideas. In retrospect, planning to run off with him had been stupid, but her sixteen-year-old heart had believed in the concept of soul mates. She'd talked herself into believing that he was hers. If she'd had any idea that he would end up betraying her for money, she would have never accepted that first ride in his car or given him her virginity.

"He was willing to say anything for the big bounty on my head." She snorted. "I was young and naïve not to realize that.

"We'd been planning to run away together for a few weeks. His family had no money, and he had a crappy home life. When he said that he wanted me to be his new family, my young heart fluttered. Besides, I didn't want to be Callindra Howe anymore. I felt like a freak. Most girls my age took dance classes and worked a summer job to buy a beat-up car. I had riding lessons. I spoke fluent French. By the time I was ten, I'd visited every continent except Antarctica. I had a trust fund and got a Porsche the day I got my driver's license."

"It doesn't sound that bad," Logan drawled.

"In retrospect, it wasn't. At the time, I felt isolated. I worshipped my dad, but he'd been remote since my mother's death. And my younger sister, Charlotte, had turned rebellious."

"So when your boyfriend paid attention to you in order to get laid and get closer to your money, you thought he was the answer to your problems?"

"Pretty much." And her stupidity still stung. "Anyway, the night my father and sister were killed, I was late for our family dinner. The second the meal ended, I told my dad that I had to finish studying for a test. I ran back upstairs to call Holden and give him the green light. At a little after ten, I pretended to go to bed like all was normal. I'd packed the night before and I was ready to leave. I grabbed my backpack and was shoving in a few last-minute items when I heard the first shot downstairs, in my father's room. I thought I had to be mistaken or my sister had turned the TV up really loud. Who would be in our house shooting? I heard Charlotte head down the hall and for the stairs." Callie clenched her fists. "She screamed suddenly. I heard another gunshot, this one much closer. She didn't scream again. I peeked out the door to see if I could help her, but the blood . . ." Callie pressed her lips together. "She was only fourteen."

Her throat closed up and tears threatened, but Logan squeezed her hand. "Go on."

"I wanted to run to her, but the killer started charging down my hall. So I grabbed my pack and climbed out my window, down the big tree to the ground. I'd done it a thousand times.

"He shot me just before I made it to the ground. Flesh wound to my hip. It stung like a bitch, and I bled off and on for days, but I kept running for my life. Holden was waiting for me in his car one street over. I got in, sobbing. I called the police and told them everything. They immediately suspected me when I told them I'd fled the scene. They wanted me to come in for 'questioning' and swore I was just 'a person of interest,' but within an hour, the media had me labeled a suspect. I was too dazed and scared to face interrogation. The whole thing was a blur, and I had no witnesses who could say I hadn't killed anyone. I didn't want to face the fact that my family was gone. So I ran."

"No one suspected Holden? After all, if your father died, you stood to inherit a lot of money."

She shook her head. "He parked in front of an elderly couple's house. They spied on the teen 'vagrant' slouched in his beat-up Mustang for twenty minutes because he was blasting Usher in their very white upper-crust neighborhood. They were sure they'd be horrifically murdered any second."

Logan's mouth flattened in a grim line. "Then?"

"Within an hour, we traded vehicles with a drunk guy in a bar's parking lot, Holden's car for his old truck. The guy was wasted enough to say yes. After that, we headed from Illinois to Indiana."

Callie hadn't told any of this to a single soul—ever. Hell, she'd barely let herself think about it in years. Just saying the words hurt like peeling off the layers of her skin one at a time until she was a bleeding, oozing mass. The worst part was, she could spill her guts, and Logan might not believe her. He could call the police because it was the right thing to do. They would take her to jail. And who knew what would happen then . . . except that it wouldn't be good.

"Then a few days later, your boyfriend ratted you out?" he asked.

"Yeah. I was still bleeding, my hip infected. Holden heard about the reward for turning me in and he called." And damn if she wasn't still bitter about that. "When I stepped out of the shower for my shampoo and overheard him on the phone, I threw on my clothes, took the truck, and split."

"Keep going," Logan demanded.

"From there, I dashed to the next town over and paid cash for a little sedan. I had about thirty grand with me, money I'd taken from my father over a few months so Holden and I could start a new life. My dad never missed it.

"Since it was winter, I bolted south. Spent some time in Kentucky. When people there got suspicious, I adopted another name, colored my hair, and slipped over the border into Tennessee. Mississippi, Louisiana, Arkansas, Oklahoma . . . Any place I could find a rent-by-the week motel and a transient job, that's where I went, at least until I thought someone might be onto me. Then I'd be gone again."

"How did you find Thorpe?"

"I waited on some lifestylers while working at a twenty-four-hour diner shortly after I got to Dallas. Some were still in their fet garb at three a.m. when they walked in. I was curious, so I asked questions. They gave me answers. One of the unattached Doms invited me to go to Dominion with him. Out of curiosity, I said yes. He turned out to be a troll, and it didn't take Thorpe long to throw him out, but I begged to stay. I'd finally found the perfect place to hide. A secretive community where no one expects to know your real name and no one is going to out you. I could dress different, change my hair, wear a lot of makeup, and no one would raise a brow. Not a soul who knew me as a child would ever admit to knowing what a fet club was, much less think to look for me there. Thorpe asked a lot of questions at first. I made up a lot of lies. After a while, as long as I did my job and promised to give him a heads-up if I planned to skip out so he could hire someone else, he left it alone." She sighed, struggling to hold it all in. "Then came Sean."

"Your Dom?"

The sting of tears lashed Callie. She blinked to hold them back. "Supposedly, yes. I've dodged assassins and bounty hunters before and always managed to get away. This one is a different breed. He's determined enough to find me again. That's why I need your help. The man who's supposed to protect and care for me, who's pleaded with me to trust him?" She shook her head. "He's trying to kill me."

Chapter One

Three days earlier

CALLIE trembled as she lay back on the padded table and Sean Kirkpatrick's strong fingers wrapped around her cuffed wrist, guiding it back to the bindings above her head.

"I don't know if I can do this," she murmured.

He paused, then drew in a breath as if he sought patience. "Breathe, lovely."

That gentle, deep brogue of his native Scotland brought her peace. His voice both aroused and soothed her, and she tried to let those feelings wash through her.

"Can you do that for me?" he asked.

His fingers uncurled from her wrist, and he grazed the inside of her outstretched arm with his knuckles. As always, his touch was full of quiet strength. He made her ache. She shivered again, this time for an entirely different reason.

"I'll try."

Sean shook his head, his deep blue eyes seeming to see everything she tried to hide inside. That penetrating stare scared the hell out of her. What did he see when he looked at her? How much about the real her had he pieced together?

The thought made her panic. No one could know her secret. *No one.* She'd kept it from everyone, even Thorpe, during her four years at Dominion. She'd finally found a place where she felt safe, comfortable. Of course she'd have to give it up someday, probably soon. She always did. But please, not yet.

Deep breath. Don't panic. Sean wants your submission, not your secrets.

"You'll need to do better than try. You've been 'trying' for over six months," he reminded her gently. "Do you think I'd truly hurt you?"

No. Sean didn't seem to have a violent bone in his body. He wasn't a sadist. He never gripped her harshly. He never even raised his voice. She'd jokingly thought of him as the sub whisperer because he pushed her boundaries with a gentleness she found both irresistible and insidious. Certainly, he'd dragged far more out of her than any other man had. Tirelessly, he'd worked to earn her trust. Callie felt terrible that she could never give it, not when doing so could be fatal.

Guilt battered her. She should stop wasting his time.

"I know you wouldn't," she assured, blinking up at him, willing him to understand.

"Of course not." He pressed his chest over hers, leaning closer to delve into her eyes.

Callie couldn't resist lowering her lids, shutting out the rest of the world. Even knowing she shouldn't, she sank into the soft reassurance of his kiss. Each brush of his lips over hers soothed and aroused. Every time he touched her, her heart raced. Her skin grew tight. Her nipples hardened. Her pussy moistened and swelled. Her heart ached. Sean Kirkpatrick would be so easy to love.

As his fingers filtered into her hair, cradling her scalp, she exhaled and melted into his kiss—just for a sweet moment. It was the only one she could afford.

A fierce yearning filled her. She longed for him to peel off his clothes, kiss her with that determination she often saw stamped into his eyes, and take her with the single-minded fervor she knew he was capable of. But in the months since he'd collared her, he'd done nothing more than stroke her body, tease her, and grant her orgasms when he thought she'd earned them. She hadn't let him fully restrain her. And he hadn't yet taken her to bed.

Not knowing the feel of him deep inside her, of waiting and wanting until her body throbbed relentlessly, was making her buckets full of crazy.

After another skillful brush of his lips, Sean ended the kiss and lifted his head, breathing hard. She clung, not ready to let him go. How had he gotten under her skin so quickly? His tenderness filled her veins like a drug. The way he had addicted Callie terrified her.

"I want you. Sean, please . . ." She damn near wept.

With a broad hand, he swept the stray hair from her face. Regret softened his blue eyes before he ever said a word. "If you're not ready to trust me as your Dom, do you think you're ready for me as a lover? I want you completely open to me before we take that step. All you have to do is trust me, lovely."

Callie slammed her eyes shut. This was so fucking pointless. She *wanted* to trust Sean, yearned to give him everything—devotion, honesty, faith. Her past ensured that she'd never give any of those to anyone. But he had feelings for her. About that, she had no doubt. They'd grown just as hers had, unexpectedly, over time, a fledgling limb morphing into a sturdy vine that eventually created a bud just waiting to blossom . . . or die.

She knew which. They could never have more than this faltering Dom/sub relationship, destined to perish in a premature winter.

She should never have accepted his collar, not when she should be trying to keep her distance from everyone. The responsible choice now would be to call her safe word, walk out, quit him. Release them both from this hell. Never look back.

For the first time in nearly a decade, Callie worried that she might not have the strength to say good-bye.

What was wrong with her tonight? She was too emotional. She needed to pull up her big-girl panties and snap on her bratty attitude, pretend that nothing mattered. It was how she'd coped for years. But she couldn't seem to manage that with Sean.

"You're up in your head, instead of here with me," he gently rebuked her.

Another dose of guilt blistered her. "Sorry, Sir."

Sean sighed heavily, stood straight, then held out his hand to her. "Come with me."

Callie winced. If he intended to stop the scene, that could only mean he wanted to talk. These sessions where he tried to dig through her psyche became more painful than the sexless nights she spent in unfulfilled longing under his sensual torture.

Swallowing down her frustration, she dredged up her courage, then put her hand in his.

Holding her in a steady grip, Sean led her to the far side of Dominion's dungeon, to a bench in a shadowed corner. As soon as she could see the rest of the room, Callie felt eyes on her, searing her skin. With a nonchalant glance, she looked at the others sceneing around them, but they seemed lost in their own world of pleasure, pain, groans, sweat, and need. A lingering sweep of the room revealed another sight that had the power to drop her to her knees. Thorpe in the shadows. Staring. At her with Sean. His expression wasn't one of disapproval exactly . . . but he wasn't pleased.

Sean sat, then pulled her onto his lap, supporting her back with a strong grip around her waist. He cupped her chin in his palm and sent her a pointed glance. "Eyes on me, lovely."

She complied, trying not to think about the fact that it was getting harder and harder to meet his stare and not give herself to him for real.

Originally, she'd allowed Sean into her life because he irritated Thorpe, who sometimes looked at her as if she were the brightest star in the sky, then always chose another woman to master. She'd wanted to make him jealous. Hell, she'd wanted to see if he even gave a shit. Sean had walked into the club with his quiet sophistication and dry humor, taken one look at her, and never glanced at anyone else. It had done her ego a world of good—until Thorpe had removed his protection and allowed Sean to collar her. Without so much as blinking, he'd let her go.

So why the hell was Thorpe watching her now?

"You're away with the fairies, Callie. Get out of your head," Sean growled. "Focus on me. Or we'll end tonight now."

That would be better, smarter. And everything inside her rebelled at the thought of Sean leaving. She clung, in fact. After all, she never knew if she'd have a tomorrow with anyone.

"I'm sorry. I don't mean to be preoccupied."

His face softened a bit. "What's troubling you?"

A million things she could never confess. She plucked at the first excuse off the top of her head. "You don't want me."

He grabbed her face in his hands. "You have no idea how untrue that is, lovely. I fantasize about laying you out under me and sinking so deep inside you that you'll not ever forget the feel of me. Never doubt that I want you."

His words made Callie flush hot all over. "Don't you think sex would bring us closer?"

A wry smile crossed his wide mouth, and she couldn't resist brushing her fingers through the waves of his dark hair. He was so blindingly handsome. He'd been her perfect revenge against Thorpe's indifference. She just hadn't planned on him stealing his way into her heart. And now she had no idea what to do.

"It's a tempting notion, isn't it? But I know me too well. Once we start that, I won't stop. And we've far too much trust to grow between us to be distracted. I also know you. Sex is easy, isn't it? True intimacy is hard. I don't think you've ever had it, and you're a bit too good at dodging it. I'm looking for more than a fuck, Callie. I want the real thing, and I won't rush because my cock is aching."

She had to find the only sensitive man in a BDSM dungeon. She would have been better off with someone who just wanted her to kneel, call him Sir, and liked to dish out a good paddling now and then. Perversely, that had never attracted her. Sean's big heart did, and she feared that she would break both his and hers before the end.

Maybe this time will be different. Maybe the past will stay there. Four years is the longest you've stayed in one place. Maybe it's time to stop running and finally live.

Callie drew in a shaking breath. "I'll try again. *Really* try. Tell me what you want, Sir."

"That's a girl." Sean eased her to her feet and led her back to the padded table.

A glance up proved Thorpe had gone. Probably for the best. He was far too controlled and sexual for her. If she ever truly put herself in his hands, he'd pry her soul wide open in no time at all. She couldn't take that risk.

"Lie flat for me, lovely."

As soon as the gorgeous Scot helped her onto the cushioned surface, she stretched out. He quickly secured her cuffed ankles. That didn't fill her with too much panic. Then he grasped her wrist and began to clip in one of the cuffs. Almost immediately, her trembling began again. Callie gritted her teeth and fought to give in to Sean. She wanted to. God knew she did.

It wasn't that she didn't trust him. But what if someone recognized her? What if the police busted up the joint? What if she needed to flee and couldn't?

"Close your eyes. Take a deep breath."

She ought to be wondering what she was going to do if she failed again and he left for the night. Or for good. She didn't want to be without him, and that kind of desperation was *so* dangerous . . .

Callie forced herself to comply. Instantly, her other senses jumped in. A woman in the far corner was having a very noisy orgasm. A male sub in the vicinity of the row of St. Andrew's crosses grunted with every lash of the whip from his top. Somewhere nearby, she heard one of the dungeon monitors speak in low tones. Her own labored breathing gradually canceled it all out. Her thundering heartbeat did the rest until she focused solely on Sean.

"Good. What's your safe word?" he crooned, leaning closer.

"Summer." Callie swallowed. She missed that horse. The little brown filly had been her most constant companion after her mother's death. No doubt, the mare was dead now. She'd never had the chance to say good-bye to her four-legged friend.

She let loose a ragged breath.

"Excellent," he praised as he bound her cuffed wrist to the table.

Her entire body tensed. She dragged in a harsh breath. Her heartbeat ramped up even more. Her palms began to sweat. Excitement and fear mingled into a heady cocktail, drugging her veins.

"You're making progress. I'm proud of you." Sean cupped her cheek. "Relax. Trust me. Put yourself in my hands."

How wonderful that sounded. How tempting . . . She nestled into his touch, forcing back a swell of devotion that was nothing more than a waste.

Callie wasn't one of those women who didn't know why her soul cried out to submit. It didn't take Freud to understand that a girl who'd spent nearly a decade being entirely responsible for her own welfare in a life-or-death struggle sought to turn all of that over to a Dominant partner for his broad shoulders to bear. Of course, she also wanted her family alive and whole as well. She always wanted what she couldn't have.

Gawd, she needed to turn out the lights on this pity party and give Sean all she could now. Tomorrow, she'd apologize for being much less than he needed, then sever the ties between them—before she could no longer find the will. Of course she'd lie and wish him well in his quest to find another submissive who could be his true love. Watching that would be too painful, so she'd soon have to leave. Sadly, Thorpe wouldn't miss her much, either. No one would. Exactly as she'd planned it.

The realization wrenched her heart.

Callie had been desperately ignoring the writing on the wall for months. She'd allowed herself to become emotionally compromised and far too relaxed. Sean kept prying deeper into her psyche. If she wasn't careful, it wouldn't be long before he put two and two together. The questions he asked already made her nervous.

Maybe the time to depart Dominion had already come. No, she *knew* it had. She needed to leave everything behind. Pack up and move on. The sooner the better.

"Callie . . ." His tone was a warning.

She heaved in a cleansing breath and shoved every thought from her mind, centering herself on his presence and her need to submit to him just this once before she ditched him for good.

"I'm fine, Sir." Before she lost her nerve, she raised her other arm above her head, an offering of her trust in him.

"Finally." His fingers curled around her, warm and protective, his thumb stroking over the vulnerable inside of her arm before he fastened down her last cuff. "Thank you, lovely. You look beautiful bound for me. Your trust is heady."

And scarier than hell. "I know it's not much."

"Shh. From you, it's a great deal. I know that was hard for you."

"Can I open my eyes for just a minute?"

Sean paused. "Do you need to see me?"

Frantically, Callie nodded, fighting the insidious panic seeping from her veins.

"Open them, then. We'll go slowly."

Her lashes fluttered open, and she focused on him in the bright dungeon. Square face, sharp jaw, dark goatee, strong nose, muscled body. A furrow seemed permanently notched between his heavy brows. A little scar sat under the corner of his right eye, and she would have sworn it came from the nick of a bullet if he seemed like that kind of guy. Everything about him looked so masculine and aggressive. Yet he treated her so tenderly. If she had special-ordered the perfect man, he would be Sean. No doubt he'd wondered a hundred times over what he'd done to earn her distrust. The thought made her sad.

If she ever wanted to know what submission felt like, what Sean felt like, before she moved onto her next identity, she was going to have to give in this once. Simple as that.

"Thank you," she murmured.

"I'm going to blindfold you now."

A scary prospect . . . but one she felt ready to handle now. Besides, her hearing had saved her the night her family had been murdered, as well as from Holden's betrayal.

"Yes, Sir."

Sean caressed her neck, his fingertips gliding down her collarbones to the swells of her breasts, thumbing her puckered nipple covered by nearly transparent white cotton. "You're pleasing me greatly."

He pleased her, too. Everything inside her yearned to show him that. She smiled and lifted her head so he could fit a silky black scrap that looked like a sleep mask over her eyes. Its weight felt light and nonthreatening. Then he clasped her hand. Callie squeezed back.

"Have you ever been both restrained and blindfolded?"

"Not entirely, and only for demonstration purposes."

She'd actually scened with very few people. Logan Edgington had usually wanted to give her a red ass to correct her bratty behavior. His friend Xander had enjoyed arousing her body, but he'd never awakened even a corner of her heart. She'd spent a little time with some of the other resident Doms at Dominion with similar results. Eric had a fascination with ball gags that made her shudder. Zeb seemed a tad too excited by feet for her comprehension. His nibbling at her toes had icked her out. Jason had not only been a stickler for protocol, but a big fan of Shibari. It had taken Callie less than four minutes to scream her safe word. Then there was Thorpe . . . He was in a class all by himself. And way beyond her reach.

"Demonstration?" Sean sounded shocked.

Callie nodded. "Yeah. But I haven't done one in about two years."

Not since that December Thorpe had asked her to bottom for a demo . . . then afterward, behind closed doors, the kindling heat between them had exploded into a tangle of arms and lips, sighs and discarded clothes. She'd been wet and ready and so desperate for him, naked on his bed. Then he'd abruptly walked away without an explanation, behaving as if nothing had ever happened. To this day, she didn't know why he'd left her. And he'd never asked her to assist him in a presentation again.

That hurt didn't matter anymore. Old crap. Only Sean was important now.

"Were you able to bear the restraint then because you knew someone would free you if need be? If that's the case, lovely, the dungeon monitors would have my balls in an instant if they thought I was hurting you."

"I know." They were intensely protective of all the women in the club, but especially fellow staff.

"Well, then?" Sean's swift reply asked how she had managed to be tied down for Dom/sub education purposes when she could barely tolerate it with someone she yearned to put all her trust in. Her only answer was that Thorpe had been the one doing the tying. She trusted him more than she trusted anyone. He knew her quirks and had accommodated them.

But she hated Sean believing that she lacked faith in him. Callie latched on to the first explanation to hit her brain. "Logically, I know you're right. Sadly, logic doesn't always penetrate fear. It's a bit like a phobia."

He didn't answer right away, just brushed his thumb back and forth over her nipple until it tingled and she wished he'd just tear off her clothes and fuck her already. She'd wanted him for so many long months.

"Have you always been this way?"

"Since I got into BDSM." She'd lied to Sean often, but always tried to stay as close to the truth as possible.

"Do you know what caused your fear, lovely? Was it something in your past?"

Callie bit back a snort. *Pretty much everything.* "It wasn't any one event."

And that wasn't a total lie, just a realization that restraint severely inhibited her ability to flee if her murder rap caught up to her.

"Are you sure? Tell me about your childhood. Maybe something there will help me better understand."

This again? He must have asked twenty times since snapping a collar around her neck to tell him about her formative years. She managed to simply say that she was from the Midwest and was an orphan. Again, not lies . . . just not the complete truth.

She clenched her hands into fists. "The longer we talk, the more nervous I get. Please . . ."

"We *will* finish this conversation, lovely."

No, they wouldn't.

"Yes, Sir."

Sean sighed. "You're doing well, so I'll reward you now."

He leaned over her, caressed her shoulders in his big hands, then his nimble fingers made short work of the waist-cinching corset she'd chosen earlier. He began unlacing it just beneath her breasts, slowly parting the panels down her torso before he detached it from her body. The garment provided enough support under her breasts to render a bra unnecessary. When he tore off the thin white tank she'd worn beneath, his groan, coupled with his hands cupping her breasts reverently, told her that he approved.

"Always so damn beautiful, Callie."

No way to miss the worship in his voice. No man had ever made her feel so wanted.

He plucked at her nipples, pinching gently, turning the peaked nubs, controlling the flow of blood. The second he released them, sensation slammed into her. Hypersensitive and hard, the nubs tingled and bunched harder. She whimpered.

Then he bent to her, breathing harshly in her ear before he kissed his way down her neck, nipping at her fair skin until a shiver wracked her. She felt deliciously vulnerable, helpless to stop whatever he did to her body. He might deliver pleasure. He might heap on pain. And she could only accept what he chose.

So far, submitting was every bit as thrilling as she'd imagined. Yeah, plenty of folks might think she was warped, but as much as she had feared it, the surrender of her will to Sean made her feel oddly treasured. And it aroused her, especially when he pressed soft kisses around the exposed flesh of her breasts. Beside her nipples, below them, hovering just above, he toyed and teased with his mouth. He made her gasp and hold her breath in anticipation of his every hot exhalation over her skin and every sweet nibble with his teeth.

With a little pleading mewl, she lifted her hips to him, waiting for him to realize that under her tiny black skirt, she wore the barest scrap of lace over her drenched pussy.

Sean braced the heel of his palm just above her mound and pushed down gently. "I promised you a reward, lovely. Not necessarily an orgasm. Do I have to punish you to make you understand?"

He'd spanked her a few times, but she hadn't considered it much of a punishment. Instead, the release of fire under her skin went right to her clit and made her throb with unrelenting desire. Always sharp, Sean had quickly come to understand that ignoring her or acting with utter disinterest was far more effective in changing her behavior. The more she cared, the more disappointing him crushed her.

"No, Sir." She just wanted to feel him in every way he'd allow.

"I'd rather not. I have a special plan for you, but I'll need you to be a wee bit patient." He chuckled. "Though I know you'll find that a torture all its own, I'll make it worth your while."

Callie grimaced. Her impatience around Dominion was well-known. A childhood of indulgence hadn't prepared her for the special hell of delayed gratification. Sean specialized in spacing out her rewards until she sometimes felt like screaming. Then again, the breath-stealing orgasms were always worth the wait.

She just wished he'd let her return the favor. No matter how hard his cock looked or how much desire-induced sweat drenched his skin, he never availed himself of her body. Just like he never asked to see her outside Dominion's walls. Not for the first time, she wondered if he had a wife or girlfriend tucked away elsewhere. She was too afraid to ask.

With a snarl, Sean removed his hands. "What the hell is in your head that's so engrossing you keep drifting away from me? I want your full attention, Callie."

Continuing her policy of honesty when possible, she gave him most of the truth. "I wish I could touch you."

"You mean you'd like your hands free, to escape being bound?"

"No. As hard as I found it to allow, I'm enjoying your restraints. I just want the chance to give you the pleasure you give me."

He sucked in a sharp breath. "Be good and perhaps I'll let you."

The way his voice shook, Callie hoped that meant he wanted her at least half as much as she wanted him. "Please . . ."

"Behave, lovely. You're not in charge here."

She pressed her lips together, did her best to lie silently and let him have his way. She expected him to use those slightly rough palms of his to abrade and arouse her until she pleaded. Then he'd do his best to ask questions designed to get in her head. She usually had to work to keep her wits about her and give him nothing more than a scrap of information so he would finally grant her screaming pleasure.

That wasn't on his agenda today.

Instead, Sean released her ankle restraints and detached her wrists from the table. Arms encircled her, then he helped her to her feet. She didn't often find herself topless in the club, so the feeling was hugely foreign . . . but not unwelcome. The cool air brushed her skin, beading her nipples more. It was an intriguing contrast to the pure heat rolling off Sean as he led her to dangling chains in the ceiling.

Poised behind her, he worked the snap hook attached to her bindings through the chains, securing her arms above her head.

"Spread your legs and keep them there." His words brooked no refusal, despite his calm tones. He never had to yell to make his point.

Biting her lip, Callie complied, but she didn't understand his intent. She knew she shouldn't, but she brushed her face against her extended arm to work the rim of the blindfold down, then she peeked at him over her shoulder.

Sean snapped her mask back in place. "Stop, you minx. Eyes front. You'll see me when I want you to, not before. Right now, focus on staying out of your head. Feel your body instead. Your skin, your breath, your pleasure. If your thoughts start intruding, try to block them." He pressed his chest to her back and cradled her breasts. "I want to give this gift to you, lovely, but you have to do your part."

If this was her one night of submission to experience all Sean Kirkpatrick had to offer, then she would do her very best.

"Yes, Sir."

"Good. Would you like ear buds with music to help you concentrate?"

And take away her ability to hear? "No."

"All right. Take a deep breath and let it out. Clear your mind. Feel your muscles let loose."

Like preparing to do yoga.

Theirs to Cherish

She did everything exactly as he'd commanded. It put her in a relaxed state. Well, as relaxed as she could be.

"Good. Do you know what this is?"

Wide strands of something soft skimmed her from neck to ass. Air filled her lungs as she raised up, trying to extend the caress.

"A flogger."

"Deerskin, yes. Has anyone ever used one on you?"

"No, Sir."

"Wielded properly, it's not an implement of pain. Are you afraid?"

Of the flogger, no. But his intent was another story. If he'd gone out of his way to point out that the instrument didn't have to hurt, she didn't think he intended to test her pain threshold. And Sean had promised her a reward. Callie had a suspicion she knew where this was headed.

It scared the hell out of her as much as it made her yearn.

But she would give in tonight, see if she could separate her body from her mind in that floating paradise others called subspace. *Just this once . . .*

"I want whatever you'd like to give me."

She sensed more than felt his approval. "Fine, then. Don't count."

The words had barely cleared his lips before the tails of the flogger struck the fleshiest part of her ass in a slow thud. Sean repeated the motion—full across her butt, in the low curve of her spine, up her back and down again. Never hard, never even making her sting. Rhythmic, sweet, lulling, the flogging was like a slow dance cradling her in its arms until she began to block out everything but the way he made her feel. Her heart beat in time with the tresses kissing her skin.

Callie didn't have to work very hard to block out thoughts. Sean perfectly understood her body, exactly when, where, and how hard to work the falls over her.

Her head started to swim away from her body, and she let it go for a moment. She sank toward the abyss just beyond her, calling out to her. The sensation was like having a couple of glasses of wine, but heavier and more compelling. More alluring.

Darkness swam around her thoughts. Minutes might have passed. Or hours. She didn't really feel her body anymore. The earth held her by the soles of her feet and her cuffed wrists, or she would have floated away to beautiful nothingness.

Vaguely, she felt Sean's hand glide up and down her hot, sensitive skin, an acute rise of burn and sensation. Her head rolled forward. She felt every instant of her slow, deep breathing, almost like a waking nap—except the intoxicating euphoria. *How wonderful . . .*

"You look stunning, Callie."

A drunk little smile curled her lips.

"This is what I wanted to give you, lovely, some respite from your head." His lips slipped up the back of her neck. He wrapped his broad hand around her and under her chin until he tipped her head back. Then he kissed his way down her jaw. "I would give you more."

Please . . . She didn't have the strength to open her mouth and beg.

"But I need something from you. Come back to me just a bit," he coaxed.

Callie frowned. It was the last thing she wanted to do, but the sweet splendor of silence in her head was too tempting. Complying took so much effort.

"Let me into your heart, Callie. Into your head. I've asked you for nothing since we began our journey together."

And he'd given her so much.

"You draw me like no other. I want to know everything about you. I don't want business to take me away from you before I've had a chance to learn you inside and out. Before I've had a chance to truly bind you to me."

She sighed. He plucked at every one of her heartstrings, and she let him. Such exquisite words. How could she not give him a little?

"We'll start small," he assured. "Did you have a pet as a child?"

Pet? The first recollection to hit her brain spewed from her lips. "I found a kitten."

"How old were you?"

"Not quite six. I couldn't keep her. Mom was sick. I woke up one morning and she was gone. I cried. Mom died anyway."

"I'm so sorry, lovely. Of what?"

Callie shied away from remembering. "God takes the fragile ones back into his fold. Dad always said that. It still made me sad."

"Of course." He petted her. "Do you have any sisters? Brothers?"

Chilled air suddenly smacked her toasty skin, jostling her brain. Awareness rushed back into her head. Why did he want to know?

"Both." Of course, Dad never knew that she'd heard about his teenage romance that resulted in a son no one ever talked about. She hadn't thought about that in years, but she'd spied on his son once. Apparently, being an illegitimate Howe sucked because he'd been a bitter man.

"You're sure?"

Callie tensed. Why would he think otherwise? His tone and the enormity of his question hit her. It might seem trifling to most, but if he suspected at all who she was and she didn't tread carefully, she might give him enough to confirm her identity.

Would he sell her down the river for the two-million-dollar bounty?

"I'm cold."

Sean took a step back. The flogger fell over her back, her ass, alternating, thudding, seeking to calm her again. At first, it stung against her hot skin. Then she had to resist the divine slide back into her silent cocoon.

"Relax," he crooned.

Callie didn't dare. She bit her lip to stay present, but she pretended. At least the flogger warmed her enough to stop her shivering.

"Did you take any special trips as a child?"

"No." She'd wanted to go to Disney World. Dad preferred Europe and museums where she had to be quiet. A whole summer in the French countryside when she'd been fifteen had seemed nearly coma inducing.

"Did you go to public school?"

Never. Her mother would have rolled over in her grave. "Mom was too religious to allow that. Guess it didn't stick very well."

Her answer was true . . . in a sense. Her mother had worshipped at the altar of Prada and been a firm believer in the church of Versace. She would never have allowed her or Charlotte to rub elbows with the middle-class kids who lived in the tract houses a few miles away. That had sucked, too. They looked like they had more fun.

"Callie, you're in your head again." And Sean didn't sound pleased.

"Sorry. The cold rattled me and I just . . ." *Got scared with all the questions.*

That made her even more dejected. Most likely, the man just wanted to know her. But just in case she was wrong, she had to lie. The truth was too risky.

Great basis for a relationship, Callie. Yeah, he'd really love you if he knew your past.

She'd be long gone before he could.

He sighed. "You get cold easily. I often forget because you make me sweat."

A moment later, he shuffled around to the front of her body. She drank his nearness in with a moan, smelling the musk wafting from him. Her mouth watered, her pussy wept. She wanted him so badly, had truly sought to please him . . .

"I genuinely tried. I loved the floaty feeling you gave me. I never thought I'd find subspace." Callie wished she could touch him. "It hurts me to disappoint you."

Sean peeled the mask away, and she blinked until she adjusted to the glaring lights. His shirt was damp, his cheeks flushed. A submissive dip of her head as he unsnapped her wrists from the chains proved his cock lusciously hard.

"You came a long way tonight, lovely. It's my own impatience that makes me want you so completely right this instant. But your effort pleased me."

"I'm sorry I couldn't give you more." She blinked up at him uncertainly as he unfastened one of the cuffs and blood rushed back into her arms.

Disappointment in herself chiseled away at her composure. Even when she'd given herself permission to let go and fully surrender to Sean, she'd been unable to.

"I wanted to." Useless tears welled in her eyes.

With a soothing sound, he drew her against his body, and she relished his warmth. When he pulled her into his embrace, she felt the protective wall around her heart softening, crumbling. Just once, why couldn't she give this wonderful man who'd showered her with tenderness and pleasure a little fucking bit of herself? She was so closed off that even she could barely reach the real her buried inside. Certainly, she didn't know how to share, even with a man as kind as Sean.

"I know you did." He cradled her head in his hand. "Don't cry, lovely. Let's get comfortable and talk."

He didn't give her a chance to argue, just pulled her along beside him, back to the bench in the corner. He removed the last cuff still dangling from her wrist and those around her ankles. Her shoulders were slightly sore. The skin on her backside still leapt with tingling life.

Sean reached for a blanket in a nearby stash, wrapped it around her, then pulled her into his lap. "Don't beat yourself up. Yes, I wanted more. But tomorrow will come."

Not for them, it wouldn't.

"I could share myself more readily if you shared with me," she ventured. At least it sounded like a good excuse.

Settling back on the bench with a raised brow, he drew her against his chest. "Is that so?"

"What we have feels so . . . one-sided. I don't know anything about you."

He drew in a sharp breath. "I was raised by my grandparents in Scotland. My father served in the military in far-flung parts of the world. My mother preferred London to parenting. I attended local schools, finished university, learned how to hold my own in a fight and drink a few pints without getting too pissed. I work in project management."

Callie gathered up her courage. "Are you married? Taken?"

Sean let loose a hearty laugh. "Has that been worrying you all this time? No, lovely. I was engaged about a decade ago, but I was already married to my job by then. We ended things amicably. I've been alone since. And my life was empty as hell without you."

That shouldn't get to her. He shouldn't. But damn, he did. She might as well be honest about this, too. "I didn't know how much my life was missing until you walked into it. I need more of you."

If they had nothing beyond tonight, she wanted him in every way he would give himself now.

Scrambling off his lap and between his feet on the concrete floor, Callie braced her hands on his knees and glanced at his cock. Then she blinked up at him, pouring her desperation into this one entreaty. "Please . . ."

Chapter Two

SEAN stared down at Callie, his breath trapped in his chest, his cock about to explode. Her blue eyes, framed in thick black lashes and silently pleading, pierced his chest. Hell, they dug into his heart. He had to hold his fucking head together. But he wanted her more than he thought possible. More than he had words to express.

Of all the damn women to fall for . . .

Normally, he'd remind her that he was the Dom, and she shouldn't wheedle for the terms she wanted. He knew a pretty piece of manipulation when he heard one. But Callie wasn't herself tonight. Her breakthrough actually worried him. On the one hand, he'd finally peeled away layers of armor to reveal the soft woman beneath her bratty attitude. On the other hand, everything about her—especially that haunted look in her eyes—reeked of desperation. Of good-bye.

His gut twisted. Had something spooked her? Or someone, like him? There were a lot of reasons that letting her go wasn't an option. If he had to rearrange his priorities, so be it. But no matter what, he must keep Callie beside him.

"Lovely . . ." He didn't know what to say. His throat felt tight. His breath thickened as her fingers dug into his thighs.

She didn't reply, just silently beseeched him with those sad eyes. How much unhappiness had she known to be so walled off from everyone? Right now, Sean could only imagine, but he wanted to *know*. And he wanted to heal her.

If he put her off now, she'd only bolt sooner. As it was, he suspected that she planned to be gone when he came back for her tomorrow. But if he gave in to her tonight . . . That was the wild card.

He'd ask her if she planned to flee, but she would only deny it. He knew Callie so well in some ways, yet she remained the most intriguing mystery in others.

Sean swallowed his doubts down. Fuck it. If he had this one chance to keep her, he was going to take it and deal with the metric shit ton of consequences later.

"Never mind." She began to scramble to her feet, the unmistakable hurt on her delicate face wrenching.

He braced a hand on her shoulder and pushed down gently. "Stay. I haven't said no."

Her gaze skittered away. "But you didn't say yes. I haven't earned it."

"That's not true. You gave me a great deal of effort tonight. You fought through fears and surrendered a part of yourself to me. I appreciate how hard that was for you."

Holding his breath, he reached for the snap of his trousers. He was crossing a dangerous line, but he silenced the concerns screaming inside him and focused on Callie. On growing his bond with her and giving her what she needed. Right now, he suspected she ached to feel wanted.

His zipper went down in a nearly silent hiss. Her gaze fell between his legs as he reached in to shove cotton out of his way and take his cock in hand. Fucking hell, he couldn't remember the last time he'd been this hard or desired a woman so much. Something about Callie had tugged at him from day one. Sean wished he could say it was the sheer challenge of conquering her. He'd always enjoyed using his wits or brawn to overcome obstacles. Who didn't like winning?

But Callie had become far more than a conquest.

Slowly stroking his erection, blood rushed south to engorge him even more as her wide gaze fell on him, imploring. He tingled just from her longing stare.

"Do you want to touch me, lovely?"

She tore her gaze away and zeroed in on his face, then she nodded.

God, this could make everything go sideways—fast. Any time he resisted Callie, it was something of a miracle. He should have known his willpower wouldn't last.

Slowly, he eased his hand away. Within moments, she wrapped her own around his length, and he sucked in a hissing breath at the contact. Her skin was so warm, her touch soft yet deft. It was a tease. Seeing her silken fingers on him, her stare taking him in . . . Fuck, it was beyond heady. Nearly seven months without a woman, and he was so ready to blow. But he had a deep suspicion that if any other perched between his feet, he wouldn't be half so moved.

With her elbow braced on his thigh, Callie glided her fingers up and down his cock, that gaze of hers boiling his balls. But it was the yearning wonder on her face that truly seared him.

On her knees now, she leaned in. She didn't ask first, just opened her mouth to him and swallowed the head of his cock past her lips. Sean choked back a groan.

He'd found heaven. Callie didn't just enclose him in her mouth or lick him. She worshipped the flesh she drew onto her tongue. She cradled it, laved and loved it, savored it, drawing it in deeper and deeper.

Sean gripped the edge of the bench, his body tensing with the pleasure. Electricity buzzed through his bloodstream. He clenched his thighs. And there was no stopping his hand as it curled into her hair, caressing her reverently as she showered him with attention, rapidly undoing his restraint.

Holy hell.

Callie took his encouragement to heart and sank his cock even deeper into her mouth until he bumped the back of her throat. She swallowed on him. He groaned out a sound of shock and fisted her inky tresses in his hands, the nearly black strands gliding softly over his fingers, as he lifted his hips and fucked her mouth in agonizing strokes.

She wasn't exactly an expert. But Callie definitely presented a dichotomy. A girl who'd lived in a BDSM club for four years had managed to retain a sweet sort of innocence. He wanted that for his own.

Damn it, he was so far gone for her. And it would be so easy to thrust into her willing mouth and let her overwhelm him with mind-bending pleasure.

Sean tugged on her hair and growled at her. "Look at me."

As she sucked up his length again, she cast her gaze at him through her lashes. With the few brain cells focused on something other than her luscious mouth, he could still see finality in her eyes. This was her last act with him if he didn't change course. She needed to be wanted, and he ached for her—not only in a carnal sense. He had to bind Callie to him.

God, this was going to send trouble clawing up his ass. But she was worth it.

Swallowing a curse, he shoved his hands under her arms and tugged her onto his lap once more.

"Sir?" she whispered, both anxious and breathless.

"You say my name when I fuck you, lovely. You scream it."

As he positioned her legs on either side of his hips, she gripped his shoulders. "But you said we weren't ready, that you weren't going to rush what we had simply because your cock was aching."

The clever minx had an inexhaustible memory.

"Are you teasing me now, Callie? Or questioning me?"

"No, Sir." She gyrated her pussy against him, and only the soft lace of whatever she wore under her skirt separated them. Her body undulated until her breasts flattened on his chest and her lips skimmed his neck. She plucked at his shirt, doing her best to remove it. Sean lost patience and ripped it away.

Almost instantly, her hot stare and curious fingers spread across his chest, tugging at his self-control. He fought to rein it back in.

Fuck, she was taking a hundred liberties without his permission, but he couldn't bring himself to care now. The lover in her was something Callie hadn't given to anyone in the four years she'd been at Dominion . . . except maybe Thorpe. There was some story between those two, but no one knew what. He'd asked. If the aloof bastard had fucked her, it hadn't been recently. Whatever the case, he'd handle the situation accordingly.

And hell, it was getting hard for him to think with her all over his throbbing shaft. Everything inside him shouted to claim her in every way a man could. Then pray to fuck it would be enough to make her stay.

"I'll do whatever it takes to make us stronger," he vowed. "You've thought all this time that I didn't want you or had someone else hidden away. I mean to show you that you're wrong."

"Please." She pulled back enough to look into his eyes. "At least this once."

Sean shook his head. "The first time of many, lovely. I swear that to you."

He flipped up her skirt and ripped away the black lace separating him from her pussy. After a satisfying tear, he tossed it to the concrete floor. Finally, Sean dug into his pocket, grateful for old habits, and yanked out a condom. With shaking hands, he shredded the foil square open and rolled it down his inflamed length, feeling her hot stare eat him up.

When he had himself sheathed, he wrapped his arms around her and tugged her closer, poising her over his cock. He slid his fingers along her hip, feeling the nick along her left side. What would it take to persuade her to tell him about that? Maybe after tonight . . .

"How long has it been for you, lovely?"

Callie looked away and gave him a particular frown he'd come to know well. It flitted across her face when he asked a painful question she wanted to avoid. "A long time."

"I won't go any further until you give me a precise answer."

She squirmed in his grip, trying to lower herself onto him. Fuck if he didn't want to let her. His body urged him to slide through her wet folds and lose his mind as her cunt gripped him. But in his current mood—one that demanded he pound her into next week—he might hurt her.

And if she admitted that she'd ever warmed Thorpe's bed, he'd do whatever it took to eliminate the man as competition. It was obvious unspoken feelings lay between Callie and her boss.

For now, Sean waited, holding her waist tightly, preventing her from sinking onto him.

"Sean . . ." She wriggled impatiently.

"I'm not fucking you yet. What do you call me?" he ground out, sweating.

Damn it to hell, resisting the minx was teeth-grittingly tough, and he had no doubt she would tax every bit of his restraint before it was over.

Callie pleaded with him with wide blue eyes. "Sir."

Her little entreaty made him even harder.

"How long since you've had a lover, Callie? I won't ask again. I'll just stop."

She squeezed her eyes shut as if hating to look at an ugly reality. "No one you know here at Dominion."

He worked to hold in his elation. "No one? Not in the last four years?"

"I tried once, but . . . it felt wrong. I stopped it. I think he was relieved." That fact embarrassed her, but the torment on her face also said something about her loneliness. She looked so fragile in his arms. "He's married now."

All Sean could feel was a thrill that she would soon be his. The relief that Thorpe had never fucked her was undeniable. He had no doubt the bastard wanted to.

"I just needed to know how gentle to be, lovely. Thank you for your honesty. I know that wasn't easy for you."

"You must think I'm broken or something."

Sean didn't think; he knew. But not in the way she meant.

"You're beautiful. I've no doubt you're much wanted among the Doms here. I feel fortunate that you chose me."

Finally, she opened her eyes, and he saw tears shimmering there. That yearning on her face made her soul look so naked. Something he was saying or doing was reaching her, and a cautious joy rolled through him.

Callie threw herself onto him, arms around him, her face pressed into his neck. She inhaled him, clinging. God, how sweet she could be. Under all that sassy attitude, she hid a fragile heart. And he was finally seeing the real her. The woman inside was every bit as stunning and soft as he'd imagined.

When she would have pulled back with an apology, Sean stopped her with a kiss—and slowly began pressing her down onto his cock.

She gasped into his mouth. Her body tensed. Her pussy closed around him, so small and tight. How the fuck was he going to survive the incendiary grip of her for long?

Beneath her, he flexed his hips, desperate to bury himself as deep as he could and accustom her to the feel of him filling her completely. After only a handful of seconds, he knew she was going to become his drug of choice. After this addicting sweetness, there was no way he could do without her again.

No doubt, he would eventually get his ass handed to him for this . . .

Callie gave a little shriek and tried to lift off his cock. Sean held her in place. "Easy. Breathe."

She wriggled, and he thought he might lose his damn mind with the way her flesh rubbed and clutched the head of his cock. Then she exhaled and slowly let the tension slip from her body.

"That's good," he praised. "Lean on me and let me take care of you."

She met his stare, her gaze tangled with his. Something about the way she silently surrendered turned him on. The man in him responded to her wordless begging for him to take everything she had. Her offering surprised the hell out of him, but he didn't dwell on that. Filling her with both his cock and affection was far more important now.

Sean lifted her up a fraction, then lowered her an inch at a time, experimenting with her clenching walls, searching her face for any discomfort. This time, he submerged deeper, his head swimming with sensations until he swore he might drown in her. Callie was everything he'd imagined and so far beyond it boggled his mind.

With his fingers biting into her hips, Sean desperately fought to hold on to his control as he lowered her even more, stopping when she inhaled sharply and her body tensed again.

"It's all right. Almost there."

She writhed on him. "I'm so frustrated. I want you so badly."

"And I want you. But I refuse to hurt you, lovely, when a little patience will do. It's been a long time. I didn't expect this to go easy."

"I wanted it to."

Sean couldn't hold in a smile at her impatience, that part of her that seemed to think or believe the world should go her way. "I did, too. Next time, it will. Now, I want you to look right into my eyes."

Callie blinked, focusing on him through the shadows. He blocked out everything and everyone except her. The sounds of whips and moans, the scents of sweat and sex, the slight chill in the air—all gone. Only she filled his senses.

Without another word, he lifted her to the tip of his cock again, then pressed down, down, down . . . This time, she helped him, folding her knees under her and tilting her hips to take all of him. He met her halfway, thrusting up into her fist-like grasp. She felt so good, his eyes nearly crossed.

He wasn't fucking Callie. He was making love to her. He was claiming her.

This changed everything.

A shudder worked up his spine, spreading through his body. With a groan, he threw his head back and let pleasure fill his veins. Jesus, this woman was potent.

Callie went wild, frantically lifting and thrusting above him. She ran her fingers through his hair, holding on as if he were her anchor to this world. Her soft pants and moans in his ear were driving him out of his fucking mind. So soft everywhere, and her scent . . . something clean and musky at once. The citrus of her shampoo blended with the feminine tang from her pussy for an olfactory high that sent his senses into a drunken daze. He could wax poetic about her for days, but he really just wanted to brand her as his own. Forgetting Callie would be impossible. Sean was damned determined to make sure she couldn't wipe him from her memory bank, either.

Grabbing her hips tighter, he took control. "Slow down."

She reared back to look at him. Her face was flushed. Perspiration dotted her forehead and her upper lip. Her dark hair rained over her shoulders, curling down her slender arms and emphasizing the milky-soft skin he loved stroking.

The more she surrendered to the raw passion between them, the more she tore away at his armor. The deeper he needed to be inside her.

"I ache." She sounded like a wounded girl who needed him to fix her problem.

In many ways, she was.

"Let it build, lovely. We've waited so long already. No need to rush it now."

Callie opened her mouth to protest. No doubt, he would have to remind her about the meaning of submission again, even if he did find her willful insistence adorable at times.

But he couldn't remind her of anything if he didn't first persuade her to stay.

Sean stilled her hips and sent her a stern glance of warning. Then he brought her down on his cock again, like a knife through melting butter. Slowly. So damn slowly a shudder wracked him again. Her keening cry zipped to his balls and straight up his stiff length. Damn it, she was going to dismantle his self-control if he didn't get a grip.

Her delicate fingers bit into his shoulders. She moved with him, graceful, sensual. Their breathing aligned. Sean watched her close her eyes and finally let him dictate their rhythm. He witnessed her slow, intoxicating loss of control.

As she undulated, the delicate collar he'd clipped around her neck twinkled above her breasts, which bounced gently in his face. He took one nipple in his mouth, melting inside as the candy-hard tip tightened on his tongue. Then he took the other tight pink bud between his lips and laved her before sucking deep. Her pussy clamped down on him. Callie was so utterly responsive, and he didn't think for an instant that she simply needed sex after her long abstinence. He wasn't going to be done here until he knew that she needed *him*.

"Sean . . ." Her little cry told him that pleasure was driving her to the peak.

He lifted one hand from her hip, tucking it under her little skirt, then dragged his thumb over her clit.

Her response was instant and gratifying. She shrieked and began fluttering around his cock, seconds from orgasm.

"Come, Callie," he growled.

As if those words held magic for her, she tossed her head back and let out a wail of pleasure. Her back arched, her breasts thrust high, and her cunt held him in a velvet vise. He gritted his teeth, clenching his fists and sweating like a bitch to hold it together.

"Sean!"

Loving the sound of his name on her lips, he rode the wave of her climax, from the short pulses through the endless clutches, to the sweet little aftershocks. Then she dissolved against him, struggling to catch her breath. The urge to explode inside her and mark her with his seed nearly overwhelmed him. Miraculously, willpower and logic prevailed. He needed more of this woman who tripped every sexual trigger in his body.

Brushing her hair away from her damp face, he forced her to look at him. Her eyes were dazed and dilated, her cheeks rosy-hot. That turned him on even more.

"How are you feeling, lovely?"

With a tired, loopy grin that did his heart good, she sighed and melted against his chest. "Fabulous."

"Good to hear." Unfortunately, he was in hell.

She stretched and wriggled. Then she paused.

Callie blinked at him. "You're still . . . You didn't . . ."

"I am and I haven't."

"Oh." Her eyes danced as she leveled him with that vixenish stare he'd come to adore. "Well, I guess I'll just have to take more of you. What a shame."

"A bloody shame for sure." He managed to tease back.

When he urged her up and down his cock again, however, the smile slid from her face. A gasp fell from her lips, then she seemed to stop breathing for a long minute.

"Ah . . . yes," she panted above him. Feminine. A goddess.

The sight aroused him so deeply, Sean knew he couldn't hold on much longer.

Trailing his thumb back to her clit, he slowly rotated until she sucked in a sharp breath, until her body jolted, and she started looking to him for permission.

God, that shit turned him on, even more so with her.

"Lean against me. Put your chest to mine and . . . yes," he praised as she complied.

Then Sean gripped her hips tightly and pistoned inside her, probing deep and quickly learning her body. Her entire front wall was sensitive, so he dragged the head of his cock along it with every thrust. But she also had a spot deep and high. She loved having her cervix nudged. He worked her, paying close attention to every reaction. Callie held her breath, closed her eyes, tensed up, then came the high-pitched pants that rang in his head like an erotic chant. Her fingernails dug into his shoulders. Her pussy clutched him.

He gripped her hair in his fist and tugged. "Look at me. That's it . . . Come for me now!"

"Sean!" Her body jerked and her cunt clamped down on him. *"Sean!"*

As soon as she screamed his name, pleasure sizzled through his blood, igniting everything inside him. Climax rocketed his system, launching him into a realm of thick, tangled ecstasy he'd never known existed. The explosion blasted through his body, deep in his chest, marking his soul. In his head, she might be his, but he knew damn well that he was now hers. Tonight had complicated the fuck out of everything. But as he surged to the peak, he didn't care at all.

"Callie . . ." he panted. "I love you!"

Chapter Three

STANDING in the shadows of Dominion's dungeon, Mitchell Thorpe couldn't miss the orgasm that wracked Callie's body, the fact that she screamed another man's name, or the unabashed way in which she shared herself with that fucking suspicious Scot. As much as he wanted to deny it, the sight and sounds damn near felled Thorpe like a hatchet to the chest.

He'd hoped that insisting on so many restrictions when he'd allowed Sean Kirkpatrick to collar Callie would frustrate the man. That the asshole would leave. Thorpe didn't trust Kirkpatrick. Something was off about the guy . . . But no matter what he'd done, Sean had proven goddamn single-minded when it came to the girl.

Damn it! Thorpe hated the sight of the other man surging deep inside Callie, where he ached to be himself. Clutching the little silk robe he'd retrieved from her room the second he'd realized she meant to let Sean fuck her, he closed his eyes, refusing to watch the bastard come inside her.

The reasons Thorpe could never have Callie were carved into his brain. And even though he'd beaten the dead horse mentally enough to recite the rationale in his sleep, he clenched his jaw and reminded himself again. There would always be fourteen years, two months, and three days' difference in their ages. Besides, he knew Callie wasn't likely to stay with him much longer. Forever was out of the question. More important, he could never give her the kind of love she craved and deserved.

Cursing under his breath, he dared to open his eyes and stare at the wild tangle of Callie's black hair brushing the fair, flushed skin of her back. Desire gnawed at him, biting deep. He'd always believed that by walking away from her that December night two years ago, he could prevent her from breaking his heart. Thorpe didn't find it comforting to be proven so wrong.

Kirkpatrick shouting out his love for her gouged him in the gut. Hearing the Scot admit his feelings for Callie aloud not only made him jealous as hell, but it proved the man had balls. Thorpe was almost in awe. But Sean obviously didn't understand her at all. Thorpe had no doubt what Callie's response to the man's unexpected declaration would be.

Right on cue, she stiffened and shook her head, then scrambled off his lap. Kirkpatrick stood and tore off his condom, trying to zip up while reaching for her with an expression meant to be gentle and calm.

Thorpe snorted. *Wrong approach again.*

It didn't surprise him at all when Callie whirled around, eyes squeezed shut tightly, arms over her breasts, and ran—straight into him.

When she would have stumbled back from their collision, he gripped her shoulders. Thorpe tried not to look at her breasts again. Why tempt himself with what he couldn't have? She blinked up at him, fear and anguish mixed on her face. Guilt followed.

"Let go," she begged. "Please."

Those words alone told Thorpe how raw Kirkpatrick had scraped Callie. Normally, she'd try all kinds of foot stomping, demanding, and plain ol' manipulation before she resorted to showing her soft, submissive side to anyone. Whatever the man's game, Thorpe had to give Sean credit for opening her emotions far wider than expected.

Over her shoulders, he eased the robe he'd retrieved in case her second thoughts about having sex with the Scot set in. Nice to see that he still knew her so well.

He sent her a sharp shake of his head. "Not yet, pet."

Callie shoved her arms through the holes and belted the robe tight, sending him a defiant glare. But tears still lurked under it. The fucking Scot playing with her heart had rattled her. Thorpe hated the asshole for it even more. His need to protect her growled, chomping at the bit to tear the collar from her neck and free her. He couldn't do that, but he had every intention of having a "chat" with Kirkpatrick.

"Why are your hands on Callie?" Sean demanded. "She's my sub."

"You're under *my* roof, and she's obviously upset."

"Which is why I need to talk to her. She and I should be sorting this out. Alone."

Normally, he would agree. But he wouldn't risk Callie by leaving her vulnerable with a man he swore had some hidden agenda. A fraud. Besides, Kirkpatrick didn't know her like he did and never would. "At Dominion, my word is law. Play by my rules or you're welcome to leave. Your choice."

Sean clenched his fists and ignored him, focusing on Callie. "Talk to me, lovely. If I upset you, help me understand why."

Thorpe felt her stiffen in his grip, then she looked up at him, her gaze imploring. He understood instantly. She'd developed feelings for this man and hated to hurt him. But he also knew that she didn't dare let him close.

"Callie, go to your room. I'll be in to see you in a minute." Thorpe motioned for Zeb, one of the dungeon monitors.

"You can't send her from me. I didn't hurt her," Kirkpatrick protested.

With a shrug, Thorpe blew Sean off and addressed the approaching DM. "Take Callie to her room. No one enters until I say otherwise. And she doesn't leave." When Callie gasped, he sent her a knowing look. "Do you have something to say, pet?"

Since she wasn't about to admit that she'd plotted to flee the club, she remained silent. But he knew it as sure as he knew himself. Kilpatrick hadn't just plumbed her physically. He'd pried her heart open, and she was preparing to react to that in the only way she knew—by running. Already, she'd mentally packed her bags. Thorpe forced down his panic and reminded himself that as long as she was still here, he could fix the situation. The easiest solution would be to toss the damn Scot out on his ear.

Callie looked ready to grind her teeth as she stomped off. Zeb followed with a grin and a wink.

Thorpe vowed to deal with her little fit of pique as soon as he'd unmasked this fraud and rid him from her life. "My office. Now."

He didn't wait to see if Kirkpatrick followed. He'd rather the fucker find the exit and save him the breath. But when he reached his personal domain and rounded his desk, the Scot stood in the portal, all but foaming at the mouth.

Sean slammed the door, enclosing them in a privacy steeped in thick air. "You have no right to separate me from Callie."

"I'm responsible for the welfare of all the subs under this roof. Until I know why she was running away from you in tears, then yes, I do."

"That's a piss-poor excuse. You're jealous because you want her for your own."

Thorpe took his time answering, sitting in his leather chair and staring the charlatan down. Idly, he wondered when and how he'd been stupid enough to tip Sean off. Xander had pointed it out, too, a few months ago. Maybe he was getting sloppy.

"I have not laid a single finger on the girl for any reason in nearly two years. So what you believe I want is irrelevant. Let's talk about what actually happened."

Sean sat, poised on the edge of his chair as if he'd rather fight. "I restrained and blindfolded her, then I flogged her. She reached a peaceful subspace. Then when she came out, I made love to her. It's been an emotional night. That's all."

Is that what the idiot thought? "That's not how Callie works. Have you been too busy fucking her to get to know her?"

"You've watched me like you're her bloody keeper, so I suspect you know that's not true." Kirkpatrick raised a brow at him. "Just like I suspect you've been too busy getting to know her to fuck her. Your knickers are in a twist now that you've lost your chance. Be warned. I mean to make her mine in every way."

Thorpe wanted to rip the guy's face off, but managed to keep his composure. "She's wearing your collar already."

"I want more, and you're standing in my way."

"I'm standing in the way because her teary dash away from you didn't indicate happiness. I'll confess that Callie is special to me. I've protected her since she came to Dominion. I know her inside and out. She's not a girl prone to crying jags. So her behavior tonight has to be a direct reflection of something you've done."

Sean pounded his fist on the desk. "I'm telling you, I finally reached her. I broke through that mile-thick armor of hers and saw the woman inside. Every minute you keep me from her is another minute she has to rebuild her walls. And to escape. I think she's planning to run."

Thorpe drew in a steadying breath, then forced himself to look at Kirkpatrick with a calm he didn't feel. The man didn't understand all the bits of Callie . . . but he was catching on fast. "What makes you think that?"

"Don't play games. If you know the girl, then you know I'm right."

Thorpe neither confirmed nor denied. But Kirkpatrick's uncanny perception troubled him. "Is that what you think?"

"I *know*. Her surrender was so sudden, as if she meant it as a good-bye."

If Callie cared for the Scot, she would absolutely give a huge chunk of her soul to him as a parting gift.

Thorpe wondered what she'd planned on giving him. A note? An empty room where her scent would linger and haunt him? A hole in his heart?

Damn it, he sounded whiny and maudlin. He would not let Callie leave without cause. As far as he was concerned, no one here but him knew she was a fugitive. And Sean Kirkpatrick was nothing more than a blip on his radar.

"I won't know if you're right until I talk to her."

The other Dom snorted. "And what good will that do? She's lived under your roof for four years. The girl is broken, and you haven't lifted a finger to heal her. Why start now?"

It took everything Thorpe had not to snarl and surge across the desk. God, he'd love to wrap his hands around the Scot's neck. Instead, he tapped his fingers on the desktop, staring down Kirkpatrick as if he were lint from his underwear.

"Since you didn't know her when she first arrived here, allow me to call bullshit." But Thorpe understood well that while she'd made strides under his protection, she was nowhere near whole.

In order to take Callie's hand and heal her, he'd have to share too much of himself with her—his heart, his truth, his secrets. He'd have to be a better man, the sort who could love her openly with every cell in his body. She wouldn't accept less, nor should she.

It wasn't that he didn't care enough about Callie to try to conquer his demons. They were simply too big. And with her past . . . she'd only leave him. If his wife of three years could walk away so easily, how badly would a girl on the run who lit the flame in his heart burn him?

Hell, she had no idea that he'd figured out her identity. But she would run the moment she did. From what he could grasp, she did that any time she felt threatened or exposed. Exactly like Kirkpatrick was doing to her now.

A little digging proved that she'd abruptly left her last two hiding places, one after only a handful of weeks. The trail before that was stone cold, and he didn't imagine that she'd stayed anywhere else for very long. If she had, she'd have left an indelible impression. She had on him almost instantly.

Sean shrugged. "I'll admit that I don't know what she was like four years ago. But if you call her 'healed' now, you need to pull your head from your arse. She needs someone to care about her, give her tender guidance."

She did, and that was part of Thorpe's rub. But he also knew something else about Callie with absolute certainty that Sean didn't.

"She requires a firm hand."

The Scot shook his head. "You're daft, man. That just fuels her defiance. It's love she needs."

Thorpe sat back in his chair and crossed his arms. "I won't disagree. Show me a woman who doesn't need love. It's the foundation Callie will build her life on—with the right man. But she needs boundaries, too. Craves them. They'll make her feel safe. That's what I've given her for the last four years."

Kirkpatrick glared incredulously. "You're wrong, man. She needs what I can give her. I intend to make her whole, and I won't let you take her from me."

At least some of that was bullshit, and Thorpe resisted the urge to spit his anger. Apparently, Sean didn't understand that if he wanted to claim Callie, she'd already be in his bed with his collar around her neck.

"I have no intention of coming between you two, and I'd like to see her happy. I merely want to sort out this situation to my satisfaction before I decide whether to return her to your care." In case

Sean's designs on Callie weren't purely Dominant, as Thorpe suspected. "So this is how it's going to go . . ." He stood and paced, happily taking the psychological advantage of standing over Kirkpatrick. Time to test the son of a bitch. "You're going to give me fifteen minutes with Callie, alone. Gloves off."

Sean jumped to his feet, fists clenched. "The hell I am!"

"Are you refusing?"

"You're damn right." The Scot turned red with anger.

"Well . . ." Thorpe smiled tightly. "Let's review. By our agreement, you're not allowed to see the girl off the premises without my permission. I haven't granted that. You won't be seeing Callie here, either, unless I deem it in her best interest. So if you'd like to continue taking her down the submissive path, then I'm afraid you don't have many options."

"You controlling wanker. You have her so tightly under your thumb—"

"I keep her protected. I'll find out why she's upset, if she's truly planning to leave, and whether she wants to wear your collar anymore. I'm a safe authority figure for her. She'll tell me what I want to know."

Kirkpatrick looked like he was torn between violent disagreement and a desire to commit murder. "I want to observe, then. Certainly you have a room or two here that allows for voyeurs."

Thorpe worked hard not to roll his eyes. "I do. Callie has lived and worked here for four years. She knows each and every one of those rooms. She knows where our conversations won't be overheard. The girl is cautious and clever, as I'm sure you're aware. She's not going to compromise her privacy. That I can tell you unequivocally."

After a long sigh, Sean looked around the room like it held the answers to his burning questions. Or like he'd rather look anywhere but at his rival. Thorpe smiled.

"You're a pushy bastard."

"Isn't that part of being a Dom?" He shrugged. "Do we have a deal, or can I escort you to the door?"

"You'd like that," Sean accused.

Very much. But Thorpe held his tongue. "This isn't about me at all. It isn't about you, either. If you care for Callie's welfare, then you won't mind me checking in with her to make sure she's all right and ready to see you again."

The man's blue eyes narrowed. "If you were anyone else, I wouldn't. But what do you mean 'gloves off'?"

"Certainly, you've noticed that Callie has . . . let's call it a strong will."

Sean snorted. "Stubborn as a mule, that one."

Thorpe tried not to smile. "Precisely. Given that obvious fact, for my conversation to have any effect on her, I need to have a full array of options available."

"You're asking my permission to discipline her?" The other man raised a dark brow.

"No, I'm not asking permission. I'm telling you I'll need to keep that as a possibility." He shrugged with mock regret. "Might as well be honest. With Callie, it's a probability."

And Thorpe wasn't lying to himself. He would thoroughly enjoy it. Anytime he got to touch the girl was a sublime thrill.

"I don't like it and I don't trust you." Sean crossed his arms over his chest in challenge.

"Let's cut to the chase. You don't like *me.* Likewise," he said bluntly. "But we're both motivated by Callie and her well-being. So let's stay on task, shall we? You want to know if she's planning to leave. I want to ensure that she's in a good mental and emotional place before I allow her to scene with you again. These don't have to be mutually incompatible goals. Give me fifteen minutes. I'll give you answers."

Everything about Sean's body language said that he used all his restraint not to throw a punch. *Pity.* Knocking the asshole into next week would significantly improve Thorpe's mood. The man knew the feel of Callie's body intimately. He'd had the opportunity to experience her surrender. He'd had the luxury of telling the beautiful girl how he felt.

So yes, Thorpe felt every bit of his jealousy.

"I don't like being backed in a corner, but you haven't given me much choice. If you don't have answers in fifteen minutes, you give her back to me. I'll soothe her and set her right."

Thorpe headed for the door. "Mr. Kirkpatrick, the first rule of negotiation is that you must have some bargaining power. At the moment, you don't. Wait for my return."

He didn't let the Scot get a word in before he strode out of his office and grabbed his phone from his pocket. His first text was to Axel, probably holed up in the security booth with a few of his compadres. He told the other Dom to get to his office ASAP and that he was free to fuck with Sean's head if he could get any answers about why the Scot had come to Dominion.

After an enthusiastic yes in reply, he tapped a message to Zeb asking what Callie was doing. The reply came quickly. Sounds like she's in the shower.

Bullshit. Thorpe knew Callie's habits well. She'd showered just before Sean's arrival. She wouldn't want to undo all that makeup when there was a chance she might see the man again. If there was one thing Callie didn't allow, it was for *anyone* to see her with a bare face.

Find out if she's packing a suitcase, he replied. The door will be locked. Do what you have to do.

This time, the pause seemed to last forever. While he waited, Thorpe grabbed a few things he might need from around the dungeon to make his point with Callie and slipped them into his pocket. Then he let his long legs eat up the distance between the main part of the club and Callie's room. Just before he reached her door, Zeb's answer came. Picked the lock. She's shoved most of her bathroom and closet into two bags.

"Son of a bitch," Thorpe cursed roundly. Sean had scared the hell out of her. He wished now that he had punched the asshole.

I'll take it from here, he texted back, then pocketed his phone again.

The door to Callie's room opened, and Zeb stepped out. With a passing nod, Thorpe greeted him, then strode inside, shutting and locking the door behind him. He shoved her desk chair against it for good measure.

The air was humid from her recent "shower." She'd flung on every light. Her two hastily packed bags sat in the corner near the door.

Callie paced in her little red robe, her manic gait taking her from one side of the room to the other. Goddamn it, she wasn't wearing a bra. He'd bet she hadn't bothered with panties, either.

Most notably, she'd stripped off her collar and was clutching it in a tight grasp. His heart stuttered. Was she removing it for good?

As Thorpe cleared his throat, he tamped down encroaching relief and told himself to take things one step at a time.

She turned to spear him with a resolute stare. "You said you wanted to know when I'm leaving. It's now. I quit."

* * *

CALLIE stared at Thorpe. He had almost no reaction to her words. *Gee, it would have been nice if you'd given a shit.* Then she squashed the thought. It wasn't his fault that she cared far more about him than he did for her. She'd known for years that Thorpe had the power to yank her heart out of her chest and crush it beneath his very expensive Salvatore Ferragamo loafers. It sucked that she'd been stupid enough to let him.

Even though she cared deeply for Sean and—if she could believe his passionate declaration—he loved her, that didn't mitigate her attachment to Dominion's owner. She'd always been a little screwed up. This just proved it.

Thorpe wandered farther into the room and sat on the edge of the bed. "I appreciate the notice, but I need a bit longer than ten minutes to replace you, pet."

"Sorry." She tossed her hair over her shoulder and stared out the dark window. He was far too beautiful to look at. "You'll find someone else soon. You won't miss me."

"You have no idea how I'll feel. Sit down, Callie."

His tone told her that no wasn't an acceptable answer. Damn it, he intended to interrogate her about Sean. Callie couldn't take it now. Leaving them both was hard enough . . .

She fought down panic and turned back to him. "I can't. I have to get away."

"Not yet." He pointed to a spot on the bed right beside him and didn't say a word until she flopped down. "Good. Sean knows I've come and that I intend to understand what happened tonight. Tell me everything."

If Thorpe was here with Sean's blessing, she wasn't going to worm out of this conversation, damn it.

As she set Sean's collar down on her nightstand, Callie mentally sorted through everything she could tell him. He must know that she had feelings for her Sir. More feelings than she was comfortable with. Thorpe missed very little, so he was no doubt aware that Sean had never taken her past her limits, ignored her safe word, or acted in any way out of line. Besides, if she was going to skip out on Thorpe after he'd kept a roof over her and ensured her safety for four years, she owed him more than a flat-out lie.

Wringing her hands, she forced herself to meet his intent gray gaze and confessed something else that had been niggling in the back of her brain. "Something is . . . off about him."

That clearly piqued Thorpe's interest. "In what way?"

Callie tapped her toes. She had to express her concerns about Sean without giving her past away. Putting Thorpe in the terrible position of harboring a known fugitive wasn't how she wanted to repay his kindness.

"He asks a lot of questions. I don't like them."

Thorpe sent her a wry smile. "If it's about your limits, that's to be expected. Pet, he's a Dom. It's his job to get in your head. Frankly, you need some untangling. You might find it uncomfortable—"

"He doesn't need to know how many brothers and sisters I have, the name of my first pet, if I ever took special trips as a child . . . He seems really focused on things that shouldn't matter if all he wants is a sub in a club."

It was nothing Thorpe did or any change in his expression, but Callie had the distinct impression that he was enraged. "Has he always behaved this way with you?"

"Yeah."

"You should have told me the first time," Thorpe scolded.

"It's not your problem."

That only made him more forbidding. "You're always my concern, Callie."

The possession in his voice excited her more than she wanted to admit. "Well, I'm telling you now. What he wants to know seems weird."

"I agree."

"Just like it's weird that he walked into Dominion and immediately had some sort of hard-on for me."

"That's not weird. That makes him a man."

She rolled her eyes. "There are plenty of other subs here."

"None of them are you."

Damn it, sometimes Thorpe could—after weeks of being a giant pain in her ass—say the nicest things. She teared up. Gawd, she was really going to miss him.

"But . . ." he went on. "I don't like the questions he's asking you, either. I don't see how they're relevant to helping you down your submissive path."

"Exactly. The other thing is . . . In almost every other way, he's too good to be true."

Thorpe regarded her intently. "Do you think he's a player?"

"No." But something wasn't quite right. "I'm not sure what to make of him, though."

Because if Sean was a cop, a bounty hunter, or an assassin, wouldn't he have either dragged her in or done her in by now?

"What did he say to you tonight that made you want to run away from him?"

Oh. Ouch. Yeah, she needed to remember that Thorpe never hesitated to go for the jugular.

"Nothing he meant to be threatening or scary."

"Good to know. Be more specific." Thorpe's tone sharpened.

"It's . . . personal."

"Dodging my question isn't an option, pet." That warning note in his voice made her shiver. "I'd rather not see you leave over whatever drivel he spewed. Tell me. Maybe I can fix the situation."

It was embarrassing enough that he'd probably seen her and Sean having sex. He'd been so close, he couldn't have missed their climatic finish. "You didn't hear?"

"Callie, I'm not getting through to you, so let me be plain. You will tell me now or I will paddle your pretty little ass."

"You can't do that!"

His smile contradicted her. "I've informed Sean that it's a distinct possibility. Besides, you've taken off his collar. If you think he's being less than honest, you don't intend to put it back on, do you?"

"Why would I? I already told you, I'm leaving."

"Not until I know why."

She jumped to her feet, gaping at him. "You'd keep me here against my will?"

Thorpe crossed an ankle over his knee and brushed an imaginary thread from his trousers. "Your tone suggests I should be uncomfortable with that idea. Until you're honest with me, I assure you I'm not. Furthermore, if Kirkpatrick is troubling you, he's nothing I can't handle. Am I clear?"

Callie blinked at him, processing everything he'd delivered in that low, almost relaxed voice. She wasn't fooled. Under his urbane, oh so cultured façade beat the heart of a predator. She'd seen him take rivals apart both mentally and physically. Thorpe wasn't someone a sane person crossed.

Callie weighed her words carefully. "Sean made me realize I'm not cut out for a Dom/sub relationship."

"Really, pet?"

She sidestepped his question. "And I'm a little bored with Dallas. Los Angeles is calling my name. Every time Xander comes by and talks about his trips to the city, it sounds fabulous. It's just time to move on."

Thorpe said nothing for a long moment. He simply stood and towered over her, that charcoal stare boring into her. "There will be consequences for anything less than totally honesty, so think carefully, Callie. Would you like to recant or amend your statement in any way?"

Shit. Thorpe knew something. Or everything. Had he heard Sean's declaration of love?

She tossed her head back and thrust her hands on her hips. This was going to be ugly no matter what. Might as well go for broke. "Butt out and stop acting like you're my father."

He stilled. "That's one role I will *never* fill, but I have no problem putting you in your place."

Callie didn't even have a moment to wonder what his silky vow meant before he hauled her into his arms and dragged her, kicking and screaming, back to her bed. He sat, wrangling her with embarrassing ease, then spread his long legs and laid her over his lap, face down.

"You are *not* going to spank me!" she insisted.

Thorpe didn't hesitate for an instant. "I am. I told you there would be consequences. You should know I always keep up my end of a bargain."

He planted his huge palm in the small of her back, silently telling her how futile her struggles were. With his free hand, he slid the silk of her robe up and over her bare ass. Her entire body tensed. What was he seeing? Thinking? And why was the thought of his discipline so damn arousing?

There was definitely something wrong with her.

"Don't I get a safe word?" she demanded.

"I'm not strapping you to a cross and unleashing a single tail on you, so don't insult me. I *know* you. I've spanked you before."

For demonstration purposes, yes. In fact, the first time, she'd giggled—until he landed a single smack on her ass. Then it hadn't been funny anymore. By the fifth swat, she'd been uncomfortably wet. By the tenth, she'd had to bite back a plea to come. Thorpe had some mysterious effect on her that she didn't understand.

"I'm not afraid. Last time you did this, you couldn't get my clothes off fast enough. When you did, you couldn't wait to run away. You're not going to do anything to me now."

Thorpe's grip on her tightened.

Crap, she was taking a *huge* chance by throwing that night in his face. No doubt, she was pissing him off. She suspected she was also arousing him, because as she wriggled on his lap, Callie couldn't miss the fact that he was hard as hell.

"Wrong," he quipped in her ear. "I'm going to spank you until you answer my question *and* apologize for your disrespect."

"You're not my Dom."

"But I am *a* Dom, and this behavior is unbecoming. Start counting, pet. Don't stop until I do."

Callie tried again to squirm away. She rubbed against his cock, and he hissed. Then his palm landed on her ass in a blistering blow.

"Ouch!" she protested, resisting the urge to rub her right cheek.

"Yes, that's why it's called punishment."

"This is Sean's right, not yours." She grasped at straws.

"Not if you've rescinded his collar. Since you said you had, I'll remind you that you live here, you work for me, and you're being very bratty. That's three strikes, pet."

She had no chance to scrape together a reply before he hit her again. Her left cheek stung, but not as much as her pride. And it didn't take long for tingles to dance across her skin. Her blood heated, and her body melted under his touch.

Damn it.

"You haven't counted yet," he pointed out. "Shall we start over?"

"I've never understand a Dom's fascination with a sub counting. You're educated. You can get to ten without me."

"You think I'm stopping at ten?" he drawled.

Callie drew in a breath and tried to calm herself. "Thorpe, please . . . Can't I have a little privacy? Isn't it enough for you to know that Sean didn't mean to upset me?"

"No. As long as you're at Dominion, that's my call. I've protected you for years and I don't plan on stopping." He paused. "It pleases me to know you're safe, but I find all this defiance when I'm trying to help you deeply disappointing."

The fight went out of her. Callie hated to let Thorpe down. Most everyone else could blow it out their ass for all she cared. But the big Dom mattered too much to her—and he knew it.

"You're being manipulative," she grumbled. "One. And two."

"I'm always manipulative when you're being both mouthy and dishonest. If Mr. Kirkpatrick didn't show you the error of your ways, I will." He punctuated the statement with another swat to her right cheek.

"Three." She knew she sounded pouty.

Thorpe always got the best of her. Half the time she couldn't decide if she resented that as much as the way their verbal fencing made her ache endlessly for him. It didn't matter that she inevitably lost their battles of will. The power radiating off Thorpe aroused her like nothing else. It always had.

But Sean had a huge chunk of her heart. What sucked more was that caring about either—much less both—of them was not only futile, it could be deadly.

Chapter Four

THORPE couldn't take his eyes off Callie's reddening ass . . . just like he'd never been able to in the past. He took a particular pride in knowing she wore his mark, even temporarily.

God, he was a sick fuck. But that wasn't going to stop him.

He had to discipline her. More important, he had to give her a reason to stay.

Her body perched over his lap, her every muscle tense. She panted. Her skin flushed. Callie might be angry as hell with him, but one thing was clear and sent a jolt of electric desire to his cock: She hadn't stopped wanting him in the last two years any more than he'd stopped craving her. And if she was going to rescind Kirkpatrick's collar, now might be his only chance to touch her. If she still ran, it would hurt like hell—but he couldn't let this chance slip by.

Dragging in a ragged breath, he brought his hand up and smacked her ass again, repeating the gesture the second the count left her lips. Slowly, her body thawed until she sank into him, her responses turning breathy.

Ten, eleven, twelve . . . He slipped into a rhythm, slow and meaningful, deliberate, measured, strong. *Thirteen, fourteen, fifteen* . . . Why was it so fucking easy to get into his Dom space with Callie?

He never had to try. The moment he touched her, it was there, a boundless pool of it. He felt her needs as if they were his own. With her sprawled across his lap, he could read her utterly, each and every nuance.

She wanted him. Yes, she'd been thinking about that goddamn Scot earlier. She was likely also wondering how she could have feelings for two men at once. As much as he disliked Kirkpatrick, Thorpe wondered that, too. But that bastard was no longer important. This tempo, his punishment, her peace—they both needed it. Then he'd bring her against his chest and care for her, cuddle and shower her with worship, find out what she needed to stay.

Callie might not be his, but he'd do whatever it took to keep her here.

"Twenty," she whispered, absolutely limp against his thighs.

Thorpe had no doubt her head was floating. Her defiance was gone. Her ass throbbed a fiery red. Her cunt seeped a sweet musk. His hand tingled. His mouth watered.

Just like the last time he'd spanked her, he was dying to fuck her. Like the last two years of avoiding every opportunity to touch her had never existed.

Letting out a harsh breath, Thorpe dragged his stinging palm over her burning backside, slowly soothing out the ache.

"Time to apologize, pet."

"I'm sorry, Sir." Her voice was slurred.

Callie sounded mostly sincere. He smiled, despite the shitty mess he found himself in.

How long could he keep this girl believing that he didn't want her with every breath he drew?

On the other hand, what else could he do? Melissa had upended his world after she'd promised to love him until death parted them, then suddenly served him with divorce papers. And that just topped the stinking pile of shit. As much as he adored Callie, he couldn't risk his heart, especially for a woman with one foot out the door.

Minus any easy answers, Thorpe gathered the pliant beauty into his lap. She rested her head on his shoulder. With his chest tight and aching, he wrapped his arms around her and kissed the top of her head, savoring her nearness.

"What did Sean say to upset you?"

"That he loves me."

Thorpe winced. He'd known that, but hearing her admit it still jabbed him. He forced himself to smooth his features and lifted her chin with one hand. "Why did that make you cry?"

Slowly, she blinked, opening her eyes, and focusing that dazed blue stare on him. "I shouldn't love anyone." Callie lifted her hand and cupped his jaw, smoothing her thumb over his cheek. "But it's too late. It has been for a long time."

His heart lurched. Jesus, her feelings weren't a surprise, not really. The unspoken emotions between them had been the neon billboard in the room for years.

He wrapped her hand in his and drew it away from his face. "You have feelings for Kirkpatrick, too?"

"Yes." Her eyes clouded over. Tears leaked out. "I'm so confused."

Of course she was. She didn't have the life experience to deal with this shit. Hell, he was significantly older and he didn't feel equipped to handle it, either.

Sean's words haunted him. *She needs tender guidance.* Thorpe had guided her, all right. But he'd never been able to do it tenderly. Boundaries and protection he could give her without compromising his heart, but seeing the love in her eyes now as she pressed her fragile body against him . . . Everything about her was killing his resolve to remain aloof.

"Callie, pet. You can't leave me." His voice croaked, and an unfamiliar sting prickled his eyes.

He slammed his lids down. Damn it, he could not afford this weakness.

"Better for you if I do." She sounded so damn sad.

Thorpe shook his head, holding her closer. "You'd ruin me, pet. In fact, I think you already have."

Callie threw her arms around him, her breath warm against his neck. He gripped her tighter. Normally, he'd wish he hadn't spilled his guts . . . but he would try if any bit of the truth kept her with him.

"You'll be my biggest regret," she whispered.

Goddamn it, that hurt.

Maybe he should simply admit that he knew she was a fugitive. Almost as quickly, Thorpe dismissed the idea. If she was insistent on running now, he suspected that divulging what he knew would only make Callie more determined to flee.

He held her tighter, taking in everything that made her uniquely Callie. The firm little curves of her body, those long lashes against her fair cheeks, her fingers digging into his shirtfront as if seeking reassurance. This close, he smelled her citrus shampoo and the remnants of the hair color he knew she used as a disguise. Her signature pink polish colored her petite toes, spritzed with glitter. And the soft little shudders of her body as she cried ripped out his heart.

"I won't give you a chance to regret me, pet. I sure as hell refuse to wish I'd done something different while I had you with me." He was already going to regret the last four years. "Lie back."

She gasped softly, her gaze shooting up to his. She swallowed. Desire mingled with despair and wracked her face. "Thorpe . . . I can't."

He tensed. "Because of Kirkpatrick?"

Callie nodded.

"You've said you're rescinding his collar. If you're leaving here, you're obviously leaving him, too."

"I know." More tears clouded her eyes.

If it wasn't just about misguided loyalty to the Scot, what else was she hesitating about? The hurt from his desertion two Decembers ago? Christ, that had to be it. Remorse wracked him.

"I won't walk away from you this time without giving you pleasure. I give you my word."

Callie stared, breath held, the moment frozen. Thorpe watched her face as a thousand thoughts zipped through her head. And he saw the second she decided that if she was severing her bond with Kirkpatrick and fleeing, then she'd rather have him once than never at all.

With a sad smile, she climbed out of his lap and onto her bed, lying across it. Thorpe turned to watch her as she held out her arms to him, a silent siren call he had no idea how or if he could resist.

On the other hand, he had his answer about her parting gift to him. Tonight, she intended to give all of herself. Her body. Her heart. Her soul.

Her response both touched and infuriated him to the core. The girl was often so damn unpredictable. Right now, he'd have to be the same.

Standing, Thorpe shucked his suit coat. Then he doffed his cuff links, setting them on her nightstand. He draped his shirt over his coat at the head of the bed. Then he checked the pockets of his trousers. What he needed still rested inside. With a bracing breath, he turned to Callie.

"Robe off, pet. Spread your legs."

Her fingers trembled as she worked the knot around her waist free. With a little lift and an arch of her graceful spine, she pulled it away from her body, gathering the silk in one hand, then letting it puddle on the floor. He would never get over how beautiful she was and the visceral reaction she elicited in him every damn time he came near her.

Callie slowly parted her thighs. His heart chugged. Technically, he should walk away and leave her untouched until she formally severed her relationship with Sean. Putting his hands on another Dom's sub wasn't ethical. The fact that he suspected Kirkpatrick of being a deceitful douche bag wasn't relevant. Thorpe realized it was possible he'd convinced himself that these were extenuating circumstances because he wanted Callie so badly. But he couldn't make himself care. This was likely his last chance to persuade her to stay. If he had to risk his reputation in the BDSM community to keep her safe from a man who might be trying to snuff her out or lock her in prison, so be it.

Her bare pussy splayed out in front of him, pink and swollen and tantalizing. Even if she remained at Dominion, this opportunity would probably never come again. If she wasn't with Kirkpatrick, she'd be with someone else. Callie wasn't cut out to spend her life alone, and he shouldn't punish her because he'd resigned himself to solitude.

Thorpe refused to take from her now, but he would gladly give.

He lowered himself to the bed between her legs. Her stare never wavered from him, but he heard her indrawn breath. As he engulfed her hip with his hand, she shivered. Then, settling himself on his chest, Thorpe took her other hip in hand and dragged her closer, until her pussy was a breath away from his lips.

"Thorpe, you said . . ."

"You assumed." He corrected. "You're not dictating the terms, Callie."

"I know." She thrashed beneath him.

"Problem, pet?"

Callie bent her knees, writhed, lifted her hips restlessly. "You make me ache."

Thorpe couldn't help but smile. "You do the same to me. Relax."

"Hurry."

"Always topping from the bottom," he chided. But that was part of her charm.

Before she could reply, he set his mouth over her pussy and began consuming as much of Callie as he could. He'd dreamed of her. Her scent had driven him to obsess about her flavor day after day, seemingly forever. But the moment she hit his tongue, it was like tasting a delicacy he constantly craved. Like Callie herself, her pussy was sweet and tart and soft . . . with just a hint of something he hadn't encountered in any other woman. And doubted he ever would again.

Her soft gasp went straight to his cock, and he raised up on his elbows, his thumbs parting the swollen lips of her sex. He lashed her hardening clit with gentle, rhythmic strokes, concentrating on growing her need. Her skin turned a rosy pink. She grabbed at the sheets with restless fingers. Her hips moved in time with his mouth. Her gasps became moans.

Lifting his lips for a moment, he nipped at her thigh and tended to her engorged bundle of nerves with sure fingers. "Does that feel good, pet?"

"Yes." Callie thrashed under him. "Please . . . More."

Thorpe smiled, eager to indulge her. He bent to her again, raking his tongue through her sultry sex. This time, he didn't bother with a slow courting of her flesh. He seized her, sucking at her clit, drawing her deeper into pleasure, wordlessly demanding her orgasm. If he had one chance to taste her, he planned to shove her to the brink, take her power, then drive it back into her so she never forgot this night.

Her moans shortened, went up an octave. Under his hands, her thighs clenched. The rest of her body tensed. Her fingers found their way into his hair and pulled. A shudder slammed down his spine. She'd be a hellcat to fuck, an active, clawing, screaming lover he'd want again and again.

And if he didn't stop thinking that, he would rip his pants off and find out for himself. Staying on course and making her feel treasured was more important than getting off.

Thorpe slid two fingers inside her. Oh, fuck, was she ever tight. He gave grudging credit to Kirkpatrick for lasting as long as he had. Being inside Callie's little sweltering cunt was one of his favorite fantasies. When he was alone and tired of all the women who joined Dominion because they'd read some fucking book and had no clue what submission actually meant, he escaped to his shower, stroked himself, and imagined her.

Probing Callie gently, it didn't take him long to learn where she was sensitive. Her bucking body and imploring whimpers gave her away.

He went after her in earnest, eating at her like a juicy piece of fruit, fucking her thoroughly with his fingers and tongue—and wishing to hell he could mount and claim her.

"Thorpe!"

She was begging for his permission. It was in her voice. In her swollen pussy. In her clutching fingers. In her heels as they dug into the mattress beside him.

Fuck, yes. He was going to make Callie splinter into little pieces before him. And he was going to enjoy the hell out of seeing her shatter—this time for him and him alone.

Keeping his fingers tucked tightly inside her, Thorpe worked his way up her body, kissing and nipping her stomach, the underside of her breasts, her nipples, her neck, then her lush bow of a mouth. God, he hadn't kissed her in forever and he'd missed it so damn much. He wanted to crawl inside her, take her, thrill her, please her.

He wanted to own her.

Imfuckingpossible.

They had here and now. Tomorrow . . . he had no idea what would happen. He was used to controlling most everything around him. But he couldn't control Callie or the future. That fact chafed him like nothing else.

Thorpe sank deeper into her mouth, prowling past her plump lips to curl his tongue around hers and capture every bit of her sweet response he could. He moaned, fitting his body against hers and slowly withdrawing his fingers from her pussy, letting them hover just over her clit, where she needed him to touch her most.

"Hands over your head, pet."

Callie complied without pausing for even a heartbeat. "Please. I need you . . ."

She did, but not in the way she begged for. She needed the limits he'd once given her. He'd stopped because she'd turned to Kirkpatrick. And he hadn't fought for her. Now she sought to leave him altogether.

You're only getting what you deserve.

Shoving aside the mocking voice, he reached into his pocket and withdrew the cuffs he'd secreted there. Before she knew what he was about, he flicked one around her left wrist, poised above her head. The other cuff he tethered to the metal frame of her platform bed with a jangle.

"What are you doing?" she asked, tugging and frowning when the cuffs clattered.

"Look at me." He demanded, setting his fingers back over her clit. "And don't look away. Do you understand?"

"Yes." Her voice trembled. Her body shook. Her eyes pleaded.

With his cock as hard as iron, Thorpe hissed in a breath and delved deep into her eyes. "Take the pleasure I'm giving you as a vow, pet. If you leave me, I will hunt you to the ends of the earth. There won't be a place you hide where I can't find you. I will never stop looking. I will never give up. I will never let you go when I can save you."

"Thorpe, don't . . . You can't—"

He cut her off by working her clit expertly with two fingers devastating either side of the little bud, then alternately rubbing extra friction on top.

"Yes, I can. I told you to look at me. Now," he demanded. "Come!"

Her eyes turned a dizzying blue, widening with every breath she hitched in, emphasized by the red flush of her cheeks. He didn't give Callie permission, but she screamed anyway. The sound rang in his

ears, echoed off the walls, and no doubt drifted down the hall. It
went on and on as her body convulsed and her clit turned to stone
under his touch, then pulsed brilliantly again and again.

Callie tumbled into his eyes as the world fell away. Only she
existed.

God, she was stunning. When she surrendered, she did it absolutely.

And the knowledge that he had to leave her now because he
couldn't trust himself not to strip off and fuck her was killing him.

Closing his eyes, gathering his will, he kissed Callie on each hot
cheek, brushed his lips over her damp forehead, then took her mouth
in one last lingering press. He stayed there, struggling to drag in air.
A moment, then another. He cherished each precious, irreplaceable
second. Callie sobbed, and his chest shattered.

Thorpe broke the kiss and pressed his forehead to hers, nuzzling her.

"You promised you wouldn't walk away," she said through tears.

"I said I wouldn't before I gave you pleasure. You're not getting
away from me, pet. Don't make me show you my ruthless side." He
thumbed the wells of her eyes dry with a soft touch. Then he draped
the comforter over her, found her purse, and rifled through it until
he located her car keys. Pocketing them, he shrugged on his shirt,
attached his cuff links, then grabbed his coat and her packed bags.

"Damn it, Thorpe. You can't undo me like that, then get up and
leave."

He headed for the door. "I'll be back."

* * *

THE second Thorpe let himself out, Kirkpatrick came stomping
down the hall, barreling toward him like a man ready for a fight.
How the hell had he gotten past Axel?

"What the bloody hell are you doing to Callie? I can hear her
screaming all over the club."

"Do you think I hurt her?"

Sean's face turned red. "I think you put your fucking hands all over her."

"Ding, ding, ding. Someone get the man a prize." He edged away from Sean, intent on reaching his office.

Kirkpatrick jabbed him in the jaw, then followed up with a mean left hook to the gut. Thorpe hadn't seen it coming . . . but he should have.

He doubled over, and Sean took the opportunity to slam him against the wall. "How dare you touch *my* collared submissive? I'm bloody in love with Callie. I know you overheard me tell her. I made certain of it."

Thorpe stared at his unwanted rival, trying to shove him off. Kirkpatrick wasn't budging. Well, the guy had some game. *Interesting note for future reference* . . . But he wasn't going to tell Sean that Callie might not be his collared submissive for long. Saying so was her place—even if he'd love to shove it in the bastard's face.

"For some reason I can't comprehend, she has feelings for you, too."

Sean snorted. "Not too many, I guess, if she decided to go straight from fucking me to you."

As much as Thorpe would love to let Kirkpatrick believe the worst, he refused to give Sean a reason to punish Callie for his own actions. "I didn't fuck her."

"You wanted to," Sean accused.

"That goes without saying. Callie is a beautiful woman. As you've previously noted, I care for her. Why are we covering this well trampled ground again?"

"Because it's my right to know exactly what you did with her." He bounced Thorpe against the wall again.

The fucker had punched him so hard, he almost felt queasy. But he refused to show weakness.

"Get off me or I'll have you arrested for assault." To make his point, Thorpe bent and shoved his shoulder into the Scot's and, using the wall as leverage, heaved the other man off him. Then he whipped out his phone to text Axel and tapped out their code for "problem."

"I don't have time for you," Thorpe said. "Let's just say that Callie has feelings for us both, and she offered us the same good-bye. I got her attention, made a few things clear, and left her cuffed to her bed alone, all safe and sound. I even swiped her car keys." He withdrew them from his pocket and dangled them in front of Sean's face.

The Scot's expression turned somewhere between sour and disbelieving. "I want to see her."

"I'm sorry. I'm still not convinced that you're in her best interest."

"And you are?" Kirkpatrick scoffed.

"No. Which is the only reason she wasn't wearing a collar when you came sniffing around. If and when I decide you can see her, I'll let you know."

On cue, Axel charged down the hall with a couple of his staff in tow. Sean came out swinging, but the guards each grabbed one of his arms.

Axel just shoved a hand in Kirkpatrick's hair and yanked. "You had to pee, huh? Let's go, motherfucker."

Thorpe smiled. No one had ever accused Axel of playing nice.

"Don't call me; I'll call you." Thorpe shouted as the men forcibly carried Sean, shouting and belligerent, from the club.

"This isn't over," Sean yelled over his shoulder, still fighting them. "She's mine!"

"Fuck off," he muttered under his breath, then extracted his phone again, making strides to his office.

Once inside, he paused, then chose a course of action. Lance had been in the dungeon earlier. *Perfect.* Callie needed care, and she'd do her best to outsmart or wheedle another sub to get away right now. Thorpe had hoped that merely kindling the sexual fire between them might persuade her to stay, but . . . wishful thinking. It would have been smarter if he'd just fucked her since that had likely been his only opportunity. *Damn it.* Now he had to tear his thoughts from her pussy and act strategically. Lance wouldn't take a lick of crap from her. He was a strong, clever Dom—and didn't have a heterosexual bone in his body. *Even better.*

Axel returned a few minutes later, winded and looking like he might have a shiner tomorrow. "Can I press assault charges?"

Thorpe slanted the other Dom a glare. "We don't need trouble here. Wouldn't you rather meet him in a dark alley?"

"Fuck, yeah. Is that option on the table, boss?"

He shrugged. "Have fun. Don't get caught. But before you go, would you ask Lance if he'd take care of Callie?"

With a nod, Axel left. Minutes later, he escorted Lance down the hallway.

Lance paused at Thorpe's door. "Expecting trouble from our little vixen?"

"Just constantly." Thorpe smiled faintly. "I have an urgent phone call to make, so I appreciate your assistance."

"Always happy to help."

When Lance disappeared, and Axel headed back to the dungeon, Thorpe indulged in one thing he never did during the club's business hours. But in this case, he figured he was entitled. He poured himself a stiff scotch, plopped into his chair, and downed it. Then he broke his own rules again and called a client to beg.

Logan Edgington answered his phone on the third ring, the noise from a television cluttering the background until he killed it. "Thorpe. 'Sup, man? It's getting late."

"I have a situation. I need some information. I'd like to speak with your wife, if that's all right."

The former SEAL hesitated for a moment. "Yeah. We were just watching a movie. Tara's due in about two months and is having some problems with insomnia. If I don't keep her occupied, she'll be up 'nesting' half the night, which is code for moving furniture without consulting me or asking for help."

"Hey," he heard Tara protest in the background. "The twins are active at night. I can't sleep when I'm being constantly kicked. I said I was sorry."

"Yeah, after I added another infraction to your quickly growing list for after these babies are born. You're racking them up, Cherry." When his wife sighed noisily, Logan just laughed. "My brother's wife, Kata, is five months behind her and still in the tired-all-the-time phase, so she conked out for the night. If you can occupy Tara's brain right now, you'll be my hero."

"I've definitely got a winner," Thorpe promised. "Are you sure she's up to it?"

Logan scoffed. "Her ankles may be swollen, but there's nothing wrong with her mind. Here you go."

After a quick scuffle, Tara's voice sounded over the line. "Hi, Thorpe."

"Hello, sweet girl. I'm sorry it's so late, but I need your help."

"Anything. Name it."

"Do you still have contacts at the FBI from your analyst days?"

"Absolutely." She shuffled in bed again. "Can't find a comfortable position. Sorry. One second . . . There. What do you need?"

"Background on someone new here at Dominion. He's a potential problem."

"So are you looking for his arrest record, criminal background . . . that kind of thing?"

"Precisely," Thorpe confirmed. "Anything you can find out, really. I've thought for some weeks that there's something about him that seems off. His story checks out on the surface, but it feels awfully pat. I suspect he's not who he claims." He hesitated. "He's fixated on Callie."

Tara grunted. "You're calling me about *her*?"

"I know she isn't your favorite person."

"Um, not exactly. She wanted my husband."

"No." He didn't want to divulge Callie's secrets, but he needed to set Tara at ease so she'd provide answers. "Actually, I believe she was trying to get *my* attention with her brattiness and misbehavior."

"Sounds like she got it."

And then some. "She used Logan to reach me because she knew he wouldn't be quiet about her antics. He was a big target."

"He still is." Tara sighed. "All right, who is this guy?"

"He uses the name Sean Kirkpatrick. I'll send you a picture when we hang up. It's not fabulous since it's security footage. I don't know much about him. Early thirties, says he's from Scotland. Supposedly, he's a freelance project manager who travels for a living." But he sure as hell had a mean left hook for a desk jockey.

"Know where he went to school? When he came to the U.S.?"

"Sorry."

"Send over the picture. I'll see what I can do."

"Thank you. Call me with anything, day or night. My time is short. I don't trust this asshole."

Tara hesitated. "Do you think he'd hurt her?"

His gut said no. For all of Kirkpatrick's faults, he seemed as fiercely protective of Callie as Thorpe himself. But would Sean separate her from him and steal her away from Dominion? Absolutely.

"Let's say I'm not taking any possibility off the table yet."

"All right. Give me a few hours. I'll see what I can dig up."

"Thanks." Thorpe smiled into the phone. Taking action felt good.

Facts would help him decide how to proceed with Kirkpatrick. Personally, Thorpe hoped the Scot had something dirty and blackmail-worthy in his past so he could hang it over Sean's head to make him disappear from Callie's life.

Then . . . he'd set about figuring what to do once he had her all to himself again.

* * *

SEAN paced the sterile corporate apartment he'd been forced to hang his hat in for the last eight months. The bland beige walls were closing in like a trash compactor about to squeeze the life out of him. He had unreturned messages and a boss who wanted to know what the fuck was going on.

Getting screwed by the competition. How's that for a goddamn update?

Sighing, he stared at his phone, willing Callie to call him. He had a million questions for her, needed to hear what was in her head. Mostly, he wanted to know if she was all right. And what that son of a bitch, Mitchell Thorpe, had done to her.

After stalking to the little desk that sat beside his bed, he sorted through a pile of file folders and came to the one he sought. Pulling it open, he scanned the information he already knew backward and forward. His nemesis was thirty-nine. His wife had divorced him and was now remarried with two kids. He came from a thoroughly upper-middle-class background. Good schools in Connecticut. Yacht club parents. Yale University graduate, then a stint as a stockbroker in New York City in his early twenties. Owner of Dominion for the last dozen years, with an interest in BDSM for even longer. But Sean read nothing in the paperwork that would tell him how to get the upper hand again.

He'd miscalculated tonight, ranking his desire for Callie above everything else. He had a feeling that by fucking her, he'd roused the competitor in Thorpe. The man didn't intend to lose.

"Too bad, asshole. That goes double for me," he mumbled.

Tossing the folder back on the desk, he paced to the front door and back again. It only took eight steps.

Shoving his hand into his pocket, he yanked his phone out and dialed Callie. Immediately, her voicemail greeting chimed in his ear. Sean cursed. Either his lovely hadn't remembered to charge her phone again . . . or she wasn't speaking to him.

Whatever the reason, he couldn't afford to let this silence between them fester or grow. But he also couldn't go back to Dominion tonight. After the right cross to Axel's eye, he figured that not only was he off the club's membership roster for a while, but he'd better watch his back. Normally, Sean would break into the club. Though challenging, it wouldn't be impossible. But if he got caught, Thorpe would throw him out for good and everything he'd worked eight months to build would swirl down the toilet. Things weren't dire enough to risk that yet.

Still, he had to find some way to reassure himself that Callie was all right.

The one silver lining was that Thorpe had prevented her from fleeing Dominion—at least so far. She intended to. Of that, Sean had no doubt. He really hated to give Thorpe any credit, but he had to since the man had cuffed her to her own bed and taken her car keys. Sean knew he would probably have opted to reason with her and shower her with affection first.

He wondered now if that tactic would have backfired.

She requires a firm hand.

Thorpe's assertion echoed through his head. Damn, but the sly bastard might be onto something.

Now that Sean had taken note, he wouldn't let Thorpe undermine him again. He was here for Callie. He intended to stay for her. And no man, not even the Dungeon Master himself, was going to get in his way.

Armed with an idea to outfox the fox, he scooped up his car keys and headed out the door. In less than an hour, he'd have Callie all to himself once more.

Chapter Five

As Thorpe waltzed out the door, Callie fumed. He'd walked away from her, after he'd promised not to. He'd utterly humiliated her—again. All that pleasure he'd poured on her, all those shiver-worthy words about never letting her get away . . . Then *poof*! He'd gotten up and left.

If he didn't have so much of her heart, she'd gleefully smack him upside the head. As it was, she didn't know how she was going to look Thorpe in the eye again without being completely mortified that she'd thrown herself at him. Seeing that it hadn't been at all difficult for him to leave her naked and ready only hurt worse. She was tired of the constant pain of his rejection.

And then there was Sean. He'd said he loved her—without hesitation, out loud, resounding with total conviction. But he wasn't going to rest until he knew every one of her secrets.

It was definitely time for her to leave Dominion ASAP.

The feelings blooming in her heart for her sexy Dom were too big, too much, too overwhelming. Was that how Thorpe felt? Callie sighed. Was Sean even speaking to her anymore? The thought that he might not tore everything out of her chest.

How the hell could she be foolish enough to fall for two men, especially when they couldn't stand one another?

Crap, her head hurt from all the circles her thoughts were turning.

When she'd asked earlier, Lance told her that Sean had been forcibly and indefinitely removed from the premises. Callie winced. She'd bet *that* had gone over well. And she could only imagine what he was thinking. Did he know that Thorpe had given her more than a spanking? It wasn't a stretch to imagine that her helpful boss had volunteered the information.

Somehow—and soon—she had to talk to Sean. If she intended to rescind his collar, she should have the moxie to do it to his face. She owed him that much before she slipped out of his life for good. No idea how to start that conversation. *I'm so sorry I almost boinked my boss after having sex with you.* She snorted. *Brilliant idea.*

The comforter Thorpe had thrown over her earlier shielded her from Lance—not that he cared. Nope, he stood over her, all leather and gloating smiles. He was enjoying being Thorpe's right hand. He'd always said she lacked discipline. Since he was a big believer in corporal punishment, she could just imagine what he had in mind.

Been there, done that already tonight. Her backside still throbbed. She didn't need more from a guy whose palm itched because he hadn't yet had the chance to spank his boy's ass.

"You don't have to stand over me, you know," she pointed out.

With a shrug of his shoulders, his leather vest skimmed his leanly muscled torso. "I enjoy pissing you off."

He always had. A practical jokester and a big tease, Lance's laughter was infectious. It would be funny someday that he was poking fun at her. Just not today.

"Gee, thanks. I assume I'm allowed to eat something."

Lance gestured her toward the door. "Feel free. You know where the kitchen is."

Callie tugged at the cuffs holding her to the bed frame and sent him an expectant expression.

"Picky, picky. I'll get the key from Thorpe." He grinned at her. "Don't go anywhere."

"Lance, I swear I'm going to throw something at you." She heaved a big sigh.

"Try it. Want to guess what will happen?"

Someone would paddle her good, probably Lance himself. *Pass . . .*

"Hurry. Please. I'm *really* hungry," she lied.

He took pity on her and stopped teasing. "Okay. I'll be right back, little vixen."

As the door closed behind Lance, she waited impatiently. Thorpe seemed determined to separate her from Sean . . . but she didn't understand. It wasn't as if he really wanted her. Why be so hell-bent on keeping her at Dominion if he had no intention of making her his own? Probably because he enjoyed giving her the ultimate mind-fuck. All the more reason to leave.

Moments later, Lance appeared with the key and uncuffed her.

"Thorpe says you're free to roam the premises. No leaving and no socializing. You get something to eat, see if there's anything pressing that needs your attention, then you come back here. Understood?"

Callie resisted the urge to roll her eyes. "Sure."

"I'll be watching you on the floor."

She didn't doubt Lance meant that, especially when he wandered out of her room, pointing a pair of fingers to his eyes, then to her own.

"I got it!" She sighed impatiently.

"That's almost insolent," he cautioned.

"Sorry." *Long fucking day.* "Hunger doesn't bring out the best in me."

"I'll let you slide this time. Don't do it again . . ."

"Yes, Sir," she murmured to placate him, throwing in a bat of her lashes. He would probably miss the finer points of that gesture, but just in case.

Lance burst out laughing as he left the room. "Oh, Thorpe has his hands full with you."

Once she was alone, Callie reached onto the floor, fishing in her purse to find her phone. Then she hesitated. What was she going to do, just call Sean and apologize? Maybe it would be better done face to face. As she was severing their bond? Very classy . . . What if he didn't want to see her again? Or even talk to her? Soon, it wouldn't even matter. She'd get another phone in a new town—a different number with a blank slate of contacts. Start over once more in a place where she knew no one. Winter was coming. Phoenix might be good . . .

She was still trying to decide how to proceed when she glanced at the little device. Dead. Crap, she really needed to remember to charge it once in a blue moon.

Depressed as hell, she plugged in her phone, then tossed on her robe and marched down to Thorpe's office. She tried the handle. Locked. And he didn't answer a single one of her banging knocks or demands to be let in. True, he might not be inside, but it was also possible Thorpe was completely avoiding her. Callie's money was on the latter.

She still planned to be gone from Dominion no later than tomorrow, but the bastard had her car keys and suitcases. And a chunk of her heart. She had to retrieve at least the first two and move on.

With an agitated shake of her head, she wandered out to the dungeon floor and cleaned up after a few customers, wiping down after some others. She gathered dirty towels and put them in the laundry room, then distributed fresh bottles of water to the coolers. She stocked bins all around with fresh blankets for Doms to wrap their subs in when it was time for aftercare. *A hopping Friday night . . .*

Axel had glared at her from across the concrete floor, scowling around what looked like a developing black eye. She didn't have to ask how he got it. His growl about her "asshole Dom" when he passed by said it all.

Suddenly, Lance strode toward her with a disparaging glance. "Your pizza is here, vixen. Or should I say your highness?"

"Pizza?" She hadn't ordered one. In fact, she hadn't thought about food at all once Lance had let her go.

Who the hell would imagine that she'd want food when her entire life was in turmoil? Not Thorpe. He knew better. Had someone pulled a practical joke on her? The first person she'd suspect, Lance, wore an expression of disapproval, not mirth.

"Yes, and the delivery guy is at the back door, insisting that he give it to you personally."

This could be a trick. What if it was some police ploy? But why a pizza delivery man when they could come in with badges flashing and guns blazing, then just arrest her? Yeah, that was a more likely scenario. Which meant the pizza had probably been sent by someone who couldn't readily talk to her.

Sean?

"Sure. Let me get my wallet."

Lance sighed. "It's paid for. I tried, but he said you'd given him a credit card over the phone."

Probably Sean.

"Right," she agreed readily. "I'm so hungry that I totally forgot. Food. Let me get that."

Shaking his head, Lance walked away.

Callie ran to the back door. Sure enough, a gangly, pimple-faced teenager stood there with a pizza box in hand. The smells of basil and oregano wafted from the cardboard as he shot her a smile.

"Callie Ward?" He looked her up and down with a leer.

"Yes," she said cautiously, self-consciously drawing the edges of her robe closer together, making damn sure everything was covered.

"For you. From a 'friend.'" He winked.

Definitely Sean.

With a stupid grin, she took the box from the boy, noting that one side was a bit heavier than the other. He turned away without another word, so she shut the back door, then headed to her room.

Locking herself inside her private domain, she lifted the lid. Inside, half a warm pizza lay, brimming with cheese, pepperoni, pineapple, and mushrooms. Her favorite. Sean had remembered. Despite the dim day, that made her smile.

The other half of the box was another story. Partitioned away from the pizza by a piece of cardboard lay a white rectangle shrink-wrapped in plastic. She stared at it, blinking a few times. A yellow sticky note on top had almost blended in with its background, but as soon as she flipped on a light, she saw that the left half said *Eat Me* with an arrow pointing to the pizza. The other half said *Open Me.*

What was this, *Alice in Wonderland?*

Callie lifted a piece of the pie to her mouth and took a bite, surprised to find that she was hungrier than she'd imagined. She moaned as the flavor burst on her tongue. *So good . . .*

But curiosity was killing her.

She plucked the plastic-wrapped bundle out of the other half of the pizza box. Immediately, the size and weight told her it was a computer. Why would he send her one? She owned a laptop. It was old, but it worked.

She pulled the device from the industrial plastic protecting it. A brand-new shiny silver unit with a familiar piece of half-eaten fruit on the front. Over that was another note that read *Turn Me On.*

Was this his roundabout way of sending her a message, despite Thorpe throwing him out of the club?

With a careful nudge of the unit's top lid, she opened it, taking just a moment to revel in how gorgeous it was. This had to have cost him a small fortune.

Peering intently at the machine, she hit the button to power it on. Someone had already gone through the setup and registration process for her. It came up with a desktop picture of a flower. The profile name matched her own.

Another sticky note across the keyboard read *Three Guesses* . . . She'd never seen Sean's playful side and she liked it.

With a smile, she bit her lip and pondered. What would Sean have used as a password. She tried his name. The operating system didn't recognize that. Then another idea came to mind, and she typed it in.

L-O-V-E-L-Y.

That did it. Seconds later, she was in. A familiar Internet video chat program tried to load. Quickly, she tapped in the club's Wi-Fi password. A second later, the software began calling Sean. He answered immediately, looking wrung out and worried, his tie loose, his hair messy as if he'd dragged his fingers through it a million times.

"Callie, are you all right?"

She swallowed down her nervousness. "Yes. Of course. I . . ." *Have no idea what to say.*

"Have you eaten the pizza? I know you, and I'm betting you haven't taken the time tonight to fill your belly."

Even when she'd handled everything wrong and hurt his feelings, Sean still put her needs first. Tears pricked at her eyes. What was she ever going to do without him?

"Not much, but I will. It smells heavenly. I've just been . . . worried about you. I saw Axel's black eye and—"

Sean laughed, his grainy image grinning on the screen. "He looks far worse than me, lovely. Of that, I assure you."

His assertion surprised her. No one ever got the best of Thorpe's security director. He'd been bouncing heads for years. How had one man who wasn't as big as Mount Axel managed to damage him and come out without a scratch? Luck, maybe.

"I'm so relieved to hear it. I've seen Axel really mess guys up before." She drew in a deep breath, her mind racing. "I don't understand why Thorpe threw you out. If anyone is at fault, it's me. You said something beautiful, and I panicked."

"You must know exactly how jealous Thorpe is."

Sean had the situation so wrong. "No, he's just concerned."

"Because he wants you. But I don't care about Thorpe now. He can't keep us apart for long. I'll find a way to you, lovely. I always will." He paused, looking at her intently. "I wish I could touch you now and show you how much I meant those words I said earlier."

Callie's heart stuttered. Sean actually loved her. He hadn't simply blurted it in the heat of passion. After nearly seven months, most of them as his submissive, it still stunned her. But hadn't she worried that she was falling in love with him herself just a few hours ago?

"I'm really sorry I ran," she murmured. "You startled me."

"Don't you care for me even a bit?" He frowned, that furrow between his blue eyes deep and troubled.

Even if she couldn't stay and fulfill the promise of the burgeoning love between them, she wouldn't be dishonest with Sean. She couldn't stand the thought of hurting him more than she was already going to. "I care about you very much. So much that it scares me sometimes."

"Ah, lovely. I won't hurt you. You can let go and fall into my arms. I'll catch you."

How wonderful that sounded. Callie pressed a hand over her trembling lips. She wished she could stay and do exactly what he wanted. But that was a stupid fantasy. The reality was that she'd already way overstayed her time at Dominion.

Her heart railed, and she wanted to scream at the uselessness of her feelings. What would Sean do if she stayed and the law caught up to her? Or, heaven forbid, if he ever figured out who she was?

So she had to remain strong and do what was best for both Sean and Thorpe. If they knew the danger that lurked around her every corner, they'd want to help. They might even insist on protecting her.

Callie refused to let them risk themselves. It was her problem, her cross to bear. Her shit to deal with.

"I'm trying," she told him.

But after today, it had to stop. By tomorrow, she had to slip out of his life, away from Dominion, Thorpe, and Dallas—everything meaningful to her. Maybe she'd go to Seattle, instead. The frequent rain would match her mood.

"I know you are." He sent her a reassuring smile. "Tell me, what did the bastard do when he had you alone in your room."

Callie froze, sure that her face looked awfully deer-in-the-headlights. If she told him the truth, there'd be trouble. "N-nothing much."

"Don't you lie to me, lovely. I'll paddle you but good. I heard your cries of passion wailing down the halls."

Damn it! She wished the video feature wasn't on. He could probably see the guilt crawling all over her face. How was she going to get out of this without riling Sean to the point of wanting to kill Thorpe?

"What did he tell you?"

Sean's blue eyes narrowed. "I expect an answer from *you*. The truth, mind you. I might be able to forgive you being confused. But if he forced you into anything, I'll take his bloody head off."

Blurting that excuse, then running away would only leave the two men behind without her as a buffer. Not a good idea when tempers were running high. "He kissed me. He . . . touched me."

"And you liked it." He ground his teeth, jaw tight. "Pull off your robe. Now."

She started to refuse, but she'd rather take Sean's anger herself than have him unleash it on Thorpe.

She stood and let the silk skim down her arms until it puddled on the floor.

"Stand closer to the camera so I can look at you. And bend so I can see your breasts."

Callie stepped forward and did as he commanded, letting him look his fill.

"Where's your collar?"

Now wasn't the time to explain that even if she'd been wearing it, the bit of bling wouldn't be a symbol of their relationship much longer. She'd explain tomorrow. And once she'd assumed a new identity, Sean would be nothing but a sweet memory. He would forget her, surely.

"I was getting ready to take a shower," she lied gently.

His mouth thinned into an even firmer line. "All right, then. Show me your belly and your cunt. Slowly."

Her entire body flushing, she adjusted the laptop lid until the webcam took in the lower half of her body as she stood frozen still for him.

"Beautiful, as always. Sit back and spread your legs." As soon as she reclined on the bed and parted her thighs, he moaned in appreciation. "Is that where Thorpe touched you?"

"Yes." Her voice shook.

"Show me how."

"You want me to touch myself?" The thought of displaying her self-pleasure was both uncomfortable and arousing.

"I do. I want to see you come and I want you to be thinking about *me* this time."

Between his possessive words and his narrow-eyed demand, she shivered. "A-all right."

"Good. I've spent months touching myself and thinking of you, lovely. I want to see you do the same for me. I want to be the only one on your mind as you feel pleasure."

Those words shouldn't excite her so much, but an image of Sean, eyes closed, body tense with need, his big hand roughing up and down his cock, made her ache.

Suddenly, touching herself wasn't a hardship. Tonight, she'd felt more pleasure than she had in the last five years put together. No way she should be ready to orgasm again. But after Sean's gruff voice grinding out such a wicked suggestion, need bubbled right under her clit.

"Now, Callie," he snapped.

She eased back on her elbows and bent her knees, craning her neck to make sure that Sean still had a view of her pussy in the camera.

"I see you, lovely. Go on."

His hard voice had deepened, his Scottish accent thickening. She swallowed against lust, then slid her fingers down her belly, right between her legs.

Sean's demand didn't exactly have the effect he desired. The second her fingers caressed her hard, burning clit, Thorpe slipped into her thoughts. The memory of his mouth on her, eating her voraciously, then sliding up her body to demand that she come for him wouldn't be banished. But in her head, Sean watched, making the demand as Thorpe slid his fingers and tongue all over her. Her skin sizzled. Her desire flared. In a perfect world, she could admit to wanting them both—and wishing desperately that they desired her.

The fantasy was totally unrealistic, but she couldn't stop it from barreling past her good sense to make her spin out of control.

With her free hand, she tweaked her nipples, imagining that Sean's fingers plucked the sensitive buds, his hot breath falling in her ear as he told her that she looked seductive while Thorpe ate her into a frenzy and swallowed her down. Then they would both fuck her, Sean filling her sensitive pussy and Thorpe driving into her ass, until . . .

Callie cried out as the peak crashed into her. She jolted, her back arching, her fingers rubbing frantic circles on the pulsing bud between her legs.

"Lovely . . ." Sean's voice sounded gruff before he groaned long and loud in pleasure.

The sound brought her back to herself. Callie blinked and sat up, then reached for her robe, drawing it over her breasts as she panted. She felt like a terrible human being. Sean loved her. She loved him—but she couldn't manage to banish Thorpe from her heart.

"I didn't say that you could move, much less cover yourself. I'm not done with you yet." He looked more relaxed, but she wouldn't call him happy.

Still struggling to catch her breath, she bared herself again. Sean had seen it all. What was there to peep at now?

"Get back in position and don't move until I tell you," he commanded gruffly.

Closing her eyes, Callie gave herself over to Sean. It would be the last time she'd ever experience submission, most likely. Even if she sometimes fought it, she craved it. She intended to savor these precious moments.

Rocking back on her elbows, she spread her legs again for him.

"Scoot closer."

The entire camera had to be one big close-up of her cooch. But she didn't argue, just complied. Then she waited.

"Like that, yes."

Sean remained silent for a long minute, and she could all but feel his eyes on her. In her fantasy, he climbed his way up her body with nips and kisses, then impaled her with that thick cock of his, making her breath rush and her back arch. She pictured Thorpe hovering over her, too, watching, tipping her head over the edge of the bed to feed his erection between her lips and deep in her mouth, muttering in the filthiest, most intimate whisper how much he was looking forward to impaling her backside.

"I don't see any bruises on you." Sean's voice pulled her from her sensual daydream.

Callie eased up a fraction and looked at Sean from between her legs. "There are none, Sir. Thorpe didn't force me."

A fact that made her feel even more guilty, but she didn't try to hide from the truth.

"Sit up and look at me." He stayed silent until she did as he'd bid. "Leave the robe off. I like you naked."

"Yes, Sir."

He sent her a reassuring nod, telling her that she'd pleased him. "Callie, he may not have forced you, but you were upset, and he took advantage of you."

"Not really." She bit her lip. "Sean, I have to be honest. I have feelings for him, too. I don't think it's one-sided."

Damn, why couldn't she just keep her mouth shut? Or break up with him and be done?

Sean's face closed up. "He had four years to give you what you needed. And he did nothing. He's not the man for you. I am. Don't let your gratitude lead your heart in the wrong direction."

It wasn't like that at all. Yes, she was grateful to Thorpe for many things, but she would have fallen for him regardless. Some invisible string tethered her to him, tugging her in his direction . . . even as another string seemed to bind and yank her toward Sean, too.

It was best that she was leaving. She could never choose between them. And if she tried, she would inevitably lose the other for good.

"I understand what you're saying," she answered obliquely. After tomorrow, it wouldn't matter.

"Good. I'm going to do my best to reason with Thorpe so I can see you. We have a lot to talk about, lovely."

He was dead wrong. It was all but over, even if that fact was breaking her heart in a million pieces. If she told him that now, it would only start an argument that neither of them would win. Next time she saw him would simply be good-bye.

"I'll see what I can do on my end, too."

"Excellent," he praised. "Now charge your phone."

"I already am." She smiled. Sometimes he knew her too well.

Sean sent her an approving nod, his blue eyes caressing her face through the screen. "Eat your pizza and get some sleep. I plan to come for you tomorrow."

And by then, she'd be ready to release him and go. "I will."

* * *

THORPE was slumped over his desk at quarter 'til three when his phone rang. The club members were gone. Axel had swept the place clean. No sign of Kirkpatrick, but Thorpe knew better than to assume he'd seen the last of the asshole. Callie had helped with cleaning and closing, then taken herself off to bed. She was too quiet and hadn't met his gaze when he'd given her back the contents of her suitcases, sans bags.

He planned to keep a very close watch on her. Lack of luggage alone wouldn't be enough to keep her here if she was determined to go.

At the first shrill chime, Thorpe started, then all but pounced on the phone. He looked at the display, smiling at the familiar number.

"Tara?"

"Yes."

"That was fast." The smart girl had always impressed him, but even more so tonight. "Thank you."

"Don't thank me yet. I've got some information for you. It's only preliminary, but . . . I don't think you're going to like it."

Thorpe's gut tightened. He'd wanted to be wrong. *Son of a bitch.* "I didn't expect to. Tell me."

"Sean Kirkpatrick's story survives a cursory glance, like you said. But once I started digging, it seems that he doesn't appear anywhere, at least under that name, until eight months ago. I also can't find a record of anyone with that name and face becoming a U.S. citizen in the last decade. The first appearance of him I have is the supposed creation of an LLC in the state of Florida earlier this year."

"He told Callie that he lives there now. He claims to belong to a club outside of Miami. His references checked out, but . . ."

"It's possible he paid someone for that."

"Exactly," Thorpe agreed.

"Almost immediately after he started the company, a major Fortune 100 corporation supposedly hired his services. Do you know how tough a gig that is to get?"

"Exceedingly. You usually have to know someone."

"Or be sucking their di— um, be intimate with them."

Thorpe managed a smile at her slipup, despite the grim situation.

Tara smoothed over the moment by continuing on. "He rented a corporate apartment in Dallas under the name of his LLC back in April." She rattled off the address, and he jotted it down. A newer part of town with lots of corporate presence and no nightlife. "He signed a six-month lease. When October rolled around, he started extending it month by month. Other than that, Sean Kirkpatrick has one relatively new credit card, no bank account, no immigration visa, no mortgage, no car loan, no record of marriages or divorces, no court dates, no arrest record, no school records . . . nothing. He's a ghost."

Sitting back in his chair, Thorpe sucked in a breath. "The way he set up his identity, do you think he's a con artist?"

"What does Callie have that he'd want to steal?"

"Absolutely nothing." On the surface. But over the last decade, the bounty on Callie's head had grown to two million dollars. What if Sean Kirkpatrick had somehow pieced together her identity and managed to trail her here?

Thorpe's blood ran cold. He swore that he'd take care of Kirkpatrick once and for all.

"I was afraid you were going to say that." Tara sighed. "Seven months seems awfully patient for a stalker, but at this point, I'm not sure if I'd rule that out. I honestly don't know what else to think."

"I've got some ideas. If you come across anything else, let me know, would you?"

"Of course. Something is definitely off with this man."

As Thorpe had suspected for some time. "I appreciate everything you've done."

"My pleasure. You know Callie isn't ever going to be my best friend . . . but I'm worried for her."

He gripped the phone tightly. "Me, too."

They rang off, and Thorpe didn't waste a minute. He left his office and crept down the hall to Callie's room, letting himself in with the key. He spied her sleeping in the moonlight, all curled up in a sea of downy quilts and soft pillows. One naked leg peeked out, from her supple hip to her little pink toes. No way he could forget having his face between her sleek thighs, but somehow he had to.

Thorpe turned and found a partially eaten pizza sitting in a box on her dresser. When the hell had she ordered that? No idea, but nothing else looked out of place. Her phone sat charging on the nightstand, and he swiped it, then dashed back into his office.

It didn't take him long to figure out that her password was his birthday. And didn't that just add a kicker of guilt to this torment cocktail? He browsed her recent calls and found one she'd missed from Sean earlier tonight. *Gotcha!*

He touched the screen, and the image changed to Sean's annoying mug as the call connected.

"Callie?" the man didn't sound groggy or disoriented in the least.

"Not quite. Guess again."

"What the fuck do you want, Thorpe? I've had it up to my eyeballs with your antics. You can't separate me from Callie. You've no right, and you know it."

Oh, he had every right, and he intended to exercise each of them to the fullest extent. He might not be her father, her husband, or her Dom, but he was her protector. And probably the only person in her life she could trust without question.

But Sean's grating lecture gave him an idea. "I've been doing some thinking. I know that I've overstepped my bounds as the owner of the club. So I'm going to allow you to see her tomorrow. Here at

Dominion. Nine p.m. You're not going to get another offer. I suggest
you take it."

"I'll be there. And don't you be trying any trickery. You won't
like what happens."

"Is that a threat?" Thorpe all but licked his lips, hoping the Scot
would give him something he could sink his teeth into.

"No. But if you're less than straight and narrow, I don't think
Callie will be too happy with you. And you can't stand the thought
that she might not look to you for all her needs, can you?"

Thorpe squeezed the phone tightly. *Fucker.* "Be here at nine."

Without allowing Sean to respond, he ended the call. That Scot
got under his skin, and he had to resist the urge to throw Callie's
phone across the room. Instead, he forced out a deep breath, then
stood, walking with deliberate steps back to her room and put the
phone where he'd found it.

He shouldn't look at the girl, but she'd rolled over in her sleep
and now lay on her back, her ridiculously long lashes caressing her
cheeks, her head angled slightly to expose the graceful line of her
throat. Pale shoulders moved softly with each breath. The quilt barely
covered her breasts, and the hint of cleavage was enough to make
him sweat.

Damn it, he had to get out of here. He had to stop obsessing.
Keep her safe. Give her a place to live her life in peace. That was the
most he could ever offer her.

The moment he closed her door behind him again and locked
it once more, he charged down the hall to see if Axel had left yet. A
quick turn of the knob to the security room, and Thorpe slid inside.
Axel wore a baseball cap. The man was a large, blunt instrument of
violence when he chose. Currently, his eyes were glued to a security
feed. His fists were clenched.

"What is it?"

"Callie got a pizza tonight."

"I saw the box in her room."

"She didn't pay for it."

Thorpe frowned. "And Callie doesn't have any credit cards to have paid for it in advance."

"Exactly."

"It's Kirkpatrick." Thorpe cursed. God, would this fucker just not go away?

"Can't imagine who else it would be."

"I've got a plan. How do you feel about searching his apartment at, say, nine tomorrow night?"

"For what?"

"Anything. Everything. He's up to no good where Callie is concerned. I want to know what."

Axel's massive shoulders slumped. "You're not going to let me trash his pad, are you?"

"Not yet, but depending on what you find, you and I together may be trashing his face."

"Now you're talking." Axel smiled wide.

"Is that a yes, then?"

Axel's expression brightened again. "I can't wait."

Thorpe felt the same. One way or another, by tomorrow night, he'd have figured out exactly who Sean Kirkpatrick was and how to permanently erase him from Callie's life. He didn't care much how he had to do it.

Chapter Six

THORPE did his best to act like he didn't want to murder Sean Kirkpatrick—or whatever his name truly was—when the imposter walked into Dominion. The man shoved something in the pocket of his trousers and adjusted his stark white dress shirt. Decent suit and loafers, but not designer. His watch wasn't Gucci . . . but it wasn't Timex, either. Which reinforced Thorpe's opinion that this man wasn't after Callie's money because he knew she didn't have any.

He hoped like hell the address Tara had dug up was real and that Axel worked quickly. Thorpe needed to eliminate the man, then find the strength to take a step back from Callie so her life could resume its status quo.

Sean caught sight of him in the foyer, standing beside Sweet Pea's empty desk. He'd sent his little receptionist on a meaningless errand because didn't want her anywhere near potential danger.

The Scot glared. "Where is Callie? You said she'd be here."

"In her room, waiting for you. But you and I are going to get a few rules straight first."

"More bloody rules? I'm done playing by yours, Thorpe. You're determined to believe the worst of my intentions because you've got your dick in a twist with jealousy, and she shed a few tears last night. If you truly care about the girl, you'll back away and let me make her happy. She looks up to you. For her sake, you and I need to stop this arguing."

The whole speech set Thorpe's teeth on edge, but the name of tonight's game was to lie low, not do anything to rouse the bastard's suspicion. So he just smiled.

"I'd rather not fight with you, either. It distresses Callie, but I won't be less than honest. I don't like you. However, if you fulfill her and have her best interest at heart, I'm willing to try accepting you. Therefore, I'm allowing you to have time alone with her in her room. I won't interrupt."

"Behind closed doors?"

Thorpe dug his fingers into his thighs so he didn't throttle Sean and nodded. "Don't make me regret my show of trust."

"Thank you. I came tonight intending to suggest a truce in Callie's honor, so I'm glad you agree. She's a stunning, bighearted lass. If you'll let her make her own choices and keep your distance, I'll give her all she needs. You've got my word on that." Sean held out his hand.

"I look forward to seeing her smile again." Thorpe was loath to shake Sean's hand, but he had no choice.

If not for the information Tara had dug up on Kirkpatrick, Thorpe was sorely aware that he might really have been willing to take the lying asswipe at face value and try to behave civilly—at least when Callie was around.

But now, that option was off the table.

An awkward silence fell between them. Thorpe ignored it, turning his back on the man and drawing him down the private hall. With a series of card keys and pass codes, he finally reached the residential section of the club and headed to the end of the hall.

He gestured to Callie's door. "She's waiting for you."

And Sean was in for a treat. Callie wore a bloodred dress that showed a healthy hint of cleavage, accentuated her small waist and petite stature, while revealing a lot of thigh. Matching lipstick and dark curls offset her fair face. When he'd seen her ten minutes ago, all Thorpe had wanted to do was strap her to his bed until she screamed out in pleasure for him—until he'd realized she was wearing that asshole's collar again. When he'd questioned her about it, she'd been vague. Had she changed her mind about leaving?

Kirkpatrick knocked on her door. "Lovely?"

The second Callie pulled it open, Thorpe's stare tangled in hers. He saw something in her eyes that set him on edge. Sadness? Before Thorpe could decipher her expression, she peeked over at the other man.

"Hi, Sean," Callie murmured, lowering her gaze in a sweetly submissive gesture that made his cock stand tall. "Would you like to come in?"

"I would." The Scot stepped inside and closed the door behind them.

Thorpe heard it lock. He wanted to rip the fucker's guts out.

Instead, he leaned against the wall in the hallway and dragged in a breath, trying to calm his rage. Hopefully, in two hours or less, this shit would be over and this imposter would be gone for good. Then he could figure out what was troubling the girl and fix it.

The only reason he'd let Sean in Callie's room was the knowledge that he could unlock her door himself in seconds. If needed, Axel's musclemen could bust it down in two minutes flat. Her windows had bars on the outside to keep creeps out . . . or in. Zeb and Lance were stationed at either end of the hall, listening and watching, just in case. The whole plan was a giant calculated risk. Yes, he was assuming that Sean wouldn't hurt Callie, since the prick had already had months if that's what he wanted. Why would he do it now, when he was cornered with no escape route? Nor could he sneak her out with him past all these watchful eyes. She'd be safe; he had to believe that.

Before Thorpe gave in to the urge to punch the wall, he whirled on his heel and marched down the hall, texting Axel. Work fast.

As Thorpe passed Lance, he pocketed his phone and frowned. "Watch over the girl for me."

Lance shot him a shrewd glance. "I'll watch over *your* girl. Admit that's what she is."

He rubbed at his forehead where a bitch of a headache was forming. "Let's focus on keeping her safe tonight and getting rid of the Scottish stallion. If we manage that, I'll think about it."

When hell froze over.

"If you won't make Callie yours, why not let her be happy with someone who adores her?" Lance challenged. "You might not like Sean Kirkpatrick, but he's in love with that little vixen."

"You don't understand." Thorpe chafed, but the less he told the others about Callie and her secrets, the better.

"That you won't claim her, but don't want anyone else to have her? Sure, I do. It's a damn shame that you prefer her being alone and unhappy to pairing up."

Why did the other Dom have to bring up the point that pinpricked Thorpe with the most guilt?

"I don't want her unhappy." Though he didn't hate the idea of Callie being alone if he couldn't have her. And yes, he knew that was selfish as hell. "But she deserves the best."

Lance shrugged. "Not arguing that. Just not sure he's any worse than you encouraging her adoration when you have no intention of claiming her." Thorpe opened his mouth to rebut, but the other man wagged a finger in his face. "Melissa, the ex-bitch, walked out on you, and it's not an exercise you want to repeat. Got it. But use your fucking brain. If Callie stayed even after all the times you rebuffed her, I doubt she's going to run out on you."

Lance couldn't be more wrong, but Thorpe didn't dare say more. "You might be surprised."

"Her heart is yours," Lance insisted, scoffing.

"Not exclusively."

And that bitter pill made Thorpe choke.

He'd had enough of this conversation. Forcing himself away, he tore into his office and tried to bury himself in paperwork. Nothing held his attention. Half-answered e-mails and discarded forms couldn't make him forget that, right now, Callie would be pressed up against a man she didn't really know. Sean might be ordering her to strip. She might be baring her body and soul for a stranger with sinister motives.

Damn it! Logically, having Callie occupy the asshole to flush him out made sense. But Thorpe hated this plan. It was wearing his nerves awfully fucking thin, as was Lance's confrontation.

He stared at the clock, watching every drag of its hands. Thirty minutes took three days. Finally, his cell phone chimed. Yanking the device from his pocket, he saw Axel's number on the display and stabbed the button to answer. "Talk to me."

"I'm in. It's his place, all right. I had to turn the place upside down to find anything, but . . . " Axel paused. "You better be sitting. I've got bad news, boss. Really fucking bad."

* * *

CALLIE trembled as Sean approached. "I'm glad you came."

"Though Thorpe all but summoned me, I wasn't going to say no, lovely. Any opportunity to see you is one I'll take."

She lifted the corners of her lips and hoped it looked like a smile. Knowing these were the last moments she'd have with Sean, that she'd already laid eyes on Thorpe for the final time, that tomorrow she'd be in another city and never see Dallas or the people who'd become her family again . . . Callie sniffled. She couldn't afford these tears and her maudlin whinefest had to stop.

"Are you all right?" Sean asked, curling a solicitous hand around her elbow.

"I'm fine. Just allergies." She forced herself to smile brighter, but it didn't seem to be working. The concern in Sean's frown deepened.

If he looked at her too hard, he would see that something troubled her. She didn't want her last memories of him to be of anger or rebuke as he futilely tried to pry the reasons for her mood from her. She had a plan; she needed to stick to it. Everything was ready, including the spare key to her car since Thorpe had never given back the ones he'd swiped from her purse. The emergency pack she'd left Chicago with all those years ago, along with a few other things to aid her disguise, was stowed in the trunk of her car. The money she'd scraped together over the years was inside as well. She'd take nothing else with her, not even her phone, filled with pictures of everything and everyone she loved. As much as she wanted to, there was no way she could risk carrying around the memories.

Shortly after Thorpe had the burglar bars installed over the club's windows, she'd loosened them just enough to wiggle through . . . in case she ever needed to leave. Earlier today, she'd tested them. She could twist through, but just barely. So even if she could take her memories with her, they would simply have to stay behind.

Besides, a clean break was always better. She'd been through this enough to know.

Callie turned to the glasses of wine she'd procured earlier from Dominion's bar and handed him the one she'd doctored in advance with two Ambien. They wouldn't hurt him, but they should knock him out and give her time to slip away. She should be at least an hour or more down the road before Thorpe discovered she was gone.

Ditching her little sedan and buying another would be her first priority. It sucked that tomorrow was Sunday. Most car dealerships in Texas were closed. She'd have to find a used lot somewhere and hope for the best. But that was later. She wanted to enjoy her last minutes with Sean. The yawning chasm of all her empty tomorrows stretched out in front of her, and she'd have to face it soon enough.

Handing his glass of wine to him, she grabbed her own.

He raised his. "A toast, lovely. To new beginnings."

She tried not to cry at that irony. "To new beginnings."

Hers would simply be far, far away.

Sean caressed her with more than kindness. Devotion and hunger lay in his smile, and she let herself bask in his gaze for a few precious seconds. If she'd been a normal girl with a normal past, she would give her heart to this man and be so grateful to have him in her life. As it was, she'd probably die alone in some big city she wasn't familiar with. Whoever found her body would never know that she was Callindra Howe. They'd never really know the woman underneath whatever fake name she'd assumed. She'd be given a pauper's burial. No one would come to her funeral because no one would care.

Gawd, she'd gotten good at depressing herself. None of that mattered. *Pick up. Move on. Don't cry.*

"Bottoms up." She clinked their glasses together and took a sip, watching as Sean swallowed some of the red wine.

"That's a mite dry, just how I like it."

Great news. Hers was super sweet, but the drugs had a bitter aftertaste, and she'd known that crushing two pills into the liquid would alter the vino's flavor.

"I want to toast new beginnings because on my way in, Thorpe and I reached a bit of a truce," he explained.

"That's great!"

If they weren't at one another's throats once she'd fled, then maybe no one would be going to prison for murder. Thorpe would discover her gone, and it should be obvious that Sean had not helped her escape. He might be angry that Sean had been unable to stop her, but no way Thorpe could blame him. They might each look for her for a time. Separately, of course. They didn't like one another well enough to do that together. But eventually, they'd give up. Their lives would move on. Hers would be forever marked by a few distinct events: her mother's death shortly after she'd turned six, her family's murder ten years later, and the day she'd left the two wonderful men she loved.

"It's a start, anyway." Sean shrugged. "I can't say that I like the fact that you work for him *and* live under his roof. I know you have feelings for him, just like I know he wants you between his sheets." He looked at her so intently. "I love you, Callie. You say you have feelings for me, too. But for us to work, you've got to choose."

Oh, she'd chosen. Now she just had to muster up the will to go through with her plan. And never lose her resolve about not looking back.

"I know. I've been giving this a lot of thought." Callie downed her wine for some liquid courage, hoping it would encourage Sean to do the same.

"And?" he asked, then took another healthy swig of wine before setting his stem on the dresser and focusing on her.

No! He needed to drink more—all of it. But when he grabbed her shoulders and tugged her closer, she knew that wine was the last thing on his mind. Now, she could only pray that he'd imbibed enough of the drug.

Callie set her own glass beside his, then looked up into his strong, familiar face, doing her best to remember every detail. Soon, she'd have nothing left of him or Thorpe but memories.

"I love you, too," she whispered.

That was the last truth she could ever give him. Now she had to release him.

Falling apart inside, she threw herself against Sean's broad chest, feeling the stalwart beat of his heart, and pressed her lips to his.

Sean ate at her mouth for a moment, his tongue ravenous, his lips possessive. Then he pulled back, panting and staring, seeming to pierce her soul. "I feel like I've waited half my life to hear you say that. Come away with me."

His soft demand shocked the hell out of her. "*What?*"

"I mean it. We've never even seen one another outside this club."

"I live here."

"We'll find a new place, room enough for two."

She gaped at him. "I-I work here."

"You don't need this job, lovely. I'll support you."

Dumbfounded, she stared mutely. He cared for her that much? It broke her heart to shake her head.

"Callie, hear me out. We can't truly grow together if Thorpe is always in our way. We need time alone, just the two of us."

"I . . ." The offer was tempting, in a way. Maybe she could start over with Sean. Maybe he would agree to move somewhere else and . . . Harbor a woman wanted for murder? Hide her when his whole life would come crashing down for it? He already asked too many questions. Sean wasn't dumb; it wouldn't take him much longer to figure her out. "I can't."

Just like she couldn't stand to break his heart now. If his feelings were genuine, he would hurt enough once he woke to find her gone.

Frustration flashed across his face. He clenched his fists. "Don't you understand? As long as he's dictating the terms, we can't really be together. We can't grow."

If she wasn't running for her life or also in love with the man Sean was trying to wrest her from, she might agree. She didn't have that luxury now. "I'll think about it. I just need time. This is really sudden."

He sighed. "All right. I've been pondering it for weeks now and I'm ready to have you all to myself, but . . . I'll try to be patient."

"Thank you." She batted her lashes at him. That was false, but she caressed her way up his shoulder and wrapped her fingers around his nape. Under her hands, he felt so very real.

"You're mine, you know," he declared, his tone strong and gruff and insistent. "I won't give up."

It shouldn't, but his declaration made her heart flutter.

"Fuck, I can't stand it. I've got to have you, lovely. Mark you as mine somehow. Strip for me."

Callie tried not to lose her cool. If she gave more of herself to Sean now, the hurt would only be deeper later. Already, she felt so damn close to crumbling that she could barely hold herself together. But she couldn't deny that she wanted to touch him one last time.

If she couldn't give him the truth, then she could give him a part of herself. Besides, she had to distract him—fast.

Pulling off her dress, she laid it across the bed. Her champagne lace lingerie followed, and the low moan that came from Sean's throat echoed with appreciation. She kicked her shoes off next and rolled down her stockings, teasing him with every movement. Callie stared at him over her shoulder, gently wiggling her hips.

"You're a right heady siren." He palmed her hip. "Every time I'm near you, I forget everything I should be doing. I can only think about making you mine."

Callie knew exactly what he meant because he often derailed her better intentions.

Sending a shaky smile his way, she forced herself to stay on track. So she pressed one last kiss to his lips, then sank gracefully to her knees.

"What's this?" he asked, looking down at her, his eyes heating.

Her stare rocketed up his thighs and lingered at the healthy bulge behind his zipper. She bit her lip, then forced herself to stare straight into his eyes. "Let me serve you."

Sean sucked in a harsh breath. "Callie . . ."

She didn't wait for him to refuse or command her to change course. She unbuttoned his trousers, then lowered his zipper with a hiss that throbbed in the silence. Without a word, he shed his jacket and shirt, casting them onto the floor, never taking his stare from her.

After she eased the charcoal trousers off his hips, they fell down his thighs. He kicked his shoes away and stepped out of the pants.

"I shouldn't be letting you control this," he said thickly. But that wasn't stopping him. "I might paddle you for it later."

Usually, she'd have a saucy answer for him. Today, she just couldn't scrape one together, not when she was so close to falling apart.

Instead, she peered up at him with her heart in her eyes. "I need to please you right now."

The hint of disapproval left his face, and he caressed the crown of her head. "I find I'm not very good at saying no to you, lovely."

The answering smile she sent him perched softly on her lips. "I'm more grateful than you know."

Before he could say anything more, Callie lowered his dark boxer-briefs down his legs, revealing the thick, long stalk of his cock. At the recollection of it between her lips, inside her hungry sex, her womb clenched. One final time . . . At least it was a small comfort to know that his last memories of her would be of pleasure.

"Suck me, then," he said.

"Yes, Sir," she murmured and leaned forward to take him between her lips.

With a long swipe of her tongue, she laved him up the long shaft, over the bulbous head that looked somewhere between blue and purple, then swirled all around until he slid desperate fingers into her hair and moaned low.

Callie closed her eyes and sank into the moment, taking him even deeper inside. She sucked hard, putting all her love and determination into every pass of her lips and curl of her tongue over his hard flesh.

"Hmm." He rocked a bit on his feet. "Feels so good. You're making me dizzy."

"Then I must be doing something right." *And so must the Ambien.*

She redoubled her effort, whimpering at the taste of him so hot and potent, growing harder and thicker. Longer. He gripped her hair tight, pulling. The slight sting of pain roused her, as did the musky scent of his skin, pooling with masculine tang in the dips and crooks between his legs. Cupping his heavy testicles, feeling them draw up bit by bit in her palm, she gave herself totally to his pleasure and let his trembling fingers guide her up and down his length until his breath sawed out of his chest. His pants became grunts, each growing louder until he moaned aloud.

"Callie . . ."

Whimpering at his urgency, desperate to feel him explode on her tongue and taste the flavor of his satisfaction, she sucked harder, bathing him with her tongue one last time. Her heart stuttered as his cock pulsed. He grabbed her hair, then gave a hoarse shout of fulfillment.

His hot seed erupted on her tongue, salty and thick. Callie drank him down, digging her nails in his hair-dusted thighs and clinging with every bit of her need.

Why couldn't this moment go on forever? Why couldn't she curl up with him on the bed, watching him sleep in sated contentment, and think about what they'd do tomorrow?

Because she could never be Callindra Howe again. She couldn't even be a woman with a real life.

Slowly, she worked her lips up Sean's length, looking through her lashes at his flushed face. His chest heaved. His eyes slid closed. Gratification spread across his face.

"Oh, lovely . . ." His voice sounded low and faint. He stumbled on his feet.

Callie jumped to steady him, then eased him onto the bed. He tumbled back, head on her pillow, his breath evening out.

Her time with him was almost over.

"I love you," he breathed out.

She leaned over him, drinking in his strong, relaxed features, firm lips, hard jaw. She cupped his face. Such a beautiful man . . .

And he'd never really know how much she loved him in return. Since he was moments from sleep, Sean wouldn't remember anything she said now.

He'd be hurt by her abrupt departure. Callie caressed his face, tears forming and falling. She should be leaving right now, throwing on her dark clothes and shimmying outside, but the thought of tearing herself away voluntarily from this bed—from him—was ripping her chest wide open and splintering her heart.

"So tired . . ." He frowned.

"I know. I'm sorry." Callie wished she could leave behind a piece of herself for him. Maybe then, she could find the will to move on, knowing she'd done what she could to ease his hurt.

An idea flashed across her brain, and she leapt up, digging frantically in Sean's pants until she found his phone. Then she shook him awake.

"Wha . . . ?"

Callie thrust his phone into his hands. "Unlock this for me. I need to make a call. My cell is dead."

"Told you. Charge it." He fought to peer at the screen and tap out the code.

On the third try, he finally managed. The phone clicked. His arm dropped to his side as deep slumber overtook him.

And that was it. Her last waking words to him were a fib. Leaving him a recording on his phone was the only way she could think to leave him the truth in her heart.

As she flipped through his apps, looking for a place to leave him a video message, she frowned when she stumbled over a picture of herself. But not a current one. It was the yearbook photo she'd taken her sophomore year, just before her family's murder had forced her to flee Chicago and all she'd ever known.

Sean knew her identity. The thought beat through her brain. He *knew*. Her fingers went numb. She dropped the phone.

Every word he'd ever uttered to her was a lie.

Oh God.

Sucking in a terrified breath, Callie leapt away from him and fell to the floor. She fumbled through his pants. Was he a cop? An assassin? A private investigator? His trousers revealed nothing—no driver's license, no wallet, no badge. She crawled over the carpet until she reached his coat. After patting it twice, she encountered a hard, cold lump. Folding back the fabric, she found the inside pocket and peeked down. A gun.

Callie bit back a shriek. Her heart beat a fast, staccato rhythm. Terror laced her veins with icy fire.

He knew who she was and he carried a gun. His plea for her to come away with him? He'd probably meant to kill her once he'd lured her away from Thorpe and Dominion. Whoever had shot her father and sister had come after her more than once to finish the job, but they'd never gotten close to her. This time, they'd found her weakness—her fucking foolish heart.

Sean Kirkpatrick, the beautiful Scot she'd stupidly fallen for, was trying to kill her. She bit back tears of betrayal and ran.

* * *

THORPE ended the call with Axel, stunned and blinking. A chill worked through his body.

Callie . . .

She was locked in her room with that son of a bitch.

Tearing down the hall, he rounded the corner, calling security as he ran and grabbing Lance, who still stood sentry in the hall.

"What the hell?" the other Dom asked.

As soon as Axel's muscle picked up the phone in the booth, Thorpe growled, "Callie's room. Now. She's in danger."

On the off chance this turned out to be a misunderstanding or a mistake, he'd worry about the repercussions of bursting in on them later.

Lance cursed. "What's happened?"

Thorpe had a terrible feeling. God, why hadn't he seen this coming? "Sean Kirkpatrick is a lying motherfucker. Nothing he's told us
about himself is true. And he's here to take Callie."

"Goddamn it!" Lance ran faster.

They reached her door at the same time as the security guards.
Panic making his heart drum loudly in his ears, Thorpe pounded on
the door. "Callie?"

No answer.

No, no, no . . . He couldn't handle it. Please let her be asleep or in
the shower or even busy with Kirkpatrick's dick in her mouth. He
couldn't deal with her being gone.

Fucking fabulous time to admit how much he loved her.

Thorpe extracted her key from his pocket. His hands shook as
he slammed it in, then turned the lock. Frantically, he twisted the
knob. He couldn't move fast enough, get to her quickly enough.

The moment he did, he took in the disheveled bed, a naked Kirkpatrick sprawled across it. Callie's lingerie littered the floor. Her
dress had been flung nearby. Her purse and phone sat on the dresser.
But the window hung open . . . and the woman he loved was nowhere
in sight.

Chapter Seven

Two hours later, Thorpe had no doubt whatsoever that Callie was long gone. In addition to her car, she'd taken her laughter, her expressive blue eyes . . . and the other half of his heart with her.

Plowing his hands through his hair, he thought acidly that if he'd been going gray before, worrying about Callie would accelerate that process. Now, Kirkpatrick was his only hope for answers. So far, he'd been unable to shake the bastard awake. In the interim, Thorpe had rifled through every inch of her closet and each one of her drawers. He hadn't come up with much.

The bottle of Ambien he'd gotten the doctor to prescribe her this summer had never been touched. He'd railed at her to take them and put a stop to her insomnia. The stubborn girl had refused. Suddenly, two of the tablets were gone. Between the wine on her dresser and Kirkpatrick still sacked out in her bed, Thorpe didn't have to guess what had happened to them. *Goddamn it.*

Axel returned, and by the grim look on his face, his search of Callie's few favorite haunts had turned up empty. He couldn't call her cell phone or track it. She'd left it here. Ironically enough, with a full charge. She'd shed her siren red dress. It still smelled like her. In her wake, she'd abandoned every other stitch of clothing she owned, except the ones on her back. Also left behind were the cards and gifts she'd painstakingly packed away for the last four years, as if each one was a treasured memento. And she'd removed Sean's collar, placing it in the center of the nightstand beside him, where he would certainly see it once he woke.

Thorpe knew exactly who was responsible for Callie's abrupt departure. She'd been . . . well, maybe not perfectly happy, but content for the last four years. Kirkpatrick had entered the scene, turned her fairly ordered world upside down, and ultimately frightened her away. Then like a wild wind, she'd swept out the door. Only Callie and God knew where the hell she was.

Would she think she was all alone now that he wasn't beside her to hold her hand?

"Nothing?" he asked Axel.

"Nada. I've looked everywhere. The guys have swept every inch of this place. The little minx crawled out the window—somehow— then she managed to avoid every one of the security cameras in the parking lot on her way to her car. The only images captured indicate that she wore black and drove out of the parking lot nearly three hours ago."

How the fuck had his careful planning gone down the drain? What, exactly, had Kirkpatrick done to spook her and make Callie flee so suddenly? Thorpe intended to get answers.

"I'm going to find her."

"I know you'll try like hell." Axel crossed his beefy arms over his massive chest. "I just don't know where to go with the search from here."

"I need to come up with some ideas. In the meantime, can you get me fake passports? When I find Callie, I'm going to move her out of the country. And I'm going to take care of her."

Axel whistled. "The documents alone will cost you a small fortune."

"I don't care. Can you arrange it or not?"

"Yeah. But you have a business to run. How the hell are you going to do that from . . . El Salvador or wherever you wind up?"

"You said once that you wanted to buy me out. Here's your chance."

His head of security held up massive hands in a placating gesture. "You're talking about throwing away everything you've worked for over damn near the last decade for a girl you haven't ever fuc—"

"Don't. Finish. That. Sentence. She's had no one to truly rely on for too long. I'm going to change that."

"If you're caught, you'll go to prison with her."

Shock pinged through him. Axel had figured out Callie's identity.

Thorpe narrowed his eyes and gave the big guy his most menacing snarl. "What are you implying?"

"Hey . . . whoa. Nothing, man. Reading Kirkpatrick's documents tonight made it obvious who Callie really is. Blew the fuck out of my mind. But I figured you knew, too." At Thorpe's sharp nod, Axel went on. "Her behavior all this time makes sense now. How long have you known?"

"Almost two years." Since that fateful December night when he'd finally put his hands and his eyes on the bullet wound that had carved a little nick out of her left hip—and confirmed all his worst fears. "You'd better not be counting that big bounty on her head."

Axel looked almost hurt. "The idea of Callie shooting anyone, much less her own family, especially for money, is preposterous. I'd *never* stab either of you in the back for a buck."

"I hope you're not fucking with me. I'd hate to have to end you and dispose of your corpse at the bottom of a lake in the middle of nowhere."

Axel snorted. "I won't give you a reason to plot my murder. Is that what you have in mind for his fate?"

Thorpe followed the other man's stare down to Sean, still all but passed out. "I'm considering my options, but I'm not ruling anything out."

"If you don't do something with him, he's going to blab."

"True. And I've got to remove him from Callie's path for good. She needs to know that she's safe, no matter where we go."

"You're in love with her?"

He figured that Axel was about the only one who hadn't guessed before now. "I'm surprised Lance didn't let you in on that. He's apparently amused. And Xander just feels sorry for me."

Being in Callie's room when it felt so utterly devoid of the woman herself was killing him. Her touch was here and her scent lingered. Thorpe paced, but pain seeped into his chest. Every moment felt like torture, and it was fucking hard just to breathe. How would he close his eyes and sleep without knowing where she'd gone? How would he be able to face tomorrow without any idea if she was safe?

"There's nothing funny about love when it goes to shit." Axel sighed heavily.

Thorpe knew the guy had a story, but he had to focus on Callie now. "Will you help me or not?"

"Absolutely. You've squeezed me out of more binds than I can count. If you need me, I'm solid. Just give me a few days to get all the paperwork in order. Focus on finding her."

"Yeah. Question is, where do we start?"

"Well, it's not like we can file a missing person's report . . ."

"No. And someone else was the last to see her before she bolted," Thorpe pointed out.

They both looked down at Sean.

"I'll make coffee. Good luck waking Sleeping Beauty," Axel drawled.

With a nod, Thorpe sat on the edge of the bed. "While you're at it, check in with your guys again . . . just in case they have anything new."

"On it." Axel sauntered to the door, then paused. "I won't give up, either. We'll do everything we can."

It wouldn't be easy. Callie had vanished into thin air many times over the years. She'd learned how to evade law enforcement, how to disguise herself well, how to connect herself with people who weren't all that friendly with the authorities.

But she didn't know how to escape a man willing to fight dirty and give anything to have her back. She'd soon learn that he'd never give up.

With a sour curl to his lips, he gave Sean a hearty shove. The man grunted, smacked his tongue in his mouth, then rolled away and resumed snoring.

Thorpe eyed him with annoyance. This shit had been going on entirely too long. He should have listened to his gut as soon as Kirkpatrick walked in the club and threw the bastard out.

Sighing, he dragged Sean to the edge of the bed and slung the man over his shoulder, fireman style. The fucker groaned and jerked, half awake and flailing.

Trudging to Callie's small bathroom, Thorpe heaved the man into her empty tub. Sean's head hit the porcelain with a little thump.

"That's going to leave a mark." Axel stood in the doorway with a considering stare.

"Oops." Thorpe smiled tightly and reached for the faucet. "Aren't you supposed to be busy?"

"Already done. I rushed back. This is more entertaining." With a bark of laughter, Axel considered Sean again. "If you're going to splash cold water on him, be careful. I was a medic in the military. He could go into shock. I've seen it happen once after a few idiots drank too much tequila on leave, then tried to wake one another up."

"Well, I only need this one alive for about two minutes. Then . . ." Thorpe shrugged.

"You have a really ruthless side, boss." Axel smiled. "I like it."

"I try." Thorpe flipped the faucet on in Callie's shower, blasting ridiculously cold water all over Sean, soaking his skin.

He came up sputtering, wiping water from his eyes and glaring. "What the fuck! Are you out of your mind?"

*Well, well. Isn't that interesting? No Scottish accent . . . The leop-*ard was finally showing his true spots.

"Not at all," Thorpe growled, then grabbed the back of Sean's head by his wet hair.

"Get your bloody hands off me."

And the accent is back. Thorpe rolled his eyes.

"Drop the act. I know you're not Scottish. And I know you're not a traveling businessman."

Sean reared back. "I've no idea what you're talkin' about. I'm from Edinburgh. I moved to Florida a few years back—"

"Shut the fuck up."

"I'd do what he says, if I were you," Axel suggested. "He's in a really bad mood."

Sean's blue stare zipped around the room. "Where's Callie?"

"Well, that's what I want to ask you since you were the last person to see her before she fled."

* * *

WITH a ripe curse, Sean jerked away from Thorpe's brutal hold and stood, turning off the freezing shower. He shook off the excess water like a dog, snickering when Thorpe and Axel both protested. Then they just looked angrier.

Well, fuck. Two against one, and I'm buck naked. The odds weren't good. How did Thorpe know he wasn't a Scottish business-man? And what else did he know?

Later. His sluggish brain was just now processing what Thorpe had declared.

His heart froze, then began pounding like a damn jackhammer.

"Fled?" He added the lilt, refusing to break cover, even if panic grated his insides. "How did you let her slip past you?"

Thorpe rolled his eyes. "I'll explain the meaning of 'the jig is up' when Callie is back home safely. I'm asking how she slipped past *you*. After all, you were in the same room with her."

Sean weighed his words carefully, trying to reconstruct the evening in his head, then he played the part of Kirkpatrick, as he had for months. "The lass must have drugged the wine she gave me. I don't recall much. Then she . . ."

He let out a ragged breath. The part where Callie had swallowed down his cock and sucked him dry, all with such a sad look in her eyes, was crystal clear.

"What?"

"That's between Callie and me, a private matter between a Master and his sub."

Axel leaned out the door, then came back dangling Callie's collar on one finger. "I don't think she's your sub anymore. She took this off before she shimmied out the window."

The sight of Callie's collar glinting in Axel's hand staggered him like he'd fallen under the weight of a giant redwood. He stumbled back. Son of a bitch, he should have listened to his instinct and pushed Callie for answers. He'd known something was troubling her.

Sean grabbed the collar from Axel and clutched it in his hand, then glared Thorpe's way. "What did you do to her?"

"Nothing I hate worse than a fake accent," the club owner muttered to the security beefcake. "I admit it had me fooled for a long time, but now it just makes me grit my teeth." Finally, the man regarded him again. "What the fuck kind of question is that?"

"The kind where you explain to me what you did to distress my wee lovely. She's been upset since last night, when you saw us together in the dungeon. She seemed more than a mite on edge tonight."

"Are you suggesting that *I'm* the one who ran her off?"

"That I am. I've no idea what she likes about you, but she does by her own admission. You pushing your attentions on her last night confused the poor girl."

"You blurting that you love her didn't? Are you going to tell me her tears then were fake?"

Axel stepped between them. "Guys, this isn't helping us find Callie."

True, and he had to keep it together. He'd invested nearly a year's worth of work on her . . . and without meaning to, his heart.

"I'm going to check in with the rest of the staff, question some of the members who were in the parking lot earlier, and make a few phone calls. Be-fucking-have, you two," Axel demanded, then strode out the door, shaking his head.

As the other man disappeared, Sean got back to the matter at hand. "Callie didn't say a word to me about leaving. We drank some wine, talked a bit, then made our way to the bed. That's the last thing I recall."

"No idea if she figured out you're a fed?"

Sean's blood ran cold. "A fed? You're arse end up. I'm telling you—"

"A birdie told me there are lots of files from the FBI about me and everyone else who frequents this club in your apartment. And of course every known fact about 'wee' Callie."

Shit, Thorpe knew exactly who he was. And who she was, too. The good news was Thorpe was protective of the girl. The bad news was that might change now that he realized he'd been having feelings for and harboring a fugitive all this time.

If Thorpe hurt her, Sean vowed to kill him.

Hurdling the rim of the tub, he jumped in Thorpe's face and, despite his nudity, shoved the annoying asshole against the wall. "I should have you fucking arrested."

No sense in faking the accent now. Thorpe had crossed the line, invading a federal agent's turf. But Sean knew he should kick his own ass, too. He should carry information in a more discreet way. He should use some high-tech way to lock it up. But he'd been raised by his grandparents. High tech wasn't his thing. Certain in the belief that no one at Dominion had seen through his cover, he'd allowed himself to slack. And now he was going to pay.

"Thank you," Thorpe spit. "That accent was driving me mad."

"It was my grandfather's, and it's spot on. I've tested it in Scotland, in his hometown. Fuck off." He stomped on the wet tile, sloshing around, before he grabbed Callie's towel off the rack. It was still damp. And damn if it didn't smell like her. Sean nearly went weak in the knees. He had to believe that he'd smell her skin again soon. She couldn't be gone forever in an instant.

"Will the real Sean step forward?" Thorpe drawled "Or is that even your name?"

"I don't have to answer that." Sean wrapped the towel around his waist, still clutching the delicate weight of her collar.

"I think you do, unless you have no interest in finding Callie." Thorpe crossed his arms, and the seams of his coat struggled to contain the bulk of his shoulders. "Because I'm not going to tell you what I know until you do."

He'd learned quickly from observation around the club that Mitchell Thorpe hid behind a veneer of civility, but under it all, he could be unflinchingly ruthless when something or someone he valued was threatened.

"Special Agent Sean Mackenzie. I have every interest in finding Callie. She's not just the subject of an investigation to me." He cleared his throat. "I love her."

"Not sure I believe you." Thorpe paused. "And I've got about a million questions, but not until we have some idea where Callie has gone."

"Fair enough."

"Did she give you any indication where she might be headed?"

"Like I said, she didn't indicate that she was going at all. I suspected, but . . . Can we head back to the bedroom so I can have my clothes? Unless you like me naked or something?"

"Fuck no." Thorpe moved out of the doorway.

Sean ambled into Callie's room, looking at the window with a frown. "She crawled out that window with the bars?"

Thorpe nodded, seeming both vexed and oddly proud of Callie. "I took a flashlight and examined the area where she'd loosened the bars in one corner. It appears that she did it some time ago to make sure she had an escape route."

"So she's always had a plan, I suppose."

"I think she always does. How else could she manage to elude you guys for so long?"

Sean nodded and located his clothes in the mess Thorpe had made searching the room. Setting Callie's collar on her nightstand, he swore he'd have it around her neck again, someday, somehow—for real. Then he slipped on his pants. "I've studied her patterns. From what I can tell, she came most recently from Oklahoma City. I don't see her going back there. I'm sure you've looked at the security footage. Did she leave in her car?"

Thorpe hesitated. "She did, but I don't expect her to keep it long."

"Agreed. It's a liability. She wouldn't want to run the risk of us putting an APB out on her or being arrested by the first overzealous cop who runs her license plate."

"No." The club owner didn't add a single other word to the conversation. Obviously, he wasn't going to lift a finger to help.

"I wished I'd listened to my gut and put a GPS tracker on her car."

"You don't have any other way to track her?" When Sean shook his head, Thorpe sighed in frustration. "Are you fucking kidding me? You knew she was a flight risk."

"I had devices in both her collar *and* her purse. She conveniently removed the first and left the second behind. If I was going to play the pointless blame game, I'd ask why you didn't check the bars on her windows to make sure they were secure. After all, you knew she was a flight risk, too."

"Fuck off."

"We don't have Axel to referee for us now. Are we going to narrow down where we might find Callie or just fight?"

Thorpe clenched his fists, looking ready to spit nails. "We're going to find her."

"Good. I've got some theories. She wouldn't head anywhere north or northeast with winter coming," Sean mused aloud.

"What makes you think that?"

"Don't treat me like I'm stupid." He bristled. "Callie dislikes the cold. And over the last nine years, we've tracked her through eight states. We've often missed her by days, sometimes even hours." Sean couldn't help but admire her guts as he slipped on his shirt. "But she always chases the warmth. You know, we've been aware for some time that she was in Texas. We even suspected Dallas, but couldn't pin her down."

Thorpe swallowed thickly. "How did you find her?"

"We got a hit on facial recognition software when you sent her to your bank to make a deposit at the end of January. It took a few weeks for the bureau to positively identify her, then another six weeks for me to watch this place, you, the others here, and her, so we could decide how to proceed."

Thorpe closed his eyes, and Sean could guess that he was kicking his own ass. "I never imagined that a simple errand would put her at risk."

"Don't blame yourself. It could have just as easily been a traffic or sidewalk cam."

But Thorpe's face said that he absolutely felt responsible and that if he ever found Callie, he wouldn't make that mistake again. Sean would bet every dime in his bank account that the man was already planning to secret her out of the country, someplace far warmer and south of the U.S., out of the bureau's reach.

He regarded his nemesis, hoping like hell he wouldn't have to detain or hurt Thorpe. It would just be a waste of time and the loss of a temporary ally.

"So you don't have any ideas where Callie might have gone?" Sean challenged, wanting to know if Thorpe was going to play nice. Obviously, the man had ideas. Time to see how much he'd be willing to share.

"Not really. The only thing I've ever been able to count on with Callie was the unpredictable. Maybe Florida. If she wanted to get out of the country, doing it from the Keys would be easier."

Sean pounded his fist on the wall beside Thorpe's head. "Bullshit! The longer you play this stupid fucking game with me, the longer she has to get away. She won't go to Florida because she thinks my home and business are there."

"Well, damn. I guess I can't accuse you of being stupid after all."

Sean just snorted.

"Are you based in Florida?" Thorpe sounded almost hopeful.

"Right here in Dallas." He smiled acidly.

"Well, hunky fucking dory. Isn't it my lucky day?"

"Hey, you don't have to like me any better than I like you. But right now, we have to work together to find her. Every minute that ticks by—"

"Is another minute she slips farther away. I know that, asshole." Thorpe gave an agitated huff and raked a hand through his hair.

"Look, whether you believe me or not, my feelings for Callie are real. I have a very vested interest in making sure she doesn't go to jail, especially for a crime there's no way she committed."

That set Thorpe on his ear. "You know she's innocent?"

"Of course. But is that really the important question?"

"Why does the bureau want her? Murder isn't really their jurisdiction."

"Now you're thinking. That's something I've asked myself over and over. I don't have an answer, and before you say a word, that's not a load of crap. I don't have the time or energy to lie to you, man. They keep giving me a line about identity fraud."

"Callie wouldn't steal anyone's identity." Thorpe frowned.

"But she's created personas and gotten fake IDs, sometimes crossing state lines before shedding them and her car, then starting over."

Thorpe looked at him as if he'd lost his mind. "And that's cause for the bureau to send in an undercover agent for months?"

"Exactly. None of this adds up for me, either. And they're treating the case like it's vital to national security."

"*What?* That doesn't make any fucking sense."

"What makes even less sense is that my directive is just to keep tabs on her and search for anything she may have taken of her father's."

"Not to arrest her?" Thorpe looked tense, poised on a knife's edge waiting for the answer.

A part of Sean wanted to let the club owner squirm in discomfort, but they just didn't have time. "At least for now. If they really believed she had violated laws, they'd want her behind bars pronto. Two and two isn't adding up. Something's rotten in Denmark. Use whatever cliché you like, but it's messed up. And I'm going to do everything I can to protect her."

"That makes two of us." Crossing his arms, Thorpe swallowed. "All right. She mentioned something about L.A. to me last night."

Sean's whole body tightened. "Does she know anyone there?"

"Not anymore. Xander moved to Louisiana. And they aren't close."

With a shrug of his shoulders, Sean considered the suggestion. "It's a possibility. They have fairly warm winters. It's far from here. It's a big city, so she can get lost."

"That makes sense."

Thorpe looked like that notion scared the hell out of him. It worried Sean, too. What if he couldn't find her there? Or anywhere?

"She'll definitely head west. Where's my damn phone?" Sean patted his pockets, then looked around the floor, then the bed. Finally, he spotted the device and nearly pounced on it. The second he tapped in his code, the picture that appeared made him swear a blue streak. "I know why Callie ran. Damn it, she fucking tricked me and figured out that I know who she is."

He flashed Thorpe the picture of her teenage self, chipper smile, dark blond hair, and those same blue eyes he could drown in.

Thorpe's sibilant curse filled the air. "That would do it."

"I scared her." Sean's face filled with regret.

"No doubt. If you think she's going west, I'm going to find her."

"You?" Sean shook his head. "This is *my* job. You need to stay here."

"Not happening. I'm going with you to find Callie and make sure you don't drag her away."

"You've got to stay here and act like everything is normal."

"How?" Thorpe demanded, looking at Sean as if he never had any mind to actually lose. "My world is upside down. Anyone who knows me knows damn well that I wouldn't let that girl go without a fight."

"Maybe, but you're crazy if you think the bureau isn't watching you, too. They don't get eyes on Callie too often outside Dominion. But you . . . every time you've hopped on a commercial flight or even taken a taxi since we identified her has been tracked and noted, just in case you leaving is a sign that she's darting with you."

"Someone inside the club snitched that we're close?"

Sean quickly assured him with a shake of his head. "Before I joined, I couldn't get anyone to talk, but the bureau surmised it. She's never stayed in one place for even half this long, so we had to assume that she was attached to someone here. You seemed like the most logical choice. The second I got in the door, I knew she'd remained here all these years for you."

He didn't tell Thorpe that he knew Callie had largely accepted his collar to see if Thorpe would care. If the bastard hadn't figured out that she was in love with him, too, Sean didn't feel the need to enlighten him. In his book, if Thorpe hadn't claimed her by now, he'd missed his chance.

"Here's a thought," Thorpe tossed out. "You stay here and look 'normal.' I'll borrow someone else's car and head west, in case they're looking for mine. I'll find Callie."

"Sure you will. While you're working out some scheme in your head where you intend to clear the country with her, never to be seen again. I promise I won't let that happen. I'll throw obstruction, tampering, harboring a fugitive—whatever I can make stick—at you. I'll also prosecute the hell out of Axel for breaking into my apartment and tampering with federal evidence. You'll both go to jail. And before you tell me Axel had nothing to do with it, shut up and spare me the lie."

"Then we're at a crossroads. You want to find her. I want to find her. You give me the 'two heads are better than one' speech, then think you're going to leave me here while you find Callie alone?" Thorpe shook his head. "At this point, I don't give a fuck if you try to arrest me. I only care about bringing her back safe. I don't doubt that she's dodged some unscrupulous men in the past who have looked at her and seen nothing but that two-million-dollar bounty." Thorpe frowned at him. "If she's not actually wanted for a crime, why the big price on her head?"

"I don't know. She doesn't have any other family to put up money, so that's another mystery that makes no sense to me. But if Uncle Sam is willing to pony up that much cash, she's somehow valuable. Someone else knows that—and knows why. People far more dangerous than bounty hunters."

Thorpe went absolutely still. "Whoever killed her family?"

"That's what I'm thinking. After all, they also shot her the night she escaped. If they wanted her dead then, why stop trying now?"

"You're right. Jesus . . ."

"According to the files I have access to, she's eluded some well-paid assassins over the last nine years. Someone wants to silence her. I just wish I knew why. I'd love to hunt down these assholes so I can keep her safe."

"We can't stand here and fuck around. This is bigger than I imagined." Thorpe didn't look like a man who ever begged, but he came pretty close now. "Two heads *are* better than one. You might know more about her background, but I know *her*. I know who she is now. I have a better idea where she'd go, what she'd do, and why."

Sean paused and reluctantly nodded. "All right. But you can't take her out of the country once we find her."

"We'll work that out later. Let's find her first."

Sean didn't like it, but Thorpe had a valid point. "My rules, though. Leave your phone here."

"What? No!" Thorpe looked at him like he'd lost his mind. "If she calls me—"

"She won't. She left her phone here with all her contact numbers."

"Callie memorizes numbers. She knows how to call me."

Sean shook his head. "The bureau is monitoring the location of your phone. Leave it here."

"Damn it! How?"

"Trade secret. Get a burner phone and tell Axel how to find you in case Callie calls you or returns. We need a car, not yours or mine."

"Axel will be happy to drive my Jag while I'm gone," Thorpe drawled.

"Perfect." Sean clapped him on the shoulder. "Let's go. We both need to grab as much cash as we can. Once we do, we'll get on the road. Hopefully, we can be out of Dallas before dawn."

"And what, just head west?"

With a nod, Sean's face turned grim. "We'll hope for a break in the information as we're traveling."

After a quick chat with Axel, they exchanged keys, and his head of security was grinning from ear to ear, promising to take care of the business and car, as Thorpe made his way to his office. Just as he set his phone in a drawer of his desk to lock it up, it chimed with a text. Sean glanced at the screen. Logan Edgington. 911.

"What does he want at this late hour?" Sean asked.

"Not sure. Might have something to do with a phone call I made earlier." He snatched his phone up again and quickly hit a few buttons, then jammed the device against his ear.

Sean didn't believe him for a second. "Put it on speaker."

"Fuck off."

"Or you stay here—behind bars. I can arrange that."

Thorpe grumbled, then hit the speaker button as the call connected. The second the other man answered, Thorpe skipped the small talk. "What's up, Logan?"

"Tara just found out through her contacts at the bureau that Kirkpatrick is really a fed named Mackenzie."

"I got that already. And he's standing right beside me."

Thorpe slanted him a stare, and Sean had to admit that he was impressed that the club owner had the forethought to look into his background. The guy might make a better partner in the search for Callie than expected.

"Well . . . I didn't know that until just now. So don't kill me."

"Not really my priority at the moment, Logan. I have to go. Callie is missing."

"I know. She came to me, terrified out of her mind. She didn't know who or what this Sean guy was." Logan sighed. "She thought he was trying to kill her, so I helped her disappear."

Chapter Eight

"WHY the fuck didn't you call me before now?" Thorpe demanded. "Hell, why didn't she come to me? I'm going to paddle her ass when I catch up with her . . ."

"Get in line," Sean groused beside him. "The little minx tricked me, drugged me, lied to me. I'm sure I can add to that list if I think about it for a few seconds more."

"Callie was scared, guys. She panicked. Based on what she told me, I understood," Logan said, trying to be the voice of reason.

There were a hundred reasons that was funny, but Thorpe wasn't in the mood to laugh just now. "And what did she tell you?"

"Are you here as a law enforcement officer or her Dom?" Logan asked.

"My priority is Callie's safety," Sean clarified. "Nothing else matters."

Logan snorted. "If you're lying, Thorpe will probably make sure that someone finds you months from now at the bottom of a lake with hundred-pound weights attached to your ankles."

Damn, Logan knew him well.

"Whatever. Spit it out." Sean rolled his eyes.

"She told me everything," Logan admitted.

Callie trusts a man she hasn't seen in two years more than she trusts me? The thought stung Thorpe like an icy rain. It fucking hurt, to be so disregarded after four years of . . . what was their relationship exactly?

If he thought about it, Callie had been his sub in so many ways. Not sexually, of course. But she'd deferred to him at work. She'd begun to come to him with her problems—not this one, granted. She'd leaned on him, sometimes letting him hold her when she'd looked forlorn or melancholy. And sweetest of all, she often tried to please him in little ways. He'd done his best to give her all the security, support, boundaries, and caring she required.

It hadn't been enough. With one sentence, Logan had stripped away his blinders and proven that he wasn't Callie's go-to confidante. It would be easy to imagine that she didn't care for him, but those teary blue eyes hadn't lied when he'd held her, and she'd cupped his cheek as she'd poured out her feelings. She did love him . . . in her way. As much as she let herself love anyone.

"So where's my Callie now?" Sean asked into the phone.

"*Your* Callie?" Thorpe asked sharply. "Remind me where her collar is now."

"Shut up and let Edgington answer," Sean snapped.

"She's on her way to Vegas," Logan supplied. "I called ahead to one of my old SEAL team buddies. Elijah is a good guy and a hell of an operative. Tomorrow, I promised to get some paperwork together for her so she could leave the country."

"Son of a bitch," Sean muttered, echoing Thorpe's own sentiment. Then the fed looked at him. "So I guess we're heading to Vegas. How is she getting there?"

"I found her a last-minute charter with a bunch of vacationers. It's a direct flight, leaving from New Orleans about . . . now. The plane is a big one. She's in the back. Hopefully, no one will remember her, especially after she bought a floppy hat at Walmart that covers half her face. Elijah will pick her up when the flight lands. He'll put her up with him. He's vacating his wife and kids from the house, just in case there's trouble. As soon as all her paperwork came together, I was going to overnight it to her."

And that would have been that. She would have disappeared from his life forever. And Thorpe realized, if that had happened, she would have been his biggest regret, too. He already had so many of them. Was he prepared to add her to the list?

"The second Callie called you to meet her, you should have let me know. You should have told me where she was, what was going on—"

"She begged me. I promised not to call you until we met and I heard her out. Once I had, I understood why she was adamant about not risking you, so I promised not to say anything. And she was right; everyone who knew her would assume she'd come to you with her problems. She usually does."

Thorpe still didn't like it. "How would you feel if Tara came to me wanting to escape danger, and refused to involve you even for your own good?"

"It's different. She's my wife."

"It's *not* different. If Xander knew how I felt about her, I guarantee you did." He cursed. "We'll talk more about this later. Where can we find Elijah?"

Logan rattled off the address, then sighed. "Look, I'm sorry. In your shoes, I'd be pissed, too. I did what I thought was best with the information I had. I'll stall her paperwork and tell Elijah to hang on to her until you can get there. Then you can decide the best course of action."

"Thanks," Sean said into the phone. "We'll call you again from the road with disposable numbers. Neither of us are taking our phones."

"Check."

Thorpe ended the call, barely resisting the urge to throw his cell across the room and smash it into pieces. Instead, he locked the device into one of his desk drawers so only Axel could access it, then looked at his rival for Callie's affection and his new partner in her retrieval. "I want to get to Callie as quickly as we can. I won't rest again until I see her."

"I feel the same. Let's go."

* * *

DAWN had inched up over the horizon a few hours ago, and they were in the armpit of Texas, somewhere between Dallas and Amarillo. Mile after mile of boring highway rolled by with nothing but small Texas towns to see, and the drive seemed interminable. He and Sean had passed the hours with a fast-food breakfast sandwich, several cups of coffee, and absolute silence. Yesterday's clothes felt gritty and stiff. But none of that mattered now. Thorpe could only pray that no one had recognized Callie and that she remained out of harm's way.

Beside him, Sean's eyes drooped like he still had a tinge of an Ambien hangover. But he continued to stare at the road as if it would somehow bring Callie back to him.

"If you want to sleep, go ahead. I got it," Thorpe said, breaking the tense hush.

Sean shook his dark head. "I've been on stakeouts in the past and had to go two or three days without much sleep, so I've been more tired."

He should probably just shut up, but they'd lost all radio reception some time ago, unless one counted the classic country twang station, which he didn't. To say the drive was stressful and boring was as obvious as calling the sky blue.

"Your sleep deprivation isn't going to help us find her any faster," Thorpe pointed out.

"Right now, I'm not sure I could nod off for any reason. We've got hours, maybe days, before we catch up to Callie. If I closed my eyes now, I'd just dwell on how disturbed I am that she believes I'm out to kill her."

"What else did you expect her to think after she realized you lied?"

"I understand logically. How many dirtbags have hunted her in the past, right? Her wariness has probably saved her more than once." A pained frown consumed the other man's face, full of deep lines and silent restraint. Callie's belief that Sean was capable of hurting her was clearly shredding his guts. "But I wouldn't tell Callie that I loved her if I'd just planned on ending her."

Mackenzie's tone asked why the girl couldn't see that. The man might have spewed a lot of crap in the past, but unfortunately Thorpe had no doubt his feelings were genuine.

"Or turning her in for the money?"

"Never."

"When did she become more than a case to you?" Thorpe wasn't interested in having a touchy-feely conversation, but it would both fill the long drive and tell him how much he could trust the guy.

Sean shrugged. "I think before I even met her. Callie was never a name in a file for me. From the moment this case came my way, I wanted to understand what made her tick. I kept thinking how damn hard it would be to lose your mother as a little girl, then so violently lose everyone else you loved before really growing up."

"And then have to run for your life and be forced to leave everyone you came to care about again and again."

"Yeah." Sean stewed for a minute. "Her circumstances hit me hard. I didn't know my parents too well, but my grandparents raised me. When they died . . ." He let out a long breath. "That was damn hard. They taught me how to love and the value of family. Anyway, I felt for Callie. But the moment I met her . . . fuck, I knew I was toast."

Thorpe gripped the steering wheel tighter, stunned by Sean's simple honesty. He understood closeness and love. Thorpe had been avoiding those for so many years, he'd forgotten what it was like to truly let anyone inside his heart—until Callie had bulldozed his protective walls and dug her way in without even knowing it. She'd quickly taken root, a weed he couldn't bring himself to pull. If he managed to find her, could he open enough to be the man, the lover, she needed?

According to most people in his past, he didn't have a prayer in hell.

"Right away, I could see that she'd been alone for too long. She isn't meant to be," Sean pointed out, his tone almost a challenge, as if he was willing to fight until Thorpe agreed.

But there was nothing to argue about. "You're right."

Sean relaxed. "Callie yearns for more."

"She does. She's afraid to connect with anyone, but her heart is too big not to share. Despite that bratty attitude she flashes, she's most content when she's making others happy."

If they could help Callie understand that they both simply wanted her safe, maybe she would come home. But that wouldn't make her whole. The girl needed the firm hand of a tender master to guide her through life and love. She was probably better off without him, but Thorpe knew that if he didn't get over his shit and try to assume that role, Sean certainly would. If the man succeeded, Callie could be lost to him forever.

The sun beat down through the back window. The remnants of the coffee tasted like cold sawdust. His stomach coiled into tight knots. Since he doubted he could be what she needed but he didn't want to live without her, where did that leave him? *Fucked.*

"I see her desire to please others," Sean agreed. "But to survive, the clever little kitten has developed some sharp claws." The fond smile on Sean's face made Thorpe both appreciate the man more and want to rip his entrails out with jealousy. "Callie will fight when she thinks it's necessary."

"Every time. But in the last four years, I've watched her blossom.

When she first came to me, she didn't smile, wouldn't talk, lied about everything. The fucking sadness on her face . . . I knew she was in some sort of trouble. It was damn hard, but I didn't push or pry."

"When did you figure out who Callie really was?"

Thorpe sent him a skeptical glare. "And admit to knowingly harboring a fugitive so you have a reason to arrest me? Not happening."

Sean tossed his hands in the air. "If I'd wanted to arrest you for that, I could have done it back in Dallas. And if I trumped up a charge and threw you in jail, Callie would never forgive me. As much as I hate to say it, I need your help to find her."

Pretty speech, but that didn't mean Thorpe trusted the fed. "What happens when we do?"

"You mean who gets the girl? That's up to Callie." Sean sighed. "She loves us both."

Another truth. The even uglier truth was that he'd never fought for her. For years, Thorpe had denied how much he cared, pretended that he knew nothing about her feelings. Why would the girl ever choose a divorced man fifteen years her senior who'd only ever rebuffed her over the hot, young agent who couldn't wait to tell her that he loved her?

"Wouldn't your superiors frown on you for getting involved with a 'person of interest'?" Thorpe asked. It was a weak argument, but the best he had.

The truth was, if Callie loved and trusted a man, she would always stand beside him. Funny how clearly Thorpe could see that if he'd acknowledged the feelings they shared and proven that she could trust him with her identity, Callie would still be at Dominion. She would never have run off before talking through the issues or intentionally leave him broken.

He might be too jaded to give Callie the devotion she deserved, but that didn't make Mackenzie good for her, either. He was just another brand of wrong, as far as Thorpe could tell.

"I'll cross that bridge when I come to it, but I won't let anything happen to her," the fed vowed, sending him a challenging stare. "I've answered your question. You answer mine."

"All right. I figured out who she was a couple of years back. Ultimately, it's her eyes."

Sean nodded. "They're so blue, you can't miss them. It's one reason she's worn colored contacts more often than not for years. So why did you let her stay once you realized who she was?"

"You think I should have tossed her out when she needed someone to protect her? Fuck, no."

"In your shoes, I would have made the same choice. It's good that she's got someone else in her corner," he admitted. "How long have you been in love with her?"

Thorpe tried hard not to grit his teeth. "Can we skip this chat?"

"You started it," Sean reminded.

"And you turned it around to interrogate me quickly enough."

Sean sat back with a grin. "Occupational hazard."

Thorpe grunted, but he felt a ghost of a smile bend his lips. He didn't like Mackenzie, exactly, but now that the guy wasn't pretending to be someone else, he didn't hate the fed quite so much. "What does Callie's file say about her that I don't know?"

"Classified."

"We're back to this game? All right, when you want to ask me something about the woman today, you'll be barking up the wrong tree."

Sean sighed. "This mission would have been so much easier without you."

"Callie would still be at Dominion if it wasn't for you."

Exasperation crossed his face. "Look, I'm not authorized to tell you anything outright . . . but I can't stop you from guessing. As soon as you tell me how long you've been in love with her."

Thorpe sent Mackenzie a speculative glance. He'd guessed that Sean wasn't above bending the rules, but found having that confirmed helpful. And even if he was no good for Callie, Thorpe ached to fill in some of the gaps in his knowledge about the girl. "Easily over three years." *Not that it's ever going to matter.* "Happy?"

"That's a long time to have a stiff dick, old man."

That jibe hit a bit too close to home. "Fuck off."

"Hey, it's good for me. Your loss is my gain."

"It's not over yet," Thorpe threatened, sadly aware that it most likely was.

Sean shrugged. "Only Callie can settle this argument. In the meantime, you want to know something in her file or not."

Prick. "Yeah. I've often wondered how Callie supported herself in other cities before she came to me. Your file say anything about that?"

"Yes. She's fallen back on the same occupation several times in several cities. Always with different names, of course. Any guesses?"

"Besides waitressing?"

"She's done that more than once, so I'll give you a point for that answer. But I'm thinking of something else."

"You're enjoying holding this over my head," Thorpe accused.

"Yep." With a grin, Sean shrugged. "Sue me."

Rolling his eyes, Thorpe focused on the empty road and the sign that told him it was forty miles to the nearest town. "Callie's great at a lot of things. She speaks fluent French, but there's not a big calling for that here."

"Nope."

"She's an organizational dynamo, and I'm sure she could do that professionally, but opening her own business would put down too many roots for her, so I'll bet that's not it, either."

"I've searched Callie's room more than once," Sean admitted. "She's extremely organized."

"She made my sty of an office the neatest it's ever been. She has a good head for math, too."

"According to her grades, she was good in most of her classes."

Thorpe smiled. "Except science, I'll bet. I enjoy some of the shows on the Science Channel, and she occasionally curls up with me during off-hours to watch. She seems lost half the time."

That made Mackenzie laugh. "I can picture that. Ever seen the program narrated by Morgan Freeman? I like that one."

"*Through the Wormhole?* Me, too." Thorpe turned a stare on him, shocked that they agreed on anything. In fact, they were almost getting along.

Sean cleared his throat. "Keep guessing. Another way Callie made ends meet?"

Yeah, moving on . . . Thorpe was uncomfortable with the concept of the two of them being chummy. "She's a disaster in the kitchen. Cereal might be too tough for her, so I'm guessing she didn't cook as a kid. And how would she have learned? I'm sure her father employed a full staff, nannies—chefs, gardeners, a personal valet—the works."

"According to her files, yes," Sean confirmed.

Which made one of his most precious memories of Callie all the sweeter. Thorpe smiled. "She knows how much I like Italian cream cake and tried to make it, along with a lovely dinner for my last birthday. The meal was horrific, and we both laughed. But the cake was actually pretty good."

His words seemed to hit Sean between the eyes like a bullet. The fact that she'd tried so hard to please Thorpe clearly left him feeling out in the cold. Oddly, Thorpe understood. Every time he'd see her dress up for Sean or kneel for the fucker, it felt like a two-by-four to his gut.

"Since she never made any money cooking, I suspect Callie could earn her living either singing or dancing. She's exceptional at both."

"Wow, you do know her." Sean looked somewhere between awed and annoyed. "Singing. That's how she paid her bills more than once. In fact, during her brief stint in Nashville, an executive for a major label saw her at a bar and offered her a record deal. She made an appointment to visit his office the next day."

"And never showed?" Thorpe guessed.

"Exactly. She skipped town overnight. I didn't know she could dance. Her files indicate that she had dance classes, but so did my cousins. That didn't help them." Sean snorted.

Thorpe laughed and found himself relaxing a bit. "The last time I saw her dance was just before you came. I hosted a charity auction for wounded soldiers and their families back in March. Slave-for-a-day kind of thing. She danced onstage and worked up enthusiasm for the crowd."

"Callie has great legs, so I'm not surprised it worked."

"Who bought her?"

"I did." Thorpe had been unable to watch anyone else touch her, so he'd given her the night off if she promised to spend it alone in her room. He'd spent it with someone else . . . thinking of her.

Sean's smile faded. "I don't like the thought that I may never see her dance."

"I don't like thinking that I'll never hear about Callie's childhood from *her*. The few times I tried to probe about her past—before I knew who she was, of course—she was either closemouthed or sarcastic."

Sean shot him a speculative look. "I'm surprised you didn't beat her ass for it."

"I was tempted."

The fed grunted. "So, Callie was twenty-one when she came to Dominion? What was she like?"

"She had a chip on her shoulder that warned everyone away for months. The girl only spoke to me because she had to. I'll never forget . . . I found her crying on the back patio after she'd been there a few weeks. Callie judiciously avoided anything remotely personal with everyone. But those tears . . ." Thorpe shook his head. "I watched her for a few minutes, then I couldn't stand it. I tried to help."

"She rebuffed you."

"Instantly," Thorpe confirmed. "If I wanted to talk about BDSM or work, she was all ears. The second I asked anything personal, she clammed up."

"When did she finally let you close?"

"I found the first chink in her armor at Christmas. God, Callie loves it. Decorates everything in sight. I praised her wildly, and she started softening."

"I didn't see anything in her file about that."

Thorpe shrugged. "I only have sketchy details about a sliver of her time before she came to Dominion, but it was obvious to me that Callie enjoys Christmas because it's a holiday for family."

"I'm guessing that since she doesn't have any, she adopted everyone at the club as her own." Sean closed his eyes. "See, this is why I could never picture her as a hardened criminal. Even if she planned to run off with that Holden prick, Callie wanted a sense of belonging. A woman like that would never kill her loved ones."

"Precisely. I was shocked that first holiday season with Callie. She fancied the place up, organized a party, made everything run like a well-oiled machine . . . then stood in the corner and watched like a little girl with her nose pressed to the glass."

Frowning, Sean shook his head. "Then she has come a long way. Callie teases most everyone at Dominion now. I guess I have you to thank for the change. I hate to admit it, but you've taken good care of her."

With the sun glaring through the back window, Thorpe flipped his wrist up to stare at his watch, uncomfortable with the man's praise. How much more could he have healed Callie if he was capable of actually fucking trying?

"How long does it take to fly from New Orleans to Vegas?" Thorpe spit out. "Three hours? Four? Shouldn't she be there by now?"

"I'd ask the bureau to track the flight, but . . ." He looked vaguely uneasy.

The truth hit Thorpe. "You're doing this under the radar, aren't you?"

"I've said enough."

"Look, we're not best pals, but we both have a vested interest in finding Callie. We've got hours of driving ahead of us and we're in this shit together. So you better be honest with me or I'll leave you on the side of this damn road and find her without you."

Spreading his knees and staring out the window, Sean sighed. "As my grandfather would have said, some of the higher-ups are a dodgy lot. They've always acted a bit evasive about this case, but over the past few weeks, something's changed. I can't put my finger on it. I just have this gut feeling that if I gave them any indication Callie has fled, it would open up a can of worms I might not be able to close. I think they'd start a full-fledged manhunt. They might even insist that I arrest her. I can't do that."

And if Sean couldn't arrest her, Thorpe didn't think he'd turn her in, even for a two-million-dollar bounty. He might be wrong . . . but he didn't think so.

"Shit!" Thorpe didn't like the sound of that at all. "Can you lean on them, find out anything?"

"I've tried. Often, agents are at the bottom of the information totem pole. Politics are always on a need-to-know basis, and they think I don't need to know."

"Are you fucking with me?"

"Right now, I don't have the energy. I just want Callie back, a decent meal, and a good night's sleep—in that order."

Thorpe wanted that, too, along with a passionate, grinding slide into Callie's undoubtedly tight pussy so he could hear her cry out in his ear while she dug her little nails into his back, just as she'd done to Sean. He didn't like another man fucking her, but he liked the fact that he'd never had the pleasure of feeling her himself even less.

Listen to him whine . . . He wasn't in her best interest. Whatever Mackenzie's flaws or agenda, the fed loved her—enough to risk his job for her. Thorpe couldn't fault Sean for that.

"So, about the ex-wife, Melissa . . ." Mackenzie began.

Thorpe choked, then took a swig of cold coffee to recover. "Nothing to say about her."

"She left, so you're bitter? Or gun shy?" Sean probed.

"Where the fuck do you get off questioning *me*? We're talking about Callie."

"I'm trying to understand you. Your bad experience with the lousy ex is the reason you kept Callie at arm's length all these years, right?"

No, but he wasn't spilling all his demons for Sean. "There's a significant age gap, too."

"Which is more your hang-up than hers, I'd bet. What else?"

Thorpe glanced at his crappy burner phone, wondering where Logan's call was that Callie had reached Vegas all right. If Logan didn't call in five, he'd ring the former SEAL. But whatever he did, he wasn't replying to Sean.

"So it's mostly your own fear." The fed supplied his own answer. "I guess that makes sense in a chicken shit sort of way. But one thing has me stumped. Why decide to get possessive *after* I entered the picture? You're off relationships because of the ex, so you tell yourself that you don't want Callie. But you don't want anyone else to have her, either. You've got your head up your ass, Thorpe. It's not fair to her."

Sean's words echoed Lance's and rang a little too true. Damn it if he didn't want to punch the man. "None of this is any of your fucking business."

"It is if you want to know anything else in Callie's file." Sean gave him an expectant smile.

Thorpe rubbed his broad forehead, wishing he could massage away the beginnings of his headache. He really wanted to toss Mackenzie from the vehicle, but that wasn't in Callie's best interest. She had to be priority number one. "At first, she'd barely talk to me. After she'd been at Dominion a few months, I used her for a teaching demo. Of course I was attracted to her from the beginning, but

Callie was a pure novice. I didn't know if she was truly submissive or was pretending because she needed a job. I found out quickly that she was. Our chemistry was . . . not like anything I'd ever experienced. It shocked me."

"So you backed away?"

"No. I should have, but Callie was far more submissive than I'd dared to hope, not to mention addicting. It wasn't long before I used her for every demo. It was the only excuse I would give myself to touch her. She still kept her distance more often than not, but damn, the way she responded to me . . . I was very seriously considering breaking my own rule about never taking an exclusive sub.

"Then I was watching some silly news program one day. They showed a picture of Callie at sixteen, the same one you have on your phone. It all clicked. I hoped I was wrong, so I invented a new excuse to touch her and see if she had a scar on her hip where that bullet got her."

"And when you found it, you cut off all but the most professional contact." Sean didn't phrase it like a question. He knew the answer.

Though Thorpe didn't like being transparent, he supposed his motives weren't that hard to deduce.

"Yes. She was always going to leave me. It was just a matter of when." As soon as he'd had to stop touching Callie, Thorpe realized just how attached to her he'd become. And it had scared the hell out of him. He'd punished her by being an absolute bastard.

God, didn't he sound like a pussy, afraid of his own emotions?

"You didn't want to endure heartache again after your divorce." Sean didn't know the half of it.

"Something like that. But seeing you with her . . ." Thorpe let out a deep breath. "I realized then that all my attempts to deny my feelings had been a fucking waste. Happy now? Can we change the subject?"

"Almost." Sean cut a stare over at him. "If we find her, are you going to be willing to risk your heart for her? Because if you're not, you shouldn't bother fighting me for her. We both agreed that she's not meant to be alone."

Thorpe wasn't sure what the hell he was going to do. He wanted to fight for her . . . but what was best for Callie? "You're not entirely prepared to handle her."

Sean crossed his arms over his chest. "What does that mean?"

"*If* you're really a Dom, you haven't been one for long. You're a bit too lenient with the girl. Sometimes, she's a handful because she wants your attention. You give it to her and let her top from the bottom." Thorpe tsked at him. "I've also noticed that you're not comfortable with all the equipment in the dungeon. If we find her, are you going to be willing to expand your boundaries to be what she needs? If not, you should leave her to me."

That made Sean indignant. "Fuck you. I may not have been an acknowledged pervert for two decades, but I'm more than willing to 'expand my boundaries' to hang on to Callie."

"*Pfft.*" Thorpe rolled his eyes. "You've been at this . . . what? Less than a year?"

"Actually, I got interested a couple of years back, went to a few clubs in Florida with some friends. But long-term undercover assignments didn't exactly leave me a lot of time to get my kink on."

Thorpe opened his mouth to drop Mackenzie with a scathing remark about wannabe Doms, but his phone rang. They both pounced for it, but he was closer and pressed the button to answer the call. "Logan?"

"Put it on speaker," Sean demanded.

"Can you both hear me?" Logan asked.

Feeling a supreme irritation that damn near choked him, Thorpe hit the speaker button and laid the phone on the console between them. "Yeah."

"I'm here," Sean advised. "Is Callie with your friend?"

"I put her on the plane. One of the flight attendants says she remembers seeing Callie napping at the very back. There was no way she could have gotten off that bird in midair. But Elijah said she never met him in baggage claim, like I instructed her to."

"You don't know where she is?" Sean growled.

"She's missing?" Thorpe echoed his incredulous tone.

"Yeah." Logan sounded somber. "But that isn't the worst news. Elijah spotted some dude in a uniform he'd never seen flashing Callie's picture to the passengers just as they cleared the secure area of the terminal. The guy asked a lot of questions."

Thorpe's veins ran icy with foreboding, then he snapped his gaze to Sean. "Uniform? Like military?"

"That's the impression he gave me, yeah," Logan confirmed. "But not one he'd ever seen. That, along with everything else, sends up a big red flag for me."

"Me, too. How is this possible?"

"I don't know. It doesn't make any sense." Logan sighed. "I didn't tell a single other soul besides Elijah and you two that I'd put her on the plane."

"Thorpe and I haven't been out of one another's sight since." The fed's expression said he didn't like any of this.

"And Elijah wouldn't talk. He's tight. Besides, I didn't even tell him who she really was," Logan explained. "Callie didn't mention anything about being hunted by anyone else when she told me why she wanted to leave Dallas. Could the feds be after her, Mackenzie?"

"If they were, I should be the first to know. Even if I was out of the loop, they wouldn't come after her in some uniform."

"You're right," Logan agreed. "Everyone Elijah talked to from the flight seemed wary or shaken after the uniformed dude left. Whatever mess that girl has gotten herself into, she's in *way* over her head. You've got to get to Vegas and find her before this asshole does."

Chapter Nine

SEAN thanked God that Thorpe had rich friends when they landed in Las Vegas a few hours later. After Logan's pronouncement that Callie was at large somewhere in Sin City, he and Thorpe had both been ready to crawl out of their skins. Two minutes later, Thorpe had placed a call to Xander Santiago. Sean remembered him, his brother, and the pretty blonde sub they shared from their visit to Dominion over the previous summer—mostly because Callie had left the club with the other woman and disappeared for damn near twelve hours.

That turned out to be a bonus. Because Callie had taken such good care of Xander and Javier's wife, London, the billionaires had been more than willing to lend him and Thorpe their plane. It had been fueled up and jetting to Amarillo, Texas, in no time. They hadn't waited long at all before the small luxury plane arrived to spirit them away to Vegas.

After a fitful catnap in midair, they touched down around noon. As he tossed his carry-on over one shoulder, Sean raced Thorpe to the exit and down the airstairs. Thorpe had shoved some necessities of his own in a briefcase and now clutched it in his fist as he sprinted for the parking lot. Anything they needed and hadn't packed they could buy—except time. And every moment that ticked by they spent away from Callie made it less likely they would find her at all, much less before some uniform who already seemed half a step ahead of them did. At the twenty-four-hour mark, it was likely the trail would grow cold, and they'd already eaten up half their time on fucking travel.

"We've got our plan," he reminded Thorpe, tamping down his anxiety. "Let's stick to it."

The club owner nodded absently, running for the stranger waiting in the distance. Logan's friend Elijah was big, bald, and menacing. The former SEAL didn't look like someone he'd want for an enemy. Nor was he much for small talk, which suited Sean just fine.

Within seconds, they'd taken the keys to the man's truck and paid him to rent a car. The idea wasn't perfect, but it wouldn't leave a completely obvious trail for anyone to follow. Since someone in a uniform had known to follow Callie to Vegas, the guy might also be keeping an eye on him and Thorpe, too. They'd have to lie really fucking low in order to both find her and figure out who followed her.

The moment they reached Elijah's Jeep, Sean slipped behind the wheel. He'd done an undercover stint in Vegas about two years ago and knew his way around the city reasonably well. The second Thorpe's ass hit the passenger seat, the man had his burner phone open and was calling folks in the local fet community. Sean doubted that Callie would fall back into a kink environment. She might find it comfortable, but he suspected she would choose to be as unpredictable as possible. It had kept her alive and free this long.

In the meantime, Sean pulled out his own phone as he tore away from the airport and started calling some less-than-legal guys he'd met here previously. He asked questions delicately because he wasn't about to tip off known criminals about a woman with a two-million-dollar bounty on her head. No one had seen a new girl in town working the seedier side of life who matched Callie's description, but Sean didn't think it would be long. She hadn't had time to plan her escape to the last detail. She'd have to fall back on existing skills for fast cash until she could come up with a better plan.

Thorpe slammed his phone on the console with a curse.

"I take it that means you came up empty-handed?" Sean asked.

"Yes, damn it. I know a club owner named Talon who's connected to nearly everyone in the life here in Vegas. But he hasn't seen or heard about anyone new who fits Callie's description in the last day or so. Then again, she'll already have some sort of disguise."

Undoubtedly. He and Thorpe would have to factor that in. "We've made our initial contacts. Now we're going to have to split up. You hit the fet joints and kink bars, make the rounds there in case she's hiding out. I'll hit dive bars, nightclubs, restaurants—anyplace that might have filled the need for quick help in the last day or so. We both just need to look past any disguise for that familiar face."

"Absolutely. She won't get away from me again."

"Callie won't be working on the Strip," Sean warned. "She'll have found somewhere just off, maybe downtown, somewhere with a bit less sophisticated security, where she could make money without drawing too much attention to herself."

"I'll check into a few bars I know. If I come up empty, we'll keep trying until something works."

"And if you find her, you better not skip the fucking country. You got that?" Sean threatened. "It's likely going to take more than one person to protect her, and if someone in a secret branch of the military wants her, then you bet your ass they can reach you down in South America."

"I know," Thorpe said, obviously resigned. "I've already thought of that."

Sean nodded grimly and drove straight for the downtown area that had seen its glory days early in Vegas's history, sixty years ago. Overall, the hotels were a little seedier, as were the people. Callie could easily get lost in this sea of humanity. A wig, a few new clothes, some colored contacts . . . No one would know her—or care. She wouldn't stay long in this city. Callie must know that he and Thorpe would come looking for her. And if she knew someone official sought her and had shaken Logan's protection, then she would want out of this city even faster. They had a few days. A week, tops. As soon as she saved a little money, she would slip out of town. Or out of the country.

"Fuck," he muttered to himself and stepped on the gas, lurching the car into heavy traffic.

* * *

TWO hours later, Thorpe had indigestion from a lousy piece of pizza he'd eaten while pounding the sidewalks. The two kink-oriented bars he knew were both half empty during the afternoon. It had taken forever to search the cavernous places. He'd seen some pretty girls with Callie's height and build . . . but not the woman herself. Talon had greeted him at the Slip Knot with a drink in hand. Thorpe had declined the scotch and asked his friend to keep a lookout.

Finally making his way outside, he pulled out his phone and called Sean. Voicemail picked up after a couple of rings, and he took a taxi back to the parking lot of the hotel where Sean had left Elijah's vehicle. When he got there, the Jeep was empty. No Sean. No keys. *Great.* Now he either had to stand here and wait or pound the pavement more.

As he pushed away from Elijah's silver SUV, a realization hit him. Picking up his stride, he dialed Sean again, who picked up on the first ring.

"Jesus, I just finished listening to your voicemail. A little patience."

"I think I've got an idea. Where are you now?" Thorpe had no more than asked the question when he looked up to see Sean striding through the parking lot.

They both hung up, and the fed looked at him with an expectant brow. Thorpe tried not to bristle.

"We're not being smart," he told Sean.

"Then enlighten me. What are we not doing right?"

"Think about it. Callie drove to Logan for help, but he put her on a plane. She doesn't have a car."

"I see where you're going with this." Sean's eyes lit up with possibilities. "She won't waste money taking a taxi to and from whatever job she's managed to scrape together. And she would have had to lay her head someplace last night."

Thorpe looked around the area with a look of horror. "Where the hell would she stay in *this* neighborhood?"

"Not at a casino hotel. They're too public and probably a bit expensive. She likes extended-stay hotels, especially ones that aren't part of a chain," Sean reminded him. "I know this area. I can think of a few off the top of my head. I've got an idea. Follow me."

God, wherever she was, it was likely a dive, some motel that doubled as a rent-by-the-hour haven for local pimps. Thorpe gritted his teeth and followed after Sean. They walked the pavement until they came to the first place.

The exterior was a faded pink. The sign advertised color TVs and air-conditioning as its big selling features. The tarred parking lot had long ago cracked and buckled under the heat of punishing Vegas summers. Iron railings overlooking droopy balconies were covered in rust. The swimming pool was an off-putting shade of blue-green.

The old man behind the counter looked half asleep, and he couldn't have cared less that he had customers. He barely lifted one eye away from the little TV. His jowls hung over his wrinkled hand as he glanced their way.

"We're looking for a missing person who might have checked in yesterday. She's twenty-five and petite, with a fair complexion. Very pretty. May or may not have black hair and blue eyes."

"Look, I rent rooms, not girls. Back in my day, I would have liked a broad like that, too, but I haven't rented a room to anyone under fifty in at least two months. And I definitely haven't had a dreamboat want to stay here. Can I get back to my show now? I'm missing Final Jeopardy."

"Thanks for your time. If she comes by, can you please call this number?" Sean jotted his digits down on a sticky note that lay on the cluttered counter, then slid it toward the old man. "It's urgent."

"Sure." But he didn't look away from his show, listening instead to Alex Trebek.

Thorpe gritted his teeth as he and Sean exited. "That was a waste."

"Maybe not. Callie might skip around for a while to confuse everyone on her trail. We'll visit this old fart again in a few days if we haven't found her."

Trying not to be disheartened or give into exhaustion, he nodded. "Where to next?"

Sean led the way to a handful of motels that advertised weekly or monthly rates. All dives he didn't ever want to call home. All looked as if they'd had their heyday during the golden age of the Rat Pack. Both gave them similar speeches. *No one new renting here who fit that description, yadda, yadda, yadda.*

"We need a plan C," he told Sean.

The other man sighed heavily and raked a hand through his dark waves. "We're both exhausted. I'm famished. Let's take a load off and talk this through."

Food didn't hold much appeal for Thorpe now, but he could use a cup of strong coffee.

They made their way to a little greasy spoon. As long as they were there, they inquired about Callie. Of course, they came up empty-handed.

"I still can't figure out why someone military might be looking for her," Sean said quietly once seated at a table in the corner.

"I'm as lost there as you," Thorpe vowed. "It barely makes sense to me that the FBI wants to keep tabs on her. I guess the fact that her father was a multibillionaire is noteworthy, but . . ."

"Why does the bureau care? Like I said, I don't have any answers. And anyone in the military hunting her down seems way out in left field."

"Exactly. I don't see how she could have gotten mixed up with anything or anyone under my roof. Before you came, I watched Callie just about every moment of every day. And if I didn't have eyes on her, Axel or one of his guys did. I did my best to protect her and keep her out of trouble."

"You did." Sean sighed. "Let's assume this pursuit has something to do with her family's murders. They were carried out by professionals. You could almost say with military precision."

That didn't make Thorpe feel better. "Any chance they're trying to protect her from something?"

"Why wait nine years to even try?"

Good question, one without a logical answer. "When you put it like that . . ."

"Let's assume they're after her and that they're dangerous. I'm guessing they just now got a lead on her. Otherwise, why wouldn't they have come after her at Dominion?"

"But how the hell did they find her in Vegas before she'd even arrived?" Thorpe asked.

"I've wondered that, too."

"We don't know how Logan got her onto the plane, but he's a clever bastard. He could have somehow managed to bypass the security screening. Or maybe she used ID from a previous alias."

"It's possible that something at the airport alerted whoever is hunting Callie. But there's another scenario. Tell me, how much can we really trust Logan?"

"Implicitly. I'd vouch for him all day long." When Sean still didn't look convinced, Thorpe tried another tactic. "Why would he set Callie up with a safe haven and volunteer all the information to us if he just wanted to collect the bounty?"

"You're right. Hell, I feel like I'm grasping at straws. Nothing makes sense."

With a frown, Thorpe leaned across the table, pausing when the waitress came by to pour more coffee. "Let's come back to how they found her later. The other big question is, why are they after her? Did her father have anything to do with the armed forces? Did he have any money in defense contracting? Have any sway with senators on the Armed Services Committee? Rub elbows with generals?"

"I'd have to go back and double-check her file, but none of that rings a bell." Sean sighed. "I don't want it, but I need some fucking sleep."

As much as Thorpe would rather keep searching for her, he needed some shut-eye, too. He would be no good to anyone until he got it, and neither would Sean.

He looked at his watch. Late afternoon. "There's a good chance that wherever Callie is now, she's lying low and resting. If she's singing, she'll likely be doing it at night."

"I agree. Since that will be her first choice of jobs, rather than serving food on her feet all the time, let's go with the idea that she's not working right now. After a nap, you and I will meet up again. Six sound good?"

Thorpe didn't want to pause, but they both needed to be sharp. "Yeah."

In silence, they walked to a cheap hotel nearby and secured a couple of rooms. The place was decent but older, took cash, and didn't ask many questions since they'd paid for a week in advance. It was hardly the Ritz, and he couldn't have cared less.

Once inside, Thorpe made a few more phone calls, one to Xander, who hooked him up with Javier. Carefully, he asked questions about Daniel Howe without mentioning Callie herself. The elder Santiago brother had been in the defense contracting business for over a decade, but he'd never heard anything about Callie's father dipping his toe in that water, financing such a venture, or hobnobbing with influential senators or military officials. Another dead fucking end.

Next door, he could hear Sean talking as well. Fuck, this place was musty and old. Normally, he'd never stay here, and it broke his heart to think of Callie curled up someplace even dumpier than this.

Why had she run without talking to him at all? Had she truly believed that he didn't care enough to keep her safe?

With a tired sigh, he wedged himself into the small shower and tried to wash his funk away. No such luck. His mood was still crashing. He felt every single second that ticked by and started to picture the rest of his life without Callie. God, even the thought made him insane. No way he could do without her in his life. He'd move mountains, part oceans, rip his own damn heart out of his chest to have her back.

But even if he did, he still wouldn't be the right man for her.

Stepping out of the shower, he wrapped a threadbare white towel around his waist and plodded over to his bed. Just as he sat in exhaustion to call himself every kind of dumbshit for letting her slip through his fingers, his phone rang. The number looked like Logan's.

"Hi. You got something for me?" he barked.

"You sound fucking miserable."

"I am, Logan. I'm in a rattrap with a splitting headache. I need sleep, and all I can think about is Callie out there, believing that she's totally alone. What if the military brass looking for her found her before we did? I don't even want to think it, but I don't know why they want her, where they would have taken her, or—"

"Take a breath, man," Logan cut in. "Callie made it out of the airport in one piece. I just got off the phone with Elijah."

"You're sure?" Hope sprang inside him for a sweet moment.

"Yeah," Logan assured. "He found someone in airport security who was willing to let him view the footage of the terminal just after her flight landed. She came off the plane in different clothing, complete with a fake belly and somehow smaller boobs. No idea how she managed that. She'd ditched the hat, donned a blond wig, put on a crap-ton of makeup and sunglasses. Elijah said it took him a few passes through the footage to spot her, but he did."

"Callie managed to prepare for this trip, at least a little. Her resourcefulness shouldn't surprise me." But it sure relieved the fuck out of him. She'd gotten away from her potentially dangerous enemy—at least for now.

"I shouldn't be surprised, either. The Callie I knew only excelled at wanting her way and throwing a hissy until she got it. But I only saw the same bratty act she peddled to everyone else. You know the real woman."

Thorpe closed his eyes. He did, but it had taken a long while to learn her. After she'd gotten a bit comfortable with him and Dominion, she'd slowly let her guard down. She'd let him in a bit more when she'd laughed at his jokes, passed time with him on the sofa, or chatted with him when she couldn't sleep. Then again when she'd had the flu, disagreed with him about her sometimes disrespectful behavior, or teased him about his "stodgy" music. And still more when he'd bound her for demos, held her, kissed her . . . barely stopped himself from claiming her when she wasn't his. He had seen her heart and that's when he'd fallen in love.

"I'm glad she got away," he said thickly.

"Clean," Logan confirmed. "After stopping off at the first bathroom inside the terminal, she walked out no longer carrying her backpack. She'd gotten a red duffel from somewhere. According to Elijah, she dragged it behind her and made her way toward the meet point in baggage claim. She intended to follow through with my plan. I can only guess that she took precautions on the plane just to be safe, then realized the man in uniform just outside the terminal was looking for her. She changed course and walked right past my buddy, then out the door. In the last frame of footage she's viewable, she's walking down the long line of taxis. No idea which one she eventually got in."

So they couldn't track the vehicle.

Every word felt like a death knell to Thorpe's hopes of finding her again. "Goddamn it, Logan. She's got to be terrified out of her mind. And I can't even fucking find her to help her. She's alone and worried, maybe even running out of money. Does she even know where she's going to sleep tonight? She might even be making plans to get out of Vegas now. And I'm too clueless to help her. What kind of protector am I?"

"Cut yourself some slack. You've done everything you can to find her. I'm going to look for this military asswipe. Elijah is checking the airport security footage for a picture of him, so we can piece together who he is and why he wants Callie. If we get something, I'll send it your way. Elijah is local if you need more assistance in your search." Logan tried to sound both calm and reassuring. "Callie is smart and she knows how to stay alive. We'll find her and bring her home."

As Thorpe hung up, he hoped that was true. The alternative was too horrific to contemplate.

* * *

SEAN dragged his ass out of bed. He could have slept more. His body screamed for it, but Callie's face haunted him. The feel of her in his arms, the sounds of her saucy laughter in his ear, the haunting beauty of her expressive eyes locked with his as he filled her body . . . Shit, how had he gone on a simple baby-sitting mission and ended up in love?

For over a decade, he'd been married to his job. He'd lost a fiancée once upon a time to his badge. He'd lost touch with all his old pals, his cousins, and anyone who had once occupied his "normal" life.

But in barely more than a handful of months, Callie had rewired his priorities. She mattered. She filled the half of him he hadn't even known was empty. She'd resurrected him just by being her sweet, bratty, kind, unpredictable self. Damn it, he had to find her—before someone with intentions between nebulous and nefarious did.

All through his blistering-hot shower, he groaned under the spray and tried to think of places he might look for his lovely. After he and Thorpe had caught a nap yesterday afternoon, they'd resumed their search that evening, pounding the pavement and opening the door to nearly every casino, dive bar, and twenty-four-hour diner they could find within walking distance. At four a.m., they'd finally agreed to pause again. He'd told Thorpe he would work on a new plan, but the truth was, he was running out of ideas.

Where the hell could she be? Worry knotted his guts and pinged in his head like a pinball bouncing between bumpers, setting off one alarm bell after another.

Thirty minutes later, Thorpe scooted into a booth across from him in the hotel's diner. Though dressed immaculately, the man didn't look any better rested than he felt.

"Anything new from Logan or Elijah?" Sean asked hopefully.

Thorpe answered with a grim shake of his head. "Nothing new since yesterday. Maybe Callie is on the Strip."

He'd been over this mentally a thousand times in the last twenty-four hours. "Highly unlikely. Anyone who'd employ her down there would insist on having proper identification. Since Callie left her fake driver's license back in Dallas knowing we'd track that name, she'd have no use for it now. It's possible she has another alias, but she wouldn't keep it for long and she wouldn't have asked Logan for help if she felt secure in the identity. Besides, the video surveillance on the Strip will be far sharper and more sophisticated than anything in the older section of town. The security presence in joints up there is palpable. Callie wouldn't go there voluntarily. She's too smart."

"That makes sense." Thorpe sighed tiredly, then absently thanked the waitress who took their orders and filled their coffee cups. "Seems like we've combed every inch of these streets. I don't know where else to go."

The only places downtown left to search were the *really* unsavory and unpalatable. The dangerous haunts for the depraved and criminal element. But he kept that to himself. Thorpe already looked ready to lose it. The strain of being unable to locate Callie was wearing on him, too. If Sean had ever had any illusions about Thorpe's feelings, he didn't now. As much as he hated to admit it, the man genuinely loved her.

"I've got a few more possibilities." Sean tried to shrug casually. "You get any sleep? It's going to be another long day."

"I crashed for three hours. After that . . . off and on." He took a swig of coffee, wincing as the steaming brew hit his tongue. "I kept having dreams about Callie needing help, being alone, crying. I couldn't take it. I know she's a very capable woman, but . . ."

Sean shot him a rueful smile. "I'm in the same camp, man. I woke up wondering if I'm crazy. How well do I know this girl? I know the person she showed me. I loved *that* woman. But is she the real Callie?"

Thorpe paused for so long, Sean wasn't sure he intended to answer. "I want like hell to lie to you and tell you that everything you saw was BS. But that's not what's best for her." He sighed. "Yeah, you saw the real Callie, especially that last night on the dungeon floor. She lowered her walls for you. With anyone else, she'd gnaw her own arm off before trembling or showing vulnerability. She'd avoid that kind of eye contact, and run screaming from that much . . . intimacy. She cared what you thought, how you felt. Her taking off probably doesn't say that to you, but I know Callie better than anyone else. Believe me, you saw her."

Suddenly, Sean understood one of the many things that ripped at Thorpe's guts. "You're not used to sharing that soft, secret side of her. You wanted it for yourself."

The big man across the table paused, froze, then crushed the empty plastic creamer container in his fist. "If I couldn't have any other part of her, I was willing to accept that. Seeing her wanting to please someone else felt like a never-ending kick in the balls. But you're better for her, so . . ."

Yeah, he should probably let that go. It was in his best interest to let Thorpe think he'd ruin Callie or whatever bullshit trolled through his head. But the man had been brutally honest with him today, and they'd been through too much in the last thirty-six hours for that crap. They weren't friends, but they shared a new respect forged in fire. Both of them knew bone deep that the other would do anything—everything—to keep Callie safe.

Sean swallowed. "You're not bad for Callie. She looks to you for so much—comfort, security." He had to force out the next truth. "Even love. She wants you in her life. I'm probably the interloper here."

With a tight squeeze of his eyes, Thorpe blocked him out, looking as if he worked hard to hold himself together. "I love her more than I believed myself capable of loving any woman. You have no idea how difficult it is for me to say that, but I feel compelled to confess since you called me a coward and rubbed my nose in my feelings like dog shit. I'm painfully aware that Callie needs the tenderness you've given her. I'm not capable of it." He rubbed at his forehead. "Ask my ex-wife, for starters."

"Tenderness isn't all she needs." Sean prayed he had everything inside him she required to be whole. Nights at Dominion when he'd wondered exactly how to give her boundaries that would both bind her to him and let her fly free . . . That's when he'd felt unsure. That's when he'd wondered if Thorpe was the better man for her.

"Oh, she needs a lot more." Thorpe snorted. "Starting with a thorough paddling."

"Damn straight." He picked up his coffee cup, and clinked it against Thorpe's, who still clutched his in hand.

They each took a sip and resorted to silence, as if this much getting along was unnerving.

Their food arrived, and Sean wasn't terribly hungry. By the way Thorpe pushed his eggs around his plate, it looked like the other man couldn't find his appetite, either. Still, they forced the meal down, knowing they'd need the energy. Nothing was said about how long they would stay here and what they would do if Callie was still missing in a week, in a month . . . or longer. Sean wasn't about to give up, and he'd bet his badge that Thorpe wasn't either.

"I'm trying to decide if it's good or bad that we haven't run into anyone in a uniform looking for Callie," Thorpe said suddenly.

"I've had the same question, but I have to think it's good."

"I know she managed to leave the airport without a hitch, but how do we know someone hasn't already found Callie and . . ."

Captured her? Killed her? Sean swallowed. Fuck, Thorpe was all but reading his mind. But he didn't want to voice any of those fears. "We just need to keep looking. Stay strong and be persistent. We have one thing going for us that no one else does."

Thorpe lifted miserable gray eyes to him, looking like the gloomiest day. "What? Give me anything to feel good about."

Sean was no cheerleader, but in this case, he refused to believe anything except they'd gotten a jump on the asshole hunting her down for one reason alone. "Callie isn't just a case to either of us. She means something. Hell, everything. We know her desires, her habits, her secret yearnings. She can't bury all those parts of herself forever. When she needs . . ." Sean nodded, willing Thorpe not to lose faith. "When she comes up looking for a sense of home or connection or affection—whatever—we'll be waiting."

But twelve hours later, he was losing hope. They'd hit even the worst of the worst places downtown. Terrible, seedy, dirty, filled with the dregs of humanity. He couldn't picture Callie here. She'd shine too bright, be too beautiful. No way she could hide here for long.

As they continued pounding the pavement, they stumbled

across a motel with a blinking turquoise neon sign that proclaimed it *Summer Wind*. Given the fact that this was Vegas, it had to be a nod to one of Sinatra's classic tunes, but its faded façade made Thorpe stop in his tracks.

"Callie's favorite season," Thorpe murmured.

"'Summer' was her safe word, too." Sean swallowed, hope brimming.

Thorpe zipped a sharp stare in his direction. The knowledge looked like it hit the big Dom right in the gut. "It fits. We have to look here."

It was a crapshoot, but Sean totally agreed.

The place looked beyond run-down. It had to be cheap. But it seemed like the first place in over twenty-four hours that made sense for Callie to have come.

He and Thorpe pushed their way inside. Wow, it was easily one of the crappiest motels he'd ever seen. The windows hadn't been washed in the last two decades. In the lobby, the carpet beneath his feet was sticky. The air reeked of cigarettes, vomit, urine, and cheap disinfectant. Rent by the week or the hour—apparently the management wasn't picky about how long anyone stayed as long as they paid.

Inside stood a woman who was probably in her late thirties but had lived so damn hard she'd easily be mistaken for fifty. She lounged against a scarred white Formica countertop permanently stained yellow, wearing a thrift store castoff of a tank top that showed cleavage wrinkled from too much sun. The woman's lined lips wrapped around a slim smoke and she sucked in hard before blowing the smoke his way with a bored stare.

"You two looking for a room?" Her voice rattled from her lungs. "If you need more than an hour for your 'business,' you might have to come back. We're pretty full up."

Beside him, Thorpe choked, looking ready to throttle the

woman. He sliced her his most displeased Dom face. In seconds, the woman lowered her cigarette and stared at him warily.

Sean stepped between them, shooting Thorpe a glare that told him to be fucking reasonable. "No. We don't need a room to share. Or any room at all." He reached into the pocket of his trousers and pulled out his badge. "FBI. I'm looking for someone."

The bleach blonde with the gray roots looked ready to piss her pants. "I swear I told Johnny to be careful who the hell he hired. Who is it, the new repairman? I suspected he might be a con man, but I didn't know."

"Focus, woman," Thorpe snapped. "We're asking the questions. You will answer us precisely and honestly. You will not speak unless spoken to. If you're dishonest, we'll have problems, you and I. Is that clear?"

The woman gave a rattled bob of her head. "Um . . . yeah."

Thorpe turned to him with a grim smile. "Proceed."

The situation wasn't funny, but Sean repressed the urge to grin. Thorpe had gotten the woman's attention, that was for sure. After a handful of words, she couldn't wait to give him a healthy dose of respect. He supposed Thorpe's commanding presence was one reason so many subs sought him as a Dominant. And it was probably one of the reasons Callie had latched on to him. Deep down, she needed to believe that someone watched over her, looked out for her, and would rein her in if she'd gone too far. She ached to know that someone could save her if push came to shove. But Callie was so damn headstrong that whomever she turned to would have to truly exert his control before she'd heed it. Thorpe would have no problem doing that. He'd relish it.

The thought niggled at his brain as he withdrew a recent picture he'd printed of Callie, one he'd clandestinely snapped on his phone at Dominion. She wore a little Mona Lisa smile, her full, rosy lips somehow taunting and affectionate at once, tempting him. Her eyes glittered with life and vitality. Her glossy black hair shone against her pale cheek. Inch after inch of the most unspoiled skin he'd ever touched drew his stare all the way down to the hint of her cleavage. His memory supplied the rest—sweet pink-berry nipples, flat belly, slender hips, sleek thighs, snug pussy. Sexual power in a petite dynamo of a female.

Thorpe nudged him. "Get on with it."

Pulled out of his musings, Sean nodded, then sat the image down on the counter in front of the desk clerk. He held his breath.

Her eyes flared with recognition, and she looked at him, suddenly in a hurry to be forthcoming. The apprehensive glance she slid Thorpe's way explained why. "Yeah, I know her."

"And? Go on. When did she check in?" Sean demanded.

"Two days ago. Middle of the night."

Bingo! "Go on."

"She was dragging a red duffel. I think she's a blonde now."

He and Thorpe exchanged a glance. She'd disguised herself, as they'd suspected. But his excitement was reflected in the other man's gray eyes. They were finally getting a lead on Callie. Sean's heart pumped. His skin tingled. Hell, even his cock engorged. Instinct told him they were close.

Thorpe braced his hands on the counter with deceptive calm. He stood tall and imposing. His mood stretched tighter than wire suspending a bridge. The woman's jaw went slack as she stared up at him, blinking so rapidly, Sean was surprised her false eyelashes didn't take flight.

"You'll tell us everything you remember," Thorpe commanded. "Now."

The woman bobbed her head again. "Sh-she asked for a corner room near the stairs. I happened to have it. She asked about a place to eat and somewhere to find work. I sent her across the street to the diner."

The one that had seen better days decades ago and had a collection of homeless drunks littering the parking lot.

"She's waitressing there?" Thorpe barked.

"N-no. My cousin Marty runs a club about two blocks down and he's always looking for pretty girls, so I sent her there."

"Did she go?" The Dom's voice dripped ice.

"Yeah. She's working until two a.m. Marty . . . um, called me to thank me about an hour ago. After less than three shifts, she's already a customer favorite. He called her a gold mine."

Thorpe gritted his teeth, and Sean could only imagine what was running through the man's head. Probably the same what-the-fuck thoughts dashing through his own.

"The name of the club?" Thorpe wasn't sounding any warmer.

The brassy blonde swallowed and stared up, almost pleading silently for Thorpe's leniency. "G-glitter Girls. Go out the door, take a right and head—"

"What the fuck kind of place is that?" Thorpe cut in with a growl.

"I know exactly where it is." Sean discreetly elbowed the Dom as he smiled at the clerk. "What's her room number?"

She focused on him and softened. Sean shoved down his fury to send her a gently encouraging expression. If good cop-bad cop worked, he was all for it.

"Two-seventeen," she murmured. "Out the door, to the left, then up the stairs. It's right at the top."

"Key." Sean held out his hand.

"I-I'm really not supposed to—"

Thorpe raised a menacing brow, promising retribution if she continued to protest. The woman jumped to action, reaching under the desk with trembling fingers to extract a key. She dropped it in Sean's hand, then cut her gaze to Thorpe, her eyes pleading for approval.

"Is her room paid?" the Dom demanded.

"Through tomorrow night."

Damn, had Callie intended to skip town in another twenty-four hours or less?

"Very good. You can consider her room vacant in the next hour." The smile Thorpe bestowed on her then was brilliant, praising as he tapped her chin gently. "Thank you for your help . . . Your name?"

She lapped up that smile like a kitten with fresh milk. "Doreen. Sir."

If anything, Thorpe's smile widened. "You've been very helpful, sweet girl."

"I tried," she breathed with a wobbly smile.

Sean tried to hold in his astonishment. Instead, he leaned across the counter to the clerk and slapped a hundred-dollar bill on the counter between them. "And you never saw us, Doreen."

She looked at him blankly, then back over to Thorpe. All the man did was send her an expectant stare, and she nodded vigorously. "Never."

Sean palmed the key and turned to Thorpe, still holding the woman all but hypnotized. "Let's go."

Chapter Ten

THORPE turned to him as they made their way out of the motel's disgusting lobby and headed for the Jeep. "So where's this club?"

"In a minute. We've got to clear her room first." Sean inclined his head toward the stairs to the upper level of the joint.

"Fuck whatever's in her room. We need to get to Glitter Girls now, before she gets away again."

Sean glanced at his watch. "I want to reach her, too. You know that. It's not quite one, and she's working until two, so we've got some time. But we can't leave behind any trace of Callie that anyone looking for her could find. If there's no trail, there are fewer followers."

Thorpe gritted his teeth. "I don't like it."

"I don't either, but what are our other choices?"

It annoyed him, but Sean had a point. Thorpe conceded with a sigh. "All right. The good news is, it will probably take five minutes or less since Callie won't have spread her stuff out. Hell, she was with me nearly three months before she put anything in a drawer."

Sean stared at the upper story of the motel as the chilly desert wind whipped through his light jacket. "Let's make this quick."

Nodding, Thorpe followed Sean and darted for the stairs, taking them two at a time until he reached the cracked cement level. The rusted railing had once been painted a bright blue, but had faded and chipped over time. The blue drapes with their blackout backing in each of the room's filthy windows looked dirty enough to be a breeding ground for bacteria and insect eggs. A few doors down, a man and a woman were arguing at the top of their lungs. In the distance, a gunshot sounded, then tires screeched.

Thorpe knew why Callie had chosen this place, but he still wondered what the hell she was doing here. There had to be someplace else out of the way that wasn't quite so ghetto-gutter.

In the moonlight, he approached the first door at the top of the stairs and barely made out the tarnished brass numbers.

"Callie chose the corner room, the one with stairs in either direction," Sean commented.

"Obviously, she'd scoped the place out in advance."

"Clever, clever girl."

As they charged toward the room in question, Thorpe tossed him a nod. "You know she is. Don't underestimate her."

"No." Sean shook his head. "I've made that mistake for the last time."

They hit the door, and Sean shoved the key into the lock, then pushed it open. As soon as he did, Thorpe squeezed past him and flipped on the light. He wished he hadn't. The carpet looked some indiscriminate color that might have been beige once. The walls were covered in faded oak paneling. The ceiling showed signs of water damage. A dilapidated swamp cooler controlled the room's temperature—sort of. The drapes were a faded blue floral that would make even a great-grandmother cringe. The bedspread was a cheap polyester imitation of polka-dotted and zigzagged stripes. The light fixture in the bathroom was minus its decorative cover. A roach crawled across the wall above the mussed, unmade bed.

"What a fucking dump." Sean stared around the room in stupefied horror.

"This is the way she lived before she came to me," Thorpe said with a hollow voice.

"I knew that on paper, but holy shit."

"How could she go back to this after everything . . ." Thorpe pressed his lips together, refusing to lose control of his anger—or feel too hurt. "When I get my hands on her, she won't sit for a week. And that's the beginning of what I've got planned for her."

"Better make that two weeks. I have some ideas of my own."

Thorpe shoved aside the fact that Sean hadn't objected to him spanking Callie. Yes, she'd taken off her collar, but she hadn't discussed it with Sean, who probably didn't see their relationship as over. Thorpe knew that the girl would never belong to him, but he refused to let this behavior slide without putting in his two cents—and then some.

Quickly, they searched the room. He found her backpack in the closet and grabbed it. There was no sign of the red duffel she'd mysteriously acquired in the airport bathroom. She had nothing else personal anywhere in the room. Even her toothbrush had been stowed back in the appropriate plastic holder in a zippered pouch. The used bar of soap told him that she'd taken a shower. Over the odor of mildew and stale cigarettes pervading the motel, he smelled a light trace of her.

As Callie's scent registered in his brain, boiling blood filled his cock. A caveman urge to grab her, bind her, and fuck her until she understood all the reasons she could never run away from him again seized Thorpe.

"She was here," Sean confirmed, sniffing the sheets.

"I've got her stuff." He indicated to the pack slung over his shoulder.

Sean gave him a thumbs-up, then headed for the door. Thorpe followed, hot on his heels. Back in the lobby, he tossed the key to Doreen with a stern warning glance. The woman looked somewhere between breathless and ready to shit her pants when he left. She wouldn't talk without substantial incentive. Not a perfect solution for keeping Callie safe, but the best he could do now.

Back in the Jeep, Sean had started the engine and turned on the lights. Thorpe tossed Callie's backpack in and shut the passenger door as the other man threw the vehicle into reverse and peeled out of the parking lot.

The journey to Glitter Girls seemed like the longest two blocks of his life. When they reached the seedy dive bar, his worst fears were confirmed. The windows were covered up and painted the same color as the exterior walls. A big neon sign over the building advertised TOPLESS GIRLS! Thorpe swore.

It was a fucking strip joint. Callie better hope for her sake that she was merely waitressing.

The lowlife clientele slinking in seemed like a mixture of locals and tourists. They all looked as if they'd served time. None of them appeared to take bathing too seriously.

As they reached the front door, a big bouncer stood grunting out a "request" for the cover charge over the raucous music. Ten bucks with a two-drink minimum. The guys in front of them pulled out a big wad of cash he'd bet they had obtained in less-than-legal ways.

As he and Sean each pulled out a bill and ran in the door, the smoke, stale beer, sweat, and glitter assailed him. Goddamn it, this place was the worst sort of dive.

On the sagging stage, someone named Whipped Cream, who wore two little pasties designed to look like her namesake, was taking her final bows. Her mother definitely hadn't given her that name—or that shade of ruby-red hair. She didn't look like she had all her teeth.

The deejay sounded bored as he told the audience to give it up for the woman. The smattering of applause broke into chatter. A few bills littered the stage as Thorpe studied the girls serving drinks, hoping . . . But he didn't see any waitress who had Callie's face, build, or innate grace.

Fucking son of a bitch.

Sean looked around, too, obviously worried. "Where the hell did she get off to now?"

Thorpe didn't think Doreen would have been dumb enough to call her cousin and tell him to warn Callie. "I'm hoping she's in the restroom. Or getting someone a drink."

"If she's already become a customer favorite, I doubt she's serving drinks," Sean managed to growl out with his teeth grinding. "If that's the case, she'll probably go on when the night's in full swing, toward the end of her shift."

In twenty minutes or less.

Damn it to hell, he was right. "We don't know her stage name, so we have no idea who to ask for."

"Unless I barge into the back with my badge and drag her out of here."

The idea had merit. Thorpe looked around, trying to gauge what the management's reaction to having an FBI agent in their midst would be when a waitress came by for their drink orders. Truth told, he didn't want anything, but ordered a bourbon and water, knowing he wouldn't drink it. Sean asked for a vodka tonic, then motioned her down to him in a moment between the music.

"I'm wondering, pretty lass, if you'd mind to give me a wee bit of information." Sean slipped into his Scottish accent and smiled at the acne-prone waitress, who looked barely legal and totally dazzled. The fed flashing a bit of cash sealed the deal.

"I'll tell you anything. My bra size is a thirty-six D. They're real."

They weren't, but Thorpe wasn't going to bother debating the girl's assets.

"You're right fetching, that's for sure. But I'm inquiring about the new bit of fluff. For my friend here." Sean gestured to him.

The waitress made a sour face and rolled her eyes. "All the customers are, like, totally insane over Juicy. It's not as if she's got a magical pussy."

Juicy?

Thorpe cast a glance over to Sean, who looked ready to disagree with the waitress, but he managed to force another smile onto his face. "Juicy, you say? Tell me more. My friend is quite interested."

"That one is antisocial. She's pissed all the girls off. Whipped Cream and Sparkle Swallows both can't stand her. Two days here, and she's already got more fans than everyone else. Now if you two want nice . . ." She smiled, showing off slightly bucked teeth.

"What does she look like?" Sean asked.

"Blond, blue-eyed, stacked." The girl sighed. "But she's not special."

"When does she come on?"

The waitress opened her mouth to answer, but the deejay's voice over the speakers drowned her out. "She's new. She's exciting. She's your wettest dream. Give it up for Juicy!"

Sean stiffened, looking like his fury had climbed ten notches. Since Thorpe felt like strangling the deejay and killing everyone who stood between them and the stage, that suited him just fine.

And if Juicy and Callie were one and the same, slipping away unseen with the girl in tow had just become impossible.

The music cued, and Britney came on with some damn suggestive lyrics. Then the curtain parted, and out strutted the next act. Despite the bright lights glaring, all the makeup, and the skimpy costume, Thorpe knew instantly it was Callie.

She definitely wasn't waitressing.

Tingles zipped down his spine. He itched to wrap his fingers in her silky hair. Even being in the same room with her made him titanium hard, so if he hadn't known in every other way that he'd found Callie, his reaction made it damn obvious.

As he watched her onstage, the waitress stomped her foot and huffed off. He barely glanced at the other girl. Callie held him rapt as she gyrated for the crowd wearing a schoolgirl uniform, complete with a plaid skirt. Her blond wig hung in long pigtails. The whistling and catcalls ramped up, and she pasted on a come-hither smile. But her eyes . . . they didn't invite. Because he knew Callie, he could read that expression. She looked both unnerved and scared out of her mind.

Beside him, Sean cursed a blue streak and leaned forward, gaze drilling into her. Thorpe felt the man's displeasure. It mirrored his own. Rage bubbled and turned, and he knew that Callie would feel every inch of their disapproval the second they got their hands on her.

"Her file doesn't indicate that she's ever stooped this low," Sean snarled.

Thorpe didn't take his eyes off her. "I don't think she's ever been this desperate."

Sean nodded grimly, and they watched her slowly reach for the top button of her blouse.

Tensing before she even had it undone, Thorpe wondered if he'd survive the next three minutes. He fidgeted in his seat, eager to storm the stage, take her down, and let her feel the full measure of her consequences. "What's the fucking plan?"

"It would be better if we didn't make a scene," Sean bit out, gritting his teeth. "But the minute this music is over . . ."

"We're going to grab her ass and haul her out of here. I'm all over that."

"I was counting on it."

Callie slipped the top button free, then another, and a third. The seconds ticked by, one after the other, in a horrific show that slowly revealed her milky flesh and had all the men in the room shouting that they wanted something "Juicy." Every muscle in Thorpe's body screamed at him to stop this travesty, even as his head silenced his inner Neanderthal and told him to keep his ass in his seat. They couldn't make a scene.

With a sexy little spin, Callie whirled away and let the white shirt slip off her shoulders. She looked back at the audience with an

exaggerated wink. Even terrified, there was something unmistak-
ably special about her. She had a sweet quality and a goodness that
her difficult life hadn't killed. But the girl still exuded sex from the
sparkle of her eyes and the pout of her glossy lips, all the way down
to her swaying hips and pink-tipped toes peeking out from black
patent stilettos. Denying just how much he wanted her wasn't possible anymore. He'd never met a woman he couldn't resist—until Callie. Thorpe feared that walking away from her again would be like
trying to swim against a raging tidal wave.

To the beat of the music, Callie flipped up her illegally short
skirt and flashed the audience her sinfully small thong—and her ass
cheeks—before the plaid fell softly over her backside again. The
whooping and whistles revved up. A bouncer nearby stood mutely
and watched.

"Show us your tits!" someone near the stage shouted.

"Gimme a piece of that luscious ass," another demanded.

The idea that these dregs now had Callie in their spank bank
made him feel somewhere between nauseated and homicidal.

"Damn it all." Sean gripped the table, looking ready to combust.
"This three minutes is taking for fucking ever."

Thorpe couldn't agree more. "It will end." It *had* to.

But would it before they lost their minds? He wasn't sure about
that, especially when the shirt slipped from the crooks of her elbows
and onto the buckled stage, leaving her top half clad in nothing but
a nearly sheer lace bra. When she turned back to the audience, there
was no mistaking the pinkish cast of her plump nipples.

Callie arched her back, running her palms down her breasts,
over her flat belly, then pressed her fingers toward her pussy. The
audience started whooping at decibels near frat-party levels. Thorpe
began to sweat. Jesus, he knew what her sweet pussy tasted like, and
his mouth watered for another chance to make a meal out of her.
Of course, every man in this room wanted that opportunity. One

started pounding on the stage. Others joined in, slamming the wooden surface to the beat of the music, demanding more of her.

Fuck, this was getting out of control, and it took everything Thorpe had to stay in his seat.

A man in a cheap suit with a pimp moustache and a shaved head crowded closer. He thought he was the shit, clearly. With a confident leer, he leaned across the corner of the stage, holding up a hundred-dollar bill. He said something to Callie that Thorpe couldn't hear over the music. Her eyes widened. More disquiet filled her face, but she danced in the dude's direction.

With a shimmy, she lifted her skirt in front of him and circled her hips, spinning around until she backed up to him. Then she crouched, wiggling her ass seductively in his face. Her eyes slid shut. To anyone who didn't know her, she might look as if she were in the midst of passion, but Thorpe saw differently. He had no doubt her skin was crawling and she was barely resisting the urge to run like hell.

Just because she wasn't enjoying herself, however, didn't mean she was going to escape punishment. She had a protector and a Dom, both of whom would do anything to help her. Had she trusted either of them? No. She'd just left. Sean, he sort of understood. Hell, Thorpe hadn't trusted the man himself until . . . what? Maybe yesterday. Or the day before. His days were running together. But Callie had known him for four fucking years. In all that time, she hadn't learned that he cared, that he would do anything to help her?

She was damn well going to learn now.

Obviously, she had panicked. He understood that—to a point. But he refused to accept excuses from Callie. She was going to learn to rely on the men who loved her. Whatever happened next, whether he never got to lay another hand on her after her punishment to-night, he would teach her once and for all to look to him if she ever found herself in trouble again.

The slime ball with the skinny black tie and the C-note in his hand shoved the bill into the back of her thong—then copped a long caress of her ass. With the other hand, he brushed his way up her thigh, looking at her like she was a particularly prime cut of filet.

Thorpe felt steam coming from his ears and fucking lost it.

As he jumped to his feet, Sean was right beside him, fists clenched. Thorpe kicked his chair out of the way and prowled toward Callie, shoulder to shoulder with the other man.

Callie leaned away from the letch feeling her up, cringing back. Trying to cover her reaction, she sent the man a little smile over her shoulder, then danced away. Thorpe felt his fists tighten with the need to beat the fucker to death.

Sean was faster, grabbing the son of a bitch by the back of the neck and snarling something in his ear. The thug tried to fight back, but the fed proved himself all kind of badass, blocking the guy's every move, then slamming the creep face-first onto a nearby post. Thorpe raced over, more than happy to help. He was gratified when Sean yanked the skunk back to reveal a broken, bleeding nose. In fact, he hoped Sean had done permanent damage to the asshole for daring to touch Callie.

Frantically Thorpe looked for her again. And he found her, damn it. Her trim back and undulating spine told him she now courted the men on the other side of the room, still holding her skirt up and wriggling her hips until a few more men shoved more bills in the string of her thong. They howled as she enticed them, and more guys approached the stage with money in fists, just wanting the chance to get close to Callie.

While Thorpe had been distracted by her, Sean and the letch got into a scuffle. Apparently, the fed had been busier watching Callie than the greaseball's elbow to his gut. As Sean grunted and dodged the guy's flailing fists, Thorpe approached. So did the bouncer.

"No fighting," he shouted over the music. "Take it outside."

"Yeah, get your fucking hands off me, prick!" said cheap suit. "I gave the pretty slut some money. So what?"

Oh, that was it. Doms sometimes called their submissives "slut," but as a form of endearment, however odd that seemed to others. Not everyone understood, but that was true of the whole lifestyle. Even if he would never call Callie *his* slut, no other random dick was going to malign the girl when he didn't know her at all and had no idea how far from the truth that was.

"Don't touch her again." Sean looked ready to kill.

"Get over it," the lowlife ranted on. "You don't own her.

"Actually," Sean tossed back, "I do."

Thorpe threw a punch, hitting the fuckwad square in the jaw and sending him reeling to the ground with the force of the blow, out cold. The bouncer turned to him with a menacing glare and reached to throw him out the door.

Fuck, he should have held his temper. He couldn't afford to get tossed out.

Thorpe turned back to Callie. She whipped her gaze in his direction to decipher the commotion. Their gazes connected, and electricity fired his veins. Shock widened her eyes and bleached the color from her cheeks. Then her gaze zipped over to Sean. She gasped as if she'd seen a ghost.

Despite the fact that she hadn't finished her number and the music still played, she turned and darted for the curtain and the back of the club.

The bouncer rightly put keeping the talent working above restraining a few guys from fighting, so he ran after Callie, catching her in his beefy grip just before she could slip backstage.

She struggled and cursed, demanding to be let free as the crowd collectively booed her retreat.

"Show us your tits!" repeated a man in the front row with a one-track mind.

The bouncer dragged Callie back toward mid-stage, then stood between her and the curtain. "Finish your damn number or Marty is gonna fire your ass."

Predictably, the moment the big beefcake released her, she made another run for it, this time darting for the stairs that led to the club floor. She valued her freedom way more than this piss-ass job.

But Thorpe was one step ahead of her. He stood at the bottom of the stairs, blocking her exit off the stage. And in those shoes, jumping down five feet to the ground would be impossible.

They had her surrounded.

Sean quickly assessed the situation, then leapt onto the stage and reached into his pocket to flash his badge to the hunk of beefcake. "FBI. Unless you want trouble, give the girl to me."

The big guy stiffened as the music screeched to a stop, his eyes narrowing as he took in Sean, then his badge. He stepped back and tossed his hands in the air. "We just hired her, man. We don't want any trouble. Take her."

Callie tossed Sean a defiant glower and over the din of the crowd, she warned, "You stay away from me."

"Not going to happen, lovely." The words were a vow, spoken as Sean prowled closer, but his expression was pure warning. He meant to assert his will.

She froze, then her gaze darted around the room. Thorpe's gut knotted. Goddamn it, she was going to make a run for it.

He opened his mouth to warn Sean, but she was quicker, taking off one of her wicked shoes and tossing it in Sean's direction. Callie's makeshift weapon smacked him in the shoulder, then she planted her hand on his chest and shoved him off balance. While Sean scrambled to right himself, she tore off the other stiletto and raised it menacingly at the bouncer. He charged her and grabbed her wrist, clamping down harshly to stop her from pelting him. So she kicked him in the balls.

As the incredibly stupid hulk dropped to his knees, he clutched his genitals and groaned. Callie sprinted past him and through the curtain, disappearing backstage.

Thorpe darted up the stairs after her, tearing past the drape in time to see her shove the weathered industrial back door open and race into the alley behind the building. He swore and took off after her.

The metal door was swinging shut, and Thorpe pushed it open, then hit the alley. Under the spotlight of a bug-infested bulb, he looked left, then right before he caught sight of Callie dashing away on her bare feet in a fevered panic, artificial blond pigtails swinging against her pale back only saved from bareness by the strap of that tiny, sexy bra. Damn it, she was either begging to step on glass or be raped by some criminal in the shadows. Of course, she was in full flight mode and not using all her logic, but what the hell was she thinking?

One thing became immediately clear: Callie was younger and surprisingly fast. But if he let her through his grasp again, he'd be fucked seven ways from Sunday.

He charged after her as fast as his stride would take him, rapidly gaining ground on the barefoot girl. She was about to reach the end of the alley, which didn't worry him . . . until a taxi rolled by. Of all the rotten fucking luck.

Somehow, he had to stop Callie. On feet, he wouldn't catch her in time. Neither would Sean, whom he could hear chugging down the pavement behind him. Once Callie made it inside that taxi, Thorpe knew she'd be gone forever. She'd definitely be taking his heart with her. And Sean's. *Motherfucker.*

Between the lights of other businesses and the moon, he could see that the alley was blessedly empty. So he did the one thing he thought might stop the panicked girl in her tracks.

"Callindra Alexis Howe, stop and look at me this instant."

Chapter Eleven

WHEN Callie heard Thorpe shout her real name, her heart screeched to a stop. He knew? She turned, still backing away, tangled up in his gray eyes. How? When? What had given her away?

Damn it, his life had just become twenty times more complicated—and dangerous. She didn't want that for him.

Stricken, she shook her head, struggling to take in air. "You're wrong. That's not me."

Thorpe approached her in long, determined steps, his face granite, his hand outstretched. Behind him, Sean, that deceitful snake, charged toward her like a train with a headful of steam. She spun around and darted away again. What the hell was he doing here? With Thorpe? She couldn't allow either of them to get their hands on her.

Callie raced for the cab fifty feet away, still idling at the corner and waiting for the light to turn green. Dressed only in a bra and a little short skirt, she could probably get his attention. Maybe. In this neighborhood, maybe not. Good thing she had money in her thong. She'd have to pick up her "go" bag at the motel, lay low for a while, then find a bus station . . .

"Don't you lie to me," Thorpe shouted out to her. "And don't run!"

"Don't believe Sean," she tossed over her shoulder.

"That nick on your left hip came from a bullet, delivered when your family's killer shot at you. I felt it with my own fucking fingers."

Two Decembers ago, when he'd touched her intimately. That explained so much, like why after so many passionate kisses, each an exquisite promise, he'd walked away without a word and left her aching. And why he'd cut off nearly all romantic or sexual contact since.

For the past two years, Thorpe had never even hinted that he knew the truth. And despite the stupidly huge bounty on her head, he had never turned her in, either.

Sean would the moment she stood still. She'd seen his badge at Glitter Girls. Obviously, she'd been wrong about him. He might not be an assassin trying to kill her or a bounty hunter out for a quick payday, but he'd damn sure arrest her the first chance he got.

"Stop!" Thorpe thundered.

His footsteps drew closer and closer, but she didn't dare heed his words. "Let me go."

"Never."

At the iron resolve in his tone, Callie's heart roared harder. She glanced over her shoulder. Sure enough, he was closing in—fast. And now, Sean was nowhere in sight. It didn't matter. She was nearly to the taxi . . .

With maybe ten steps to go, she landed on a rock. It gouged her heel, slicing the skin open. The sting screamed up her leg. She tried not to let the pain stop her, but when she slammed that foot down on the asphalt again, the pebble embedded deeper in her skin. The sharp ache nearly made her crumple to the ground. She slowed, hobbled, until Thorpe was nearly on top of her.

Panicked, Callie opened her mouth to scream to the taxi driver—to anyone who would listen. Sean jumped out from behind a Dumpster and clamped one arm around her waist like a vise. The other he bracketed over her mouth.

"Stop!" he panted.

His breath was warm on her face, his body like a furnace against her chilled skin, now sheened with perspiration. Her senses registered succor and safety. They wanted to melt into him. They yearned for his gentle touch, his fiery kiss . . .

Every one of which had been a lie.

Her brain screeched that she should pry herself away and run. Callie bucked wildly so she could free her mouth and tell Sean to go to hell. But he held tight. Thorpe blanketed her back, bracing his hands on her hips. She tried to stand strong and defiant, but he wrapped his suit coat around her shoulders both to warm and immobilize her. Immediately, the garment steeped her in his body heat. Their hot breaths caressed her skin. Their heady masculine scents swirled together as their taut bodies surrounded her.

"Don't move," Thorpe growled. "You're in enough trouble as it is."

She shivered at those words. Then, mere feet in front of her, the taxi dashed away, taking with it her only avenue of escape.

Finally, Sean slowly drew his hand away from her lips, staring down at her with blue eyes, piercing her despite the crappy lighting and shadows. She steeled her heart against his once beloved face. She'd always associated him with patience and gentle care. Now she knew he was a con artist with a badge, callous enough to steal her heart just to bring her in.

"Take your fucking hands off me."

Face tightening with displeasure, Sean narrowed his eyes at her. "Looking to add to your punishment, lovely? I don't recommend it. Your ass is already going to be sore."

"You and your former fake accent can go eat shit. I took my collar off, so you have no business touching me."

"That's not precisely how it works, Callie, and you know it," Thorpe murmured in her ear.

She turned her head to the man she'd once trusted and loved above all others. "You're on his side now? I never imagined that you'd be gullible enough to fall for his lines, too."

Behind her, Thorpe leaned around to look at Sean. "There won't be any reasoning with her in the next ten minutes."

Sean grunted. "Or in the next millennium, I imagine. This isn't a smart place to talk."

"Good point."

"Stay with her. I'll bring the car."

She could all but feel Thorpe smile. "I'll make sure she doesn't go anywhere."

Callie's jaw dropped. When the hell had they gotten so chummy? And why did Thorpe trust the liar?

With her head still reeling, Sean jogged off. She struggled against Thorpe's grip, holding out hope that another taxi would zoom by. But even if she was lucky enough for that, she didn't think she could outrun him with her foot smarting.

"Why are you helping that rat?" She'd always believed that Thorpe would be on her side, and knowing otherwise felt as if someone had pried her heart from her chest with a crowbar. "He wants to see me in prison."

"Sean wants to protect you, pet. Just like I do. Don't look at me like that," he demanded. "You didn't ask any questions before you jumped to conclusions. You just ran away. And you were dead wrong."

"He fooled you like he fooled me."

"If he'd wanted to arrest you, he could have done it anytime over the last seven months," Thorpe reasoned. "He could have brought in a small army of agents and let them haul you out. I wouldn't have been able to stop them. If you think he's in an all-fired hurry to lock you up and throw away the key, ask yourself why he hasn't already done it."

Callie tried. There was logic in what Thorpe was saying, but she'd been running for so long. Her flight response was so ingrained. Panic still pumped through her system. The thought niggled in the back of her head . . . What if Thorpe was wrong?

"Pet." His low voice soothed. "Think about it."

"Then why didn't he tell me he was some sort of agent?"

"Because you would have run immediately if you'd discovered he was FBI. We all know that, especially Sean. You don't trust well, Callie, and we understand the reasons. But things are going to change now. Neither of us will ever risk you. If we haven't turned you in for two million dollars yet, we're not likely to."

Headlights bobbed up the worn alley before a silver Jeep she didn't recognize stopped beside them. Sean stuck his head out the window. "Someone already called the police. They're two blocks over. Get in."

As Callie's blood ran cold, Thorpe cursed and shoved her toward the vehicle. She dug in her heels.

"Callie!" Thorpe growled. "Get in the fucking car."

She probably stood a better chance of eluding the local police than the FBI. She might be able to convince the Vegas PD that she was the victim of some random attack in this alley. It was possible they'd release her before they figured out who she was, and she'd be long gone before the truth hit them.

But that would leave Thorpe . . . where? In jail? And what about Sean? If he really wasn't trying to turn her in for the cash or a pat on the back at work . . . The implications were staggering. Would the police think the guys had kidnapped her or something? What if they couldn't get away? What if she couldn't? A million thoughts raced through her head, and she couldn't quite grasp any of them. On the one hand, she'd relied on herself for so long, she didn't really know how to relinquish her control. On the other hand, as Thorpe had pointed out, they hadn't given her up or let anyone haul her away, so why would they start now?

Crap, she wasn't sure what to do.

"Trust me, Callie," Sean stared at her through the driver's side window. He held out one hand to her, his earnest expression willing her to believe him. "Whatever you think, I swear that I'm not here now because of my job. I would do anything to keep you safe."

His words made her melt a little more than they should. Gawd, she wanted to believe him so badly. If she was wrong and she climbed into that SUV, it could mean the end of her freedom. She hadn't managed to elude capture for this long because she made decisions with her heart.

A shout from Glitter Girls' parking lot had her head zipping around and her gaze trying to penetrate the dark and distance. Thorpe, however, just lost his patience.

With a grunt, he picked her up, yanked open the door to the backseat, and tossed her in. She braced herself on the leather bench, scrambling to the far side of the SUV as Thorpe jumped in and slammed the door.

Callie didn't like any of this—too sudden, no time to think. She didn't run off with other people. She'd managed to escape the fateful night her family had been killed and she was still alive today because she'd stayed one step ahead of the cops and killers after her. She wasn't about to drag Thorpe through the mud. And she was still on the fence about whether to believe Sean.

Lunging for the passenger door on the far side of the car, Callie grabbed the handle, preparing to tumble out into the chilly November evening again and dash the distance to . . . somewhere. Wherever Thorpe and Sean weren't.

Sean merely locked the doors to the car, killed the headlights, then rocketed into the night. At the first corner, he flipped on the headlights again and merged into traffic, blending in with every other car chasing Lady Luck on the Vegas streets.

"Are you insane?" she shrieked at Thorpe. "Do you understand what will happen if the authorities find out that you're knowingly aiding a fugitive's escape? It was one thing when you could say I lied to you. Then you could have been the victim. Then you wouldn't have gone to jail." She glared at Sean in the driver's seat. "And if you're not going to arrest me, do you realize that you could lose your job? What the hell are you two doing?"

"You want to take this one?" Sean looked at his new "pal" in the rearview mirror. "I need to make sure we're not being followed and try to decide where we can go from here."

"With pleasure."

"Good. I have a feeling our time is short. Did you already pack up everything in your room and put your belongings in the car?"

"I did."

"That makes two of us. Carry on."

Thorpe nodded at him, then turned to her with a Dom glower so menacing she found herself inching back until the car door ensured that she had nowhere else to go.

Callie gulped. "What? I-I took care of myself. I couldn't very well expect the two of you to—"

"Be reasonably concerned human beings who wanted to keep you happy and safe? Talk to the two men who will always put your welfare above everything else?"

Damn it, he was determined to make her feel somewhere between stupid and irresponsible. "Sean was a liar. How was I supposed to know he wouldn't turn me in?"

"I'm sorry for the subterfuge, lovely. But I had to create a cover to get into the club and keep everyone from getting suspicious, especially you."

And didn't she feel like an idiot for falling for it—and him? "Great job, Mr. Kirkpatrick. You had me fooled."

"Mackenzie," he corrected. "Sean Mackenzie is my real name.

Here." He passed her a little leather case. She flipped it over as he turned on the interior light.

Callie clutched the document in her hand and read it with a sense of something between *OMG* and *holy shit*. It was true. Sean Mackenzie truly was a Special Agent for the FBI. She passed his credentials back with numb fingers. He grabbed it and killed the interior light.

Then darkness settled around her, leaving her to battle her thoughts again. *Holy shit* finally beat out *OMG* as her final reaction. And anger that she'd been duped. Apparently he'd done it without much difficulty and probably even less regret.

"I guess that's why you were able to give Axel a black eye." What else was there to say?

"I taught hand-to-hand combat for the bureau for two years."

Which meant that he was damn good at it. And here she'd thought he didn't have a violent bone in his body. Callie snorted. That proved she had almost no clue about him. In fact, there were probably a thousand other facts about Sean Kirkpatrick—or Mackenzie, rather—that she didn't know. "Who are you? Obviously, I don't know."

"You do." His voice was so soft, compelling her to believe him. "Everything except my name and occupation was the real me. I never lied about how I felt."

She wanted to believe him. But the truth was, she'd fallen for a charming smile, a fake brogue, and a whole lot of smooth lines. If his tenderness and caring had seemed like more, well . . . wasn't that the point of winning her trust and breaking her barriers down? "Whatever."

"It's a lot more than 'whatever,' Callie. I swear to you."

"Even if finding out that Sean wasn't who he claimed, that doesn't excuse you for running off without talking to *me*, pet," Thorpe jumped in. "What's your justification there?"

"I didn't think you knew who I was, so I tried to keep you from this mess. Was I supposed to guess that you cared about me?"

She hadn't thought it possible, but his face became even more forbidding. "Don't you *ever* say that to me again. I sheltered you for four years, Callie. I tried to teach you, help you, comfort you. What part of that indicated to you that I didn't give a shit?"

"I knew you cared as a friend, but I didn't think you—" She tried to untangle her thoughts as he leaned across the seat toward her. "The night you . . . that it seemed like we were going to . . . you know." She still hated thinking about that humiliating event. "Then you just walked away and never explained, never touched me again, so—"

"Because I didn't fuck you, you imagined that I didn't care anymore?"

"Pretty much, yeah." She shrugged. "I might have believed that a lover would go out on a limb for me, but not merely a boss or a friend."

"There are so many things wrong with that statement." Thorpe cursed, shaking his head.

"Being your lover clearly didn't give me any extra perks in the trust department," Sean piped up from the front seat. "In fact, I think you gave me even less than Thorpe."

"Well, yeah," Callie defended hotly. "Everything between us was pretense and bullshit. Don't try to convince me that I've wronged you."

"He's not telling his superiors that you've run or that his cover is blown because he's trying to minimize the chances that the FBI will suddenly want you brought in."

Maybe that was true. Even if it was, she wasn't ready to be less angry. No, hurt. Damn it. "So I'm supposed to thank you for your kind lies? Was it difficult to get hard on command? Was fucking me a chore?"

Sean slapped his palm against the steering wheel. "That's it. I've had enough. Thorpe . . ."

"On it," he assured the other man. "We're done with your lack of trust."

"And your bratty mouth," Sean added. "Don't forget that."

"Absolutely," Thorpe agreed. "You will apologize this instant to both of us."

"Like hell! You two don't like the way I communicate. Guess what? Your style sucks, too. You lie." She pointed at Sean, then turned her stare on Thorpe. "And you clam up."

Thorpe grabbed her by the arm. "You've refused to rely on the men determined to help you."

"I didn't ask for help," she pointed out.

"You've refused to apologize, and you've insulted us."

"You insulted me, too. Because I'm going to defend myself, I'm bratty?" She rolled her eyes. "I'm not the only one slinging words around here."

"I might have lied, lovely, but I didn't drug you," Sean reminded darkly.

"Neither of us stripped for a room full of scum. And it was your third shift in two days?" Thorpe raised an intimidating brow at her.

A gong of foreboding resounded in her gut. Shit, they'd done their legwork. Sometimes, she lost her temper and forgot important details . . . like being at the mercy of two pissed off Doms. Of course, Thorpe probably wouldn't punish her. In fact, he'd probably never touch her again. But he'd sure give Sean lots of craptastic ideas about how to do it effectively.

"I wasn't enjoying myself. I was making money."

"To skip town, right?" Thorpe's question was sharp as a blade.

"It's what I do."

"Along with driving us out of our fucking minds," Sean growled.

"It wasn't intended to be a personal affront!" she insisted.

"So we were supposed to shrug that you'd left and move on with our lives. Do you know how worried we've been?" her former boss asked.

"Oh my gawd, you both sound like overprotective hens."

Callie braced for Thorpe's explosion. Instead, he drew in a bracing breath, nostrils flaring, then with a taut profile and rigidly controlled body, he directed his gaze to the front seat. "Sean, reasoning with her isn't going to work."

"Agreed. Go ahead. I need to focus here, but I've had more than enough."

"Excellent. Minus the gloves?"

He sighed. "I doubt anything less will register."

"I couldn't agree more. It's bound to get noisy."

Sean smiled faintly. "I'll enjoy that."

He glanced at her in the mirror at the same time Thorpe regarded her with a frightening smile. Callie felt like an actress who'd forgotten her lines, pinned by a spotlight.

"Apologize, pet."

It wasn't a suggestion. But there was no way she was going to say "sorry" for doing what she thought necessary. "I'm sorry if whatever I did upset you."

"And?" Thorpe's grip on her arm tightened.

"I'm sorry if I misinterpreted your actions."

"Anything else?" His voice dropped to a silky baritone that served as its own warning. "Anything you'd like to say to Sean?"

Callie's belly tightened, but she refused to lie. "No, I think that's it."

"Then it's obvious we need to lay down a few rules and expectations." Thorpe settled against the backseat, legs braced wide, then grabbed her shoulders and gave a mighty jerk until she tumbled face down across his lap.

"Oh hell, no!" She writhed, trying to twist upright again.

Like that was going to help. He'd dealt with a thousand squirming submissives. There would be no escape. She already knew that from experience.

Expertly, he splayed a hand in the middle of her back, pinning her to his lap. "Hell, yes. It's past due, pet. You've more than earned it. Your attitude needs serious adjusting."

Thorpe punctuated his assertion by lifting her little skirt, yanking the bills out of her thong and throwing them on the floorboard, then giving her right cheek a quick, blistering swat. Before she'd even finished gasping, he spanked the left. *Ouch!* Her ass stung. Heat flared. And not for one second did she think that he was done.

"From now on," he began, "you will keep uppermost in your mind that anything that affects you concerns us. We care. Is that clear?"

Even if she was a little thrilled at the conviction in his words and more than a bit excited at the way he restrained and handled her, Callie wanted to tell him to jump off a bridge. She was about to say something satisfyingly dismissive when he smacked the flat of his hand against each of her cheeks again. A yelp slipped from her mouth.

"I'll take that as a yes." A smirk resonated in his voice

Damn him!

"You will never leave our sight without proper permission. If you ever run away again without doing the courtesy of talking to us both, your ass will be a glowing shade of red for a month, I promise."

Was he serious? "I don't need babysitters."

"Since you could have gotten yourself molested in that terrible club or in the fucking alley behind it, if not for us, I'm going to disagree."

"But I didn't."

"I didn't give you permission to speak." Thorpe's voice dropped another octave.

Another few swats to her backside had her flesh stinging again . . . and her pussy weeping. Why did Thorpe's discipline always turn her on? Why couldn't she hate him for it and tell him to go to hell?

"And lovely? There will be no drugging anyone, no taking your clothes off for strangers, and absolutely no lying," Sean insisted from the front seat. His voice held a harsh, authoritarian edge she'd never heard from him before.

"If you remove so much as a shoe in front of another man without our permission, you will feel my wrath."

And to prove his point, Thorpe rained a series of short, sharp blows down on her backside, one after the other. Callie couldn't stop the gasps, the moans. Her blood felt like it had caught fire. Her skin burned. Still, Thorpe kept at her ass, pounding one wallop after another on her vulnerable backside until she thought she would melt all over him. She barely reined in the urge to cry out in pleasure.

"Mine, too," Sean vowed. "You're likely to feel it as soon as I don't need to focus on the road, in fact."

Well, wasn't that something to look forward to?

"I didn't give either of you permission to touch me," she pointed out.

"Lousy attempt, pet," he tsked at her. "You just keep digging a deeper hole."

"*I* gave him permission," Sean clarified. "And I don't care if you *think* you removed your collar. We didn't talk about it. *You* decided without consulting me. Last time I checked, you weren't the Dominant in this relationship."

"This is ridiculous. I'm not a possession."

"No, but you're a submissive in need of a great deal of discipline. I have no problem giving it to you, pet."

"I have no problem either, Callie. I was too easy on you before. That's going to change," Sean promised.

Her heart lurched. They absolutely meant business, and a bit of her really wanted to let them take her under their wing and rely on them for her safety. If she wasn't Callindra Howe, she might dip her toe in the water. Okay, so she'd probably dive in. But that wasn't her reality.

"The hell it is! I only managed to stay free for nine years because I never got sentimental. I leave everything and everyone behind and sever all ties once I'm gone. Thorpe, it's not that I don't believe you'd do everything possible to keep me safe. But I can't let you ruin your life. I left because I'm trying to do the right thing so you can get back to normalcy."

"He didn't ask you to throw yourself on the sword, lovely." Sean's voice softened before it hardened again. "Neither did I. We won't let you cast either of us aside because you think it's 'safer.' What you're really doing is being stingy with your trust and protecting your heart. I won't have it."

"Nor will I," Thorpe added. "I might have been your boss and your friend, but you're lying to me and yourself if you think we weren't more."

Was he finally admitting there was something between them? Callie closed her eyes. *What crappy timing . . .*

"So?" she tossed back. "You ignored it yourself for years."

"I did," he admitted. "And I'm done."

Her heated ass throbbed in the cool night, and she felt Thorpe's stare on her bare skin. The yearning nearly choked her, but this wasn't just about her. She couldn't stand to see them get sucked into the morass her life had become.

Callie figured she could play this one of two ways: either keep fighting tooth and nail and get her ass beat more for her defiance or give in until they let their guard down. Then she'd run again. Sean hadn't asked her to throw herself on the sword, and well . . . she hadn't asked him for that either. If he really had been protecting her and was here against his orders, she couldn't let him jeopardize his job any more than she could risk being involved with an FBI agent. And she refused to gamble her heart on Thorpe, one of the most emotionally unavailable men she'd ever met. No good would come from that.

"Yes, Sirs."

Above her, Thorpe stilled. "I don't know whether to praise your breakthrough or wail on your ass again for lying."

"I think I know," Sean quipped.

"I think I do, too. But time will tell. Just for good measure . . ." Thorpe palmed the burning flesh of her backside, then spanked her again with unyielding discipline before jerking her skirt down and sitting her on the long seat beside him. "Behave, pet."

She fidgeted from the stinging burn making her skin tingle and couldn't sit still.

"Thorpe, is the naughty girl's pussy wet?"

He zipped his gaze up toward Sean, who met it in the rearview mirror. No words were exchanged, but Thorpe must have seen what he wanted because he nodded and sat back with a little smile playing at the corners of his lips before he turned to her.

Callie's eyes widened. In what alternate universe was Sean going to let her former boss even think about her girl parts? Punishment was one thing, especially while he was driving, but . . . The thought of Thorpe's hand right where she ached for him most made her clit swell and sizzle. He turned and pinned her with a feral stare.

She shook her head, knowing she looked more than a tad panicked. "No."

If he got near her, he'd know she had just lied to him again. There would be more punishment. But the truth was too embarrassing.

"Spread your legs and let me feel for myself, pet."

Oh hell. She flipped her stare up to the rearview mirror, hoping to catch's Sean's disapproving scowl. Despite the spanking and his question, he wouldn't really let Thorpe touch her there, would he?

She did snag Sean's gaze, but he merely looked at her expectantly. "We're waiting."

"And not patiently," Thorpe drawled.

Callie's heart started beating harder. Her silky thong was already beyond damp and wasn't going to absorb any of the excess moisture. Even in the darkened backseat, Thorpe would see if she tried to use her skirt to wipe away the evidence.

She pressed her lips together and frowned. "All right, I am."

"So you lied?" Damn, that Dom voice of his went straight to her clit. The ache coiled up.

A few possible responses ran through her head, but she'd seen Thorpe operate enough to know that excuses wouldn't work. Compounding things with another lie would only make her eventual punishment—and there would be one—worse. So she settled on the only thing that might persuade him to show a little bit of mercy.

"I'm sorry," she whispered. "I'm confused. I was . . . ashamed."

He grabbed her chin. "Explain."

Shouldn't it be obvious? "You haven't touched me in two years, except the night after Sean and I, um . . ."

"Made love," he supplied from the front seat oh so helpfully.

"That was the night you came under my tongue and fingers." Thorpe stared into her eyes, forcing her to remember the way she'd writhed for him and screamed his name.

Mortification froze Callie. Would Sean be mad? Or would this weird alternate universe where he and Thorpe were having some bizarre bromance continue and lead Sean to do something once incomprehensible, like high-five the Dungeon Master?

She cleared her throat. "Other than that, you've shown almost no sexual interest in me for so long. It's kind of embarrassing that your spanking, um . . . aroused me."

Thorpe looked like he wanted to say something, but he didn't. After a long pause, he simply glanced at her thighs. "Spread them. I won't ask again."

"You're really going to check?" She blinked at him, then back up at Sean in the mirror.

"I asked him to, lovely."

"So yes," Thorpe provided, then looked at her impatiently.

Her heart chugged like a herd of wild horses. It had been one thing to spread her legs for Thorpe when she thought it had been good-bye, when she thought she'd never have to see the knowing gleam in his eyes again or worry that he thought her a silly, inexperienced girl for being so easily excited by him. Now . . . she got the feeling that he intended to plow his fingers through her feminine folds and enjoy the hell out of her response. For her hesitation, he'd only want to arouse her more, bask in her helpless reaction to him.

Would she rather have more punishment or more embarrassment? The former would only lead to more of the latter, so she might as well get this shit over with. It wasn't like she had any way of preventing him from tying her down and doing whatever he wanted to her pussy the minute they made it out of this car and found a flat surface.

Slowly, Callie parted her thighs until her knees were as wide as her hips. She couldn't bring herself to look at him, and realized that every hang-up about sex she'd ever had was coming back to haunt her.

Her father had never talked about the taboo subject. Holden may have been her first, but the fumbling in his backyard that early fall evening hadn't taught her a lot except that losing her virginity hurt. She'd tried casual sex once over the years with Xander. She'd wanted Thorpe so badly and hadn't known how else to get his attention. Thirty seconds and one fake orgasm later, she'd called it off, knowing that she couldn't bring herself to fuck one man when she wanted another. Xander had been fine with ending it, too, leaving her to wonder if she lacked sex appeal altogether. Then came Sean. He'd given her a pleasure so excruciating, Callie still caught her breath just thinking about it. She hadn't ever known such ecstasy existed. And she'd craved him since. But Thorpe? Gawd, she was almost afraid to discover all the ways he could turn her body inside out.

"Please . . ." The word slipped out as she stared into his eyes.

What the hell was she doing, showing her vulnerable side to a man well-known for his ruthless domination?

"Please what, pet?"

Her entire body shook. Thorpe made her nervous; he always had. Such a big, forceful presence. It was hard not to want to please him. The not knowing whether she mattered to him as something more than a responsibility troubled her. One minute he'd wanted her, the next he hadn't. He had once again when Sean had come on the scene. What did Thorpe really feel for her?

Exhaustion and hunger tore at her. The pain making her heel throb was nothing compared with the ache in her pussy. It was impossible not to acknowledge how important Thorpe had been to her. For a girl who usually uprooted every few months, four years to feel unrequited love was a damn long time.

A tear streaked down her cheek, and she wiped it away. "I don't know. I'm so confused."

He let loose a heavy sigh. Then he wrapped an arm around her and tugged her against his tall, hard frame. "On my lap, pet."

Callie was dying to know what he was thinking, feeling, wanting. But he wasn't going to tell her. "Yes, Sir."

As she scrambled into his lap, he cupped a gentle hand around the back of her head and guided her onto his shoulder, wrapping his suit coat around her once more. "Are you cold?"

"A little."

"I'm turning up the heater, lovely. All you had to do was say something."

That gentle note was back in Sean's voice, tugging at her. Emotions she didn't know how to comprehend piled up, right on top of all her confusion. Mentally, she couldn't hold it all up or in anymore.

"Thank you." She sniffled.

"Give me your feet." Thorpe held out one hand where she could snuggle them into his palm.

She shook her head. "I don't want to get blood on you."

"Blood?" he questioned sharply.

"M-my foot. I stepped on a rock. It's nothing."

"I'll be the judge of that."

"I'll add first aid supplies to my mental grocery list," Sean said.

"Do you have any idea where we're going?" Thorpe inquired, curling his arms around her more tightly.

His embrace was like heaven. It might be stupid, but the only thing that would make her happier would be to have Sean cuddled up to her, too.

"I have a few thoughts. Callie, do you like to swim?"

"No." Her sister had nearly drowned as a toddler in a little koi pond in the backyard of a neighbor's house. She'd tried like hell to rescue Charlotte—and almost drowned herself. She'd been terrified of the water since.

"She can't swim," Thorpe supplied. "I managed to drag her to the lake once with some of the regulars from Dominion. She spent the entire time as far away from the railing of the boat as possible."

"Perfect," Sean said with a smile in his voice.

The words filled her with disquiet. Not because she thought either of them would willingly hurt her, but if they isolated her someplace where she couldn't escape and put their heads together to collaborate on what came next . . . Callie had a feeling she—and her heart—might be in real trouble.

Chapter Twelve

FOUR hours later, Sean stared down at Callie's sleeping figure almost swallowed whole by the surprisingly big bed. She was worn out, and when he bent to remove the terrible blond wig, she didn't move a muscle. That alone told him how fatigued she was, as did the gray smudges under her eyes. He tossed the synthetic hair in the corner and carefully removed all the pins until her dark tresses spread across the white sheets. She looked so beautiful, it broke his fucking heart.

Thorpe stood beside him. "Is she still asleep?"

He nodded. "She's exhausted."

"Well, she's not the only one." Thorpe twisted his powerful torso, stretching and stifling a yawn. "We got her back, and that was a feat in itself, but we've still got a shitload to do."

"Yep. Now that we've got distance between us and Vegas, we can sort through the facts and decide what comes next."

With a nod, Thorpe headed out of the bedroom in grim silence, then out onto the dock, into the night. Sean followed. From the deck of their rented houseboat, moonlight glowed over the dark waters of Lake Mead. Now, just before the dawn, everything was shimmering and quiet, a hush of night before the riot of life that came with

day prevailed. It was a welcome change from the last frantic few
hours.

"I don't think we were followed," Thorpe observed.

"As deserted as the road from the highway to this private dock
is, we would have seen anyone on our tail. Let's just hope no one re-
alizes that we've left Dallas yet or figures out how to track us down."

After snatching Callie from behind Glitter Girls, he'd developed
a plan to hole up and began to set it in motion. After her punishment, she'd given into weariness and all but passed out on Thorpe's
lap. She hadn't awakened when they'd stopped at a twenty-four-hour
superstore on the southeast side of Vegas. Once there, Sean had
grabbed a ball cap and windbreaker from his bag and emerged thirty
minutes later with a cartful of everything they would need for a
week of isolation. If they needed more provisions, he'd deal with that
later.

After leaving the vehicle's keys in a magnetic box in the wheel
well, they'd hopped in a taxi. Using the burner phones they'd picked
up in Dallas, both he and Thorpe had made a few calls as they traveled southeast. The big Dom dialed Axel to check in. After finding
out all was well at Dominion, he rang Logan for updates and gave
him the number for a new prepaid cell. The former SEAL jotted
down Thorpe's new digits, swore to call only if it was an emergency,
and said he was still looking into the guy searching for Callie at the
airport.

Meanwhile, Sean reached out to Elijah to explain where they'd
left his Jeep and to advise him to call Logan if he learned anything
more about the military goon he'd seen flashing Callie's picture at
baggage claim.

Those tasks completed, he'd used his new phone to put through
his final call, this one to a business he'd seen advertised in a bro-
chure at their hotel. He'd awakened the old man in the middle of the
night with a bullshit name and promised a wad of cash in exchange
for a houseboat for seven days.

Shortly after that, they'd arrived at the marina with Callie and their bags. They set about casting off from the docks in grim silence. The minute the sun rose, Sean vowed to steer this fifty-foot luxury vessel to a secluded spot so they could get down to work. It wasn't a perfect solution, but without known phone numbers, Wi-Fi, or other means to trace them, he hoped they could hide until he and Thorpe could figure out how to make Callie safe for good. Sean had no clue how long that would take or what they'd have to do. He was risking everything by disconnecting from his superiors. Not only could he be fired and Thorpe lose his business, but it was possible they'd be hauled off to jail for obstruction and hampering an investigation. Still, Sean didn't see any alternative if Callie was going to have a future and he wanted to be a part of it.

But this road trip/search-and-rescue mission had shown him that tomorrow wasn't simple. Sean knew he would never have gotten this far without Thorpe's assistance, and he was surprisingly glad to have the man helping him keep her both safe and in line.

Over and over in his head, he kept replaying the way the Dom had punished Callie in the Jeep. She had lay sprawled across Thorpe's lap, her backside all but bare to him, her cries resounding in the dark. Not even a blind man would have missed Thorpe's peace at having her under his control, being the master of her beautiful vulnerability.

Callie hadn't been immune, either. He'd asked if she was wet to establish that fact. The other man hadn't had the chance to check, but Sean would have bet his job and his life that she'd been turned on by that manhandling. Thorpe had probably known it, too.

Yes, Sean suspected that Callie would have responded to his own discipline and submitted to him as well, but that quickly and with that much abandon? Sure, she'd complained about Thorpe's punishment—that was Callie—but far more than sexual desire glued them together. They yearned for one another. Somewhere in her stubborn heart, Sean knew that she loved him, too. After all, she'd blossomed beneath his tender care just days ago, giving her body to him and a tantalizing chunk of her soul.

He and Thorpe had already acknowledged they both loved her. And if she loved both of them . . . where the hell did they go from here?

Together, he and Thorpe eased into the galley to put away the groceries, ensuring all the food-related bags had been emptied.

"I think that's everything." Sean glanced around the room. Together, they grabbed most of the other bags—toiletries, clothes, and other necessities—along with the bottle of tequila he'd bought during his middle-of-the-night stop. "We should talk."

Thorpe gave a tight nod. "Where we can keep an eye on Callie."

"Agreed." Sean's thoughts raced as he backtracked to the bedroom in which she slept, Thorpe trailing behind him down the narrow passage. Inside, he walked to the far side of the bed, set the bottle on the nightstand, toed off his shoes, then climbed in beside her, trailing his hand across the chilled skin of her back. The other man stood, watching Callie with a hunger so strong, it was visceral.

In her sleep, she shivered, and Sean gathered her closer, sliding down to plaster his body against hers, wishing he could hoard her. But other than him, who did that benefit?

"Damn it, she's freezing," he told Thorpe. "Can you look at her foot? When you're done, I'll find some blankets for the bed."

"Yeah." Thorpe dug through the plastic bag dangling from his fingers until he found some cotton balls and antiseptic. With a wince, he flipped on the overhead light while Sean shielded Callie's eyes.

If the sight of him holding her bothered Thorpe, it didn't show. Instead, the big Dom simply cleaned her wound. He tended to her need, shelving his own, even when she moaned groggily and tried to squirm away. Sean watched the man's big hand curl around her ankle to steady her so he could try to heal her. The visual metaphor struck Sean in the gut. Over the years, Thorpe had done that for Callie in nearly every other way. It was one reason she loved him. Sean wondered if his own broken trust with the girl could be repaired. Would she ever see that, even though he'd given her a fake name, his feelings for her had been very real?

Once Thorpe was done with his first aid, he turned off the light, casting the bedroom in shadow again. Sean flicked the rocker switch for the nightstand light, casting a dim artificial glow over the bed.

"It's not serious," Thorpe said. "Her heel will be tender for a few days."

Sean nodded. "Good to hear."

The other man looked away. Out of discomfort because Thorpe didn't want to see him cradling Callie's scantily clad body? Or out of respect because Thorpe believed she wasn't his? Either way, the other Dom didn't waste time squabbling or backbiting. Matters now were far too serious for that.

"Um, the guy who rented us the boat—Werner, wasn't it?—said there was another bedroom down the hall, right?" Thorpe tugged at the back of his neck. "And a shower? If we're done here, I think I'll just grab those and—"

"We're not. Stay." Sean tempered his demand. "Please. We really do need to talk."

There was no place in the small bedroom for Thorpe to sit except the bed. He stood, arms crossed, until Sean motioned to the mattress on the other side of Callie and passed him the bottle of tequila.

With a sigh, Thorpe sat on the edge and wrangled open the bottle, taking a long swallow.

"Sorry, I haven't got any salt and lime."

Thorpe shrugged. "It just slows down the drinking."

He held out his hand for the bottle. "Amen to that."

After taking a long swallow, he passed the tequila back to Thorpe. The alcohol was already warming him, but she still trembled with the chill.

"Callie needs a blanket," Sean said. "Let me find one."

Thorpe made to rise. "I'll do it."

It would have been so easy to let the other man see to the task, but what did Callie need? The answer wasn't simple . . . but seemed so obvious. Sean swallowed hard.

"You keep her warm. I'll find it. I think I remember where Werner said he stashed the rest of the bedding."

Sean jumped up and prowled in the room's little closet. He found a stack of blankets on a shelf, but loitered to see what Thorpe would do. The other man set the bottle aside and sank farther onto the bed. His gaze fell instantly on Callie, but he kept his distance until the girl shivered again. November had turned cold, especially out on the water. The boat had a heater, but Sean hadn't found it yet. She still wore next to nothing. And judging by the look on Thorpe's face, he was hard-pressed to forget that.

When she trembled again, he gathered her in his arms, closing his eyes as she settled against him with a little sigh. The contentment on his face spoke volumes to Sean. Even though everything was up in the air and filled with danger, in that moment, all was right with Thorpe. And Callie. The sight didn't bother Sean. She was safe and content—and he was surprisingly good with that.

When the big Dom looked settled, Sean scooped up the blankets and spread a couple over her. She burrowed under them, looking even more relaxed.

Moments later, he sat beside Callie, who remained nestled against Thorpe, and combed his fingers through her silky hair. "I need to say a couple of things."

Thorpe tensed. "Shoot."

"First, we have to figure out who's after Callie and why. My money is still on whoever had her family offed."

"Mine, too."

"Which means we have to dig deeper into Callie's background. We'll have to ask her questions when she wakes up."

"Oh, she'll love that," Thorpe drawled.

"I'm sure. But as painful as she may find the mental jaunt through her past, I think it's important. There's no way she doesn't know something. It may just take the right questions for her to remember it. Once we figure everything out, we'll go from there."

"Don't you think she's tried this a million times?" Thorpe looked up at him as if he was stating the obvious.

Maybe he was.

Sean shrugged. "I'm hoping that more heads are better than one. We can't fail to try just because she hasn't succeeded on her own. I've been studying this case for close to a year. I'll have a better idea of the questions that need to be asked. Maybe that will make a difference."

"Maybe." Thorpe shrugged.

"I didn't say it would be overnight. In fact, I'm betting it won't be. But however long it takes, I'm in this for the duration."

"Because you love her?"

Nodding, Sean held out his hand for the tequila. Without displacing Callie, Thorpe rolled over and plucked up the bottle from the floor, passing it over her supine form.

"Same as you." Sean took a long swallow of the clear liquid from the bottle they shared.

Thorpe didn't comment directly. "I'm not sure if she's ready for either of us to feel that way. She doesn't know how to let herself be loved because she never really has been."

Sean didn't even have to think about that. "As a woman? No."

"I'd love a piece of that Holden pecker who tried to sell her out for cash as a teenager. I'd wring his fucking neck."

"Actually, I'd like to get way more creative," Sean mused. "I'd rip his throat out through his asshole after I've carved out his spine with a screwdriver and gouged out his eyes with a spork."

"Remind me not to piss you off." Thorpe looked both horrified and suitably impressed.

Sean smiled. "As long as Callie comes first, we won't have a problem. She needs that. Based on her file, I think the only person, besides us, who openly loved Callie was her mother."

"She was only six when the woman died." Dismay spread across Thorpe's face.

"Exactly." Sean took another long swig of booze. "She and her sister had more of a mother-daughter relationship. By all accounts, she really loved Charlotte, but when the girl hit twelve, she started rebelling and they'd been having major arguments about her behavior." He paused. "According to the autopsy, Charlotte was nine weeks pregnant when she died."

"At fourteen? I know that happens, but . . ." Shock sent Thorpe's brows into a frown. "Do you think Callie knew?"

"Only she can answer that. Lots of speculation about who fathered Charlotte's baby . . ."

Thorpe's frown became a scowl. "You think it was Callie's prick of a boyfriend?"

"Holden apparently spent a lot of time at their house, and he was obviously an unscrupulous bastard. I'd say anything is possible."

Thorpe ruffled a hand through his mussed hair. "Son of a bitch. If that's the case, it could be another reason she doesn't trust well. Being betrayed by her boyfriend *and* her sister at such a young age would be harsh."

"It wasn't as if she could rely on her father, either. My information says that, after her mother died, he left the girls' care to hired help and began hanging out with people willing to take his money, primarily medical researchers. Seems he became obsessed with discovering the cure for cancer in his late wife's name."

"Oh hell." Thorpe shook his head. "The girls were so young. They had lost a mother. They needed reassurance, guidance, and love. No wonder Callie wanted to run away from home and believed the first guy with a stiff dick who claimed to love her. She learned her lesson the hard way. How the hell is she supposed to recover from that while running for her damn life?"

"I'm not sure she has. I've tried to heal her as much as I could, but as you know, it's a big fucking job." Sean sighed. "She needs constants, people she can count on without fail."

That thought seemed to sober Thorpe even more. "You're right."

"So if you want to head back to Dominion, tell me now. I'll get you to land after sunrise. As long as you keep your mouth shut, I'll understand."

"What? I haven't come this far to bail now. I won't abandon Callie. Axel can manage Dominion without me. Lots of folks there will help. And Sweet Pea might seem like the most submissive creature ever, but she can run that place like a drill instructor when she has to."

Relief flooded Sean's system. They both agreed that Callie had to come first. They might not have a lot in common, but they shared that belief. Now the conversation got tricky . . .

"Good. I've been thinking about this. I need your help with Callie. Sometimes you're the only person who can reach her." Sean sighed and tried to figure out how to say all the other things crowding his head. He should probably have a bit of sleep and a stiff cup of coffee before he even tried, but time wasn't on their side. Once Callie woke, they'd have a fight on their hands. The dust between he and Thorpe had to be settled now.

"I'm here for her, whatever she needs."

"Even if that's both of us?"

Thorpe hesitated. "What do you mean?"

"She'll probably need us both to protect her from whoever is searching for her," Sean began. "I think it's safe to assume that if they killed her family and took a shot at her, they want her dead, too. The more people she has watching her back, the safer she'll be."

"Agreed."

"And you know how secretive she's always been—for good reason. But if we're going to pry her open so she'll tell us about her past, we're going to have to earn her trust. I'll need your steady hand."

Thorpe sat up and peered across the darkness at him. "Meaning?"

"After months of giving her my cover story, her trust in me is shaky at best right now. We can't wait to grow it again before we find out what she knows. We need that info now." Thorpe didn't answer, but Sean could see the man's mind turning. "You know I'm right."

"Yeah." Thorpe swallowed.

"Just like you know where I'm going with this, man. This woman has never had what she needs. As a little girl, she needed a mother, but hers died of cancer. As a teenager, she needed the support of her family, but her father was too distant, while her sister probably stabbed her in the back. She needed to finish growing up in a safe environment . . . and you know how that story goes. Now Callie needs us for more than protection. She needs us to finally make her whole."

"Jesus . . ." Thorpe blew out a breath and raked a hand through his hair.

Sean pressed on. "You said yourself that I lacked the knowledge to properly guide her. But you don't. She trusts you. And she loves you, too."

Thorpe didn't say a word at first, just held out his hand for the bottle. Sean passed it back, watching the other man guzzle down more tequila as he, no doubt, turned over all the possibilities in his head.

"I'd ask if you're fucking serious, but you obviously are." He shook his head of mussed hair. "I don't recommend inviting me inside your picket fence, Mackenzie. I'm not good for her."

That assertion was ridiculous. He and Callie fit together perfectly.

"Right now, I'm just trying to keep her alive," Sean hedged. "If you want to go your separate way once the danger is done, I'll help you find the door."

He had mixed feelings about making that offer. Thorpe walking out on Callie would crush her. But if that happened, he'd just have to find some way to help her deal. Regardless, that was another problem for another day. He had enough to juggle now. He just had to trust that once Thorpe got close to her, he wouldn't be able to walk away.

"But I want you to think about this. The only place where your age difference means a thing is in your head. And your worry about giving her enough tenderness? It's bullshit."

Even if it wasn't, Sean would be happy to supply Callie plenty of affection. After all, if he couldn't give her something, Thorpe might well edge him out of her heart. Or maybe that was his own fear talking because then he closed his eyes and remembered her trembling surrender, her cries that she loved him. He might have started out with Callie as a substitute for the needs Thorpe wasn't fulfilling, but their relationship had progressed into something far deeper than he'd ever imagined when she'd been just a name on a file folder and a picture of a pretty girl.

"Cut to the chase and tell me what you're saying," Thorpe chomped impatiently. "Spell it out. I don't want any gray between us."

"We share her one hundred percent—at least for as long as she's in danger. Everything we do for her, we do together. But you can't half-ass this. You have to give her your all."

Thorpe stilled. "So . . . you want me to discipline her?"

"When she needs it, yes."

A deep breath. A pensive stare. A gulp. "Are you me giving a green light to sex?"

There was the question he'd known would surface sooner or later. How much of Callie was he willing to grant the other man . . .

Now it was Sean's turn to hesitate. Honestly, he didn't know how he was going to feel seeing Thorpe's hands on her, his cock tunneling inside her. He might feel like slashing the Dom's throat. But he also might take comfort in doing the right thing for Callie and watching her bloom. Either way, he had to put her first. If they didn't force pertinent information about the past out of her, she might not live through this ordeal. His jealousy would be awfully moot then.

"Tell me something," Sean finally said. "Would you top another pretty submissive and dismiss the possibility of sex before you've even started the relationship? Would Callie believe you were committed to her if you refused to give yourself in return?"

"Shit." Thorpe took several long drags from the bottle, looking floored. "So that's a yes to sex."

Despite the gravity of the conversation, Sean was almost amused by the man's tension. "Is that a problem?"

"Oh, fuck no. Not at all." Thorpe shot him a dirty glare. "But you knew that."

"Just checking." He grinned.

"She may think she's taken her collar off, but I respect the fact that she's still owned."

And Thorpe sounded like he'd rather spit nails than admit that.

"So what are my limits?" the other man asked.

With a shrug, Sean rolled through the possibilities. "Only one: Everything we do with Callie, we do as a team. No Lone Ranger acts."

Thorpe paused, frowned for a moment, then nodded. "I'm in. We need to make Callie feel safe enough to open up to us. It's important that we establish our control and get whatever information she's got in her head out soon. You're absolutely right about that. It's our only chance of her listening to us if danger follows her here. Beyond that . . . I've been hungry for her for years."

So it was settled. They would share in Callie's care. They would both Dominate her. They would both partake of her. And they would do it all together.

"You ever had a ménage?"

"Sure. Just for fun." Thorpe tapped his thumb against the bottle. "This is different."

Sean was glad he saw the distinction. "Completely. I don't know how complicated it will be. But we'll figure it out."

"For her, we have to."

"Exactly. The sun's coming up." Sean gestured to the graying sky outside the bedroom window as a mixed cocktail of relief and anxiety flowed through his veins. "First, we need some sleep before Hurricane Callie wakes and figures out where she is."

"Sure. Yeah." Thorpe braced himself on the mattress and pushed upright. "Do you want me to get out of your way and let you bunk down with your girl?"

Sean shook his head. Apparently, it was going to take Thorpe more than a few seconds to adjust to the idea of sharing her completely. "We both take care of her. This is our bed now. You need to stay with Callie in case she wakes up. She'll be disoriented at best and furious at worst. Get her under the sheets, make sure she's comfortable. Now that I've got some sunlight and I won't run this boat into the shore, I need to anchor it someplace as secluded as possible." He grabbed his shoes and thrust them on. "Back in ten."

Sean didn't wait for Thorpe to reply before he darted out the bedroom door. He picked up anchor and cruised the lake until he found a wide inlet with tall, craggy rocks on either side. He navigated to the middle, still away from shore, then dropped anchor again. It wouldn't hide them from someone in a helicopter, but anyone else on the lake would be hard-pressed to find them.

Nearly forty minutes had passed. Exhaustion weighed his every limb, and nothing sounded better than tumbling into the bed with Callie and sleeping for long, uninterrupted hours before waking to make love to her.

When he hit the bedroom again, he stopped short in the doorway. Thorpe had fallen asleep on the right side of the bed with Callie spooned against his chest. They both looked peaceful, exhaling together in harmony.

The worry Sean had been trying to restrain jabbed at him. Naturally, he had concerns about letting Thorpe too close to his woman. Would she ultimately choose the other man instead? Or would Callie always need them both? Nearly three sleepless days hadn't equipped him to answer that question now.

With a weary sigh, he shut the drapes, then shed everything except his boxer-briefs. He slid under the sheets, rolling over to kiss Callie's forehead. She moaned quietly, then scooted closer to him as if seeking warmth . . . while Thorpe's arm remained snug around her, his legs tangled in hers, his breath ruffling her long, loose hair. Sean drifted in the peace and slept.

* * *

COCOONED in warmth, Callie woke and squinted against the filtered light making its way through the curtains. The little bit she could see around her didn't look at all familiar. It certainly wasn't Dominion. No, wait. She'd left there and she wouldn't rehash all the reasons that had been necessary. It damn well wasn't her skuzzy dump of a Vegas motel either. And why did the ground seem like it was swaying slightly?

She forced one eye open—and the sights just kept getting weirder. A shirtless Sean slept on one side of her, his hard chest pressed to her own. His powerful torso rose above a soft, faded blanket. He looked damn good for a liar.

Behind her, hot breath spread unexpectedly across her neck. With a little jerk, she stared over her shoulder. Thorpe. Asleep in a rumpled white dress shirt and dark trousers. The five-o'clock shadow darkened his sharp jaw more than usual.

The men she loved surrounded her. It was like a fantasy. It had to be a dream. They hated one another . . . or they had back at Dominion. The time since her departure from the club rushed back to her, her memories lingering on the ride in the silver Jeep last night, on Thorpe smacking her ass and Sean approving every gesture with his stare in the rearview mirror.

Last night, they'd been a team, united by their determination to capture her and bring her back to safety. Or so they claimed. Thorpe, she believed. Sean? She really didn't know him or have any idea how much of what had passed between them was a lie. It had felt so very real. He'd sworn it was. And she had to admit that if he'd simply wanted to bring her in for the bounty or prestige, he probably would have done it in Dallas. He certainly wouldn't be letting Thorpe tag along, either.

But even if he actually loved her, as he claimed, and even if every word Sean and Thorpe said was true, she couldn't stay. Her life was too dangerous, and she wasn't going to drag them into her muck. They had some foolish notion in their heads to be noble, heroic. By all appearances, they cared. Whatever their motives, Callie couldn't let them.

Carefully, she inched to the end of the bed and crept off the mattress, shivering and steadying herself. Crap, it was cold this morning. She reached for the first garment she encountered, Sean's shirt. It even smelled like him. Where were her shoes?

Inhaling his musk as she slipped it on, she glanced at them both, regret nearly bringing her to tears. They'd worked hard to track her down and "rescue" her, not really understanding that the job of saving her was bigger than them both, even with their forces combined. Their effort humbled Callie, and the guilt for leaving them again nearly took her to her knees. But she wouldn't be able to live with herself if she was the reason they found themselves behind bars.

The floor beneath her dipped again, a gentle rocking that confused her. Where the hell had they brought her? Tiptoeing to the window, she eased the dull white drape aside and peeked out. Water—and a lot of it.

Callie sucked in a stunned breath and tried to shove down her panic. *Shit! Okay, keep it together.* If they were on a boat, maybe they were docked. There had to be a way off, right? In her head, though, she heard Sean ask again if she liked to swim . . .

On silent feet, she dashed out of the room, down the little passageway, then found a door leading out to the expansive deck. Water everywhere, at the front of the boat, either side . . . Callie sprinted to the back of the vessel, heart pounding three times for every step she took. But all she found was more water. The nearest land, formidable rock formations that would be a terrifyingly steep climb, looked a hundred feet away—at least.

Her heart pounded so furiously that her blood vessels felt close to bursting. Her entire body flooded with adrenaline. Memories of nearly drowning as a kid and the brackish water filling her mouth, stinging her eyes, and rendering her lungs useless overwhelmed her.

If she wanted off this rocking prison, she would have to swim and climb and haul ass through the desert without shoes, water, or sunscreen. Hell, she was doomed.

Callie couldn't stop herself. She opened her mouth and screamed. And screamed. And screamed.

Suddenly, she felt a hand cup over her lips, trapping in the sound. "Are you trying to bring every police officer and bounty hunter within a hundred-mile radius down on our heads?"

Sean. He growled the words in her ear as he bracketed her back with his solid warmth.

On her right, Thorpe stormed up and turned on her, looking disheveled and pissed off. He grabbed the back of her neck in a firm grip. His gray eyes looked thunderous as he pinned her in place with his stare. "Calm down, pet. Not another sound. You're safe here. We intend to keep you that way."

Surrounded. Trapped. Escape had been the only way she'd survived for nearly as long as she could remember. Now, these two seemed determined to keep her here on this floating hell and ruin their lives in the process.

She twisted away, dislodging Sean's hand from her mouth. "Don't do this! Let me go before you regret it."

"I told you not to make a sound," Thorpe reminded, his voice heavy with disapproval.

Behind her, Sean's disappointment seeped into her, too.

She hated hurting them. The submissive in her especially hated disappointing them. Logically, it didn't make sense, but that didn't make the feeling less real.

"Let's get her inside."

Sean nodded. "Just in case this lake isn't as deserted as we hoped. The last thing we need is a fellow boater hearing her and calling 911. If they come down on our heads and find her, I may not be able to control what happens next."

Without exchanging another word, he wrapped one hand around her back, then bent and slid his other arm behind her knees. He lifted her against his bare chest as if her weight didn't strain him at all. His shoulders bulged and his jaw tightened as he turned and made his way back inside the living quarters. He stared down at her with reproving blue eyes and gave her a slow shake of his head.

She would have squirmed and scrambled out of his arms if she thought it would do any good, but Thorpe walked right behind them. No doubt, he'd haul her back if she tried to run—and provide her some sort of extra "motivation" to stay. And if she did flee, what then? Swimming to shore and walking back to civilization without any protection from the desert sun or a cent to her name just wasn't an option.

"We're not hashing this out again, lovely," Sean said. "We told you last night that you were not to leave again without our permission or there would be consequences. Do you remember that?"

"This isn't about me being disobedient. It's about you two losing everything to try to save me when you can't. No one can. I appreciate you wanting to help, but I wouldn't be able to handle it if you wound up convicts over something futile."

Sean sighed heavily as he lowered her to the bed and looked at Thorpe. "She's not listening."

"She has that nasty habit at times." Thorpe approached her and took her chin in his hand. "Your situation isn't futile. Have some faith in us."

"Thorpe—"

He sent her a sharp stare and held up a finger to silence her. Damn if it didn't work. He'd run hot and cold with her for years. Why the hell did she still respond to him so completely?

"It's not open for discussion. When was the last time you ate?" he asked.

With a frustrated sigh, Callie mentally retraced the previous day. "Breakfast yesterday. Then I had a handful of almonds about three o'clock."

They both looked at her with glaring disapproval before Sean clenched his fists. "Damn it, Callie."

"It just wasn't the most important thing on my mind." Their frowns deepened, and their concern for her made her feel small, as if she'd messed up even more. "Sorry."

"Not yet, but you will be," Thorpe promised before he turned back to Sean. "How are your kitchen skills?"

"Passable. I've been feeding myself since college." He shrugged. "I won't poison her."

"Good. Mine are terrible. It's why God invented takeout." Thorpe smiled wryly.

"I can feed myself, guys. If it will make you feel better, I'll grab something and eat it all like a good little girl if you'll just let me go."

"Not this again." Sean sounded at the end of his rope.

"She doesn't understand . . . yet," Thorpe drawled. "First, she needs food."

"And a shower," Sean added.

"True. God knows how many fucking germs were breeding at Glitter Girls." Thorpe speared her with a glare. "Eventually, we're going to have a long discussion about why you chose that place."

"You mean you intend to punish me again." She rolled her eyes.

"And then sometimes she catches on so quickly . . ." Thorpe smiled Sean's way.

"I've been sure for a while now that she chooses not to 'get it' at least half the time because she's just stubborn." Sean sighed.

Callie balled her hands into fists. "Stop it! You're not my Dom anymore—if you ever truly were. I took off my collar. And before either of you tells me again it doesn't work that way, you both know that BDSM is safe, sane, and consensual. I'm not consenting. And you." She turned to glare at Thorpe. "Yes, you're the big bad Dom or whatever. But damn it, that doesn't give you any right to keep me against my will. You have to let me go!"

They both tensed, then Sean shook his head. Instead of persuading them to release her, she'd hurt him. Pain was carved into his expression. By all appearances, he'd sacrificed everything to help her, and she'd thrown it in his face. Thorpe, too. A glance at her boss didn't show him any less ruffled. He mostly looked pissed off, except his burning eyes . . . Anguish lay there.

Callie dragged in a tight breath, everything inside her feeling as if she'd screwed up again.

"That's not going to happen," Sean vowed softly. "If you still want to leave once you're safe, I'll take you wherever you want to go and leave you with my well wishes."

If he wanted to arrest her, would he really make that offer? He'd have to be the worst kind of con artist . . . and foolish or not, Callie just couldn't believe that about him.

Thorpe stared, his face closed up tight. "Until then, you're staying here with us. We intend to keep you safe and solve this mystery. You can count on that, pet."

Their selflessness—along with a hefty dose of guilt—flogged her all over again.

"Guys, please." Tears prickled her eyes. "I don't want you to do something that will destroy your future."

"We don't want you running for the rest of your life. And I don't want to have this conversation again. Our decision won't change. If we have to keep you against your will . . ." Thorpe shrugged.

"You can't do that forever. You both have lives." She sighed tiredly. "Mine is screwed, but yours don't have to be. I can't prove that I didn't kill my father and sister. The crime is way cold, and no amount of investigating now is going to—"

"The FBI doesn't want to arrest you," Sean cut in.

"What?" She couldn't have heard that right.

"If the bureau took an interest in this case and wanted you behind bars, you'd already be locked up. I was just sent to watch you, look for any clues, nothing more. They wouldn't give me that directive if they believed you'd committed a terrible crime."

The news impacted her like a two-ton bomb, both blowing her away and creating one hell of a crater in her thoughts. "The Chicago police still have an APB out on me."

"They want to question you, but that's not my jurisdiction. I only care about my orders. Uncle Sam hasn't given me any indication that you're regarded as a criminal."

Callie blinked. She wasn't actually wanted for murder? After nine years, she didn't even know how to process that possibility. "Then why the huge bounty on my head? Because of that, I almost bit an assassin's bullet in Birmingham. I literally ran out of Arkansas with a pair of bounty-hunting goons chasing me. I've crossed paths with both sorts over the years and—"

"Both are definitely after you, pet," Thorpe cut in.

"And I think someone powerful is behind the bounty or I wouldn't have been assigned to keep tabs on you."

"Why didn't you tell me any of this?" she asked, crossing her arms over her chest.

"I wasn't at liberty to blow my cover, lovely. I'm still not . . . but I won't lose you."

"We'll have a nice long chat about everything later," Thorpe cut in. "In fact, we're going to talk about many things. For now, believe that you're not going to jail and that you can trust us with your life.

Other than that, we're not saying another word until you've showered and eaten."

"Well put," Sean agreed, slapping Thorpe on the back.

When had they become the Domination Duo, able to command shivering subs with a single glance? Weirdly, they not only seemed able to tolerate one another, they functioned like a team.

"Understood?" Thorpe asked.

Callie gaped at them. She didn't have any illusions that she'd find the conversation pleasant. She knew it would be pointless. After all, she was accustomed to living alone, running and hiding for her life. The guys were tough, but not cut out for that life.

"If you want to help, then let me have a car and fifty bucks. You go home and try to figure out who wants me dead. Once that threat is stopped, then . . ." *What?* She'd just look them up? In another ten years, they'd probably both be married with kids and wives who wouldn't appreciate a Callie blast from the past. "Then I'll be safe."

Sean and Thorpe exchanged a glance. "I appreciate your independence, lovely—to a point. But not when it comes to danger. Until now, you've done well keeping yourself safe, but you won't be doing it alone anymore."

"That's final. Don't ever run from us again," Thorpe added.

Like she could keep that promise. "A-all right."

"All right, *Sir*? Isn't that what you meant?" Thorpe raised a demanding brow. "Not only did your response lack conviction, it was also short on respect. Unacceptable, pet."

Callie cast her gaze down. A thousand thoughts thundered through her head. They'd spent time and money, encountered violence and put themselves on the line to help her. Yes, it was for nothing. They were being stubborn, bossy, foolish, and pig-headed. And she wanted to throttle them. But she also hadn't thanked them for all they'd tried to do for her, much less shown respect.

Both flustered and humbled, she looked from Thorpe's forbidding countenance to Sean's questioning stare. Easier to start where she could see a little softness. Then she'd figure out how to proceed from there.

She rose to her knees on the mattress and scooted closer, lifting her arms to Sean. "Thank you. I've put you through a lot. I know what you've risked. I wish you hadn't."

He crushed her against him. "I told you why, Callie. I love you."

So easy-breezy for him to just put it out there. She'd never had the luxury of saying those words openly to anyone. They implied the promise of tomorrows she'd never had.

Callie could only hope that somehow her life wasn't doomed to end badly. Even if it was, she had his affection and devotion right now. How many years had she spent utterly alone and aching for someone to give a shit about her? Too many to count.

Was she really going to throw it away? Couldn't she have them for a day or two? Couldn't she give Sean the love filling her heart in return? Thorpe the obedience and devotion he deserved?

"I fell for you at Dominion." She cupped Sean's cheek and met the sincerity of his blue stare, so open. His dashing little smile creased the corners of his eyes and lifted her heart. "I love you, too."

Sean caressed a broad hand down her tangled hair, deepening the connection of their stares. Inside, she could *feel* him, his caring, his understanding. She'd been lucky when the FBI assigned him to watch over her and had a feeling that he always would if she let him.

Now for the hard part. Callie only hoped that Sean would understand that her feelings for Thorpe didn't mean that she cared for him less.

She drew in a shaky breath and turned to Thorpe, already searching for the words to tell him how grateful she was for all he'd done and somehow confess everything he meant to her. Before she could unscramble her thoughts, Thorpe zipped around and strode out the door, shutting it with careful quiet behind him.

Chapter Thirteen

Callie's heart dropped in a sickening fall. Guilt flayed her again. Damn it, she hadn't meant to hurt Thorpe's feelings.

"I need to . . ." *What?* Apologize to Sean for also being in love with Thorpe? Say she was sorry for moving beyond carrying an unrequited torch for her protector? Sean didn't want to hear her pour out her feelings for Thorpe any more than her former boss wanted to hear her wax poetic about the fed she'd once called her Dom. Could this get any more complicated? "I didn't mean to make him uncomfortable."

"You didn't. Thorpe is just beating himself up. He wants to tell you that he loves you, too. But he's afraid."

Those words stunned her. Presumably, Sean had spoken in English, but it might as well have been Greek. How would he know anything about Thorpe's feelings? Why would he care? And how did he have it so wrong?

"No." Callie stepped back, shaking her head. "Thorpe doesn't love me like that."

"He does, exactly as I do. Like a man loves a woman. He's got a hang-up or two, I gather, but he loves you. Just like you love him."

With a little gasp, she blinked up at him, struggling to find

words beyond her shock. He'd figured that out and he wasn't furious? "Oh, Sean. I'm so sorry if I've hurt you. I don't know what to
say. I—"

"You can't apologize for your heart." He kissed her forehead.
"I've known that you love us both for a while. So has he. Would I
enjoy having you to myself? Of course. But I've asked myself long
and hard what *you* need. Thorpe gives you something I can't."

She clung to him, grabbing his arms. "But you give me things he
doesn't. I don't want to lose—"

"I know, lovely. You won't. What sort of man would I be if I
put my own anxiety and jealousy above your fulfillment?"

Callie stared up at him in wonder, blinking through a sheen of
tears. "You amaze me."

He gave her a sad smile. "The world hasn't shown you a lot of
kindness, so you don't expect it in others. You've had so much taken
from you. If I have to bend my pride to be the one to finally make
you whole, I'll be fine."

A sudden thump sounded just outside their insulated little galley, and they both turned to see Thorpe shaking his hand . . . like
he'd just punched the wall and hurt his knuckles.

Her heart ached for him, but he'd walled himself off from her.
He'd always been an island, never quite letting others close. She
couldn't help him if he wouldn't let her behind his defenses.

"I think he's been worried that you'll leave him, Callie. You
wouldn't be the first woman to do it. And he seems to believe that
he's a bit too old and rough around the edges for you. He just needs
a little reassurance. You'll have to give it to him."

Callie blinked up at Sean, who smiled softly. Was he for real?

"You won't feel betrayed?"

"What good would it do me?" He shrugged. "Having two of us
to protect you makes sense. If I force you to choose between us, not
only could I lose you altogether, but I think you'd only be halfway

happy. I never thought it possible for someone to love two people at once, but when I see you with us, I know you sincerely do. Not sure yet how everything will work in the 'real' world, but let's get you past this danger and we'll see."

Her heart nearly burst open. Callie hadn't thought she could love Sean even more. But she'd been wrong. She tightened her arms around him. "How do you understand me so well?"

He chuckled and cupped her cheek. "I've been studying you for a year now. You've been my life. And maybe my obsession a wee bit. From the start, I wanted to be jealous of your connection with Thorpe, and maybe I should be. But I've seen how, when he and I work together, we balance one another to make your world right. I think that will make us both happier in turn."

Callie teared up again. "I don't know how to thank you for being so wonderful and—"

"You can start with a shower." Sean grimaced. "Get that God-awful inch of makeup off your face. Have Thorpe help you. Tell him to be sure you get nice and clean. Then . . . we'll see what happens. Just don't take no for an answer." With a wink, he turned her, smacked her ass, and sent her in the other man's direction. "Go."

* * *

THORPE couldn't stop the jealousy rolling through him like an ugly black cloud. It wasn't because she loved Sean. He'd known that. And he could actually admit that the fed was not only a decent guy, but good for *her*.

What made him resentful as hell was that he couldn't be that open with her about his feelings. Not once in three years of marriage had he been able to tell Melissa that he loved her. It wasn't like he didn't know why.

He sighed. A tenderhearted girl like Callie would need that reassurance. He didn't have it in him. Sean had given him the green light to fuck her, so Thorpe would damn well take advantage of that golden opportunity whenever possible. But it couldn't lead anywhere.

All too soon, he'd be forty, and she'd barely be through her mid-twenties. Sean suited her better from an age perspective. Callie looked happy with the other man. Because she meant everything to him, Thorpe refused to burden her with his bottled-up heart. When they untangled her from the mess that had ripped her world apart for years, he would quietly support Sean and fade into the background.

But he'd never stop loving her.

When Callie approached him on deck, the wind whipping her dark hair around her shoulders, he closed his eyes. Looking at her and knowing that he'd already lost her was killing him.

"Mitchell?" She touched a hand to his arm.

No one ever called him that . . . except her, except when her mood was soft. The sound of his name on her lips was like a siren song. Her sweet caress clutched his heart and sent desire sizzling up his arm, streaking under his skin.

"What?" he barked more than he meant to.

Callie opened her mouth, then snapped it shut. "Thank you for helping me. I wish for your sake that you hadn't, but it means the world that you'd risk so much for me. Now I'll make you happy and leave you alone."

Like hell. He grabbed her wrist before she could get away. "Where are you going?"

"Well, since Bora Bora is out of the question right now, Sean wants me to take a shower. He had some strange notion that you needed to supervise me and make sure I got squeaky clean, but I've been bathing myself for a long time. You don't have to bother. I'll manage."

Callie tugged free and turned away. She hadn't spared any words of love or affection for him. No surprise. He hadn't done anything to engender them. Still, as Callie eased through the door and into the galley again, it fucking hurt to watch her walk away. He should protect her and strictly limit their interaction to punishment and sex. It wouldn't be easy, but better for her. Less terrible when she paired off with Sean for good and shattered his heart.

But right now, her attitude needed to come down about ten notches. Sean had kept him around for a reason. Might as well start earning his privileges.

Inside the galley, Callie and Sean exchanged a few words. She gesticulated in agitation. The fed raised a brow, then stared at him out the window. A moment later, the girl rolled her eyes and stomped down the narrow passage toward the bedroom.

Insolent little brat. Thorpe stooped through the door and marched after her.

"I've got her," he assured Sean. "She'll fucking shine by the time she steps out of the shower."

"Good. We still owe her a lot of punishment, along with a thorough interrogation . . . which will probably lead to more punishment. I don't want any trace of Glitter Girls on her or it will just piss me off more."

Since he could still picture her onstage, wearing next to nothing and wiggling her ass in the face of a guy who looked like the poster boy for pimpdom, Thorpe couldn't disagree. "Same here."

"Good. While you take care of that, I'll finish cooking. Then . . . it's on."

Absofuckinglutely.

Thorpe strode down the hall, into the first bedroom and its adjoining bath. He found Callie staring in the mirror in the tiny bathroom, peeling off false eyelashes.

"You didn't wait for me to bring you to the shower."

She turned to him and raised her chin. "I know where it is. And your 'fuck off' demeanor didn't exactly invite company."

"You've got thirty seconds alone to empty your bladder before your shower. After that, I'm coming in."

Callie rolled her eyes. "Why? I won't run again. Where would I go?"

Maybe not, but after her Houdini-like escape from Dominion, followed by his nearly three sleepless days of frantic searching for her, Thorpe wasn't inclined to let her out of his sight. Besides, Sean had given him this duty, and he wasn't giving up the chance to look at her naked. "Good to hear. I'm not budging."

"I can shower alone."

"But you're not going to." He glanced at his watch. "Go. Clock's ticking."

"Ugh . . ." She sighed and closed the door in his face. Near the thirty-second mark, he heard the toilet flush and she yanked the little door open. "Happy?"

"Do I seem thrilled, pet? In the past few days, I've had almost no sleep or food, and I'm running thin on patience, too. Don't test me."

And his bad mood was exacerbated by how ratcheted up he felt. He'd gone to sleep thinking about the moment he could finally slide his bare skin over hers before plunging his cock into her tempting pink pussy and at least pretend that she belonged to him. He'd awakened thinking exactly the same thing. Unless he wanted to torture the fuck out of himself, he'd better quit that line of thinking.

Dismissing that from his mind only left him with the nagging worry about the danger lurking around every unseen corner. It all gnawed at his composure.

"Sorry," she murmured, casting her gaze to her toes. "Sir."

"Shower," he barked.

Callie hesitated. "One question."

He crossed his arms over his chest. The last damn thing he wanted was a dialogue. Dangerous ground. But he must have a secret masochistic streak. In his book, some contact with Callie was better than none.

"What?"

"Sean has made it very clear why he's gone out on a limb to help me. But you've done so much for me for years. You've said that you want me, but . . ."

"Fishing to find out how I feel? After running away from me without a word?" After she'd told Sean that she loved him while he had to listen? "We've always been friends—"

"You said last night that we were more."

A tactical error on his part. His blood had been rushing at the thought of having her in his grasp again, sprawled across his lap for his discipline. Why hadn't he kept his damn mouth shut?

"Leave it alone, Callie. Shower before Sean finishes your breakfast and it gets cold."

"I love you," she choked, her stare all but imploring. "That's hard for me to say."

His heart stopped. Joy, hope, love all flooded in—until reality crashed back. He would never be the tender lover she needed and deserved. And Callie was young. She might think that she loved him now, but in a dozen years? He'd be able to join AARP, and she'd still be able to bear children. They would never work. And that was just one of their problems. Someday, she'd realize he wasn't a good fit for her and leave. If he didn't stunt things between them now, it would hurt far worse later.

"You've had plenty of practice with Sean," he shot back.

Her chin trembled as she raised it and crossed her arms over her chest. "Why do you always make me feel like some urchin tugging after you for your affection?"

"You have a Dom, Callie. What I feel doesn't matter."

"Isn't that convenient for you? That way, you don't have to admit that I mean something to you beyond a friend. But you wouldn't go this far out on a limb for me unless I meant more, despite what you've claimed in the past. Every time you've kissed me, it wasn't like a platonic pal. And that certainly wasn't how it felt when you spanked me or put your tongue on my—"

"What do you want from me?" he growled.

"The truth."

He pressed his lips in a grim line as he struggled to restrain the urge to grab her and snarl out his love while he filled her cunt full of every hard inch he ached to give her. "This is not open for discussion. Shower. Now."

"You always avoid me. Oh, discipline me, of course, but don't talk about your feelings. They're scary," she mocked.

"Callie," he growled, hating how right she was.

She shrugged him off. Sean's shirt, swimming on her petite form and hanging to her knees, slipped off one shoulder. The long sleeves nearly swallowed her hands. Though she'd rolled back the cuffs, the garment was still huge. But as she eased the buttons from their moorings, Callie peeled the cotton open bit by bit, exposing fair, rosy skin. Finally, she shook it off. The white fabric cascaded down her arms and fell to the floor. She stood before him in a nearly transparent bra and a tiny thong.

Thorpe swallowed. Jesus, Callie killed his self-control. She tested him, pushed him. Did her best to lure him in. Didn't the girl see that Sean would give her all the tenderness she needed, all the gentle affection he couldn't?

Her little pink tongue peeked out, wetting her lower lip. His cock jerked. With a challenging stare from beneath her dark lashes, still coated with way too much mascara, she turned to start the shower. Soon, steam filled the little bathroom.

With her back to him, Callie reached behind her to unclasp her lacy, ridiculously sexy bra. It dropped to the floor, and she wriggled out of the thong with an extra sway to her hips. Thorpe's stare caressed the dark hair that fell in a sleek veil over her fair shoulders, then ended to reveal the exaggerated nip of her waist and flared to the lush curve of her hip. He began to sweat. Her smooth, firm ass—still with a hint of pink from his hand last night—made his cock unbearably hard. He sucked in a harsh breath.

Callie turned her head, lashes fluttering up. She sent him a hurt stare. So sexy. So tempting him. So fucking wrong because unless Sean was beside him, taking Callie with him, he couldn't touch her.

"Go on. There's only so much water on this boat. I want some, too." And he thanked fuck that the stall was barely big enough for one. If it had been roomier and she invited him in . . . Yeah, that would only end with his cock buried in some orifice that he had no right to even be contemplating without Sean's presence.

Callie stepped in behind the clear Plexiglas and groaned as the hot water cascaded over her soft skin. He watched as she tipped her head back, sluiced water down her throat, her breasts, over her flat abdomen, her thighs. Damn, he needed a distraction.

"Soap?" she murmured.

Right. The toiletries Sean had bought earlier. He'd set the bag somewhere . . . In the bedroom, on the floor, he found the plastic sack and carted it into her. He fished out a scented bar, along with a citrus-scented shampoo and conditioner. Sean had even bought a couple of packs of disposable razors and a few cans of shaving cream.

He started handing items to Callie. She opened the door and took them in silence, then bathed without a word, quickly scrubbing all the makeup from her face and the Glitter Girls grime from her body. She washed her hair, shaved, then basked in the hot water for a minute more. And Thorpe couldn't take his eyes off her. Something about the girl—no, everything about her—was sexy as hell, and fantasies of spreading her across his bed, restraining her, then indulging in every last pleasure he could think of fried his brain.

The flavor of her slick folds still lingered in his memory, haunting him. Thorpe had discovered in Vegas that when he wanted to make himself unbearably hard and so horny that jacking off eased none of his restless edge, he thought of that. And he thought of how she'd looked as she came for him.

Suddenly, she groaned, and he yanked his thoughts from his daydream. Thorpe peered closer, visually penetrating the steam to find that she had her hand between her legs, slowly rubbing her clit. Even through the fogged-up shower door, he could see her skin flushing, her nipples peaking. Her breasts rose, then her shoulders fell. She leaned against the white fiberglass of the stall and spread her legs wider with another little moan.

He nearly fucking lost it.

"Callie, you don't have permission for that."

Her sultry eyes fluttered open again, not quite focused. "Why do you care?"

Goddamn it, she was goading him. He couldn't fuck or discipline Callie when he was alone with her. Yes, he had once been willing to cross Sean when he'd thought the fed was a dangerous player. Now? He scrubbed a hand down his face, sweating. But he couldn't stab Sean in the back. They had an agreement, and he'd live up to his part.

"Neither of us said you could self-pleasure."

"Sean didn't tell me I couldn't. And according to you, we're back to being just friends. I don't ask my pals for permission to masturbate." She sent him a sly smile. "Oh, I also don't shower in front of my buddies, but here you are."

Fucking son of a bitch. She was right—not about masturbating. That was something every sub understood was a no-no without their Dom's permission. But he couldn't claim to be just her friend, then oversee her shower with sick, voyeuristic glee. Or make love to her later, even with Sean, and claim that it didn't mean a thing.

Her soft moans lengthened, deepened. Thorpe couldn't take his eyes off her as she dragged her fingers over her clit in slow, sensual circles. Water poured down her skin. Her breathing roughened. Her nipples beaded even harder. Hell, he was going to lose his ever-loving mind. If he had the right, he'd give Callie the paddling of her life. Then the fucking to match.

Since he couldn't, Thorpe absolutely refused to endure this torment a minute more.

He yanked open the clear, rigid door between them, grabbed her wrist, and hauled her out. Her drenched form brushed his chest, instantly soaking his clothes and skin. As he dragged her near, he couldn't miss her dilated blue eyes flaring. Or her rosy cheeks. Her lips were so fucking tempting, parted and red and too damn close to his own.

Swallowing down his lust, he grabbed her shoulders and shoved her against the wall. "You're done teasing me like this."

"What? I'm just relieving tension. It's been a crappy couple of days." She arched her hips toward his aching cock. "Don't mind me, *friend*."

Her swollen, saturated cunt brushed against his dick. A half-groan, half-growl tore from his throat.

When the hell had he ever wanted a woman even half this much?

Thorpe knew the answer. It wasn't comforting.

"You've been incredibly naughty. Topping from the bottom. Self-pleasuring without permission. Lying to me."

"Like you lied to me about merely being friends?" she challenged, brow raised. "What are you going to do about it?"

Damn it, Callie was asking for it. Begging. He slammed the bathroom door, enclosing them together in the tiny space. The move was risky, but the only way he could open the cabinet doors. Finally, he reached inside and fished out a bath towel, then wrapped it around her, covering some of her delectable nakedness. Not enough, obviously, because he still wanted to fuck her into next week, but this was the best he could do now.

Focusing on her freshly scrubbed face, he knotted the white terry cloth just above her breasts, then yanked on it. "Let's go."

She dug in her heels. "What are you doing?"

"Making sure you get discipline."

Thorpe lifted her and dragged her against his chest. Because Callie was Callie, she resisted him with everything she had, fighting like a hellcat. Against him, she smelled clean and womanly, and as he passed by the bed, he gnashed his teeth to keep from throwing her on the softly rumpled sheets and taking her in every way he knew how.

Instead, he dragged her toward the galley, fighting off her claws and kicks to the shin.

He squeezed her tight against his body. "You have a Dom who loves you and you're taunting me to take something I shouldn't."

"It's not like that. Stop manhandling me." She gritted her teeth and squirmed for freedom, succeeding mostly in mashing her breasts to his chest.

Thorpe dug his fingers into her hair and tugged, stilling her. She was going to get the spanking she deserved. Maybe, if the gods looked down on him, Sean would let him dish it out. And if he was more sexually frustrated than indignant on the other man's behalf, well . . . Callie didn't need to know that.

Once they reached the galley, Thorpe tossed her into the room, trapping her between his body and the small faux wood table attached to the wall. In front of the utilitarian stove, Sean looked up with a spatula in his hand, now wearing trousers, and staring at them with a questioning expression.

"Callie needs discipline," Thorpe spit out.

"Does she?"

He shoved down his frustration that he had to explain himself. Couldn't they just get to the part where Sean tugged the towel off of Callie's naked body and smacked her lush, damp ass with his hand so he could see her breasts sway and her face flush, watch the shock of the sting become unbearable arousal and . . .

Thorpe swallowed hard. "She tried to give herself an orgasm in the shower."

Sean slanted his gaze to Callie, then back again. "Oh?"

"Yes, knowing full well that I watched her." He closed in on her, trying not to notice how soft her damp body was or how well she fit against him.

He hoped to hell that he and Sean would fuck Callie soon. Maybe once would be enough to satisfy this clawing hunger bleeding his self-control dry. Maybe . . . but highly doubtful.

To his surprise, Sean merely looked down at whatever was in the pan in front of him and began working with his spatula.

"Don't you get it?" Thorpe questioned indignantly. "Subs are not supposed to touch themselves without explicit permission."

"I'm aware," Sean said calmly, flipping over some egg concoction, not seeming at all ruffled.

"Callie was topping from the bottom, doing her damn best to entice me when she was supposed to be getting clean."

"Hmm . . ." Sean mused, salting the omelet.

How could the fed not be pissed off at that? He'd never struck Thorpe as stupid, but suddenly he was rethinking Sean's IQ.

Thorpe tossed his hands in the air. "She kept stroking herself even after I told her to stop. She completely disregarded me."

Sean smiled faintly. "Minx."

"And? We've got to be firm with her. She needs it or she'll run all over us." Thorpe felt ready to burst a blood vessel.

Sean reached for the pepper and shook some on top of the eggs. Thorpe had to restrain the urge to throw the pan against the fucking wall. How could Sean be so damn calm? If he wasn't going to act, this co-topping crap was never going to work.

"Lovely?" Sean turned her way.

"Yes?" She sounded oddly quiet. In fact, it struck Thorpe as unusual that she hadn't said a word since he'd dragged her into the galley.

"According to Thorpe, you need discipline quite badly."

She bit into her plump lower lip, and Thorpe had to look away. Water dripped from her hair, down her pale, graceful shoulders, disappearing into the cleavage visible above her towel, now slowly unknotting and inching down her breasts.

"Yes, Sir," she murmured.

Sean turned to look at him. "I can't leave these eggs or they'll burn. Thorpe, we've had this discussion. You're more than equipped to give her whatever she needs while I finish up here. Then we'll eat."

Sean turned away, staring back into the pan. Callie blinked, then turned to look at him.

A thousand volts of electricity shot straight to Thorpe's cock. He clenched his fists. "You want me to spank her again?"

"Whatever you think is proper punishment for her behavior. Once you're done, I think you should give her that orgasm she sought. She probably needs the release, and I always like to see Callie in pleasure."

Thorpe nearly choked on a thick lump of lust. Hadn't the son of a bitch seen his erection through his trousers? He must have; it felt the size of Texas. Damn it, if he ripped that towel off Callie and put his hands anywhere on her, much less made her come, Thorpe wasn't sure he could stop.

Where the hell was his self-control? His stare roved all over Callie, her damp skin, her dark tresses clinging, breasts half visible, and those blue eyes of hers wide and crushing his ability to think of anything except having her naked under him, clawing at his back, and begging for more.

"I can definitely do that, but let me be plain," Thorpe said between gritted teeth, feeling way north of insane. "I want to fuck her."

He didn't dare meet Callie's stare or he wouldn't be responsible for what happened next.

"You made that clear last night." Sean reached to open the microwave and insert a paper plate filled with bacon. "If you punish her now, we'll deal with the rest later."

Then Sean winked at the girl.

What the hell kind of Twilight Zone shit had this morning become? Whatever. It didn't matter. Sean had agreed that her behavior needed correcting, so he'd fucking take care of it.

Thorpe sent Callie a hard grin that she would find impossible to interpret as comforting. "Fine. I'm all over this."

"Glad to hear it. Breakfast should be ready in five." Sean set a few pieces of bread into the toaster.

But Thorpe wasn't listening anymore. He had a few precious minutes to put his hands all over Callie. He didn't intend to waste even a second.

"Drop the towel. Every hesitation, bratty remark, or lapse in your manners is only going to make my discipline more unpleasant. Are we clear?"

"Yes, Sir." Her eyes went soft and wide as her fingers loosened the towel.

The terry cloth unraveled from her body, slithering to the ground. And there Callie stood before him, her petite form shaking and blessedly bare. Need seized his insides. She belonged under his hands, his body, his command. He'd fought it for years. But as her gaze clung to him now, silently pleading for both his hard boundaries and his mercy, he couldn't deny how badly he wanted the right to touch the girl.

"On your knees, pet." He'd dreamed of saying those words to her forever.

Slowly, gracefully, she knelt before him, her stare unwavering. Without a word, she pleaded. Her desire and anticipation were a punch to his gut.

Thorpe never took his eyes off her as he yanked a small chair from the little table and sat in it, leaning forward with elbows on his knees to drill her with a hard stare. He steadied himself with a deep breath, finding his balance and center. Knowing he had so few boundaries right now with Callie was immersing him in the most heady Dom space. One wicked idea after another raced through his head.

"Good. What I say will be absolute, Callie. No arguments. No

questions. No comebacks. This isn't a demo, and I'm no longer playing. Do you understand?"

"Yes, Sir." Her voice sounded so breathy and acquiescent. Need
seared itself on her face. This passionate Callie was the one he
knew—and loved. The one he burned for.

He sat back in his chair and patted his thigh. "Sit on my lap."

She rose. It wasn't quick. Nor was it so slow that he could call it
a hesitation, but close. Her lips parted and questions nearly tumbled
forth. Callie stifled them. Instead of asking whatever she wanted to
know, she merely perched her pretty bare ass on his thigh gingerly,
then looked to him for reassurance.

"Yes, like that." He swallowed back the command to kiss him, to
tug down his zipper, to stroke his straining erection before she eased
him into the blistering silk of her pussy. But all of that would be what
he wanted—not what he'd been granted. Not what *she* needed. "Now
turn to face Sean and put your legs on either side of my knees."

Callie responded more quickly this time, rotating on his lap,
then settling her back against his chest. Thorpe hissed in her ear as
she rested her bare skin against his thin, damp shirt. He gripped her
hips, barely restraining the urge to shove his cock against the ripe
curves of her ass.

He widened the stance of his thighs, parting her legs at the same
time. Sean looked up from the eggs, watching raptly. His face told
Thorpe that he didn't really give a shit if the eggs burned.

Settling his lips against her ear, he whispered, "Tilt your head
back on my shoulder."

Callie shivered, but she obeyed without pause. Her shaky little
exhalation left him no doubt that his domination aroused her. Unable to resist anymore, he ground his dick into her pert backside,
then caressed his way up her waist, her ribs, until he palmed her
breasts and trapped her nipples between his thumb and forefinger,
turning and tugging.

"You touched yourself to torment me. Didn't you, Callie?"

"Yes, Sir." Her breathy reply made his gut and his need tighten.

"Why, to taunt me with what I shouldn't take or to seduce me?"

He felt her draw in a deep breath, then undulate on his lap, sending hot sensation skittering through him again. He tightened his grip on her nipples, and she gasped.

"Lovely?" Sean prodded.

"Both," she admitted with a little cry. "I hated the thought that you wouldn't show me whether you want me or not."

"So you tried to corner me. Very naughty." One hand left the soft curve of her breast.

"But—"

"Not a word." His voice reverberated through the little room. "Running away, stripping in public, staying in hellholes, fighting me, frustrating me . . . You've done nothing to earn an orgasm."

"Good point," Sean conceded. "Scratch that off the list."

She moaned in protest.

"You've earned this, pet." Thorpe spanked the pad of her pussy with his fingers in a stinging blow that awakened and inflamed.

Callie gasped, arched, thrusting one breast deeper into his grasp. He gritted his teeth. She responded to him even more beautifully than he remembered, way beyond his wildest dreams. Despite her craving for tenderness, she seemed completely capable of taking the edgy side of his nature—and still asking for more. At the thought, what little blood remained in his body rushed to his cock until he felt staggered and dizzy.

Again, he lightly smacked her pussy enough to sting sweetly. And again. Each time, her folds plumped and slickened a bit more. He couldn't miss the way her clit swelled and hardened. So he kept on.

"Please, Thorpe . . ." she panted.

"That's Sir to you right now. And I promise, you're going to beg, little girl. For my mercy and for the pleasure I can grant you . . . if I choose. Eventually."

She shuddered, and Thorpe tried to hold it together, fighting the urge to bend her over the little table and work his way into her tight cunt until she'd taken every throbbing inch he had.

"Yes, Sir," she moaned.

"Better." He settled his palm over her swollen folds, gratified to feel her slickness coating the slide of his fingers onto her clit. Gently, he circled her sensitive nub. It hardened to stone. Then he slowed his caress, plying with a swirling, stroking, downright leisurely brush of his fingers. Her breathing grew more labored.

"You've played with me for the last time, pet. First, you left me without so much as saying good-bye, despite the years I spent sheltering you. Then I found you stripping, of all things, in a place not even clean enough to house rats. I chased you down a fucking alley and told you never to run from me again. What did you do the minute you woke up this morning?" When she hesitated, he barked, "Answer me, Callie."

"I ran, Sir."

"Yes. You're in a shitload of trouble, little girl."

Callie grabbed his thigh, whimpering as he curled a pair of fingers into the snug depths of her cunt. "I'm sorry."

"I didn't give you permission to speak. I'm not done listing all the reasons I'm displeased with your behavior so you'll understand exactly why I'm going to make this punishment difficult. Don't interrupt me again."

She writhed and trembled in his arms. "I won't, Sir."

"Then you teased me while you showered, driving me to the brink of sanity. If you'd had any idea just how exasperated I've been—worried out of my mind and chasing you all over the damn place, wanting you so fucking much and knowing you were just out of my grasp . . . I've reached my limit, Callie. No more."

He plunged his fingers deep inside her, rooting around until he found the bit of smooth, sensitive tissue high on the front wall of her passage. He rubbed in mercilessly unhurried circles.

Toast popped up. Sean plated food. Thorpe gritted his teeth. He wasn't ready to let Callie go. She hadn't been punished enough for all her transgressions . . . and he couldn't bring himself to stop touching her.

"Breakfast," Sean said as he set her plate on the table.

"Did you happen to buy clothes pins or chip clips when you went shopping?" Thorpe snapped.

"No, but I found some while prowling around in the drawers here," Sean said.

"Perfect. I need two."

Sean turned and rummaged in a drawer as Thorpe shoved Callie's hair from her neck. As he continued to drag his fingers ruthlessly over her most sensitive spots, he swept his lips up her neck, then nipped at her lobe. On his lap, she gyrated restlessly. Moisture gushed all over his fingers. Her breathing ramped up. She had to be getting close. Now it would get fun . . .

After a slam of the drawer, Sean turned back. His stare fell on them, his blue eyes turning dark with arousal. "She looks beautiful."

"She feels like the most exquisite hell," Thorpe groaned.

"Callie always does." With a little smile, Sean held up the clothes pins. "Where do you want these?"

Chapter Fourteen

"On her nipples," Thorpe instructed Sean. "Suck the buds first. Get them good and hard. Make her feel every pull of your mouth all the way down to her clit."

Callie thought she might explode. Thorpe was doing everything in his power to drive her beyond her ability to endure his sensual torture, and now Sean was pitching in to help out. Having both of their hands on her, their bodies crushed to hers, had been a fantasy nearly beyond her wildest imagining for weeks.

A big smile stretched across Sean's face. "I like the way you think . . ."

"I've got a ton more ideas," Thorpe assured.

She'd just bet.

Callie panted now, every breath a labored cry as he worked her pussy, fondled her clit, and breathed across her neck. He made her suffer, ache. She wanted to cry out, but held in the need. In every way possible, Thorpe was reminding her that he was not only a Dominant, but a Master—the sort of man who would crawl into her head, read her every need, dangle it in front of her until she knelt and pleaded and submitted, then he'd turn her inside out as he fulfilled every dark fantasy.

Drawing up the other kitchen chair and dropping into it, Sean looked completely on board with that plan.

"Excellent," he murmured as he leaned forward, closer. "Give me your breasts, lovely. Arch to me."

With a whimper, she did. She couldn't help it. Sean grabbed her sides, pulling her closer. He didn't pounce on her aching nipples right away, though she wished he had. Instead, he hovered over her, palmed back the damp hair that had worked onto her face and plastered to her breasts, then fastened his hand around her nape. He plowed his way past her lips, seizing, taking, wildly devouring her mouth. She melted, gasping into his kiss as Thorpe's fingers plied her clit with ruthless efficiency. He backed off again when she held her breath. Perspiration sheened her skin, and she keened out with unfulfilled need.

Sean lifted his head, and he gave her a lopsided smile of triumph. For good measure, he fondled her breasts, pinching her nipples. "Not so eager to run now, are you, lovely?"

Wasn't it obvious? She couldn't move now if she wanted to, not when satisfaction was so close and they held the key to her pleasure. To her heart.

"Answer him," Thorpe barked in her ear, then grazed his teeth over her sensitive shoulder.

Callie shuddered. She thought she'd experienced pleasure before, but this . . . Poems and songs were written about the sort of ecstasy they suspended just out of her grasp. Wars were fought. Kingdoms fell. She had no idea how to do anything but plead and beg for them to put her out of her misery.

"No, Sir. Please. Please . . ."

Sean chuckled but didn't answer her directly. Instead he bent to one of her breasts and took her nipple in his mouth. His suction pulled on the sensitive crest, then zipped a line of fire all the way down to her pussy. *Oh, gawd.* She only thought she'd been on the knife's edge of need before. Now?

Unable to help herself, she filtered her hands through his hair and tugged him closer, wishing desperately that she could make him suck more. Or less. Or whatever would ease this relentless need driving her to madness.

Instead, Sean backed away and inspected his work. His smile tightened, and he lifted one of the clothes pins to her. Callie's eyes widened, and a protest sat on the edge of her tongue. The little wooden implement would act like a nipple clamp. She had so little experience, despite living and working at Dominion. She'd never been clamped in any way. No doubt, it would sting at least a little or they wouldn't bother.

"Please . . ." she begged.

Thorpe stiffened, his voice a dark growl in her ear. "Take your punishment, Callie. You've given us no choice for days. Now it's your turn."

"Exactly," Sean agreed as he cupped her breast and applied the first clothes pin.

It pressed down on her nipple. Not pain exactly, but a constant, somehow tugging pressure that jolted straight to her clit. Callie gasped.

With rough fingers, Thorpe pinched her other nipple. The second he released it, Sean sucked it into the burning oven of his mouth and pulled. She dug her fingers into Thorpe's thighs, trying to take in all the sensations at once. The arousal climbed yet again to something dizzying she'd never imagined possible. Callie groaned, mewled. Neither man heeded the sounds. They seemed intent and eager to keep pushing her. Thorpe set his greedy fingers back over her clit, his circles on her flesh even more torturously slow. Gawd, she couldn't take much more.

"Sean . . . Thorpe," she panted. "I—"

"Burn and ache?" Thorpe breathed into her ear. "Oh, I know. The way I've burned and ached for you for fucking years. I want you to know what it was like every hour of every day I had to be near you, trying to figure out how not to go insane because I couldn't have more."

Sean cut off any possibility of her reply by applying the second clothes pin to her other nipple.

The pressure times two did more than multiply the pleasure. Somehow, it turned exponential. Her blood flowed like lava. Her pussy throbbed with the pent-up need for release. Her already sensitive nipples ached even more as Sean toyed with the clothes pins, making them gently tug on the hard tips of her breasts, twist and tighten, before he rubbed his fingertip over the top of each.

Callie dug her nails even deeper into Thorpe's thighs, writhing and arching.

"Breakfast time, pet. Sean is going to feed you. You're going to eat every bite . . . no matter what we do to you. And no coming," Thorpe said sternly. "Is that understood?"

Was he out of his mind? Her gaze bounced up to Sean, pleading for respite, mercy—anything. Gently, he shook his head.

"You'll do as he says, lovely." Sean picked up the plate of still steaming eggs. "Open wide."

Automatically, Callie parted her lips. He slid in a strip of bacon. She bit, chewed, swallowed—but didn't taste anything. Her body felt like a volcano. Her clit burned with the most towering, delicious ache, exacerbated by the pressure on her nipples and Thorpe's unrelenting fingers driving her up into a sky with no ceiling. When she fell, the crash would be monumental, life altering. She felt on the verge of begging them to allow her to give them anything—or everything—just for ease. Instead, she wriggled on Thorpe's lap as Sean followed the bacon with an intimate brush of his lips and a stare that made her shiver.

"You're so beautiful, Callie. I like you all flushed and subdued. And I can't say that I dislike you being helpless and at our mercy." Sean chuckled, then fed her a bite of buttery toast.

She smelled more than tasted it and choked it down, only to

encounter a bite of hot eggs on the fork he shoved past her lips moments later.

"Open wide," Thorpe insisted.

Callie would have called him a bastard son of a bitch asshole if she could have found the words and wasn't convinced that they'd only heap on more punishment. But Thorpe deserved that and more. Once they'd let her come, she would have to think of something really creatively suitable to repay him for this loathsome torture. If he didn't stop soon . . . Callie really had no idea what she would do or how she would make it through the next five minutes with her body on fire and ready to explode.

"After she eats, do you want me to cook us something?" Sean asked Thorpe as if he didn't have a care in the world, fondling her breasts while he spoke.

Thorpe shook his head. "I'll find something quick."

"Good thinking. I'm not convinced that we'll have finished torturing Callie by the time she's done eating. I think I've got just the thing."

Barely missing a beat, he reached onto the counter and yanked a box into his lap. Seconds later, they were both munching on protein bars with one hand . . . and stroking her to insanity with the other.

In the middle of all that, Sean still fed her. Bite after bite passed her lips. She chewed fast and swallowed even faster, hoping that when she finished this meal that maybe there would be an almighty orgasm in her future.

Lifting her with him, Thorpe rose behind her, withdrawing his hands from her pussy and his lips from her neck before he set her back in his chair. Whimpering, Callie protested. Sean filled her mouth with another bite of egg, then toast. He washed it down with coffee from his cup. Then he took her lips again in a mind-numbing kiss, fingers tumbling into her hair, tongue plunging deep.

She threw herself against him, and their chests met. Her clamped nipples met his hard flesh, and a fresh riot of sensation ripped through her. She gasped into his kiss.

Suddenly, Thorpe returned and resumed his position behind her on the chair, his muscled slab of a chest—now bare—pressing into her back. Her skin sizzled at the contact. She hissed. A thousand feelings pelted her—the pressure on her tight nipples, the slight bitterness of Sean's insistent coffee-flavored kiss, the press of Thorpe's hair-roughened chest against her back, and the slide of his fingers on her pussy once more.

The burn of desire decimated her. She couldn't have fought or refused them anything. All she could do was surrender, hope they would take her, and finally relent—give her the pleasure their every touch promised.

"You need us, don't you, pet? You're coming apart. I feel your heat. I hear your breathing. I can taste your excitement."

"We're going to make you scream for us, lovely," Sean added.

"Please . . ." Callie heard the pleading note in her voice and didn't care. Whatever brought her relief and sanity, whatever urged them to fill and fulfill her, that's what she needed now.

"But not just yet." Sean swallowed down the last of his protein bar and tossed the wrapper on the table, then looked Thorpe's way. "You finished eating?"

"Yes." Thorpe's wrapper joined his a minute later, and she heard him swallow in her ear.

"Let's go. We need a bed."

Callie's pulse jumped. A dozen images all leapt to the front of her fantasies as she interpreted what Sean's words might mean, but the one above all others, dazzling her with want, shimmering hope and promise was the thought of them both giving her all of their desire and making love to her.

"Please . . ." she wailed again.

"Fuck," Thorpe swore.

Gawd, she hoped so.

His palms heated the insides of her thighs with a possessive caress before his fingers slid back into her drenched folds and he ma-
nipulated her clit until she was a breath shy of an orgasm she knew
would rob her of all sanity.

Bucking for more, keening with the need so acute she saw black
spots dancing at the edge of her vision, she reached blindly for Sean
and fused their lips together in a searing kiss that had her swallowing his lust, feeling his heartbeat against her own, hearing the blood
roar in her ears.

"Fuck is right," Sean muttered as he tore his lips free and lifted
her to her feet.

The second she stood upright, Thorpe grabbed her shoulders
and spun her to face him. He clasped her face in his hands and
stared down into her eyes. "Unless you stop me, I'm going to fuck
you until you can't stop screaming. Last chance to say no, pet."

"Why would I stop you? I need you."

Thorpe shook his head. "I'm too old for you."

"You know what the hell you're doing," she argued. "I trust you."

He scowled. "I'm not a tender lover."

"If you make me come, I'll relish every second."

"Only if you're good, lovely," Sean taunted in her ear.

Then his fingers found their way to her nipples, toying with the
clothes pins clamping them. The pressure there fed the ache below,
which he found with his next touch. The caress teased her with just
enough sensation to make her knees weak and her blood surge . . .
but not enough to send her over the edge.

"You're so fucking beautiful." Thorpe leaned closer, his lips hovering just over hers. "I've wanted you so badly . . ."

Callie melted against him as his gaze and Sean's hands both caressed her. She *felt* beautiful. They gave that gift to her just by being here with her. She believed they adored and treasured her. Now
she knew they'd do anything to keep her safe. Did they have any

idea how desperately and for how long she'd wished to feel like that? In all the times circumstance had forced her to flee whatever rattrap she'd temporarily called home and the strangers who might have become friends in different situations, she'd never really imagined she'd feel like the most precious person in the world to anyone.

"I've wanted you, too. Why did you never—"

"Eventually you'll leave me," Thorpe choked out.

"I've never wanted to. That's one reason I stayed at Dominion much longer than I should have." Callie stood on her tiptoes, inching closer, their stares all but welded together. "And I'll never want to again. If something happens and we're separated, please believe that I didn't ever want to be apart from you."

She brushed her lips over Thorpe's. He didn't need any more encouragement. He met her halfway and claimed her mouth with a possessive sweep of his tongue, drinking her in as if he'd been parched for her. As if she was the elixir that would keep him alive.

Callie soaked him in, drowned in the heady swamp of the need tugging her under. As she did, Sean caressed his way up her torso to pluck at the makeshift clamps again as his teeth nipped her neck. A shiver shuddered its way through her body. A dizzy fever overcame her. Yet nothing had ever felt so perfect. This was more than a fantasy coming true. She loved them both, and having them with her, wanting her, working together to give her pleasure . . . the rightness clicked into place. She belonged between them.

If only life or fate or God above would grant her this completeness for the rest of her life, she'd take every opportunity to make them feel this wonderful in return.

The thought was almost absurd. She had now, this moment. Tomorrow was a crap shoot at best, and the odds were stacked against them. She'd better seize this glorious sliver of time while she could.

Thorpe lifted his head, breathing hard, his chest sawing up and down. He ripped his stare from her, then glanced over her shoulder to Sean. "What's next?"

Her breath caught. Hope suspended her from a tightrope. She didn't dare say a word or even whimper for fear she would wake up from this lovely dream.

"You want Callie, as I do," Sean pointed out.

"More than I want all my tomorrows," Thorpe vowed, those gray eyes burning down into her.

She clutched his shoulders a bit harder and felt herself sway toward him. His fingers bit into her hips.

"Lovely?" Sean turned her back to face him.

Worry lay in his blue eyes. Uncertainty. That expression said he feared that no matter what he did, he would lose her.

He might not have always been honest with her, but she'd seen the man under the badge when he'd first come to Dominion. It had been evident in the gentle way he'd encouraged her to open up, in the patient way he'd coaxed her until he understood. She'd feared his questions and where they might lead, yes. But she'd feared losing her heart more. In the past few days, he'd risked so much to help her. Maybe she should be more wary, but over the years she'd developed a decent danger meter. Now that she wasn't freaking out and had started using hers . . . she knew he might be the best man to ever happen to her.

Callie cupped his jaw. "I'm yours, too, Sean. Always." *At least in my heart.*

Relief spread across his face, and he took her mouth in a slow, searing meeting of lips that made the last few minutes of hesitation evaporate. A well of yearning and desire flowed from her to both of them and back. Callie couldn't fail to feel it. This was right. It was time.

"You are," Sean confirmed, then grinned at Thorpe. "I kept in mind this possibility when I bought provisions."

What the heck did that mean? Callie frowned, trying to puzzle out his cryptic statement as Sean reached onto the counter behind him and plucked up a plastic grocery bag, tossing it. Thorpe caught it, parted the plastic handles, and looked inside. Rising on tiptoe, she peeked, too.

Box after box of condoms lay inside.

Thorpe's gaze bounced up to Sean. Then a massive grin broke out. "It looks like we'll be really busy."

Sean answered with a smile. "I certainly hope so."

Blood rushed through Callie's veins as she blinked into the bag. The sight was both thrilling and daunting. "I think that's enough condoms to glove up a platoon for an entire year."

"I doubt it, pet, but we'll work like hell to keep up. Get ready." Thorpe tossed the sack back at Sean, then scooped her into his arms and carried her to the bedroom.

Sean followed them, tearing into the first box and dumping a handful of the foil packets onto the bed beside her head as her back met the mattress. She looked up at the men. Thorpe's stare penetrated her the way his cock would soon.

Beside her, Sean half covered her, his lips swooping down for another kiss. Callie met him, giving herself over as she felt the bed on her other side dip under Thorpe's weight. Through his trousers, his erection pressed against her thigh, big and hard and hot. She moaned, grabbing at Sean's hair with one hand and Thorpe's shoulders with the other.

It should be awkward. She should be nervous. But no. They flowed together, seemingly of like minds and wants from the second they hit the sheets. No bumping, no conflict.

The arousal filling her now was both residual from the guys' ardent fondling and the deprivation of her orgasm. But more, it stemmed from having their scents combining in her nose, her skin heated by the dual press of their own, the way they began to pass her lips back and forth with devouring kisses. Everything felt right.

Finally, Thorpe lifted his mouth from hers. He zeroed in on her breasts before sliding a sly stare to Sean, who grinned. Callie stilled. When had they developed this silent guy-speak that—

The moment they plucked the clothes pins from her nipples and bent at the same time to suck her flesh deep, she screamed. She arched. Blood filled the nubs as their lips surrounded them. Suction tugged, the sensation reaching down like a direct caress to her clit. *Oh, hell.*

Then they made that a reality, Sean surging a pair of fingers into her pussy and Thorpe wiggling his way over her clit. Gawd, she was going to combust.

"Guys . . . please," she panted. *"Please."*

"I'm not convinced you've learned your lesson properly, pet. Are you, Sean?" Thorpe growled, making her shudder with need.

"No." He tongued his way around her nipple. "I'm not sure yet that you understand the full extent of your infractions, lovely. I owe you a red ass for drugging me and running away without talking to me. Or Thorpe, for that matter. I'm also not sure we've repaid you properly for taking your clothes off in front of a room full of dregs and losers."

"I'm sorry. I swear. But—"

Thorpe captured her lips and devoured her mouth in an intoxicating kiss.

"Good thinking, Thorpe. Callie doesn't need to be talking just now." Sean pinched her nipple before he laved it again, then hitched his fingers high inside her pussy, finding the spot designed to send her reeling.

Callie's head swam. Blood charged her system, converging between her legs. She twisted, silently begging.

"When I'm convinced you're truly sorry, then we'll see about your orgasm. Until then . . ." He nipped the side of her breast. "Get on your hands and knees."

Thorpe slid his fingers over her clit one last time, then sent Sean a frown. But he played along. "That was a direct order, pet. Move."

Her brain struggled to swim through the arousal drowning her body. Finally, the command penetrated her—because their cocks sure weren't yet—and she rolled over between them, presenting her ass in the air.

"Ah, you look so damn pretty like this." Sean's voice had thickened, deepened, as he ran a hand under her body until he palmed her pussy again.

"You do, Callie," Thorpe agreed. "You look ready to serve and please us. Would you like that?"

As much as her body cried out for orgasm, the opportunity to give them everything they wanted and yearned for made every submissive cell inside her clamor. She could find her own kind of reward in satisfying the men she loved. In fact, her whole body felt as if it glowed at the prospect.

"More than anything, Sir. I'm sorry if I worried or upset you by leaving. I meant to protect you both."

Sean leaned down into her face, his mien surprisingly stern. "What you did was utterly fail to communicate. How can we help you or keep you safe if you don't let us?"

Callie opened her mouth to reply, but the sharp crack of his hand on her backside made her yelp instead. Had Sean just spanked her? Yes, and much harder than she would have thought, than even Thorpe had in the past.

"Quiet now," he demanded. "You'll take your punishment like a good girl. Spread your knees apart." Sean waited until she'd complied, then widened them a bit more until her stance was to his liking. "Better. You can apologize to Thorpe now."

She looked up to see the two men exchange a glance. Then a look of supreme satisfaction lit up Thorpe's face. "Yes, you can, pet."

He reached for his zipper. It fell in the hush. Callie held her breath as he worked the pants down his hips and revealed his thick cock, standing hard as he took it in his fist. The swollen purple head made her lick her lips in hunger.

Thorpe shoved his fingers in her tresses and fisted them in his grasp, drawing her down toward the engorged stalk of flesh he palmed slowly up and down. Her stomach clenched. Her pussy wept. For years, she'd had this fantasy of being at Thorpe's feet, on her knees, completely at his service. Her breath caught as he brushed his cock over her lips, a tease . . . then gone.

Without thought, she reached up, trying to take his shaft in hand and thrust it into her mouth.

Thorpe pulled up on her hair, denying her, at the same time Sean slapped her ass again.

"Don't be greedy and impatient, pet. If you're apologizing to me, rushing me before I'm ready isn't the way to convince me you're sorry." He released his tight grip on her hair, then clamped his big hand around her face, fingers squeezing the muscles of her jaw. "Open up. Suck my cock. Make me believe you're repentant and eager to please."

"I'll have to believe it, too, lovely, or there won't be any fucking in your future," Sean added. "Go on. And not a sound while I take my pound of flesh."

This tag-team discipline probably shouldn't turn her on so much, but why deny that it made her needy and turned her inside out. Too bad whimpering and begging wouldn't do her a damn bit of good. Only obedience would.

Callie hadn't had many opportunities to really put herself in another's hands and turn over her will. She wanted to now so, so bad. Yes, they were going to make her wait and ache and beg. But whatever they did would also draw them all closer together . . . for however long it lasted.

She poured her heart into the pass of her tongue over Thorpe's cock, licking him lovingly, closing her eyes as if she could preserve the moment forever. Behind her, Sean smoothed his palm over her heated flesh, spreading the warmth. She held in a whimper and restrained the urge to raise her hips to him for more. He slid his fingers down her ass, to her pussy, skimming over her swollen labia, her engorged clit.

The moment was magical. Callie felt touched all over. She felt adored. And she surrendered completely to the moment. To them.

Stretching her lips wide, she took Thorpe deep, relishing his hard length filling her mouth. Every corner burst with his scent and taste, so masculine, a bit salty, so very big and musky and perfect. Holding back her moan became impossible as she eased her head back, sucking until her tongue tingled, then dragging her teeth over the sensitive head. Thorpe cursed on a groan.

Callie sensed more than saw Sean lean around her body to watch. Knowing that his stare fixed on her ignited something in her belly. It was impossible not to want to put on a show and make him remember the moments she'd had her mouth around him, too.

Soon, Thorpe shuttled his cock from between her lips in a rush, as if he couldn't feel enough of her. He cursed, his fist tightening in her hair. His excitement ratcheted up her thrill.

Then Sean kissed his way down her side before resuming his position behind her and settling into a rhythm. Methodically, he swatted her backside until it burned and tingled and lit a fire in her blood.

Fighting the urge to squirm and plead for mercy was becoming nearly impossible. With their every touch, Callie submerged herself in the most delicious euphoria. She wasn't sure she could take a deep breath around the bliss. Dizziness swamped her head. Thrill fevered her blood.

And she loved every minute of it, just like she loved them.

"Pet . . ." Thorpe's voice deepened, roughened, to something so intimate. She'd listened to the man's every intonation for four years, but never heard that particular note. She loved the idea that it was something he'd reserved just for her. "Callie, baby. You're killing me."

She smiled around his thick flesh so hard on her tongue and

laved him again with all the feeling swirling and pooling inside her. He groaned and tugged on her hair again, vacating her mouth with a pop.

Callie moaned in protest without thought, blinking up at his big, heaving chest as he worked hard to breathe past the arousal. His jaw was clenched, his nostrils flared. His gray eyes looked stormy and had darkened to something on the verge of a tempest.

No way she could stop herself from falling helplessly into his gaze. "Please don't stop me."

"I damn near came down your throat." He brushed his thumb over her lower lip. "Someday, I would love to shudder and climax right inside that pretty mouth. Not today."

She bit her lip and tried to swallow down her disappointment. The idea of Thorpe granting her his pleasure—of pushing him past his restraint—aroused the hell out of her. But she hadn't earned the right to ask for anything she wanted. This was punishment. Very sexy, amazing punishment, but almost more difficult to bear than anything else she could imagine. They dangled a dear fantasy in her face, then yanked it away. This morning would be full of orgasm deprivation. They would stop her anytime she ached for something too much. She would endure it because she regretted worrying and hurting them, even if it had been for a good cause.

"I understand, Sir."

He caressed the crown of her head, then settled at her nape and urged her up for a kiss.

"Are you satisfied she's sorry?" Sean asked, still palming her heated backside and adding a swat every now and then.

Now that she wasn't focused on heaping sensation all over Thorpe, the blood and desire throbbed in the cheeks of her ass. A neon billboard would have been more subtle. She gasped, wishing she had the distraction to focus on again. But Sean only ran his hand between her legs once more, settling his fingers over the jewel of her clit.

"I think I might see a little remorse," Thorpe drawled. "But I'm not convinced that she's sorry enough. I want to be sure that she never intends to run again."

Callie swallowed a cry. She didn't want to flee from them. But if she brought danger or trouble to them and could fix it by leaving . . . she would have no choice.

"Absolutely." Sean twirled lazy circles at the top of her mound, right where she needed it most, but never with enough speed or pressure to send her flying. "We'll just have to work her harder until we're convinced that she truly understands where she belongs." A groan tore from his chest. "Your pussy is so slick, lovely. Perfect."

Sean lifted her up, resting her back to his chest. He fondled her already sensitive nipples, plucking and pinching. Her head lolled back against his shoulder, and she arched into his touch. She'd barely figured out how to absorb all the hot sensation he forced on her when Callie felt thick fingers nudging her folds in a deceptively insistent touch. Thorpe's deft, soft stroke against her clit incinerated her ability to hold her tongue.

"Please . . ." she panted, then looked at him with dazed, beseeching eyes.

"You're pretty when you beg, pet." A little smile played at his lips. "I'll look forward to hearing more of it."

"Me, too," Sean vowed. "On your back."

Together, they helped her lay supine across the mattress. Thorpe took over the gentle torture of her nipples, flicking the crests, then bending to nuzzle the swells before sucking them into his mouth one at a time. At her feet, Sean gripped her ankles and spread her legs. And she was suffocating in her own need, unable to make her thoughts churn beyond all the ways she craved them.

When they had her positioned to their liking, she moaned, incoherent sounds of pleading she hoped they understood. Finally, she heard the soft tear of a condom wrapper. Then another. Thorpe climbed off the bed, and she managed to lift her head enough to see him stand at her feet near Sean, who shucked his clothes in record time. Both of them arranged the prophylactic over the strong surging stalks between their legs.

Thank goodness there's sex in my future. Without it, Callie was ready to scream or cry or lose her mind. She absolutely knew better than to touch herself. Thorpe had made it entirely clear in the shower that was a big no-no.

Sean eased onto the bed beside her and propped his head on his hand, his blue eyes glittering with mischief and hot with desire. "Spread wider, lovely. Make me believe that you want us to fuck you."

He hadn't even finished the sentence before she bent her knees and parted them as wide as she could.

Thorpe caressed his way up her thighs and settled between them, the head of his cock nudging her weeping entrance.

"Take me, pet. Take every inch. Please me."

She blinked up at him. "There's nothing I want more than to please you both."

"Callie . . ." he moaned as he impaled her and closed his eyes, grinding. "Fuck."

Finally, after four agonizing years of waiting, Thorpe was inside her.

She gasped in a huge breath, trying to accommodate him all at once. But with the blood engorging her folds and swells, Thorpe had to fight his way in. A hard thrust, a slow withdrawal. He gnashed his teeth together. His face pulled tight with concentration. He opened his eyes, his stare locking in on hers, penetrating her soul as his cock did the same below.

"Can you feel him, lovely?" Sean murmured in her ear, a tantalizing suggestion. "Can you feel how much he wants you?"

"Yes." She melted under Thorpe, desperate to take every inch of him.

"That's how much I want you, too. I can't wait to sink into your tight little cunt and feel you close all around me. You know how I'm going to fuck you? I'm going to hammer my way in with a hard stroke that will make you catch your breath. Then I'm going to ease out so slowly, the head rubbing against every sensitive patch. I know what sends you off."

He did. God help her, he did. And Thorpe was catching on very quickly, working each inch in with an agonizing plunge and a lip-biting pull until, with every thrust, he managed to settle right against the one spot designed to send her soaring. Then he finally withdrew to the tip and plunged deep in one growling shove and claimed her completely.

He settled right against her cervix and awakened another barrage of nerves centered there. Together they fired and tingled. Callie rocked with Thorpe, tilting up to urge him deeper.

"You've already discovered that she likes it deep," Sean said.

"Fuck, I love it that way. Holy hell . . ." Thorpe threw his head back as he inched back and pushed in again. "Callie, pet, I fucking imagined this so many times, you have no idea."

"I thought of you, too," she cried out.

He fitted his hands beneath her hips, grabbed her ass, and shoved inside her, stroke after grinding stroke.

"You look beautiful, Callie," Sean whispered in her ear between Thorpe's juggernaut thrusts, then plundered her lips. "Yes, that's it. Your cheeks are so flushed. Your lips are so sweet."

"Sean . . ." She didn't know how to say all the words of need and love bubbling up in her throat.

Somehow, he knew. He dipped his head again. Her eyes fluttered closed, and he kissed both of her lids. "I've only ever wanted you happy. Whatever you need, it's my pleasure to provide. I will always take care of you."

How could she be on the verge of tears and orgasm at the same time? Every tingle and burn, each sensation and ache built in her clenching pussy, her swirling head, and her overflowing heart.

"I will, too, pet. Anyone who wants to wrest you from me will be in for the fight of their life," Thorpe vowed as he rode her from one dazzling stroke to the next. As she fluttered around him, her body preparing to soar in the heaven they'd created, he pulled free. "She's awfully close."

"Not yet," Sean chided her.

Panting, Thorpe rolled to her right, occupying the space beside her, shoving pillows out of his way and spilling them to the floor.

Before she could wonder what he was doing, Sean climbed between her legs and surged balls deep in one breath-robbing thrust, crashing against the spot he knew would make her tremble in want. She couldn't stop her cry of need.

"Your orgasms are ours, pet," Thorpe reminded. "He hasn't given you permission. He's in charge of your pussy now. Patience."

"But—"

"No." Thorpe nipped at her lobe, and his heavy breath cascaded down her neck, making her shiver and squirm. "Do you think protests are going to induce us to let you come? Who are you here to please?"

"Both of you, Sir."

"Exactly. It pleases us to see you writhe and flush and need."

And goodness knew she was doing exactly that, ready to do anything for relief as the feelings surged through her body and the need to come threatened to overtake her. She clamped down on Sean, rising to meet each thrust. She dug her nails into his back, peppered kisses over his cheeks, down his neck. The orgasm was right there, even closer than before. She gave a high-pitched cry.

"Now, lovely, didn't Thorpe just explain? You don't want to disappoint us, do you?" Sean withdrew and rolled to her left.

"No," she sobbed. "But it's so big. Overpowering."

Callie couldn't catch a breath, couldn't think. She wriggled over to Thorpe, rubbing against him. He pushed her to her back again, then loomed over her, supporting himself on his bulging arms as his knees parted her thighs and he drove in with one savage shove that had her clawing his shoulders.

"Look at me," he demanded.

She did, anchoring herself to him like a lifeline and trying to hold back the tremendous pressure dammed just under her clit. Frantically, she searched his face for mercy.

None. He was going to push her up harder and higher. Even as she mourned, she delighted in his control.

Nor did Callie dare disobey. She really didn't want to. She'd waited forever to feel Thorpe deep inside her, looking at her like she held his heart. He reached down to cup her hip, the one with the nick in her flesh from that terrible night. He fingered it, soothing it back and forth for a moment.

"That's it, pet. Stay with me." He pistoned inside her with ruthless, thorough strokes that had her clawing for more.

Beside her, Sean tipped her chin in his direction and covered her lips with his. She closed her eyes for a moment and basked in their attention, in the adoration that poured from them both, and let it soak into her.

As he lifted his lips, he smoothed a kiss to her chin, then pressed it up, giving himself access to her throat. He skated his lips across the sensitive skin there, then worked back to the tight beads of her nipples silently begging for relief . . . for something.

Thorpe reared back on his knees, never breaking stride, and thumbed her clit. "So hard. So needy, aren't you, my sweet pet?"

Callie honestly couldn't speak. How did he expect her to hold it together and answer such an obvious question?

"The last thing we want now, lovely, is defiance. Answer Thorpe," Sean breathed against her nipple, then nipped at it with his teeth before soothing the tip with the rub of his tongue.

The jolt of sensation went straight to her clit, where Thorpe polished it to a lightning thrill with a slow rub that made her insane.

"Yes," she managed to gasp out. "Yes, Sir."

The blood and need began converging again, building, building, gathering like a storm. Everywhere she tightened, prepared, breath held. Just one more stroke . . .

"Son of a bitch," Thorpe heaved as he withdrew from her sweltering flesh and plopped down beside her, panting as if it took everything he had to bring himself under control.

"No!" She couldn't help the protest that slipped free.

Sean grabbed her chin as he rolled back on top of her and slid home in one devastating stroke. "Yes, Callie. Remember your penance? Your punishment?"

He thrust inside her with strong, deep plunges of his cock that did absolutely nothing but push her ardor higher. Vaguely she remembered why she owed them. But the inferno raging inside her made her yearn for more—for everything.

Callie forced herself to draw in a breath and center. Above it all, she softened at the notion of being all they needed. Of course she knew that she offered them what they might have gotten elsewhere, but no surrender would ever be given with more heart or love than what she offered.

"Yes, Sir."

"Good, lovely. Hold still."

Sean gripped her hips and began a unrelenting pace that made her spine twist and her insides melt. She wrapped her hands around his shoulders, then caressed down to his muscled backside to pull him in even deeper, despite the fact that he'd have nowhere to go. The need to feel him deep was pathological, biological.

Thorpe tunneled his hand into her hair and tugged her face his way until he seized her lips and took control of her mouth, forcing her to open to his kiss, feel the crush of his lips, take the plunge of his tongue, and give him all her soft acceptance and feverish passion in return. He growled into her mouth.

"Don't come, Callie," Sean insisted.

That demand was getting harder and harder to meet. Pulling from Thorpe's lips, she tightened, focused, squeezing her eyes shut and praying she could obey. It wouldn't be for lack of trying . . .

Inside her, Sean thickened. He pumped harder. A second later, he cried out in a deep sound of agony as he stiffened and pressed himself as far inside her as he could, rooting around as if he'd found home. His cry of ecstasy echoed in the bedroom. Callie whimpered like a wounded thing to hold back her need to join him, to celebrate this moment that might not ever come again.

With a groan from the bottom of his chest, he exhaled against the side of her neck, and managed to push himself up enough to press the lightest brush of kiss on her lips. He worshipped her with a starkly blue stare.

"I love you, Callie," he murmured in her ear.

Then he rolled away.

Callie lay still, her toes curled and her fists clenched to ward off the horrific need roiling inside her. *Mind over body. You can do it.* She dragged in more breaths, fighting to control the arousal and the throbbing flesh between her legs, insisting on more.

She hadn't come close to recovering before Thorpe made his way into the crook of her spread thighs again and hovered above her. With total abandon, he plowed into her. In a lightning-fast barrage of thrusts, he took everything he needed from her, including her sanity.

Callie curled her arms around him. His back was slick with sweat and effort. He heaved in a breath with every shove inside her. And damn it, he swelled inside her as his strokes became even more insistent.

Like Sean, he meant to find his orgasm and leave her body needing and her soul bleeding as a lesson. She'd earned it, but gawd it hurt—in a strangely glorious way. Giving them control of her climax was her giving herself. If they needed that power, if they had to have a show of her penitence, she vowed to suffer.

Sucking in a breath as Thorpe's strokes shortened, deepened, pounding, pounding, she waited, eyes clenched shut and struggled to give herself over and hold her pleasure back.

Sean tangled his lips with hers so very gently. "Come, Callie. For us."

Had she heard that right? She opened her eyes wide to see the soft smile on his face. *Yes.* He'd given her a gift because he loved her, not necessarily because she'd earned it. She'd torn off his collar because he'd lied to her—in the name of duty. But he hadn't lied about what really mattered. He had been true to his heart. While she had run, hidden, and tried to cut him out of her future and her feelings.

And still he managed to forgive her. No wonder she loved this man.

"Now, pet!" Thorpe thundered into her pussy. "Damn it, Callie. Yes. Oh, fuck. That's it. Perfect. Now," he groaned long and low. "Come!"

The pressure grew, pleasure surged. It was as if a weight had been lifted from her body. From her soul. She was free to fly, to soar and bask in their adoration. The submission she'd always craved giving but never had the freedom to grant, made her spill into bliss with more abandon than she'd ever experienced or imagined.

She peaked, then screamed as she hurtled endlessly through the pleasure. She roared out in body-twisting ecstasy. Thorpe was there to catch her, grounding her with a sure embrace and plunging strokes. He prolonged the exquisite sensations by digging against her most sensitive spot. She cried out, shuddered, dizzy, floating, flying again . . .

Sean kissed her jaw, squeezed her hand, praising her with whispers she barely heard as she tried to catch her breath and find a way to bring her soul back into her body.

Finally, Thorpe grunted, then collapsed over her and rolled to her side. Together they surrounded her, cuddling her, both trailing their lips across her skin. She turned to each, back and forth, as the floodgates of her heart opened wide for the first time in her life. Tears spilled, joyous, her smile wobbling. She clutched the moment tight, wishing she could bask here forever.

Chapter Fifteen

LATE that afternoon, Sean wandered into the galley in search of Callie. His world righted on its axis when he spotted her near the sink, gulping down water. A smile slid across his face that was probably sappier than hell, but he didn't even know the right words to describe how beautiful she was to him with the tangled gloss of her hair spilling down her back and her lithe form silhouetted under his once-pristine dress shirt.

He slipped his arms around her waist and kissed her neck. "I can't get enough of you, lovely."

But he was certainly trying. After their first go-round in the bed, he and Thorpe had rested with her between them. They'd all drifted off, and Sean had awakened to a nose full of Callie and a cock harder than stone. She'd welcomed him with open arms, her kisses so clinging and poignant. It hadn't taken Thorpe very long to join in, availing himself of her mouth while Sean drowned in her pussy and took for himself an orgasm like the one he'd allowed Thorpe to give her. He'd given her several more for the sheer pleasure of it.

Every touch she'd bestowed on him felt infused with her love. He'd never wanted that devotion from another woman. But like everything else with Callie, she was simply different. She filled some void in him he hadn't known was missing.

She set down the bottle of water, then turned in his arms with a little smile. "Well, you bought a year's worth of condoms and you did warn me . . . Not that you'll hear me complain."

"I hope not." He gripped her hip and settled a kiss on her swollen lips. "Are you all right?"

She sent him a saucy grin with blue eyes dancing mischievously. "The sex isn't exactly scarring me for life, if that's what you're worried about."

"Good to know, but no. Let's start at the beginning. Why did you run from Dominion without talking to me? Or to Thorpe? I hate that you felt that you couldn't trust me."

"You lied, Sean." When he opened his mouth to argue, she cut him off. "I know what you're going to say. It was your job. You weren't untruthful about your feelings. I get all that. Just understand that I thought you might be an assassin or something. And if that was the case, I certainly wasn't going to give you the opportunity to shoot me while I was busy asking why you knew my true identity and had a gun. And I refused to put Thorpe at risk by running to him for help."

Arguing with that logic would get him nowhere. She'd kept herself alive by being cautious. And walking away from everyone who'd ever mattered. He was going to have to break that last habit. Maybe when he'd begun having feelings for her, he should have come clean. Or maybe she would have just run sooner. It was all moot now. They were finally getting everything out on the table. He wanted to clear it so they could stop the danger to her and have a future.

"I know. But I can't have you running off again. I don't think my heart can take it, lovely."

She cupped his cheek and frowned. "Sean, think about what

you're saying. Hell, what you're doing. By your own admission, you've been married to your job for the last decade. I can't let you give that up for me. It's your *career*. Your future."

"No, you are. Make no mistake. I won't give you up. If you don't love me and want to leave, I can't stop you. But I refuse to walk away from you because my boss might be pissed off. I won't abandon you when you've got danger breathing down your neck. Someone wants you dead."

"Yeah, and I don't know who or how to stop it. The best thing I can do for you is give you all the time and love possible, then quietly leave. If you'll say I gave you the slip and let me have a head start—"

"Do you not love me?" he cut in.

"I do, Sean. More than I can even tell you." She gripped his face in her hands, her eyes tearing up. "But the day my family was murdered and I ran, I gave up my future. I didn't really understand at the time, but I can't argue with the facts."

She pressed the softest, saddest kiss on his lips—meaning it as the beginning of her good-bye.

Sean refused to let that stand.

He jerked back. "I'm not going to stop fighting for you."

Tears swam in her eyes. "I think you should. You've already given me an incredible gift with your love. I don't get involved with people. It may not seem like much, but it's very scary for me to tell you that I love you. I'm saying it because it's true and important to me that you know. I don't even have the words to tell you how touched I am that you've risked so much to help me. Or that you let Thorpe share this time with us. Why? You hated him back in Dallas."

The last few days had been a blur, and he'd been so tired sometimes and stressed that he didn't always know his name. But he was totally clear on this answer. "Because you love him. His experience and control lets you feel safe. You've known him for so long that trust is easy." He shrugged. "Besides, having someone help me watch your back has been beneficial. And having another pair of hands to spank your ass when you get out of line has come in handy, too."

Sean tried to pass the last line off as a joke, but Callie wasn't smiling. "I've loved him for a long time. Please don't think that means I love you any less. And I want you to know that no matter what happens with Thorpe or the future, it won't change how I feel about you."

Sean smoothed back her hair and met her with a smile. "Thank you, lovely. I needed to hear that. I wish it sounded less like you intend to leave me. You have such a big heart to give. Thank you for sharing it with me."

"You made it impossible not to fall in love with you. I've never felt this way, as if you came into my life . . . and supported me so perfectly. Suddenly, the ground under me felt solid. I wasn't lonely or lost anymore. I was afraid to trust you. I've wanted to give you everything I could in return, but I didn't know how to get past my fear. And now, I don't ever want to let go."

"Then don't. Share your mind and heart with me. Give me your trust and honesty. You've been alive, but you haven't really *lived*, Callie. I want to help you do that and be with you every step of the way."

Callie hesitated for a long moment, looking up at him like he was her everything. "If you're really not going to save yourself and let me go—"

"I've made myself clear." He shook his head.

"Then I'm yours." Callie threw herself into his arms, burying her face in his neck. "I'll stay as long as you'll have me."

Sean's heart swelled. He could have never guessed that this case would change not just his workaholic ways, but show him all he'd been missing. Callie had awakened him to love.

"Be prepared to grow old with me," he murmured in her ear. "I swear I'll keep you safe so we can have that future together."

"I'd love that more than anything. And I'll try every day to make you happy."

Sean caressed her silky hair and her velvet cheek. "As will I. But I don't want you to be crushed if Thorpe doesn't stay with us. He loves you, too, but he's quite resistant to the 'picket fence.'"

"I know." Callie tried to shrug as if it didn't matter, but Sean knew better. "I never expected him to want me, much less stay. I mean, he probably opened a BDSM club because it was a great way to meet like-minded women and play with a different one every night."

"I don't know why he opened Dominion. He definitely wants you, but he's kept his distance because he's just a man with his own insecurities. And you have the power to hurt him."

"Me? He's ignored me for the last two years. When he first cut me off, I missed him so much, it was like physical pain. Then I wondered if subconsciously I wanted his love so badly because my relationship with my father had been so fucked up and now he was dead or something else stupid and Freudian like that. But then it didn't take long to realize the feelings were totally different. That I just . . . wanted Thorpe. You're right that he's always made me feel safe." Tears spilled down her cheeks, and she swiped them away. "Sorry. Crying to you about Thorpe seems insensitive. Trust me, I'm more thrilled to have your love than I can ever express."

Sean kissed her forehead. He could feel her pain and uncertainty just standing close to her. Exhaustion played a role, sure. But there was more. "I don't want your gratitude. I'll love you, regardless. I want you to know that, if Thorpe doesn't stay, I'm going to use this time to learn what he gives you and try to provide it. We'll manage, all right?"

Even more tears fell. "You're the best man I've ever met. I don't know what I did to deserve you, but I'm the luckiest woman in the world."

Sean kissed her reverently. She pressed her lips to his in a gesture that worshipped and communed. She clung to him. In that moment, he had no doubt whatsoever that he had her heart and that he'd made the right choices, difficult though they'd been.

"That question intimates that you think you deserved the last nine years. You didn't. You've had a bad lot, but you've still kept a kind heart. Watching you smile, working to earn your trembling trust, always trying to guess what unpredictable mess you'll get up to next . . . it made me appreciate *you*. Besides, you're damn sexy."

"Ditto in double for you." She winked his way, then leaned in, resting her head on his chest.

Sean wrapped his arms around her and just felt her heart beat against his for a long, silent second. He didn't expect their near future to be full of peace, but he drank in this moment when most was right with his world.

"You know, I should be more put out with you." She sighed. "A houseboat? Really?"

He chuckled. "I had to be sure you weren't going to get away from me, and I can't watch you twenty-four seven. Since you don't swim, bringing you out on the lake was the next best thing. In the middle of the week with winter closing in, I think we may be the only boaters out here."

"Sneaky." She said it almost like a compliment. "But I guessed that after the computer in the pizza box."

"I liked that myself." He grinned. "But if you want to talk about sneaky . . . what was in my wine?"

"Ambien."

Callie was the only woman he knew who could wince and flash a smile at the same time and somehow make it look adorable.

"Minx." He shook his head. "Don't do it again or I'll have to paddle your ass but good."

The mischief on her face was like a flirtation all its own. By all rights, he should at least need a good shower and a decent meal before he wanted to fuck her again. But no. He was already contemplating whether the kitchen counters were the right height to spread her legs and plow between them.

"If that's supposed to be a deterrent, it's not working," she whispered.

Sean laughed out loud. This was something else he loved about Callie—her playful side. He'd been so damn serious for so damn long. Not much to joke about fighting crime on a federal level, but somewhere along the way, he'd forgotten to stop and smell the roses. Callie's life had been far more dangerous and stressful than his own, but she still found ways to smile. He admired her grit and intelligence. If his grandparents were still with him, they would have loved her.

"You know we're going to have to talk about everything, don't you? The night your family was killed, anything you can remember that might be relevant? Who came after you as you moved around— anything that might help us pinpoint who wants you dead."

"Yes," Thorpe said, entering the kitchen wearing only a pair of trousers and looking freshly showered. "As much as I've enjoyed being distracted by your beautiful body and the incredible sex, now we have to tiptoe through your past."

* * *

THORPE sidled closer and pressed a kiss to the top of her head. Then he tipped her chin up to him so he could look into her eyes. "I always hoped I'd get to ask you questions so I could truly understand you, pet. But not in circumstances like this."

Callie ached to ask why he'd never told her that he knew her true identity. But she couldn't, not anymore than she could be greedy and demand more from him if he wasn't prepared to give it. Besides, it was more important to focus on whoever was chasing her. She might not be able to stop them, but finding out who it was would definitely help her evade trouble in the future. Thorpe wasn't going to suddenly and magically fall in forever love with her. Contrary to what Sean thought, Thorpe wanted her; he worried about her. He cared. And that was it.

"I've thought about that night over and over. Everything seemed normal until I heard the gunshots downstairs. I thought my dad was in bed, so I was just about to sneak out the window and meet Holden."

Thorpe actually growled. "I'm going to find out where that prick is now and repay him for what he did to you."

He was such a protector, and it was one of the things that drew her. He'd always been ready to tear the head off anyone who hurt her. When he was around, it was so easy to trust that he had everything absolutely under control. Sean reminded her that there was tenderness in the world. He'd made her believe that she mattered to someone. He was her pillar of strength. And her tomorrow.

"Actually, I think justice is being served." Sean grinned.

She sent back a wobbly smile. "I agree."

"You know?" His blue eyes glinted with surprise.

"I've tried to look him up every now and then, when I could make my way to a public computer at a library so that nothing could be traced back to me. I really do think he got his just rewards." She faced Thorpe. "His parents moved to Kentucky about six months after he bailed on me. Within a few months, he'd gotten some girl pregnant. She had no money and a really mean father. They got married not too long after that, and I'm pretty sure it was at the business end of her daddy's rifle. After three kids and seven years, she left him and took everything they had. He was too stupid to hold down a job, so he robbed a convenience store with a handgun. He's all locked up. He was always pretty, so I'm betting he's really popular in prison."

Thorpe seemed to turn that story over in his mind. "I wish I could have gutted him myself, but we have bigger fish to fry now. Let's go back to the night your father and sister were killed. Is there any way Holden could have been involved?"

Callie shook her head before Thorpe had even finished the

sentence. "He's far too dumb to be that stealthy. He wasn't violent, just greedy. I know now that he was more interested in my family's money than in me. He always wanted whatever he didn't have to work for. If he had broken into our house with a gun, he wouldn't have shot my family, taken a swipe at me, then fled. He would have stayed to rip off whatever he could. He got caught at the robbery because the cashier, who looked like a female sumo wrestler, decided that she wasn't going to take his shit and tackled him. She pinned him down and called the cops. Besides, that night . . . witnesses placed him a few streets over, and there's no way he could have done all the shooting, then beat me back to his car without being winded or having blood splatters."

"What about his friends? Would any of them have helped?" Sean asked.

She shook her head. "He didn't have any guy friends anymore. He'd slept with all of their girlfriends or sisters at some point. He was universally regarded as a douche."

"And you liked him why?" Thorpe looked like he was grinding his teeth.

"He was cute and had really pretty eyes. When you're sixteen, that's important." She shrugged.

"Did he sleep with your sister?" Sean asked.

Callie let her eyes slide shut. "I don't know." She drew in a deep breath and forced herself to face them again. "Right after school started that year, I came home from cheerleading practice early one day and found Holden there with Charlotte, supposedly waiting for me. She looked flushed, and he seemed winded. They told me they'd just come in from outside. The temperature was still hot. I wanted to believe them. Knowing what I know now about Holden, I'm sure he tried to seduce her."

The guys exchanged a glance, and a gong of foreboding rang in her stomach.

"What? Spit it out. What do you know?"

Sean sighed. "According to Charlotte's autopsy record, she was nine weeks pregnant when she died."

A wave of incredulity overcame Callie. Tears stung her eyes. She had a hard time breathing. In some ways, she was too shocked to be anything but numb. But as if she couldn't stop the march of time and emotions, a blade of betrayal stabbed her right in the heart.

"Then it had to be Holden. I knew she had a crush on him. I won't ask what he was thinking; I know. He must have laughed at taking the virginity of two sisters. But what the hell was Charlotte thinking?"

Thorpe shrugged. "That she would be important to him, perhaps. Come here, pet."

When he tried to pull her into his arms, Callie resisted and twisted away. "Don't. Not now."

"We're not Holden." Thorpe's gray eyes looked like thunderclouds under the scowl of his dark brows.

"She just needs time," Sean argued. "It's a lot for her to take in."

Callie shot him a grateful look as she wrapped her arms around her waist and tried to absorb the fact that she'd been deceived by the sister she'd loved. But Charlotte had always been a difficult child, always lashing out as if punishing the world for taking her mother. She'd always required more love than any one person could give.

"In retrospect, I should have realized that she'd be vulnerable to someone with a smooth tongue like Holden. But I didn't want to imagine that either of them would do that to me." She sighed raggedly, trying to cycle past the blow that probably shouldn't have been a blow at all. But the revelation, even all these years later, was still like a bomb going off inside her. "I think I knew about two hours after we ran away from my house that I'd made a huge mistake with him, but I was in shock and terrified."

"Of course," Sean soothed, but he didn't try to touch her. He only made himself available in case she wanted the support. Bless him.

But she wasn't ready.

"Is there any chance that Holden and your father argued about Charlotte's pregnancy?" Thorpe asked. "That Holden shot him, then maybe he and your sister wrestled over the gun?"

"No. There were no voices in the house, just gunshots. My father was a quiet man, and he might not have raised his voice with Holden if he'd known about Charlotte's pregnancy, but Holden would have yelled. He was rebellious and wanted to be heard. And heaven knows that Charlotte would have put in more than her two cents. Neither one of them could shut up. Besides, he wouldn't have been smart enough to wipe the gun clean and plant it in my room to frame me."

"The crime scene reports make the whole event sound methodical. Professional," Sean said in agreement. "Whoever did this knew exactly what they were about."

"They came to kill. There were no struggles or scenes. As far as I know, they didn't try to extort money from my dad or rob the place. He had millions worth of art in the house and an underground safe with a lot of cash in his office."

"Whoever killed him blasted their way into the safe," Sean confirmed. "But the cash was still there, as well as the art."

"Whoever did this wanted something specific." Thorpe crossed his arms over his chest, visibly restraining the urge to hit something since he couldn't find the someone who deserved it.

"I can't imagine what." Callie shrugged.

"And no one else had an ax to grind with your father?"

She'd really tried to figure it out, and of course she didn't know everything about her father, but . . . "The only possibility I can think of is a woman. After my mother's death, Dad didn't date or really get involved. He kept a mistress in a loft by his office downtown. About twice a week, he'd disappear for a few hours. He'd get cranky when he moved one out and had to find another. That happened about every six months, as soon as one got comfortable enough to want more out of the relationship than baubles and sex. I overheard him once on the phone. He told whoever she was that she wasn't his first mistress and wouldn't be the last. The woman moved out the next day. But that was at least three or four months before his murder. He had a new mistress by then, I'm sure."

"This wasn't a crime of passion," Sean pointed out. "It was a surgical strike."

"Any greedy family members you're aware of?" Thorpe asked.

"Dad was an only child. Mom was an orphan. So no. I'm not supposed to know that I have an illegitimate older half brother. He's definitely bitter, but last I heard, he had two kids and sold cars for a living. Why would he wait into his twenties, then decide to come after his father? If he's pissed about missing out on the money, why resort to murder rather than blackmail? He wasn't mentioned in my dad's will."

Pacing, Thorpe speared Sean with a glance. "And the bureau has no other suspects?"

"We've combed phone records and financial transactions. Nothing suspicious. Your father didn't keep tight security, much less video surveillance, so that's a dead end. The staff we interviewed were either gone or asleep when it happened. Their hands were all tested for gunpowder residue and came up clean. They were openly weeping when they realized your father was dead. It's not impossible one of them was guilty, but again, wouldn't they have stolen something if they'd gone to the trouble of killing him?"

"They loved him." Callie shook her head. "They had been with him for decades, in most cases. He didn't part with our nanny until Charlotte turned thirteen. Most of our classmates didn't have a nanny much past ten. And the only reason Dad let Frances go was because she had to take care of her elderly mother. One thing about my father, when he loved someone, he was as loyal as the day was long."

Sean scrubbed a hand down his face and joined Thorpe, pacing in the small galley. They bumped shoulders and grunted a

nonverbal apology at one another. "We've got to be missing something. Let's try looking at this from a different angle. Tell us what
made you bypass Logan's contact at the Vegas airport."

"That was really weird. I had my disguise, just in case. I know
security in airports can be ridiculously high-tech, so I was all ready.
I changed on the plane. Since I was last off, no one noticed. I stopped
in the bathroom to check myself and found a red pull-along someone had shoved in the trash can because one of the wheels was stuck.
But it disguised my duffel, so I swiped it. I was ready to meet Elijah.
Logan had shown me a picture of him before putting me on the
plane. I had his number, too." She shrugged, remembering that day.
"When I hit baggage claim, the first thing I noticed was some big guy
in a uniform. I drifted toward the smoking area and watched him
through a window. Imagine my shock when I realized that he was
flashing a picture of me—taken in the New Orleans airport just a few
hours earlier."

"And you panicked," Thorpe guessed.

"Hell yeah! Instead of waiting around, I left. I was worried this
guy would figure out the connection between me, Logan, and Elijah,
and hunt us down. I didn't want to make the guy's life harder since
I knew he had a wife and kids."

"So you went into the city with the idea of getting a job as a
stripper?" Thorpe raised a brow at her.

Boy, for a man who'd seen a lot of nudity at Dominion, he
was acting like it was a big freaking deal that she'd taken half her
clothes off for a few dollars.

"Mitchell Thorpe . . ." She put her fists on her hips.

He grabbed her arm. "Watch your tone, pet. I have no problem
putting you over my knee again. If your ass isn't sore enough yet for
you to mind your manners, I can fix that."

A fact she was beginning to know well. "I'm just saying that I've
worn bikinis with less material to Dominion pool parties, and you
didn't have a spaz then."

"No, I just watched you like a hungry dog all afternoon, then went back to my room and jacked off. But I digress."

Seriously? Callie blinked at him. She hadn't guessed that he had more than a fleeting thought about her sexually in the last two years.

"The amount of clothing isn't the issue," he continued. "It's the intent. You meant to arouse other men with what I considered mine. I know Sean felt the same."

"Exactly, lovely. You could wear a skimpy bathing suit at such a party, and if you meant it for us, I would probably smile. And get into a fight with any asshole who thinks he's going to lure you away. But a striptease for money for all those strangers . . ." Sean gnashed his teeth.

Had they gone to the same caveman school? Apparently so. They'd both graduated with honors, too. "Look, I didn't have a lot of money, so I had to get to the city and find work fast. I had to secure a place to live, buy food, and make enough money for a bus ticket out of town. It wasn't like I hopped on that stage as a big 'fuck off' to either of you."

They exchanged a glance. It was clear that neither of them liked the direction of this conversation. Thorpe bristled, crossing his arms over his chest to glare down at her with a gaze that promised hell later.

Callie melted back in one of the galley's chairs, biting her lip. She'd pushed the Dom in him too far. Best if she shut up and picked her battles. If she was smart, she'd change the subject now and distract him. "Don't you want to talk about the man in uniform at the airport?"

Sean rolled his shoulders, as if trying to shrug off tension. "He didn't look familiar?"

"No." She shook her head, grateful to him for the return to business. "Just the uniform. It looked military . . . but it didn't exactly seem standard issue." She tried to picture what was different in her head, but drew a blank. "Something was off. The color, maybe?"

"Were they BDUs?" Sean asked.

Callie frowned. "What?"

"Camo," Thorpe supplied.

"No. They were a pale blue."

Sean scowled. "Like the Coast Guard? Pale blue shirts with navy pants?"

"No. Both the coat and pants were the same color. More of a pale grayish blue. And they were dressier, for sure. Almost formal. The coat had patches and medals and stuff."

"You mean insignia?" He looked amused.

"Yes. Lots of chevron stripes and braided rope and crap."

"Did you recognize any of it?"

Callie held up her hands. "When would I have had time to study military uniforms?"

"Point taken." Sean scowled. "Did he wear a hat?"

"Yeah. One of those beret things. It looks funny on a guy built like the side of a mountain. He thought he was a real badass, too. I could tell."

"Did you overhear him give his name or rank or branch of service?"

"No, he didn't say any of that. He told people that he was meeting his girlfriend, but that she hadn't come off the flight. A few people remembered seeing me get on, so he knew I'd been on the plane. He had old ladies searching the bathroom. When some dude headed for the smoking lounge, I slipped out with my bag and caught a cab. You know the rest."

"And you've never seen that uniform before?" Thorpe asked.

Callie paused, scanning her memory. "No, I think I have. But it seems like it's been forever ago. I just can't place it."

Now that she remembered it, she flipped back through memories, years, locations. Not since she'd arrived at Dominion. Not while she'd been running before then. At home. With her father.

"Wait! A man came." Her heart pounded. "To our house. Not long before the murders." The memory sharpened, coming into clear focus. "An older man—not like the young guy from the airport. But I think they wore the same uniform. My father took him into his office. They argued. I remember it because Dad almost never raised his voice. He did that day. When I asked him about it later, he just said the man was pressing for a political donation and didn't want to take no for an answer. I let it go."

Sean frowned. "Did you ever see the older man in the uniform again?"

"No. My father was largely a recluse. He met with very few people, especially at the house. When I was a kid, the only person who came over with any regularity was some sort of medical researcher, Doctor . . . Aslanov, I think." Callie frowned. "But he stopped coming around when I was ten or so."

Sean searched around for a piece of paper and jotted some notes. "Yes, I know who he is. Doctor Aslanov researched cancer. I know your father funded quite a bit of his work for about five years."

"Yeah. Like he thought it would bring my mother back."

Thorpe came closer then and wrapped his arms around her. "I'm sorry, pet."

About her mother? Yes, she was, too. He seemed very sorry about Holden and Charlotte, as well. They both did. She drew in their sweet empathy.

Callie softened in his arms, and Sean joined them. They cocooned her in warmth and acceptance. Love. She kissed them each briefly, then backed away. They still had work to do.

"I think it's fair to say that the man who came to your house in uniform didn't drop in on your dad for a political donation," Sean said. "Any guesses about why he was really there?"

"None. I didn't get involved in Dad's stuff. I was a typical teenager, too wrapped up in my own."

"So . . . if we don't know who visited your house in uniform and we don't know what he wanted, let's talk about what the police found at the crime scene after the murders."

"You said my home was ransacked?" Callie frowned and wrapped her arms around herself. "I remember that big, gorgeous house like it was yesterday. Double grand staircases with white marble, wrought iron railings, and so much natural light. The house always seemed so . . . pristine. It was a reflection of my mother, and Dad never changed it. I can't imagine it torn apart."

"I saw the pictures," Sean said softly. "They didn't have a lot of time in the house before the police arrived, but they searched in every nook and cranny, every drawer, closet, and niche."

That shocked Callie. "They had to have worked fast in over sixteen thousand square feet."

"Sounds like they knew the layout of the house," Thorpe surmised.

She shrugged. "It was public record. *Architectural Digest* had done a spread on the house about a year prior. It showed the floor plan."

Sean sighed. "I'm looking for logic. Why would anyone come in, kill the occupants of the house, then tear it apart to take one item?"

"I don't think anything had been stolen. What did they actually take?" She searched her memory for all the treasures her father had in his possession. As a man who'd come from enormous wealth and had a talent for growing it, he'd had some priceless treasures. But if the killers hadn't taken any of the art or the cash, what had they sought?

"An Imperial Fabergé egg. It's worth about . . . eighteen million dollars, give or take a few pennies. I can't imagine someone stealing it for profit, but we've never seen the egg for sale, even in the most illegal channels. It doesn't seem likely that hardened criminals would break in and kill simply to decorate their mantel."

Callie flushed. "They didn't take it. I did. It's in my backpack. My backpack! Where is it? I left it in my hotel room in Vegas and—"

"We brought it with us, lovely. Take a breath. Relax," Sean advised. "Why did you take the egg?"

"It was my mother's. It was all I had of her."

"It's rare and incredibly expensive. You've been carting it around for nine years while living in slums?"

She sighed. "I know. But it's not like I could have rented a safe-deposit box or anything. My consolation was that if anyone ever thought about swiping it, in those neighborhoods, they probably wouldn't have had a clue what it was. After all, it's one of only about six dozen to survive the Bolshevik Revolution."

Thorpe's eyes widened. "You had that egg in my club for four years?"

Callie nodded. "It was kind of a relief. No one was going to steal it from there. They didn't dare come in my room or you would remove their heads from their bodies in the most unpleasant way possible."

"That's true," Thorpe concurred, smiling as if pleased with himself.

It was . . . cute.

"I never imagined *you* took that egg," Sean admitted. "One way the bureau tracked you was your pattern of leaving everything behind. You were reported as a missing person about a half a dozen times, so we got to know your MO. You never took personal mementos when you moved from one location to another."

"Well, my father had so many of my mother's photos locked away, as if he couldn't look at them without grieving all over again. But Mom told me just before she died that the egg was mine. I probably should have left it behind, but I couldn't."

"Is there any chance that whoever killed your family wanted that egg?" Sean wondered aloud.

"I don't know why they would. It's valuable, but if they didn't want art or money, why go after a relic? For me, it was just sentimental. That egg was her pride and joy."

"They open up. Could there be something inside it?" Sean asked.

"I don't know." She shrugged. "I've tried to pry it open repeatedly. I even took a screwdriver to it once and got two stitches and a tetanus shot for my trouble. It's stuck."

Sean gripped his chin and let out a breath. "There are a lot of pieces to this puzzle. We're onto something. It's right here. I can't quite figure it out yet. Why don't we have some brunch? I'll grab a shower. After that, we'll hunker down and think some more."

"Good call." Thorpe glanced around the galley. "I hope cereal is okay. You know Callie and I don't cook."

"For shit's sake, I'm sending you two to cooking school when we get out of this mess."

"Sounds fun. I've always wanted to learn." Callie smiled, then turned to Thorpe.

"Don't count me in," he snapped. "I'm fine just the way I am."

Meaning he didn't want to see her after the danger had passed? She looked away, biting her lip.

An awkward silence prevailed, and Sean sent her a sympathetic glance. Maybe she should just try to put the brakes on feeling anything for Thorpe, accept that he mostly wanted sex from her, and stop hoping for more. If Thorpe didn't need her, then she'd do her best not to need him.

Callie opened her mouth to say she'd try to cook breakfast and invite Thorpe to jump into the lake, but a phone rang. The guys both looked at one another. It could only mean trouble. Their expressions said that.

Then Thorpe took off running for the bedroom, following the sound of the ring. Sean followed like it was a footrace. Callie trailed after them, hating the icy slide of dread in her veins.

"Axel?" Thorpe shouted into the cheap plastic phone.

A pause, followed by a grunted acknowledgment. Then a much longer pause. Then shock transformed Thorpe's face.

"Are you fucking kidding me?" he barked into the phone.

Axel answered in a way that only made Thorpe more angry. His cheeks flamed red. He clenched his fists and looked like he might grind his teeth into dust. Holy hell, she'd never seen Thorpe that pissed off.

"Keep me posted." He stabbed a finger at the keypad to end the call, then looked up at Sean with a bleak stare.

"What?" Sean barked as he wrapped an arm around her, already trying to brace her for the news he expected would upset her.

"In the middle of the night, someone broke into Dominion. They trashed Callie's room and my office. Axel had a hunch, so he drove by your apartment. Searched and destroyed, too. Whoever has been after you, Callie, knows we're all gone. They're looking for something, probably whatever they didn't find when they killed your family. Now they're coming for us."

Chapter Sixteen

AN hour later, Sean retrieved her backpack from the stash in the bedroom. Gently, he shoved the remnants of cereal and toast to one side, then set her ragged bag on the little table and took a deep breath. Beside him, Callie looked tense and scared.

"What is it, lovely?"

"Aren't we sitting ducks here on the lake? We should abandon the houseboat and get far away from here."

"Medieval lords built castles using bodies of water as part of their defense. It would be difficult to mount an attack on the water and even harder to sneak up on us. We're hidden by boulders and mountains. No one is likely to find us without a helicopter, and even then, we'll just look like a boat on the lake."

"But they still might investigate it. In the past, when I've had someone breathing down my neck, I would change locations every day or two until I felt sure that I'd lost whoever was chasing me."

"You haven't done anything criminal, and I don't want you running like you are one anymore."

"Guilt or lack thereof has nothing to do with it," she insisted with a wave of her hand. "Whoever is after us will hunt us down. I think we should get off the boat and leave everyone guessing by going in three separate directions—"

"No!" he and Thorpe both barked together.

Sean turned his gaze to the other man. Thorpe's jaw clenched firm and resolute. He might not think he wanted to commit to Callie yet, but he'd fight to keep her safe. He'd even die for that cause. Because he loved her. The big lug was just too stubborn to do anything about it. At least right now. Time would tell . . .

Sean pushed the thought aside. Not the most important problem at the moment.

Except that if Thorpe broke Callie's heart, Sean knew he'd have to work even harder to heal her. She would cry and believe that she wasn't . . . something enough. Good, smart, pretty—whatever adjective filled in the blank and made no sense. Callie ticked all of those boxes for Sean, and if Thorpe's pig-headed avoidance made her feel like she lacked any of those qualities, Sean would take pleasure in beating the hell out of him. Kind of a downer, really. He'd started to actually like the guy.

"Maybe this egg has something to do with your family's murder." Sean changed the subject. "Let's focus on that and not make any other decisions until we inspect it. Maybe there's something special about it besides the obvious."

"Agreed." Thorpe nodded.

Callie pursed her lips, then looked away with a sigh. "We have to pull our heads out of our asses. Let's examine the egg once we get off this floating dead end. We're wasting time, guys."

He and Thorpe exchanged a glance, then the other man reached across the table to tangle his hand in her dark hair. "If we didn't have more important tasks at hand, I'd devise a fitting punishment for you, pet."

She pursed her lips. "For expressing an opinion?"

"For expressing it so disrespectfully."

Exasperation crossed her face before she stuck out her tongue at him. The gesture was somewhere between playful and impertinent, and Sean bit back a chuckle. No one could ever accuse Callie of being boring or predictable.

Thorpe tugged harder on her hair. "So you want to do this right now? I can occupy your tongue if you can't keep it in your mouth."

"Oh, I'll bet you can." She licked her lips. "Ready when you are."

"Why would I reward you?" He raised a brow at her, then prowled through the little galley. A few moments later, he pulled open a drawer and pulled out more clothes pins. Then with a yank on the little refrigerator door, he produced a bottle of Tabasco. "Stick your tongue out at me again, pet, and I'll put these to good use."

Callie gaped at him, indignant. She looked like she had a few choice words, but finally clapped her mouth shut with an angry little huff. Sean bit back another laugh. Even when she was a brat, she was adorable. But if he'd been alone with her, he would have had to nip her defiance in the bud. Thorpe's tactics were interesting, and Sean made note of them in case he needed them for future reference. In case Thorpe wasn't here to administer the attitude adjustment she needed.

With a sigh, she curbed her annoyance and focused on the situation again.

"I understand." She stared at Thorpe, who merely raised an expectant brow at her. "Sir."

"Better." He smiled and turned Sean's way. "Proceed."

It was impossible not to smile back. "On it. What do you know about this egg?"

"Not a lot. My mom talked about it, of course. But I was so young. She started getting sick when I turned five. As time went on, she became quieter. Mostly, I remember her holding me and telling me how much she loved me and to never forget that." Callie teared up, then sniffled. "Sorry. I haven't let myself think about those times in forever."

Thorpe stroked a hand down her spine in reassurance, then kissed the top of her head. There was no way he didn't love her. Dumbass prick. Even when he held himself back, Thorpe's devotion showed.

"So you don't remember anything about the egg specifically?" Sean asked softly.

"I think she said this one was from Easter 1912 or 1913— somewhere around that time frame. Dad bought it for her from a collector in Europe shortly after they were married. I guess she'd seen one on their honeymoon and fallen in love. This one came up for sale, and Dad gave it to her as an anniversary gift or something. When I was really little, she had it on a display stand that lit up on the mantel in their bedroom. She redecorated their whole bedroom around it. The room looked very stately. But when she got really sick, Dad had everything redone. He couldn't stand to see her lying in a bed surrounded by black."

Sean understood that. If faced with the prospect of losing Callie, he'd want to throw away everything dark and see her in nothing but sunlight and smiles for as long as he could.

"After she died, Dad moved it to his home office," she continued. "It sat on the corner of his desk for years. Charlotte and I weren't allowed to touch it. Then one day, he brought it to me and said that since Mom had wanted me to have it, I could keep it in my room as long as I was responsible. I've been trying to pry it open since."

"And you never succeeded?" Sean asked.

"Nope. I lied about how I gouged my finger bloody. I didn't dare admit I'd taken a screwdriver to the egg. But I'd dreamed up this fantasy that my mother had written me a long letter or poem— something she intended me to have that she tucked inside her favorite object. It sounds silly, but when you're doing things like getting your first period and surviving your first crush without a mother's guidance, it's rough."

"I'm sure she was with you in spirit, lovely." Sean wanted to hold her, wrap his arms around her. Hell, he wanted to carry her to bed and love her tenderly until he somehow convinced her that he meant to fill every void in her heart.

"And you're not aware of anything else unusual about the egg?"

"Other than it being a rarity in general, no."

"Tell me how else you've tried to open it." Sean felt her eyes on him as he unzipped her backpack and peeked inside.

"Besides the screwdriver, I've tried soaking it in water and brute force. It's, like, glued together or stuck. Something."

"Hmm. The eggs were made to open. They often contained some jeweled surprise," Thorpe pointed out.

"Right. I remember something inside the egg when I was a kid, but I can't recall details. It was shiny and pretty. After Mom was gone, I know my dad stashed pictures of her around some of her favorite objects. Once he gave it to me, I wondered if he'd left a picture of her in here, but I never could get the damn thing open to see. That just made her feel more gone to me." She sniffled again.

"We'll see if we can do better." Sean reached into Callie's backpack and pulled out some clothes, a wig, makeup, her toiletries, a box of colored contacts. Then he encountered a wadded-up towel.

"It's in there," she said as she stood on her tiptoes and peeked in.

With a nod, Sean reached down to the bottom and braced his hands under the towel, then began lifting it up. It was bulky more than heavy, and he felt himself sweat a bit, knowing that he held millions of dollars and something infinitely precious to Callie in his hands.

Resting the towel on the table, they all peered over it as Sean unwrapped the bundle. An intricate black and gold design in diamond-shaped sections decorated the top half of the egg. The lower half was a smooth black lacquer with solid gold braiding edging the bottom. As he turned it in his hands, Sean held history. These had been made for the Russian tsars for fifty years. They'd been valuable even a century ago. Now that so few had survived the bloody October revolution that had changed Russia, as well as the upheaval and wars since, the object verged on priceless.

Maybe her family's killers had sought this all along?

Thorpe dropped a comforting hand on her thigh, then looked his way. "Have any other ideas about how we might get this open?"

Sean winced. "As much as I hate to use more muscle on an object like this, I don't know what else to do." If there was nothing important about the egg itself or what might be inside, they were at a dead end. And he wouldn't know how else to give Callie hope. "I've got a multi-tool with me. We can start there."

Thorpe nodded. "Let's do it. I'll see if Werner keeps any tools lying around that might help, too. Callie, clear the table and put the dishes in the sink."

She nodded. Sean watched Thorpe squeeze her hand before he disappeared from the room, presumably to search for Werner's Craftsman collection on the boat, likely near the engine. He watched her forlorn face as she stared at the egg and touched it wistfully. He could plainly see how much it reminded her of the parent she'd loved and lost so young.

Jogging to the bedroom to pull the multi-tool from his bag, he grabbed a few other things and returned to find Callie rooted to the same spot.

He eased down into the chair beside her. "Lovely?"

"What if this doesn't work? What if it's nothing more than a pricey egg? If it's empty and of no value to whoever is after me—"

"Then we examine all the evidence again. We keep trying. I refuse to fail. I will not give up until you're safe. Do you hear me, Callie?"

She responded immediately to the sterner note in his voice with a valiant little nod. "Thank you, Sean."

"Is that who I am to you now?" He pulled her collar from his pocket and dangled the glittering white gold with its petite lock from his finger, directly in her face. Something less delicate was more customary perhaps, but it didn't suit her. "Is it?"

Hope lit her eyes. "No, Sir."

"I mean to fasten this around your neck again. You should never have removed it in the first place. Believe me, I never relinquished you from our bond in my mind or heart. So you best not be doing that either, lovely."

"I tried to," she admitted in a soft, broken voice. "But I couldn't. You're impossible to stop loving."

The words were difficult for her to speak, and he loved her all the more for finding the courage to say them. "If you want it back, ask me."

Callie scooted closer and looked at him with earnest blue eyes in her naked face. Even without all the black eyeliner and glittering shadow, she was stunning. His own eyes were a darker shade than the crystal Caribbean waters hers resembled. He wanted to drown there.

"Please, Sir, will you return my collar to me?" She ended her plea with a submissive bow of her head.

Sean drew in a huge gulp of air. As much as Callie had been forced to fend for herself most of her life, she wore her armor of independence with pride. She fought making herself vulnerable— despite how badly she wanted and needed to. He sensed the soft side of her that craved not just a lover, but someone she could rely on day in and day out for the rest of her life.

He would stand in front of her, never wavering, until she knew he meant to be that man. Then he would marry her and never leave her side.

But one thing Sean knew for certain: whether she was the fiercely independent Callie Ward or the more vulnerable Callindra Howe, she would never ask to belong to a man unless she not only cared, but trusted him.

Elation swirled through him as he tipped her chin up to him. "Will you remove the collar again without first talking to me?"

"No, Sir."

"Will you finally put yourself in my care and believe that I will always see to your needs?"

She blinked up at him solemnly. "Yes, Sir."

Sean cupped her face in his hands. The room was heavy with their connection. Gravity weighted each word she spoke. In retrospect, the first time he'd offered Callie a collar, she'd given him a saucy wink and a sway of her hips with her "yes." Now he saw that it hadn't been an invitation to touch her, but a way to keep emotional distance between them. She hadn't taken him seriously then.

Her reaction now couldn't be more different. And he was so proud to have earned her heart.

"On your knees, lovely." He glanced at the floor. "Bow your head."

She sent him one last clinging stare with those big eyes, a silent plea that he treat her fragile heart well. Then she slid to the vinyl floor gracefully and dipped her head low.

Sean unclasped the collar and fixed it around her neck, settling the bit of bling in place. The action was silent, but the importance of the moment shouted through his system. Callie was his again. And she would stay that way.

As he bent to kiss the crown of her head, Thorpe clambered to the door and stopped short, clutching a little bag of tools. He fixed his stare on Callie, his face stricken. The man swallowed. Pain gathered in the furrow of his down-slashed brows, his eyes darkening with something that looked a lot like anguish.

Sean frowned. The girl had always been his submissive. Seeing his collar around her neck shouldn't be new for Thorpe. Since the man had completely refused to claim her in any way for years, why should he begrudge anyone who did? Or expect Callie not to seek happiness? But he understood Thorpe's fear that the woman he loved

was slipping through his fingers. Sean knew he couldn't change
Thorpe's mind for him, but he could leave the door open as long as
Callie needed him.

"I found a hammer and a chisel." Thorpe said finally, his voice
sounding scratchy, strained. He set the bag on the table. "We'll use
them as a last resort. I'm sure Callie would rather not break the egg."

She whipped her head around and scrambled to her feet. She
looked braced for Thorpe's anger or a fight. The man did his best to
give her a gentle smile. The expression was a bit rusty from disuse,
but Callie relaxed.

Sean pulled her beside him. "Let's start with this little blade."
He held up one of the ends of his multi-tool. "I'll try to wedge it into
the space where the two halves of the egg meet. The piece is obviously well crafted, so I'm not sure we'll actually be able to work anything in there. But it's worth a try."

He focused completely, tuning the other two out to try to shove
the thin blade into the nearly nonexistent gap. He only succeeded in
bending the little knife. They tried taking some household chemicals
to the ridge where the two halves met until the galley smelled like
they'd been spring cleaning. They paused, then inspected it again.
Nothing.

With a sigh, Sean accepted the notion that they might actually
have to damage the multimillion dollar egg. It was an expensive
gamble. "If this is simply wedged shut, rather than holding something important, you realize that we'll have ruined a historically
significant object that could keep you living plushly for the rest of
your life for no reason?"

She blinked at him. "Unless I can figure out why someone wants
me dead, I can't come out of hiding to sell the object and live off the
proceeds. And if I do stop this person or people, then I stand to inherit my father's estate. And even independent of that, he left money
in trust for me."

Sean stepped back, a bit stunned. Callie's words made perfect sense, but he hadn't really put two and two together to consider her net worth once the smoke cleared. Her father had been a multi-billionaire, all his money carefully and successfully invested at the time of his death. The funds had been frozen since, presumably pending Callie being cleared of wrongdoing . . . or found guilty of murder. Some of her father's favorite charities and supposed friends had begun legal plays to petition the courts for the Howe funds, but the local police had refused to declare Callie dead with so much evidence to the contrary. They seemed convinced she was the most likely suspect, despite shaky evidence. But Sean also knew they were grasping at straws because they had nothing else.

Given all that, if the money remained invested as it had been that October, it should still be a very sizeable fortune—somewhere north of five billion dollars a year ago. The market had been fairly stable since then. *Holy shit.*

"Sean?"

He'd had a billionaire's daughter kneeling on the floor at his feet—the son of an unwed teenage mother and a philandering soldier with a girl in every military town. Instantly, Sean had a knee-jerk reaction to apologize to Callie, but he checked it. They weren't defined by their pasts or their bank accounts. They'd chosen one another because they clicked. They stayed together because they were in love. He didn't give a shit if her bank balance had ten zeroes or none.

"You didn't know that?" Thorpe looked at him as if Callie's inheritance was obvious. Because it was. For a moment, he felt like an idiot.

"Yeah, I did. It's not relevant. I guess that means we'll be doing whatever we have to in order to pry the blasted thing open."

"Hammer and chisel it is," Thorpe quipped and prowled through the bag on the table until he came up with the right tools.

"Try not to break it. It really is sentimental for me."

"I'll do my best," Thorpe said grimly.

With that, he set the chisel against the faint line that bisected the egg and tapped on it as gently as he could. The sound filled the little room to overflowing. Sean winced, not wanting to think about what sort of damage they were doing to the artifact. Metal scraped metal in a high-pitched squeak that made him wince.

After the next tap of the hammer, Callie hissed. Thorpe swore softly. Sean peered between them and saw a little dent in the gold of the rim—along with a small gap. With another tap, this one gentler, the two halves eased apart a bit.

His heart jumped, and Callie gripped his hand with such sweet hope. With her free hand, she brushed Thorpe's shoulder with a gentle touch that was equal parts adoration and thanks.

Both he and Thorpe had fingers too thick to work into the little wedge. Besides, it was her egg, her life on the line. Sean prodded her forward. "Go on. See if there's anything inside."

A more tentative girl would have perhaps shaken the delicate piece to see if something spilled out or tried to take a closer peek at the innards to see if anything lurked within. Not Callie. She plunged her thumb and finger right into the little open space. There was no way her vision could help with this task, so she closed her eyes as she rooted around.

Tension gripped the room, so pervasive it was a menacing presence all its own. Whatever they found here could make, break, or crush her. Then again, finding nothing wasn't a palatable option either.

A moment later, she gasped.

"What?" Thorpe barked.

"There's something stuck here and it wouldn't have been made with the egg. It's thin and plastic. I'm trying to get my fingers on it." She fumbled a moment more, twisting and turning her wrist for a better grip.

"Does it feel like anything familiar?" Sean asked her.

She shook her head, getting more frustrated by the moment. "I can't quite get it."

"Do we need to just break the damn thing open?" Thorpe scowled. "Because I will if it helps you."

Callie glanced at him with a face full of confidence. "No. I'll manage. You know how determined I can be."

Thorpe snorted. "Do I ever . . ."

Sean gritted his teeth. Damn it, they needed to stop bantering and hurry this along. What she found inside the egg could determine the sort of future he had with Callie. Would they be riding off into the sunset or living underground and on the run for the rest of their lives?

"Got it!" she shouted triumphantly, twisting and turning her hand a few more times.

Finally, she emerged with a flat little plastic square. It was blue and thin, and he hoped like hell they'd hit the jackpot.

"It's an SD card." Sean stated what was probably the obvious, then he blew out a breath. "Could your father have saved data on this, then hidden it in the egg?

"Maybe." She shrugged. "No clue."

"Then again, we didn't have a computer among the inventory of his possessions at your house. How would he have saved the data?"

"He had a laptop. He kept it mostly at his office, but brought it home occasionally. Why would he put data on this card instead of just keeping it on the computer?"

"Maybe this was a backup?" Thorpe surmised. "We need to read what's on this card ASAP."

"Where the hell are we going to find a computer that reads SD cards?" Sean tried not to lose his cool.

"Last night when I thought I'd be crashing in the spare room, I peeked in there. I saw an old desktop machine. Werner said he and his family occasionally take the boat out themselves, right? Maybe this is his floating office when he does."

"Let's go." Sean took Callie by the hand, making sure she still held the little blue card, and hustled her out of the galley behind Thorpe, falling in after her as the hall narrowed.

They caravanned together past the bedroom they had all shared last night. Sean wasn't sure how he was supposed to feel about the sex. He'd never imagined sharing the woman he loved with another man. But he had to admit their romp on that lumpy bed had been one of the most pleasurable of his life. Seeing Callie's fulfillment only added to the enjoyment. He itched to give that to her again.

A few steps later, they entered the second bedroom. It was smaller and darker. The head of a double bed, with a faded white comforter covered in little flowers, butted up to the paneled wall. It looked soft and worn and ready for a Dumpster. A window to the left with a desk in the corner made up the rest of the room. An old CRT monitor crowded most of the desk. The tower sat on the faintly musty carpet.

Thorpe yanked out the spindle-back chair and hunkered over the keyboard in front of the monitor that, from a technological prospective, had come from the Jurassic period. He bent and examined the computer, looking all along the sides and front for an SD card slot.

"Found it! If everything still works, we'll know whatever information was hidden in that egg soon. Give me the card, pet." Thorpe pressed the power button on the computer tower, and it flickered to life.

Anxiety skittered through Sean's system.

As they waited for the old machine to croak its way through the boot-up process, Callie nibbled on her lip and fidgeted. "Why would my father have put anything on an SD card and hidden it in the egg, then given it to me?"

"We may never know, lovely." Sean squeezed her hand in reassurance.

She squeezed back. "Did anyone break into his office and take his computer there?"

"Off the record? Yes. The authorities have kept that out of the press. But they ransacked his office—and nothing else in the building. As far as I know, everything else in the suite was destroyed, but nothing more was taken."

"How is that possible? The security was pretty tight. And if I were guilty of murdering my father, why would I kill him, then run to his office to tear the place apart?"

"Actually, we think the office was hit first, about eight p.m. that night. When whoever broke in didn't find what they wanted there or on the laptop, they came to your house a couple of hours later and . . . you know the rest."

"I was having dinner with my family before the murders, so I couldn't have been breaking into his office."

But the only people who could have corroborated that story were dead. She'd arrived at the table after the meal had been served and left before Teresita had come to clear the dishes.

"Let's see what the SD card holds," Sean said. Because if it held nothing of value, then this whole discussion was pointless.

A few tense minutes later, the computer finally finished its sequence and the desktop appeared. Thankfully, the operating system hadn't been set up to require a password. So as soon as Thorpe shoved the card in the slot and navigated to the drive, only one folder appeared, named Aslanov. Inside that were files with purely numeric names that Sean guessed were dates. After fairly consistent entries for months, they stopped abruptly fifteen years ago, then resumed again about six weeks before Daniel Howe's murder.

"Aslanov. I guess that's as in Dr. Aslanov." Callie frowned.

Deep in his gut, Sean knew where this was going and he didn't like it. "I suspect so."

"My father gave him a huge grant, a new lab . . . the works." She frowned. "But something happened. I don't know if they had a falling out or what. Suddenly, he just disappeared."

Now Sean really didn't like where this was going. "What's in that folder, Thorpe?"

He clicked on the little icon, and inside were dozens of documents with the same naming convention, looking as if they were based on dates.

"Now what?" Callie asked beside him. "With one computer, how do we tackle this? I have to know what this says or I'll go insane."

Sean caught the concern on Thorpe's face and nodded almost imperceptibly. Whatever was here might upset the hell out of her. It would likely be dangerous, too. Yes, Callie was an adult and had every right to know what they found. He had no intention of keeping facts from her, and her life really couldn't get much more perilous. He simply wanted a chance to prepare her in the event the card held something shocking.

"Lovely, there's only one screen and three of us. How about you throw together a little snack for us while Thorpe and I wade through the information. Then we'll share it."

"You two can't protect me from what I need to know," she protested.

"We won't hide anything from you or delete information," Thorpe vowed. "Just let us get an idea for what's here."

"You think I can't handle whatever this says." If her tone hadn't been an accusation, her pursed bow of a mouth definitely was.

"I'll admit to wanting to know what's here before I spring it on you." Thorpe turned in his chair to regard her directly. "Is that so terrible?"

Callie crossed her arms over her chest. "It is if you keep me in the dark."

"I won't."

"And I won't let him," Sean promised. "Let us just read it first, all right?"

She sighed. "Fine, but I want to know every word on that disc before I go to bed tonight. I *need* to know."

"We'll make sure you do as soon as we know something."

"You're still trying to shield me," she said glumly.

"Yes, I am, pet." He gave her a wry smile.

"And you're helping him." Callie pointed at Sean.

"Yes, because I agree, and no amount of your pouting is going to change my mind. You're more likely to earn yourself a punishment if you don't let up." He sent her a hard stare.

Callie looked like she bit back a thousand sarcastic replies. Instead, she managed a long-suffering sigh. "Yes, Sir."

Not the attitude he wanted, but he understood her strain. The balance of her life might hang on that card and, after nearly a decade of mystery, she wanted the chance to solve her family's murders. If closure was at hand, she had a right to it. It would help her move forward. It might give her—them—a future.

Sean watched her leave the bedroom and march stiff-backed down the hall.

"I don't like any of this," Thorpe said to him in hushed tones.

"I don't, either. But we'll have to tell her as soon as we've figured out what that says."

Thorpe nodded reluctantly. "Do you think her father put the card in the egg?"

"And glued it shut, yes. Who else would have done that?"

"Then he wanted this information hidden for some reason."

"Or kept safe. But I'm trying to decide why he would give it to *her*." Sean rubbed an absent thumb over his chin. "To be less conspicuous, maybe, in case someone wanted the information badly enough to break in? But why not put it in his safe or keep it securely at the bank."

"Daniel Howe wasn't a stupid man. Maybe he had some inkling that Callie planned to run off."

"And planned to take the egg with her?" Sean shook his head. "Daniel Howe was regarded as a bit eccentric, but what man stands by idly and lets his sixteen-year-old daughter run off with a player? That doesn't add up. But I can imagine him wanting to hide the information in plain sight. He could still access it if he wanted. But since he went to the trouble to conceal the card in the egg, I have to believe that whatever it says, he wanted that information buried."

"There's no other way to see it." Thorpe sighed. "I'm almost afraid of telling Callie what we find. It probably got her family killed."

"I can't argue, but there's no way we can keep this from her. If we find something, it will be a bombshell, I have little doubt. It might completely turn her world upside down. We have to be prepared." *She'll need us both.* Sean bit the words back. Thorpe wasn't ready to hear them.

Cursing softly, Thorpe opened the first file on the SD card. Sean looked over his shoulder. Together, they began to read.

Chapter Seventeen

AFTERNOON had come and gone when Sean and Thorpe finally stepped into the little galley. Callie had long ago stopped pacing, stopped trying to recall the terrible night of the murders . . . stopped hoping that her men hadn't found anything.

As they stepped into the small space, filing in through the doorway and looking at her with a gravity that scared the hell out of her, she stood and felt her stomach drop to her toes. "You know why someone is after me? Why they killed my family?"

"We think so, yes," Sean said heavily.

"How bad is it?" No sense in dancing around the truth or letting them BS her. Someone was after her, and she was damn tired of running, of not knowing why her life was in shambles, or not understanding how all her tomorrows had fallen apart at once.

If she was reading their faces right, anything that might resemble a happy future was nothing but a pipe dream.

"Sit down, lovely," Sean said softly.

So whatever they'd discovered was not just bad, but awful.

"I don't want to sit down. I've been doing that for hours. Damn it, just tell me."

Sean glanced at Thorpe. Though Callie wouldn't have thought it possible, he looked even more grim. Her caretaker for the last four years firmed his jaw as if steeling himself.

Panic slipped an icy chill through her bloodstream. "I'm already expecting bad, but you two are scaring the hell out of me. What is going on?"

"Your Master gave you an order, Callie." Thorpe pointed to the chair.

Did they think she was going to faint? She plopped down into the little aluminum chair with the bright blue vinyl seat and glared.

Before she could demand that they spit it out, Sean dropped to the floor in front of her and took her hands in his. He swallowed. "How much do you know about the research your father paid for when you were a child? What was Dr. Aslanov supposed to do exactly?"

"Find a cure for cancer. That's all Dad ever said. Is this . . . about the research?"

Sean hesitated, so she looked up at Thorpe. He nodded. "Your father didn't just want to find a pill or treatment that would make cancer disappear. He told Aslanov to find a way to cure it genetically to ensure that no one ever had to hear again that they or a loved one had a disease that would eat away at them from the inside. Aslanov wasn't just a researcher; he was a controversial young Russian geneticist. He had theories many of his colleagues eschewed. Turns out he was right. And wrong."

"Aslanov figured out how to genetically prevent cancer from ever happening?" Callie had to pick up her jaw. Was that even possible?

"Not exactly," Sean hedged. "If we're reading your father's notes right, Aslanov took the principles of genetic engineering used in fields like agriculture and medicine and expanded them with mixed results. Your father later described this sort of genetic research as the 'lawless frontier' of science. But he didn't know that's what his money was buying until it was too late."

"What do you mean?" Callie gripped Sean's hands, her stomach tightening in knots. "Aslanov killed him?"

The guys exchanged another cautious look that made her heart stutter.

"No," Thorpe finally supplied, looking as if he had more to add. But he clammed up.

"When your mother first got the diagnosis, she apparently wasn't given more than eighteen months to live. Your father searched for someone who believed they were close to a cure or something at least to put her in remission. But he couldn't find anyone willing to bypass all the safety precautions and government regulations to test their solution on your mother. Knowing that she was going to die if he did nothing, he veered in another direction and found Aslanov. In the previous five years, the Russian had been to some third-world countries that wouldn't bind him in a lot of red tape. According to Aslanov, he performed his research on others with great success. He told your father that with a little research and funding, he might be able to save your mother. Of course, that didn't happen."

"Her cancer progressed faster than expected."

"But Aslanov insisted he was close, so your father continued funding him for another four years." Sean paused, then glanced at Thorpe again, whose mouth took a grim turn.

"If you're editing this speech in your head, don't," she demanded.

"We're not, pet," Thorpe promised. "It's just complicated."

"All right, then. How did this research lead to the killing of my family?"

Sean stood, paced, obviously agitated. Thorpe took over the storytelling. "In researching to cure cases like your mother's, he stumbled onto additional genetic changes that your father wouldn't be interested in . . . but others would."

Callie frowned. "What others? Spit it out. I've waited nine years to find out what the hell happened to the family I loved and to stop

looking over my shoulder every five minutes because someone
wanted to kill—"

"Aslanov had a wife and three children—and financial problems. While researching for your mother, he claimed to have found
ways to mutate the genetic structure of a person to improve their
immunity, stamina, strength, and even their intelligence. No idea if
that was true, but he sold that bill of goods to someone else, we think
in the military because there were notes about an investigation on a
camp somewhere in Latin America, experiments being done to soldiers using some of the initial research. But exactly who was behind
that isn't something your father outlined."

None of what Thorpe said computed. "Wait. You're telling
me . . . what? That Aslanov sold his research to someone in the military, who later killed my family?"

"I've always said that you're quick." Thorpe nodded. "Eventually, yes."

"But why?"

"Your father found out what Aslanov had done and ordered
him to stop," Sean continued. "He pulled the plug on the research
and threatened to blow the whistle. Aslanov bowed to the pressure
and gave the remaining research his money had paid for back to
your father, who burned it, according to his notes. But Aslanov had
apparently already sold the information to his military contact,
who was expecting delivery. Here's where we have to guess a bit
what happened, but it makes sense. This military contact went to
Aslanov for the most recent data he'd purchased. When the scien-
tist no longer had it to give, they killed the man and his whole
family."

"Even the children?"

Sean and Thorpe wore identical expressions that didn't give her
a happy feeling, before Sean finally spoke. "That's the assumption.
The bodies of two of the three children were recovered at the crime
scene. The third was a five-year-old girl, but she's never been found.

The Aslanov case is something I've been looking into as a possible tie-in to the murder of your family because they shared a professional connection and the execution of the crimes was so similar. I could never prove they were linked, however. What we found on the SD card isn't a smoking gun, but we're getting closer."

Callie couldn't sit still. The information pinged around in her head like a pair of dice, rolling and tumbling. She paced, clenched her fists . . . felt Sean's and Thorpe's gazes watching her every move.

"Talk to us, pet."

"My father tried to do a good thing. He tried to save my mother and end cancer. It was probably Pollyanna and too ambitious, but someone killed him for it? I don't understand. And why would they kill my sister, too? She didn't know anything more than I did." Callie scoffed. "She probably knew less, even. Dad paying Aslanov for all that research happened when she was just a tyke and—"

"Collateral damage," Sean said softly, rising to embrace her. "That's why they killed your sister and Aslanov's family. They were all witnesses these scumbags didn't need. Whoever paid for that research had no idea what Charlotte might have known and if they'd asked . . . well, then she could have identified them. I'm sure they saw her death as a precaution."

Callie saw the whole thing as senseless—her father's murder, Charlotte's slaughter. For DNA research? Logically, she could connect the dots. Emotionally, she just couldn't understand anyone capable of pulling the trigger. "Whoever killed my family and the Aslanovs . . . what can they do with this research?"

"Piecing together the puzzle from what your father wrote? I'd say someone wanted to build a faster, better soldier. Maybe even a whole army."

Super-soldiers? The implications of that were astonishing. Possibly world altering. She'd already known they weren't dealing with amateurs or people likely to give up. But this information terrified her beyond anything she'd ever felt.

Suddenly, Thorpe's arms were around her, fitting her back against his broad chest. Warmth, comfort, protection.

Sean cupped her face in his big hands. "You're trembling, lovely. Deep breath. You'll never be alone in this."

"We're by your side," Thorpe promised. "Until you're safe, we always will be."

Callie wanted to burrow deeper between them and pray that the danger went away. Or shove out of their embrace and rail at the world until something changed. "Safe? There is no safe. We have to start being realistic here. Given who and what I'm up against, it's a miracle I've escaped them for this long. But can I really do this for the rest of my life? Like you said once, I'm alive, but I'm not *living*. I've already done this for nearly a decade. How much longer—"

"We're going to get this information into the right hands at the FBI." Sean stared down into her eyes, determination stamped all over his face. "I'll figure out who we can trust. We're going to work until we make you safe. I put a collar around your neck. Someday, I'm going to put a ring on your finger. Don't for one instant think I'm going to let anyone harm you."

His vows were staunch and so lovely that they made her heart sing. They were also most likely hopeless.

Behind her, Thorpe tensed—and remained utterly silent. He made no such promise for the future. He cared, but he didn't love her. And he'd probably never tell her why.

Hell, she might not even be alive long enough to miss him.

"If whoever this is finds out that you two have been secluded with me, I won't be the only one they kill," she pointed out.

"Stop that speech there," Thorpe growled. "We're not leaving you to handle this alone and we've already amply covered that point. Don't bring it up again."

"Precisely," Sean added. "You may not see the way to safety now, but there must be one. We're going to find it, and it starts with getting this information into the right person's hands. I'll figure out who that is. But without Internet, we'll have to deliver it in person."

That made sense, though it scared her half to death.

"I think we start by leaving here at first light. As soon as I can see well enough to dock the boat, we'll sneak back onto land. I'll find a secure cell signal then and I'll start making phone calls. At that point, we'll arrange something, whether they send reinforcements to us or direct us to a safe house—something. We'll prove you weren't involved in the murders. They'll protect you while we figure out who killed your family and the Aslanovs, then—"

"That's a lot 'ifs' and 'thens.' How do we know we can trust everyone at the FBI? How do we know that we'll ever have enough information to figure out who was willing to kill so many innocent people for that research?"

"Leave all that to me," Sean insisted.

Callie stared out the galley window to see the sun setting. She had no idea what the actual time was, but she wished she could stay here forever with these two amazing men who held her heart. She wished she could give them a lifetime of love, kneel and obey . . . and get into trouble now and then just for the fun of it. She wished she could pour out her heart to Sean every day and be the best wife and submissive possible. She yearned to heal Thorpe so that he could be whole again, so he might stay with her and fill that other missing part of her. None of that looked likely now.

But they were right about one thing; running wasn't the answer, not anymore. Whether she had eight hours or eight decades left, she wanted to spend as much of them with people she loved. These murderers had taken away her family and her past. By damned, she wasn't giving them her future, too.

She nodded at them. "All right. What's next?"

* * *

BY that evening, they'd packed up everything they needed to take when they debarked, secured the egg and the SD card, and eaten a light dinner. They sat around the galley's little table in near silence, drinking a bottle of red wine.

Thorpe couldn't help but fear that tonight would be their last together.

He swallowed, his finger rimming the top of the glass. Hearing that Sean intended to save Callie, no matter the personal risk, wasn't a blow. Thorpe felt the same. But the other man's declaration to marry her had been like a wrecking ball to his solar plexus. Once they left here and the FBI got involved, Callie wouldn't need him anymore. Oh, Thorpe knew he might give her more boundaries than Sean, but the fed would catch on. He was a smart guy. He wasn't going to let her flounder or need for long. Sharing a road trip with Sean had convinced him of that much.

Downing the rest of his vino, Thorpe thought about fighting for Callie or at least trying to stay with them both. But he knew his limitations. A woman like her deserved to be with someone who could be by her side step for step. As the years went past, he'd become less able. But long before then, she'd want someone who could show her in every way how much he adored her. With his body, yes. Every day, every night, every chance she gave him. With his words? This fucking hang-up of his was so frustrating. He needed to get over his shit. Callie wasn't Melissa; she wouldn't leave him over three little words. Even more important, she wasn't like—damn it, he even hated to think her name.

Suddenly, Callie stood, her chair scraping the floor. "I can't stand the elephant in the room. Whatever happens next is going to be dangerous."

Thorpe turned to Sean, who nodded. "Likely. We don't know if we were followed to the lake. I don't think so or they'd already be all over us. But they aren't going to give up. When we step on shore tomorrow . . . anything could happen."

Wishing like hell he could refute those words, Thorpe only nodded.

Callie looked nervous, stricken, scared. But resolute. "Then I need to say a few things."

Her voice shook, and she looked like she was trying to hold it together. The belief that she might not live through the end of this was written all over her face.

Thorpe's heart lurched in his chest. "Pet . . ."

"Please let me." She shook her head. "I need to get this out. I won't break."

"Go ahead." Sean took her hand, his thumb making soothing circles across her knuckles.

"The two of you stuck with me when sane people wouldn't. You came for me, despite the hell I put you through. You didn't sell me out when you could have. After Holden, I didn't want to trust anyone—ever. But you kept proving yourselves over and over." Tears flowed and fell down her cheeks, and damn if that didn't break his heart. "I'm sorry if I was difficult and stubborn. But you two reminded me what it was like for someone to care, and I hadn't had that in so, so long. Thank you. I will always be incredibly grateful. And I will always love you."

"Callie." Sean reached for her.

She stepped aside. "There's nothing more we can do tonight, right? No docking in the dark?"

"No. I'm not expert enough with a boat this size."

"No making phone calls now?"

The fed shook his head. "Not until I can figure a few things out, like exactly who to trust."

"Then I want tonight to be about the three of us. I want to give you both what I've never been able to give anyone." She drew in another trembling breath, her nervous gaze bouncing between him and Sean. "All of myself."

His cock stood up and partied. The idea of having Callie in ways he'd only fantasized about made his blood rush south, his head swim with dizzy anticipation, and his veins sizzle. It also made him ache. As she'd done before, she was leaving a chunk of her soul with them as good-bye.

The thought that he might lose her to a bullet tied his guts up into an army of painful knots. The thought that, if the danger passed, he'd have to give her over exclusively to Sean made him want to scream and spit nails and beat himself up for not being the right man for her.

"Are you sure, lovely?" Sean cupped her cheek.

"Yes. I trust you. I want to do one thing right. I want to take one really good memory with me tomorrow in case it's my last. Please."

How the fuck were they supposed to say no to that?

Sean cast a concerned glance his way. Thorpe sent it back, then stood. If this was the last time he got to touch Callie, he wanted to experience her in every way she'd let him.

And to give her all the love he couldn't with his words.

"To the bedroom, then." Thorpe heard the rough note in his voice. He was trying to hold it together.

"Off with you, lovely. Once you get there, kneel and wait. We'll be along."

Those big blue eyes of hers looked Sean's way, her stare a caress, before settling on him. Her expression told him that underneath her determination to experience what might be her final night to the fullest, her heart was breaking.

Fuck, so was his.

He grabbed her shoulders and stared hard. If he kissed her now, he'd take her here in the galley. He'd ravish her over the little table and bang away at her like there was no tomorrow. Because there really wasn't.

Somehow, Thorpe managed to restrain himself and merely pressed his lips to her forehead. Sean grabbed her hand and nuzzled her neck. Callie held her breath and froze. Eyes closed, she appeared to drink in the moment. He inhaled her scent and did the same.

Why did this hurt so fucking bad, way beyond the pain of Melissa leaving him? Even more than what the terrible bitch before her had done? Callie had told him once that he would be her biggest regret, but damn it, she would be his.

The moment passed, and she left the room, head held high. A thousand thoughts crowded his head. Even more emotions crushed his chest. He clenched his fists, wanting to beat the fucking wall. But it wouldn't do any good. Tomorrow was going to come.

"We can't leave her alone for long or she'll fall apart," Sean murmured softly so Callie couldn't overhear on the small boat.

"Agreed."

The other man swallowed. "Let's get down to it, then. She struggled for months before she allowed me to fully restrain her. If she wants to submit everything, we'll have to push her."

"I say we cut off most of her senses. There's no way she can fully put herself in our hands until we take away her sight and sound. Force her to rely on touch, on what she's feeling."

"She'll surrender every part of herself, I think."

Thorpe nodded. "We have to give her this one night of freedom, really let her fly."

"She's asked us for almost nothing else. So if we can save her from whoever's trying to kill her, I'll probably never refuse her anything again." Sean's smile was self-deprecating.

"It will be to your detriment, I promise. She'll fight you, but she will want to know that you have her firmly in hand."

"Why won't you stay and make sure she is?"

The truth was on the tip of his tongue, but even if he blurted it out, it would change nothing. And Sean wasn't the one to whom he owed this truth. "It doesn't matter."

The fed looked ready to argue, but didn't. "I think you're making a grave mistake by walking away from Callie, a mistake you'll regret to your dying day."

"I'm sure of that. Why aren't you calling your boss tonight and asking for an armored escort to safety come first light?"

Sean sighed, clearly not happy with the change of subject. "My boss hasn't been forthcoming with information. He's fed me some lines that set off my bullshit meter. I'm really not sure who we can trust, so I won't give away our location until we have a plan B and a good escape route. I'd rather walk into the Vegas field office where there will be lots of witnesses. Trying to off Callie will be a lot more difficult then."

"All good points. Let's go find her."

Sean nodded, but began digging around in the galley. He picked up a few items that made Thorpe smile faintly. "I need some damn ear buds."

"I've got some in my briefcase, in the bedroom."

"Perfect." The other man headed out of the galley and toward the bedroom. "I'd like to surround her tonight. Make her feel the safest and most loved she's ever been."

Exactly what he'd been picturing. Thorpe nodded.

"We should make love to her together." Sean stopped in the little hall and turned, his expression sober. "Not like we did before, not taking turns. At the same time. I want to fill her completely."

God, he'd love that. But there were complications . . . "I don't think she's ever taken a man anally."

"Probably not." Sean pressed his lips together. "I've fucked a woman that way before, but not recently. I'm guessing you've had far more experience than me in that department."

Lots and lots and lots. During the wild years of his adolescence. Even more during his angry postdivorce phase. And probably more than his fair share in his early thirties when he'd decided to control every damn facet of his life and lost his ability to really give a shit about anything.

Until Callie had walked through his door and changed everything.

"Not so much practice in the last few years."

"The last four, maybe?" Sean asked knowingly.

Hell, he really was transparent.

He just smiled tightly. "Shut the fuck up and get to her."

With a brittle laugh, Sean closed the distance to the bedroom.
When they walked in, Callie knelt by the bed, head bowed, eyes
down, dark hair cascading all around her slender body. She looked
nervous but strangely at peace.

Thorpe retrieved his ear buds from his briefcase, along with his
iPod. He kept it mostly for his visits to the gym, but he'd equipped it
with some alternate playlists, including one for dungeon play. Without a word, he handed them to Sean, who'd already set the items
from the galley on the nightstand.

It chafed to turn over control of Callie's submission to another—
not really because he couldn't stand Sean touching her. Because he
wanted to have her under his control at least once. But he hadn't
earned it. Nor did he deserve to take that much from her if he wasn't
going to stay.

"You're still dressed," Sean pointed out.

"I debated, Sir. But you didn't tell me to strip."

"So I didn't. I think tonight we'd prefer to do it ourselves."

"Definitely," Thorpe added.

Sometimes, he and Sean were so thoroughly on the same page,
it was scary.

"Stand for us," the other man ordered softly.

Callie did so on wobbly legs. Now Thorpe could really see her
nerves. It endeared her to him even more, knowing this meant so
much to her.

Sean lifted the plain white shirt up her torso and over her head,
exposing her bare breasts and their plump nipples.

Thorpe brushed his fingers over one peak. "Close your eyes, pet."

She did so without hesitation, and Sean stepped up, pulling a handkerchief from his pocket. It wasn't a perfect solution, but it was clean and useful.

As he knotted it at the back of her head, he walked a semicircle around her, then tilted her chin up to him. "Your safe word?"

"'Summer,' Sir."

"After your childhood horse?"

"You knew that?" Surprise rang in her voice.

"I know so much about you on paper. I want to know everything about the real you for myself. Thank you for the beautiful gift of your submission. I know it isn't easy for you."

"No, but I need to do this."

"I know," Sean assured. "And I need to have it."

"So do I," Thorpe said thickly, walking behind her and grabbing her wrists. "Give me your hands."

Callie took a deep breath, then as she let it out, she released all the tension from her body and gave herself over completely. She'd always been beautiful to him, but watching a woman who had never truly trusted anyone now surrender her all both stunned and humbled him.

Thorpe took her wrists in one hand. With the other, he reached around and tilted her head back so he could plant a soft kiss on her forehead. "You move me, pet. I can't even tell you how much. Please don't ever think otherwise."

A soft smile lifted the corners of her lips. Thorpe bent to press his cheek to hers. So silky, so female. Callie was the woman he'd never dared to dream about.

As Sean passed him a couple of pillowcases knotted together, he tied off her wrists at the small of her back. Then he caressed her shoulders, lifted the hair from her neck, and kissed her soft nape. Every time he touched her, something swelled in his chest. Fuck, he hated that tonight would be the last time he had her.

In front of Callie, Sean gripped the ear buds and flipped through the iPod's playlists. "Which one?"

erTh

Thorpe chose a classical mix, instrumentals that were both reflective and passionate, that throbbed and swelled before finally crashing to a dazzling end. He used it as drinking music when regret buried him. The words to tell Callie how he felt were stuck in his heart, but some part of him hoped that she would hear his feelings through these songs.

Sean nodded, then directed his attention back to Callie. "You can't see?"

"No, Sir."

"And you can't move your arms?"

She wriggled her shoulders, attempting to work free. Thorpe smiled. He didn't know everything, but he damn sure knew how to secure a sub's wrists so that she'd be comfortable, but immobile, until he was ready to let her go.

"No, Sir."

"I'm going to cut off your hearing now. You'll hear music. But you're not to use it to tune us out. It's to quiet your head so you can feel what we're doing to you. And feel how much we care."

She tensed. "Sean—"

"No, lovely. Try again." His voice, low and encouraging, was meant to soothe, but it was also full of backbone. "Will Thorpe and I hurt you in any way?"

Callie didn't hesitate. "No, Sir."

"After all we've done to keep you from harm, do you think we'll let anything happen to you?"

Palming her shoulders, Thorpe gave her a little squeeze. "Pet?"

"Never. I just wanted to ask you not to make the music too loud. That usually gives me a headache."

Her answer filled him with relief, and he glanced over at Sean, who shook his head ruefully and fitted the ear buds in place as the music started.

He let it play for a moment, then removed one. "How's the volume?"

"Perfect," she assured. "The music is beautiful."

"Very good."

After gently fitting the bud back in her ear, Sean affixed the iPod, attached to the armband he also used during his trips to the gym, around her delicate biceps. It looked far too big on her, but it held.

"She's a damn amazing woman," Sean mused aloud.

Thorpe had known that almost the instant she walked through Dominion's door. He wanted to tell Sean how very lucky he'd be to have Callie in his life, if they could just get her past this danger. But he choked and barely managed a nod.

The moment dissipated as soon as Sean kissed Callie's rosy lips—a peck, a brush, then a lingering press, before he dove into her mouth with a stroke of tongue. Thorpe left a string of kisses along her neck and shoulder, bracing his hands on her hips and pressing his cock against her lush ass, desperate for the chance to be inside her again, to take something she'd never given another man. Wanting it this much was selfish, but he didn't bother to deny how desperately she made him ache.

Sean broke the kiss to caress Callie's breasts and thumb her nipples. Her breathy gasp heightened Thorpe's anticipation. And when the other man bent to tongue one of the berry tips, he tilted her head back and captured her next gasp with his kiss. Sweet, sultry, so tempting. She gave to them, the raw surrender so heartfelt, it made his damn knees weak. Women had submitted to him for longer than he wanted to admit. But they'd largely done it for their own reasons, mostly selfish. Now that he felt a submissive truly giving her soul simply to please, Thorpe wondered how he'd ever be satisfied with anything less.

Or anyone else.

Chapter Eighteen

When Thorpe pulled away, he found Sean on the ground between Callie's feet, arms thrown around her thighs, pressing his cheek into the flat of her stomach, eyes closed, expression reverent. Thorpe couldn't help but see how much Sean loved her. It should reassure him to leave Callie in such good hands. Instead, an acid ate away at him that she couldn't be his. Why couldn't he be more right for her?

As Thorpe reached around to bring her closer against his chest, he smoothed a palm up her ribs to her breast. Callie melted into him a little bit more, giving him a soft sigh.

From her waist, Sean dragged down the overlarge sweatpants she'd swiped from his bag. He removed her panties with them, prompting her with just a touch to step free. She was gloriously bare, naked to them now in all ways. And Sean didn't waste a second. He kissed his way up her thigh and settled his lips over her pussy, lapping at her, kissing her with not just his mouth, but his whole body, full of gusto and need and promise.

Callie arched. Her lips parted with a gasp. A gentle pink spread across her milky skin as her nipples drew up tighter.

"Lay her across the bed," Thorpe demanded.

Sean looked up like he wanted to object. Then he glanced at the bed. "Yeah. It will be more comfortable for what I have in mind."

He stood, lifting Callie against his body. Instantly, she wrapped her legs around his waist and he walked with her to the mattress, still rumpled from the last time they'd taken her between them. Thorpe was there to untie her wrists and catch her as Sean spread her sideways across the bed. Her hair fanned like black silk against the bleached white sheets, her lips a succulent red. He secured her wrists together over her head again, then tied the pillowcases off to the bed frame, chafing with impatience to possess her.

As soon as she lay across the mattress, needy and writhing, Sean fell to his knees between her legs and bent to lap at her pussy again. No hesitation. No games. They were beyond that tonight.

Thorpe watched for a moment, the beauty of her skin shimmering in the low light, the power of her arousal, the way she spread herself wider and gave, all revealing the woman within.

Suddenly, her fingers dug into his thigh, conveying her sensual distress without a word. Callie couldn't see him, but she could obviously feel his presence. She must need him, and for that he was damn grateful.

Thorpe bent over her pleasure-filled face and sucked her nipples into his mouth, rolling them on his tongue, a lap here, a nibble there, alternating, lavishing sensation on them as Sean continued to worship at the altar of her cunt. Soon, she began tensing and crying out, pleading.

"She's going to come," Thorpe pointed out.

"Not yet. Distract her for a minute. I want her good and ready."

He could think of several ways to do that, but one overtook his thoughts and filled his cock with even more blood. Fuck, he couldn't remember ever being not just eager but frantic for a woman.

Tearing into his trousers, he released the button and zipper, then shoved the pants down, kicking them out his way with a snarl as he ripped his shirt from his torso, buttons pinging everywhere.

Fastening his grip around her arms, he tugged a bit and slid her closer. Callie's head fell over the edge of the bed with a cry, and he fisted her hair, tilting it a bit more. Anticipation wracked him as he stroked his cock and guided himself toward her parted lips.

As soon as he brushed the head along her softness, she opened fully for him, greedily swallowing him deep in her mouth and moaning.

"She likes that," Sean murmured. "She just got even wetter."

Thorpe couldn't do more than nod as he leaned forward, braced his hands on the mattress, and slowly began to fuck her mouth. The sensations of Callie all around his length, laving every nerve, coating him completely, and still eager to take more, was short-circuiting his brain.

Sucking up his shaft to the sensitive head, she laved it with her tongue, moaning and eager, before he plunged into her mouth again. Her lips tight, she took him as far as she could and held him there as if she sought to memorize his flavor. And she did it all so slowly. Her face, her body language, her very movements, they all shined with her love. No way his heart couldn't beat for hers in return.

Thorpe wasn't a man prone to emotion—or he hadn't been in over twenty years. Now he couldn't stop feeling. He didn't like it much. Some part of him wanted to resent her for dragging him from his self-imposed gray. But he'd needed Callie. He'd been suffocating without her. God alone knew how he was going to make it without her after tomorrow.

And if she kept sucking him like that, he wouldn't make it two minutes more without coming.

Suddenly, she gasped around his cock. Her body tensed again. Thorpe couldn't miss the rosy flush spreading across her chest or the way she lifted her hips to Sean's mouth.

With a whimper, she writhed. He almost swore he could hear her say "please" with a mouthful of his cock.

Sean pulled away, and she gave another little groan of protest that made Thorpe smile, despite his stinging arousal. She'd rarely been shy about saying how she felt or what she wanted—in her clever way. Lance had once referred to her as a handful. He'd been right.

"I'd love to let her," Sean said sheepishly. "I don't have it in me to deprive her tonight."

Thorpe brushed Callie's cheek, encouraging her to slowly release him. With another breathy moan, she did.

"She may need it now," he countered. "It's possible the double penetration will be a bit too uncomfortable for her the first time and she won't come. Besides, if pleasing her pleases you, she'd want that."

"You're right."

All of what he'd said was true, but there was a bit of selfishness in there as well. He wanted Callie to remember this night and the ecstasy they gave her over and over. She'd pair off with Sean, and they'd share a lifetime of passion. But Thorpe wanted tonight embedded in her heart forever.

"Here," Sean cut into his thoughts, shoving a plastic cup in his hand. "I'm sure you'll find something fun and creative to do with these."

Thorpe looked down. Ice. Always a favorite. "I'm sure I can."

"Maybe put them in her mouth?"

And sink his cock back into that velvet heaven after adding more stimulation? "I've got a better idea."

"Excellent." Sean grinned as he returned to the bed, petting and laving Callie's swollen pussy, driving her arousal up once more.

Thorpe stretched across the bed, settling beside her and keeping the cup within reach. As soon as she turned her face in his direction, he took her mouth with his, cementing his lips on hers and nudging her open wider. Then he grabbed one of the cubes from the cup and skimmed it over her nipple.

Her gasp filled his mouth. As unexpectedly as he'd set the cold cube on her flesh, he took it away. Callie tried to raise off the bed, as if searching for more. Sean held her hips down firmly and affixed his lips to her pussy again until she twisted, her breathing turned uneven, and she mumbled pleas that thrilled both the Dom and the man in him.

Then Thorpe set the little block of ice on her nipple again. This time, he turned it on end, dragging an uneven edge back and forth across the sensitive bud. She whimpered, then held her breath, her entire body straining toward the pleasure.

"Now?" Thorpe asked.

Sean lifted his face from her slick folds and licked his lips like a man having a really good time. "Yeah. Fuck, she's so juicy. Tell her to come."

Thorpe nodded, dragging the ice down her breast, then caressing her nipple with the edge again. Callie wriggled and gasped, both tender peaks as hard as he'd ever seen them.

With one hand, he switched the ice to her other breast. With the other, he dislodged one of her ear buds. "Let go, pet. Sean wants you to come on his tongue."

He barely wedged the little piece back in her ear and sucked on the chilled tip of her breast before she tensed from head to toe and shouted out a low, agonizing climax that seemed to last forever. Sean didn't stop, didn't waver. He just loved her clit with a nonstop devotion that soon had her bucking in aftershocks and tears streaming from her eyes.

Every time they gave their all to Callie's pleasure, he swore that she couldn't possibly experience more ecstasy than the time before. Again, she'd proven him wrong. Her capacity to open herself to them just kept growing and astounding him.

Lost in his musings, Thorpe almost missed the condom Sean threw his way. "Put it on now. I need to be inside her."

He hedged. "It will be easier on Callie if I go first."

Sean hesitated, gritting his teeth, then nodded. "Then hurry up."

Thorpe scrambled to his feet and had his condom on seconds later, studying the bed all the while. "How do you want to restrain her now?"

Doffing his shirt, the fed frowned and took in the situation with a glance. "Untie her hands. I've got a solution."

Thorpe released Callie's wrists from the pillowcases and unknotted them from the bedframe.

"Want to clue me in?"

"Oh, you're going to get this without a word." Sean grinned. "Pick her up for a minute."

Thorpe did, bringing Callie against his chest and nuzzling her neck as Sean lifted the mattress and settled a length of rope he'd brought from the galley beneath it, leaving a foot or so dangling on either side.

Just like Sean had promised, he understood. And he grinned back.

"I think I can help you. I brought a few things with me . . . just in case." Thorpe passed Callie back to Sean, then rifled in his bag until he came up with two pairs of cuffs. With a quick couple of knots, he affixed the ropes through the O rings of the cuffs, watching the other man kiss Callie with abandon. "Now, she's not going anywhere."

Sean eased her onto the mattress on her hands and knees. He fitted one cuff around her wrist. Thorpe took care of the other. Callie didn't protest. Instead, she arched restlessly on the bed, a silent invitation neither of them would ever refuse. Like Sean, Thorpe couldn't wait much longer.

He settled onto the bed behind her and gripped her hips.

"Gently," Sean warned.

Gritting his teeth, Thorpe fought with his conscience . . . and it won. "You want to do this yourself? It's your right as her Master to fully claim her."

Uncertainty slid across Sean's face. "I'd love to and I will someday. But I really don't want to run the risk of hurting her. You know what you're doing."

"It's not that complicated," Thorpe pointed out.

"I know. But she's not just fragile to me, she's priceless. You'll do a better job."

Now really wasn't the time for this conversation, but Thorpe had to know. "How are you the most selfless bastard on this fucking planet?"

"Haven't you ever lost someone precious to you and realized all the things you should have said and done when they were around? I don't want to end up with regrets."

No, he hadn't, Thorpe realized. Since adolescence, he'd been closed off, never letting anyone matter. Never letting anyone in. He didn't know what it was like to lose someone because he was not just walled off, but always the first to leave.

No wonder Sean had earned Callie's devotion. He would take care of her forever, putting her on a pedestal and loving her unconditionally.

Thorpe sighed. He felt like a terrible prick.

"She's waiting," Sean pointed out.

Looking down at Callie's sweet, round backside, Thorpe wished again he could give her more than this. Suddenly, all his regrets weighed two tons.

Trying to shove all the crap in his head aside for her, Thorpe caressed Callie's ass, then anchored one hand on her hip. The other he dipped down to her sweltering cunt and plunged two fingers inside. Her back arched. She cried out. Her flesh tightened around his digits. He began to sweat.

Rooting in her passage, he coated his fingers liberally with her wetness. He could probably find something in the galley to use as lubrication, but nature had provided well enough.

As soon as his fingers dripped with her essence, he circled her clit a few times. He wanted her not just aroused again, but as fevered as he could manage. It would blunt some of whatever pain she might feel.

With a steadying breath, Thorpe dragged his fingers through the well of her wetness again, then skimmed up to her back passage. With his free hand, he spread one cheek wide. She tensed. Her opening looked so small, untouched in any way. Was she even ready for this? Did she want any man to have this sort of dominant, primal claim on her?

"Take the damn ear buds out. I need to talk to Callie."

"But she's surrendering so well. She's giving us—"

"We don't know if she's going to consent to this, and I won't force it on her. Trust me, if she agrees to this, she's going to surrender more than she ever imagined. Even more than you hoped."

Sean nodded, then removed the ear buds and cupped her face in his hands. "All right, lovely?"

She gave him a shaky nod. "Can I see you?"

Flicking a glance in his direction, Sean asked a silent question. *What's best for her?* Thorpe nodded. Cutting off her senses was all well and good, but they'd given her that test. She'd absolutely passed, giving herself over and trusting them entirely. Now she needed reassurance. And he wanted to *be* with her, talk to her, look at her, feel that instant connection to her soul as he sank deep into her body.

"Of course." Sean pulled off the blindfold.

She raised her gaze to him, then turned to look over her shoulder. Thorpe met her stare, and electricity zinged down his spine.

He leaned over her back, thrust his fingers into her hair and tugged slightly. He set his lips to her ear. "We're going to get inside you, Callie. Deep. So damn deep. You're going to scream for us. You're going to come for us, too."

She whimpered, and to make his point, he rubbed at her clit again, then plunged his fingers into her cunt. "Yes."

"Both of us," he said. "Together. At the same time. Are you ready for that?"

She froze and tried to look over her shoulder at him again. He tugged on her hair. "Yes or no. We can discuss it if you need."

"I don't." She stared up at Sean, and Thorpe saw the man's face soften at her expression. "I trust you both."

"I'm going to take your ass, Callie. I'm going to ease my way inside and fill you like you've never felt. Sean's going to take up every available bit of space in your pussy. We're going to fuck you." *We're going to love you.* "We're going to make you feel so good. You will communicate with us. Tell us what feels good, what doesn't. If we're too fast, too slow, too hard, or just right. Is that understood?"

"Yes, Sirs."

"That's good, lovely," Sean praised her, then he bent to kiss her, taking her mouth with abandon.

Slowly, Callie relaxed under the long, devouring melding of lips. Thorpe took the opportunity to work her clit with teasing circles, a rhythmic brushing of all those nerves guaranteed to send her soaring when the time was right. Then he paused, cutting off her sensation for long moments. She groaned into Sean's mouth as if in agony. He repeated the process a few times, dragging her closer and closer to another orgasm with every delicious manipulation of her flesh and every maddening delay.

"Thorpe!"

She didn't need to finish the sentence for him to know what she begged for. "No coming, pet. You wait for us. Understood?"

Callie moaned in protest. Thorpe slapped her ass.

Sean grabbed her chin. "You will be patient or you'll get nothing. Now answer Thorpe."

Her whole body tensed, on the edge, flushed and ready and about to burst. "Yes, Sir."

God, she really was amazing. He knew they were pushing her far and fast, but she just drank in everything they gave her as if she needed to feel like she belonged with them.

Thorpe was painfully aware that he couldn't give her anything else tonight.

"Good," he praised, removing his fingers from her clit one last time, dipping them into her drenched cunt, then dragging them back to her untried rosette.

Slowly, gently, he worked his fingers in and spread them apart little by little, back and forth, over and over. They weren't going to do the job of a good set of anal plugs, and the sensations he was about to heap on her would be totally foreign. But she was as ready as he could make her now.

Fitting himself against her slick feminine folds, he slid inside her pussy, hissing out his pleasure and gripping her hips as she surrounded him. Fuck, it was heaven in here. Thorpe would love to stay and drown forever. But he remained only long enough to stroke her slowly and coat his cock with her juices. Then he withdrew.

Finally, he pulled apart the firm, pale globes of her ass and settled the head right against her puckered hole. "Arch your back, pet. Push down and exhale. I want this to go as smoothly as possible."

Callie gave him a shaky nod and did exactly as he demanded. She welcomed him. Maybe anal sex didn't say love to some people, but he knew the trust and courage she was showing, and he both admired and adored her for it. Of course, she also looked so fucking sexy, he could barely contain his need to shove inside her and pound her to the most demanding orgasm ever. But he did.

Backhanding perspiration from his brow, Thorpe began to slide inside her, a deliberate, steady push. The head of his cock eased in. She was every bit as tight as he imagined, and her body heat was already incinerating him. The sweat he'd wiped away just moments ago popped up over his skin again. Then he reached the tight ring of muscle and paused.

"Callie . . ." He pried her cheeks apart a bit more. "Keep arching. Push down as much as you can. Release a deep breath. Squeeze Sean's hand. Tell me if it's too much."

She drew in a shaky breath and nodded. "I will."

Bracing her knees a bit farther apart, she rebalanced and repositioned. Her ass pointed up to him, and he could see her releasing her breath.

Thorpe bent to kiss the small of her back, then pressed inside her again, gently tunneling down. The plum head of his shaft popped past the tight ring and . . . ah, he was gliding deeper and deeper. Callie gave a sharp gasp. A little pain—not unexpected. But he petted her hip, crooned praises to her, watched as Sean smoothed the hair from her face and smiled at her as if to silently tell her that he was beside her every step of the way.

It seemed like forever before he found himself buried to the hilt. Once he was, Thorpe couldn't help but grip the lush curve of her hips and toss his head back with a groan.

"You in?" Sean asked.

Thorpe managed to uncross his eyes long enough to nod at the man. "Get ready."

He didn't have to tell Sean twice. The man grabbed frantically for his condom and tore off his pants. Thorpe didn't pay attention to the rest. He closed his eyes and reveled in every second of Callie's burn, of her sweet surrender. God, this would be seared in his memory forever.

Gritting his teeth, he pulled back to the grip of her muscle, then melted into her again. This time, the stroke flowed. Callie breathed through it. Her moan of pleasure at the end ratcheted up his tightening arousal.

He withdrew and plunged his way into her again, this time with more speed and force. She rewarded him with another incoherent sound of need as she clawed at the sheet. Fuck, if that wasn't the sexiest thing he'd ever heard.

"Hurry," he barked at Sean. "Seriously."

"Yep." The other man wriggled under Callie, brought her head down to his, and kissed her furiously.

She dissolved into a puddle between them, moaning from deep in her throat, and undulating back into him stroke for stroke. Then Sean was gripping her hips and whispering something thick in her ear that Thorpe couldn't quite hear over the roar of his heart.

Callie gave a shuddering gasp as Sean probed her opening and worked his way into her pussy one agonizing inch at a time. Through the thin membrane inside her, Thorpe felt the other man coast up, slowly filling her with every inch of his cock until she began panting and let out a keening cry.

"Am I hurting you, lovely?" he asked, strain evident in his voice.

"It's tight. I feel so stretched."

Thorpe gnashed his teeth and fought for patience. He peeked around Callie's creamy shoulder, kissing it, then shot Sean a look.

The other man nodded. "We'll take it slow, then."

"Don't you dare!" she screeched. "Fuck me, damn it. I'm dying . . ."

She liked anal sex and double penetration. Callie had already been the woman of his dreams, but this made her his hottest fantasy, too.

"Demanding minx," Sean growled.

"Yes, Sir. Now hurry!"

Thorpe slapped her ass once as a matter of principle. "You don't make the demands, pet. But as it happens, fucking you suits us."

Sean didn't wait or reply or even give a shit what he was doing. He simply began thrusting up, shoving into her pussy with long, firm strokes that shook her body. Oh, no way was the fed getting all the pleasure.

Thorpe found the rhythm of Sean's strokes and began diving his way into Callie's ass between each. They quickly fell into sync, like a complicated trio of dancers—Sean plunging inside her, then Thorpe grinding down into her, and Callie rocking her hips for the most impact. It became a symphony of breaths, moans, skin gliding, sheets rustling. Fuck, it was like they'd done this a hundred times and knew the cadence and flow they each needed for maximum pleasure. It was utter magic.

Sweat now covered his chest and back. It was definitely on the cold side out on a houseboat in November, but July had nothing on him now. He sweltered, felt dizzy, almost fucking faint. His system was overloading with need and pleasure. And a love so strong, Thorpe knew he'd never recover.

As one, they picked up the pace, each straining until they melded together in perfect sensual harmony. Every sensation seemed to magnify the closer he got to the runaway orgasm he couldn't stop. Air whispered over his skin. His heart roared. His muscles bunched. Even the hair on his arms stood up as goose bumps covered him. This was going to completely flatten him.

Change him.

Sean grabbed Callie and kissed her again, a passionate consuming of her lips cut short by her high-pitched wailing.

"Please . . ." she pleaded.

"Yes," Sean grated out. "Now. I'm dying."

"Fuck, yes," Thorpe echoed, knowing that he was seconds from losing all control. "Come for us."

Before he even finished the sentence, a guttural cry escaped Callie, something deep and primal and immensely satisfying as she jolted and bucked between them. Sean's hoarse shout echoed his own as ecstasy blindsided him. His entire body and soul poured into her as he released. She might have given him all of herself, but he'd given her every bit of himself in return . . . everything but the three words that stuck in his throat. But Thorpe had no doubt that he loved her now, tomorrow, and forever.

Chapter Nineteen

AFTER a shower and a change of sheets, Sean emerged to find Thorpe waiting for him.

"Can we talk?" the big Dom asked solemnly.

His heart stuttered. "Sure."

"Not where Callie can hear us. Outside."

Where they'd freeze their asses off? It had to be serious, and Sean feared he knew where this was headed.

Single file, they walked through the galley, where he paused to kiss Callie gently on the forehead. "We're going to step out here for a minute, lovely. We'll be right back."

She frowned, her dark brows dipping with obvious concern. "All right."

"Why don't you wait in the bedroom? You look tired. Get comfortable." He tried to smile. "Take half the bed. You always do anyway."

"Hey!" she protested.

Forcing a laugh, he herded the other man outside, noticing that Thorpe said nothing to Callie. He barely looked at her.

The moment the door shut behind them, Thorpe walked to the

railing at the bow, then turned back to him as if preparing to launch a speech he'd rehearsed in his head.

Sean lost his temper.

"Don't you dare say it," he snarled. "One reason I brought us here was to spend time together, so you could see how perfect this is. I've given you access to every part of the woman I love, even some I've never taken. I fucking trusted you not to break her heart."

Thorpe's face closed up even more. "I didn't lie about the fact that I will never be what she needs. The danger is going to come. Hopefully, she makes it out unscathed. Then you'll take care of her. You have the capacity to love her and—"

"You're being a total chickenshit. That woman loves you. She would lay down her life for you. Tonight, she trusted you with everything she's got. Did you not understand that?"

"No, I got it. Damn it, what do you want from me, to admit that I'm fucking broken? Fine. I am." Thorpe grabbed his arm and snarled in his face. "I will not spend months or years tearing her down while I try to get my shit together. It's not going to happen. I'm doing her a favor."

Sean snorted. "Don't kid yourself. If you leave, you're going to kill her. And you're going to destroy yourself in the process. When you wake up a bitter, lonely man, I'm going to hold her tighter and tell her how much I love her. You'll only deserve every ounce of your misery."

He'd had it. No way he could look at Thorpe anymore—someone he'd considered . . . if not a friend, then a partner in Callie's completion—and not feel betrayed. Yes, the stupid lug had said he wasn't staying, but Sean had refused to believe that someone could love Callie as much as he did and still leave.

With a glare and a jerk of his arm from Thorpe's grip, Sean turned to head back to the galley.

"Wait." Thorpe's voice shook.

Sean didn't turn back to him. He didn't care anymore. "We're done. As soon as she's safe, I expect you to fuck off."

"And I will," he swore. "Just . . . let me have the rest of tonight with her."

That made Sean whirl around, jaw dropped. "Are you out of your mind? There's no way—"

"I won't touch her." Thorpe held up both hands, fingers splayed. "But she deserves an explanation. I've never told anyone what I'd like to share with her. I can't give her what she really needs, but I owe her this much." He swallowed hard, holding back a wealth of regret. "Please."

Sean wanted to punch Thorpe, make him hurt and bleed and welcome a painful death. He came so damn close. The only thing that stopped him was Callie. She'd be mad, damn her big heart. And she'd need Thorpe's explanation for closure. She wouldn't be able to move on without it.

"I really hate you right now."

Thorpe looked up at the sky, whether for divine intervention or to ward off tears Sean didn't know. Nor did he give a shit.

"It can't be more than I hate myself."

He sounded so defeated. If he was anyone else in any other circumstance, Sean would feel sorry for him. But . . .

"You know what she's been through in the last nine years." His tone sounded every bit like the accusation it was.

"I watched it for the last four. If I were the right man for her, I would have scooped her up back in Dallas, and you would never have had a shot. So don't tell me what she's endured." Thorpe drew in a shuddering breath. "I am never going to convince you that I'm doing what's best for her and to not hate me. And I'm deeply sorry. She's your submissive. I won't trespass any more than this. Do I have your permission to explain?"

Sean huffed in short, furious breaths. He struggled to put Callie's needs above his pride. It chafed him in every way possible to let Thorpe even talk to her now. "You don't need a whole night alone in the bedroom with her."

Thorpe shrugged. "Maybe I don't in order to get the words out. That's just so I can hold her and convey all I can't tell her."

"You've got an hour. Then she's all mine." He stormed back into the galley, slamming the door behind him.

Already, Callie looked like she knew she was about to get bad news that would shatter her heart. Sean swore he'd do whatever he must to pick up the pieces and make her whole.

* * *

"I need to talk to you." Thorpe reached his big hand out to her, his damp hair still slicked back, his cheeks lean with a fresh shave. Despite his grim expression, he was so achingly handsome.

Callie knew where this was going. She couldn't help but overhear his conversation with Sean from the other side of the door. The minute Thorpe's intention had become clear, a hollow sorrow had assailed her. Tears worked up from her chest, crowding her until she couldn't keep a blank face. Still, she tried like hell to press them down. All the while, she stared at his hand, wondering . . . if she didn't take it, would he still break her heart?

Finally, he approached her softly and slipped his hand in hers. "Come with me."

She dug in her heels. "You're going to leave me."

"I'm going to save you," he swore as he tugged gently on her arm. "No!"

"Will you please just listen to what I have to say?"

For once he wasn't ordering her. He wasn't using that Dom voice to demand her obedience. She wished he would, but no. Instead, his voice cracked. He sounded like he was falling apart.

Callie had no way to refuse him.

Stunned and disintegrating on the inside, she allowed him to lead her to the spare bedroom where the old computer rested. Her head raced, trying to think of a way to keep him from leaving. The pain of his departure was already pelting her all over and spreading debilitating agony. He'd been her constant for four years. Losing him was like losing a piece of herself.

Thorpe closed the door behind them, then led her to the bed, sitting down and dragging her into his lap.

"Don't do this," she begged. "Why can't you love me at least a little?"

It sounded pathetic the moment the words left her mouth, and she hated her weakness. The woman behind Callie Ward and every other alias had been tough, never allowing anyone to penetrate her armor, much less hurt her. Where was that woman now?

Gone. Deeply in love. Mired in loss.

"I wish it were that simple," he said with such aching regret. "I'm sorry."

Callie leapt from his lap and to her feet. She'd let herself fall in love twice, once with a man who couldn't love her back. Somehow, she had to pull herself together, gather her strength, and not beg Thorpe again.

"So that's it. You're leaving?"

"As soon as you're safe, yes. If it all works out, by tomorrow this time, you'll be free to be Callindra Howe again."

And she wanted that so much. She wanted the world to know that she'd loved her family and would never have harmed them. She wanted to honor their memories. But damn it, she wasn't sure it would mean anything without Sean by her side . . . and Thorpe on the other.

"Can you do me one favor and tell me where I fell short. What do you need that I don't give you?"

Thorpe cursed under his breath, then reached for her, tumbling her back to the bed and pinning her down with his thigh. She squirmed, anger flaring and making her fight him with everything she had.

"It's not like that, damn it. Would you lie still and let me explain?"

"The old 'it's not you, it's me' speech? Spare me." She struggled against him. "Let me up."

"Two minutes, please." His voice shook.

"Does it matter? If you need me to tell you that your leaving won't break my heart, I'll lie to you. I love you enough to say that. Just . . . I don't want to hear the excuse."

"You're the most amazing woman I've ever met." He stared down at her, his gray eyes so intent, almost angry with conviction. "Don't you dare think otherwise. And don't you lie to me. This is breaking my heart, too. If I was the kind of man capable of the devotion you deserve, I would give it to you, Callie. I would give you everything. I would open my heart for you and . . ." He broke away, turning his back on her and scrubbing a hand down his face. "But I'm not. Would you please let me tell you why?"

Callie felt her heart shatter into a thousand pieces in her chest. She wanted to be furious with him, rant and rail and tell him to go to hell. But it was obvious that whatever was tormenting him was killing him inside. He'd always been an island— controlled and closed off, a part of everyone around him yet not. His ability to remove himself was one of the things that made him a great Dungeon Master.

"Fine." Tears fell like hot acid down her cheeks. "Tell me."

He turned back to her with a watery gaze. "I want you to know what I've never told anyone. It's the only way I can explain that there's never been a more special woman in my life, and I will never forget you."

"Every word you say makes it sound like you love me. Whatever it is, we'll work it out. We're strong. We can—"

"The summer I was fourteen, I started my first D/s relationship. My dad worked. My mom was out with friends, doing charity work, lunching . . . whatever she did. I was stuck alone in a big house with our cook and maid. To a teenage boy, Nara was hot. Eight years older than me and fresh from Brazil. I'd been in lust with her for over a year."

Callie swallowed. She didn't want to hear this. She didn't. On some level, she knew that he needed to say it. And that she'd need to understand later when the shock had passed and she bargained with herself to find him and try again—whatever she thought would end her pain. So as much as she wanted to dash out of the room, she simply nodded. "Go on."

"My dad had some magazines. I know now they were BDSM-themed. I'd been having fantasies of tying girls up and spanking them since puberty set in. My head told me it was wrong. A good guy didn't have 'violent' urges. But that didn't stop the thoughts. And these pictures proved that I wasn't the only one who felt this way. They fueled my thoughts like never before." He tried to turn his pained expression into a rueful smile. "As teenage boys do, when they don't have anyone to play with, they play with themselves. Nara found me."

A thousand questions ran through Callie's head. Had this woman chastised him? Made him feel dirty? Blabbed to his mother? "And?"

"She was holding a pair of cuffs in her hand and said that if I wanted to experience my fantasies, she would teach me."

"She was submissive?"

"Sexually, she could be. That summer, I began learning how to be a Dom. It was a teenage boy's paradise."

"You restrained her?"

He gave a low, bitter laugh. "In the first five minutes. I spanked her, flogged her, paddled her. She taught me to use a whip, how to tie knots, how to read a sub's body language, how to anticipate her needs, how to discipline, control, and manipulate. There was nothing I couldn't do to her. *Nothing.*"

Callie blinked at him. "You had sex with her?"

"Oh, yeah. A lot of it. In about every way you can think of."

At fourteen? "Mitchell . . . She took advantage of you."

"I was no one's victim. I was a very willing participant. She gave me an education I craved. I'm not proud of it now. At the time, I was the envy of my friends." He shook his head. "By sixteen, I was six foot one and could grow a decent beard. No one questioned my age, so she took me to my first club. I loved it. She was an exhibitionist, and I didn't mind. I started learning from the other Doms. Needle play, fire play, blood play, breath play—she wanted it all. She even let me pierce her. And ménages. Lots and lots of those. She liked it when I invited friends over or took her to someone's house with me."

The woman had abused him. Of course, a teenage boy wouldn't see it like that, but there was no way he could have been ready for all that. Sex alone required some emotional maturity. A BDSM relationship even more. In retrospect, Callie had been way too unprepared to sleep with Holden at sixteen. She'd felt a bit guilty and dirty afterward—and that was with a guy she'd thought she loved.

Oh gawd. "Did you love her?"

Thorpe sighed heavily, the sound so deep with remorse. "After four years together and sexcapades all across the East Coast, I thought so. Right after I turned eighteen, I saw college on the horizon. I knew I'd be leaving home, and the thought of doing without Nara was killing me. It was all hormones and teenage angst.

"About two weeks before I left, she called me late one night. As I'd done many times, I snuck out and we met at some play party." Thorpe drew in a shuddering breath. "After the scene and the sex, I finally worked up the courage to tell her that I loved her. She'd never been one to make love or cuddle or show affection. She didn't even like kissing much. I just thought that was her."

That terrible woman had used him. How could he have imagined that he loved her? Because he'd been young and confused and hadn't known better. Her heart went out to Thorpe. She wanted to touch him so badly and tell him that it wasn't his fault, but she sensed that he wasn't done.

"Anyway, I asked her to come away with me. Nara laughed. Completely fell on the floor, giggling hysterically. She called me a stupid boy. She said she'd basically been changing my diapers for the last four years and she was done. According to her, I was too stupid to know that love didn't exist; only sex did. Then she told me that I'd better not confuse the two again because I still had a lot to learn. Apparently, my father was a better fuck."

Callie gasped. Shock stunned her system, a jolt to her heart, a twist to her stomach. She couldn't breathe. "Nara and your dad?"

"Yep. Apparently, he found her on a business trip in Rio and hired her. My mother wasn't submissive and told him if he wanted to do 'that,' he needed to find someone else. So he did. He'd moved Nara in to be his mistress and paid her well. But he traveled a lot, and she was angry at being left behind after he'd promised to show her the world. I was her revenge."

That would have been a terrible blow to a teenage boy's spirit. Barely a man, he must have been crushed by her cruelty. To know she'd used him over and over just to get back at someone else . . .

Callie had felt stupid to have been deceived by Holden and hadn't trusted anyone for nearly a decade because of it. And her ex-boyfriend hadn't been vicious, just greedy and horny. Nara had done her best to destroy him for the rest of his life.

"I'm so sorry." She fused her gaze with his, willing him to understand that she would never treat him that way. "What she did to you was unforgivable. You have to know I would never—"

"I'm not done." Thorpe was clearly trying to hold it together.

She wasn't sure she could hear more. But for him, she would. In some ways, she understood how terrible it had been to endure such venom, then to keep it all inside. She knew the loneliness, the never feeling quite whole.

"I'm listening."

"I confronted my father the day before I left for college. He was furious that I'd touched his 'property' and told me that I deserved every bit of my heartache. He mocked me for thinking that I was in love. In his view, perverts like us aren't capable of that."

"That's awful. And wrong! You may not ever say the words to me, but I know you love me. You watched over me, took care of me, risked your life for me—"

"With a knowing gleam in his eyes, my father asked me if I had known that Nara was playing me, would I still have fucked her? He knew exactly what my answer would be. And he was right. I might have been more guarded, but . . ."

"You were young."

Thorpe shrugged as if he refused to excuse himself. "After that, I went to my room. He cast Nara off the next day, sent her back to Brazil. He and I didn't speak again until my mother's funeral five years later."

More tears spilled down her cheeks. How was Thorpe even remotely warm or compassionate after all this? Because his soul was beautiful. How could she make him see that? "Did you ever repair your relationship with him?"

"No." Thorpe looked down, clenching his jaw and his fists. "He came to my wedding and told me at the reception that I was an idiot for marrying a nice girl because I'd soon be bored with her and either stray or divorce her—or both. And if I stayed, I'd be as miserable a bastard as he'd been for thirty years. I invited him because Melissa begged me to bury the hatchet as a wedding gift to her, but I hated him with a passion."

"You never told your ex-wife about Nara?"

"No." He shook his head. "She would have been horrified. She was from a loud Italian family, sarcastic and passionate, but very vanilla. I hadn't engaged in any BDSM activities since Nara. I'd sworn off it, but the fucking need wouldn't go away. We'd been growing apart because I couldn't say those three words to her. I approached her to see if she'd be willing to try a light scene. I craved it so badly. She walked out that night and served me with divorce papers a week later."

"What a bitch," she muttered.

He shrugged. "I scared her. Our sex had been tepid at best, and now she knew why. She swore that if I ever tried to spank her or tie her down, she'd press charges. I couldn't change the way she was wired any more than she could change the way I was. The worst part for me was knowing my father had been right about our marriage. So after the split, I changed my whole life and gave myself over to my addiction.

"I quit my job as a stockbroker. I moved out of Manhattan. I'd been to Dallas once on a business trip and liked it. I moved there and bought Dominion with my savings. My dad died six months later, and I inherited more money than I knew what to do with. So I sunk a bunch back into the business and made it my life. I think I was completely numb for years." He drew in a ragged breath. "Then came you . . ."

Thorpe cupped her cheek, and she gripped his hand. "Thank you for trusting me with your story. You didn't have to tell me, but I know you did to help me." And when she hurt less, maybe she would be more grateful. "Don't ever, ever think you're unworthy. You saved me, Mitchell Thorpe. You reminded me what it was like to belong somewhere again. You gave me strength. Even if you can't admit it, you gave me love."

He teared up again and swallowed down a lump. "I'm going to miss you more than I can possibly express."

"You're letting them win, your father and Nara," she couldn't stop herself from pointing out. "They hurt you decades ago, but you're allowing them to keep you in misery. I don't need the words if you can't say them. Just don't—"

"Shh." He covered her lips with his finger. "They won a long time ago. Leaving is my way of refusing to let them hurt you. This is me protecting you. Let me. It's the only way I can show you what's here." He pounded on his chest. "When I'm gone, tell Sean my story, if you need. Above all, be happy with him."

Thorpe shredded her, and still Callie just wanted to hug and soothe him. She wanted to give him her love. But if he needed to slip away quietly, she would let him. It was the only way he would allow her to show him that she loved him enough to sacrifice.

"I, of all people, understand why sometimes you just can't stay." She barely got the words out past her tears. "I will think of you every day. I will be happy with Sean because I love him. But I will always love you, too. And for what it's worth, I think you have a big heart that anyone would be blessed to share. Try to find some peace."

Thorpe finally broke down and grabbed her against him, sobbing silently into her shoulder. They stayed that way for what seemed like hours, breathing together, memorizing one another, mourning what couldn't be. He dug his fingers into her back and pressed her nose to his shoulder. Despite the discomfort, she couldn't let go.

Sean finally eased the door open. "Lovely?"

Callie sniffled and nodded at him. It was time. She and Thorpe had nothing left to say except he gave her an achingly soft kiss on her forehead and whispered one final word. "Good-bye."

Chapter Twenty

DAWN began to break over the lake, mountains reaching toward the sky and still hiding the golden orb of the sun. Light leaked over the peaks, and everything looked so peaceful. Callie knew this day would likely be hell.

In a perfect world, they would find a car and drive quietly to the Vegas FBI field office and call Sean's boss. They would look at all the evidence, know that she wasn't guilty of murder while figuring out who was. Then authorities would arrest the person or people, and she could start actually living again.

But her life had never been perfect. Whether Sean said it or not, she was expecting the worst. And even if the danger never came, Thorpe would still go.

Either way, she was going to lose today.

Sean docked the boat in furious silence, glaring occasionally at Thorpe who stood two feet behind her—a silent sentinel. All their bags sat at her feet. No one said a word.

The houseboat dipped toward the shore, nudging the rubber bumper on the dock before sliding into place. Sean killed the engine and leapt out to tie the boat off. As soon as it was secure, he approached and slung her backpack over his shoulder. Then he picked up his own, gave Thorpe's bags a pointed glower, took her hand, and led her ashore.

Nothing could have said more eloquently that Sean no longer considered Thorpe a partner. Callie stared over her shoulder at Thorpe's stony face as he grabbed his briefcase and followed.

"I've already called Werner. He should be here with his truck any minute. He's agreed to take us to the outskirts of the city. We can take a taxi from there," Sean told her.

"Let me call Elijah," Thorpe argued. "It's possible that his Jeep is still in that Walmart parking lot. It's only been thirty-six hours."

"I don't want your help," Sean snarled.

"But you need it until Callie is safe. It's not smart to wait on the street corner for a taxi like an easy target."

Sean looked like he was weighing his rage against his common sense. "Fine. Call him."

Thorpe stepped aside and withdrew his burner phone, turning away. Within seconds, he was having a low-voiced conversation Callie couldn't hear. She could feel Sean seethe as he started down the dirt road, waiting for the houseboat owner to fetch them.

"Don't do this. He's got demons bigger than you can ever imagine." She sent him an imploring stare. "Just let it go. For me?"

"He hurt you. I thought he would help heal you, but he's leaving a gaping hole in your heart."

"I'll be fine," she assured. "It won't break me or kill me. It will always hurt some; I won't lie. But you and I? We'll be happy. We'll find a way."

Tight-lipped, Sean turned his attention back to the wide cement road and the pair of headlights bobbing up and down as a pickup truck traveled over the slightly uneven surface. Thorpe ended his call and joined them.

The old man stopped the truck near the dock and hopped out with an unexpectedly spry step. "Throw your bags in the back and tell me where you want to go. We should make it fast. Some military types were in my office yesterday asking about you. I told them I didn't know anything, pushy bastards. But I'm not sure I've seen the last of them."

Fear struck deep and hard in Callie's heart. She and Sean exchanged a glance, then she looked over at Thorpe, who wore his resolution like armor. Neither would let anything happen to her; they'd give up their lives first. And no way was she going down without a fight. She was going to finally start living—or die.

"How many? What did they look like?" Sean asked.

"Two guys. One older, one younger. They both wore some fancy-shmancy uniform with the stupid little French hats."

The fear became terror. "You mean berets?"

"Were the uniforms a gray-blue?" Thorpe asked.

Werner looked between the two of them. "Yeah."

Sean put his arm around her and did his best to calm her. Her enemies were close and closing in. She wanted to be brave and face this down—and she would. But she couldn't seem to stop trembling.

"Let's go." He shepherded her toward the truck.

As soon as they'd tossed their luggage in the back, Callie followed the guys to the passenger door and took hold of her backpack. She couldn't risk damaging the egg or losing the SD card tucked inside again. That disc was the key to her future. They'd looked for a way to copy the file or backup the information somewhere else, just in case. But short of saving it on Werner's hard drive, they hadn't found the means. There had been no Internet or any other storage device on board.

Werner slipped into the driver's seat. Thorpe folded his tall frame in on the other side, sliding to the middle of the bench seat. His knees damn near folded against his chest. He had nowhere else to put them.

Looking like he'd rather eat dirt, Sean climbed in beside him until they sat with their broad shoulders squeezed together and their thighs pressed close. He pretended like Thorpe didn't exist and put her backpack on the floorboard between his feet, then reached down a hand to help her. "Come up. Sit on my lap."

She braced her foot on the running board and climbed in, doing her best to perch on Sean's thighs. Curling up against his chest, she found her senses pelted by the two men she loved. Their scents blended, the press of their bodies quickly warming the cab on this chilly morning. She'd missed that so much as she'd tried to sleep last night.

Callie wondered if this was the last time she'd feel remotely whole.

As soon as Sean managed to shut the passenger door, Werner took off, driving into the glorious sunrise spreading across the Nevada desert. It looked expansive and calm. Best of all, there was no way anyone could follow them clandestinely out here, in the middle of nowhere. There was no place to hide. So Callie tried to sink into the moment and push all the angst and worry aside. None of it would help her today. But it kept crowding in. By the time she laid her head down tonight to sleep, everything would likely be different.

Or she'd be dead.

"Elijah says his Jeep is still at the Walmart," Thorpe offered. "He was waiting for his wife to return before he went out there, and that won't be for another few days. He says its ours for the duration if we need it."

Sean didn't say a word, just nodded. She really wished he wouldn't be so angry, and she suspected it wasn't totally about Thorpe hurting her. He'd been hurt, too.

"Thank you," she said softly.

"Least I could do," Thorpe answered with a wealth of meaning behind his words.

The rest of the drive was silent. Traffic was minimal this early in the morning. Soon, the roads would be hopping with commuters, but for now, they reached the big-box chain store with barely a stoplight to obstruct them.

Once in the parking lot, they fished the keys from the magnetic holder behind the wheel well and shoved most of their bags from the truck into the back of the Jeep. Sean jumped in the driver's seat, watching the parking lot all around them for any activity. But it was dead empty, save for a few employees. Callie gestured Thorpe to the front, then crawled in the back with her pack, wishing she could curl up and sleep. She hadn't all last night, even when Sean had drifted off with his arms around her protectively. She'd missed having the other half of her soul beside her.

What she wouldn't give for everything to be different with Thorpe and for today to turn out right . . .

Sean looked at her in the backseat. "I'm hoping we can drive straight to the field office here and walk you in to see the SAC."

"SAC?" she asked.

"Special Agent in Charge. Once we do that, we'll call back to the Dallas office and—"

Thorpe's phone rang. They all froze. No one calling him at six-thirty in the morning was going to be trying to reach him for a friendly chat.

"Who is it?" Sean barked.

"Logan."

"Put him on speaker."

Thorpe frowned, then did what Sean demanded. "Hey, man. What you got?"

"A little more information, and none of it gives me a warm fuzzy. Elijah was finally able to send me a security image of the dude trolling for Callie at the airport . . . How is she, by the way?"

She smiled. Callie knew firsthand that Logan packed a hell of a wallop when he spanked a girl's ass, but he had also proven to be a friend through and through. "I'm fine. Thanks. You and Tara?"

"All good. Don't worry about us. The guy at the airport, hun? His name is James Whitney. Does that ring a bell?"

"Not at all." She'd never heard it in her life. "Should it?"

"I wasn't sure. Tara did some digging, but is having a tough time finding much. He's twenty-nine and from some little-ass town in Alabama. An Iraq War vet. He came home to find his wife and kid had left. Between his PTSD and his antigovernment ravings, most of his neighbors thought he was a loose cannon. He was arrested for drunk and disorderly and unlawful possession of a handgun, but the charges didn't stick. About three years ago, he dropped off the grid. There are rumors that he's joined some group of mercenaries. That's all I've got now. But there's something here. I can feel it."

Callie drew in a deep breath. Why would this James Whitney want anything to do with her? He had barely been much older than her when her family had been killed. "I don't understand."

"I don't, either. But there's an answer here. We'll keep looking. Do you need anything else?"

"No, thanks." There was nothing Logan could do for her from Lafayette.

"I do, Edgington," Sean spoke up. "Sean Mackenzie here."

"Name it."

"If my sub ever comes to you again wanting to disappear, politely refer her back to me."

Logan cleared his throat. "I was trying to help. I didn't have all the info. Sorry, man."

With that, they ended the call. Sean drove northeast as Callie tried not to nibble on a ragged nail and imagine the worst.

"There are a million pieces to this puzzle and I don't get it," she said finally, her voice tight with encroaching panic.

"I don't know why this Whitney character would be hunting you down in the Vegas airport. But if he was wearing the same uniform as the older man who came to your house just before your father's murder, they might be in league together," Sean mused. "After all, Werner just said that two uniforms visited him, one old, one young."

Shayla Black

"That's what I was thinking," Thorpe popped in. "And if they're related to some sort of mercenary group, maybe they wanted Aslanov's research to make themselves better or something like that."

Yeah, that made sense in a warped way. "But to kill innocent men, women, and children?"

"Greed does strange things to people, lovely," Sean pointed out. "I've been a criminal investigator for a decade. I've seen some terrible instances of that."

How fucking tragic. Her father had only tried to do something good for the world and instead, he set off a chain of murders, including his own, and set her life on its ear.

"How long will it take the FBI to read everything on the SD card, investigate, and arrest people? Weeks? Months?"

Sean didn't answer.

"Years?"

"We don't know where it will lead, Callie. You'll be free from any implication." He paused. "It's possible you may be put in Witness Protection. If that happens, I'll go with you."

Callie's heart stopped. She had spent a decade being someone else. She didn't want that anymore. The time had finally come to be Callindra Howe again, to put her family's memory to rest. To live the life her mother had hoped for her.

And if the federal government put her into hiding . . . She watched movies and read books. Callie already knew that she'd never be allowed to contact Thorpe again. That would put them both in danger.

"No. There's got to be another way. I won't do it. I'd rather die."

Sean gaped at her from the rearview mirror. Thorpe turned around and glared.

"I won't let you do that," Sean snapped.

"I have to second that," Thorpe added.

They gave one another a wary stare before Sean snapped his gaze back to the road. Traffic was beginning to pick up as rush hour began and they drove closer to the heart of the city.

"Do you know anyone trustworthy in the Vegas office you can call?" Thorpe asked. "Let them know we're coming in. Or better yet, maybe they can send someone to escort us, just in case."

Sean's face tightened. "The agents I worked with a couple of years ago have been reassigned or retired. I'm not sure who I can trust."

"You've had questions about the decisions in the Dallas office," Thorpe conceded. "But does that necessarily mean that someone here is keeping secrets?"

"Maybe not . . . but I can't say for sure."

"But we already know that killers are hot on our tail from Werner," Callie argued. "No one in the FBI will shoot us dead."

"No," Sean agreed. "But there are worse things than being shot. That's what worries me."

"You mean if someone is dirty?" Thorpe looked tense and pensive.

"Yeah. But it's possible I'm being paranoid." He sighed. "I've got an escape route if we need it, so I'll call."

Sean pulled off the road into a fast-food restaurant's parking lot. As commuters started wrapping around the building in their vehicles, waiting for liquid caffeine and fortification, he drove to the edge of the lot and kept the engine running. "Wait here."

He jumped out with his phone in both hands, staring intently at the screen and dialing something. A moment later, he pressed the phone to his ear. The conversation lasted less than thirty seconds. Then Sean was running back to the car. He tossed his phone onto the asphalt, and it splintered into a dozen pieces.

Callie gasped. "What the . . . ?"

He peeled out of the parking lot and swerved back onto the freeway, cutting off a little subcompact. "As soon as I identified myself, the SAC took the phone. That shouldn't happen. He demanded that I bring you in, Callie. I won't do it."

Her heart caught in her throat. "Like he wants to arrest me?"

"He called it 'questioning,' but something is off. He asked what we'd been doing in Vegas for the last thirty-six hours. He knew you were with me. He knew I'd shopped at that Walmart and that we'd taken a taxi from there. Which means he may even know we're in this Jeep." Sean weaved in and out of the swelling traffic. "I tossed my phone so that he couldn't trace that signal anymore, just in case they're locked on to it."

"Should I do the same?" Thorpe asked.

"Can't hurt." Sean nodded tightly.

Thorpe rolled down the window and dumped it onto the freeway without hesitation. "Now what?"

"Our one saving grace was that they hadn't been able to find out from the cab company exactly where they'd taken us. They were still doing paperwork to obtain the information. We have to ditch this Jeep and find another cab."

"Then we should probably head back toward the Strip," Thorpe suggested.

"Yeah."

Mouth pressed together tensely, Sean switched lanes and followed the signs toward the touristy section of Vegas. "It will probably take twenty or thirty minutes or so from here. Depends on the traffic."

"Once we get a cab, where are we going then?" Callie asked. "It's all fine and dandy to disappear into anonymous transportation, but where do we tell him to drive us if not the field office? Local police?"

"No," Sean said immediately. "The SAC will just swoop in and claim jurisdiction, then we'll be right back to where we started. There's got to be another way to get you free. Who else wants the information on that disc?"

Callie sat back in the seat, trying not to let panic overwhelm her.

If Sean didn't know where to turn, she feared they were doomed. "Maybe Logan could get paperwork for us to leave the country."

"I'm worried that if the killers tracked us to Lake Mead, they can follow us anywhere. The way they're operating, I don't think they have boundaries. They'll go wherever and do whatever for that remaining research."

"But you said my father burned it."

"We know that," Thorpe reminded. "They don't."

"So if we find a way to convey that the research doesn't exist anymore, maybe they will leave me alone?" That sounded awfully optimistic, but Callie still hoped deep down that Sean believed it, too.

"No," he scoffed. "You still know something about these people and what they want. You still have enough evidence to suggest they killed your family and the Aslanovs. And you're the only eyewitness who can tie both Whitney and the older bastard he's working with to this conspiracy. They will kill you in a heartbeat to bury their skeletons."

He was right. Callie fought to breathe. She wouldn't die for greed, for research that didn't exist anymore, to keep a dirty secret.

Then a solution hit her—so simple and effective. She grabbed her backpack and tore into it, pulling out her cosmetics case. "As soon as we find a taxi, I think I know where to go."

* * *

SEAN began to wonder if Callie was out of her mind. She was in the backseat getting all dolled up, carefully applying mascara with a hand mirror, then teasing and smoothing her hair with a small brush.

"You look beautiful, lovely, but I don't think now is the time to worry about all this."

A glance to his right showed that Thorpe looked as confused as he did.

"It's the perfect time. I'm going to make a big splash." She dug into her backpack and pulled out some black leggings and a simple V-neck shirt in red. She shimmied out of her old clothes and into the new, then exchanged her tennis shoes for some black sandals.

Somehow, she made clothes that had been rumpled into a ball five minutes ago look perfect.

"Why?" Thorpe demanded. "What do you have planned in that mischievous head of yours?"

Callie shook her head. "I'm still working out the details. Get me to a taxi. You'll see."

"You should clue me in. After all, I have some experience at eluding bad guys," Sean said ironically.

"I've put my trust in you for the last thirty-six hours. Now it's time for you to do the same for me."

Sighing and grumbling, Sean continued heading northwest, toward downtown. Traffic was definitely picking up now that it was after seven a.m. They slowed to the speed he'd drive on a residential street as he headed north on I-515. Fucking mess.

Ten minutes to go, max. Then they could disappear into a cab, get lost in a sea of humanity, and hopefully whatever the devil was in Callie's head would save the day.

Another glance in the rearview mirror alarmed him. A black sedan two cars back and to the right. They'd picked it up a few minutes ago—along with a lot of other cars. But this one . . . every time he switched lanes, so did the sedan.

With the hair at the back of his neck standing up, Sean slowed down. It wasn't hard with this many cars. The lane of traffic beside him was moving a tad faster. But the black sedan slowed, too.

Growling a curse, Sean changed lanes again, getting directly in front of the dark car. He glanced in the rearview mirror, hoping to see someone blabbing on the phone, a woman putting on her mascara, or someone reading their texts—anything that said this driver wasn't really paying attention to them. Instead, he saw two men in an unfamiliar bluish uniform, one fancier than the other. He tensed.

"What is it?" Thorpe asked.

Sean didn't really want to talk to him, but Thorpe was another gun and more muscle. He needed that more than resentment now. "We've got company. Callie, have you worked out your plan?"

"I need to make a phone call. Neither of you has a phone anymore?"

"They're destroyed." Thorpe looked grim.

"Keep getting to the taxi. I'll figure out how to make this work."

An exit appeared on the right. He sped up and put on his blinker, pretending that he intended to change to the fast lane on the left. At the last moment, he jerked the wheel right, cutting off an SUV, then bumped onto the off-ramp, flooring it.

The other car hit the brakes, tires screeching, then followed them off the ramp.

"Fuck," Thorpe said, turning to look out the back windshield.

That summed it up. Sean navigated the traffic, dodging cars, changing lanes, screaming through a yellow light to try to lose their tail.

The black sedan simply ran the red and continued on, firing a semiautomatic out the window.

"Jesus, they could kill anyone!" Sean cursed, thankful that the bullets had missed. "We should hit the Strip soon. If I can't shake this tail, we won't have time to retrieve our luggage from the back. Callie, hand Thorpe your backpack. As soon as I stop the Jeep, everyone bail out and run."

In the backseat, Callie gave him a nod. Besides lushing up her lashes with mascara, she'd rimmed her bright blue eyes in her signature black liner. Her eyes stood out in her pale face, broken only by the red gloss on her lips. Now wasn't the time to notice how damn beautiful she was, but he couldn't help it. She looked especially lovely with her delicate face full of determination. Hell, he really was madly in love.

As Sean raced down Tropicana Avenue, he also realized that

finding a quick place to ditch the Jeep on the Strip might be tough. Time to improvise.

Sean hung a right onto Las Vegas Boulevard the second he could, grateful that traffic wasn't too heavy. When he saw the street sign for Las Vegas Boulevard, he hung a sharp right onto the edge of the Strip. A screech of tires behind told him the sedan was doing its best to follow suit.

"Where the hell are you going?" Thorpe barked.

"Looking for a place to lose the Jeep and pick up a cab," he said grimly.

Thankfully, the traffic in the tourist areas wasn't as heavy at this hour. Random cars and the occasional cab drifted by. Some hungover partiers were doing the walk of shame back to their hotels.

The grandeur of the Bellagio jumped out at him, the famous fountain show idle this early in the morning. He floored it down the relatively empty side street leading to the hotel, past the standing streetlamps meant to be charming. Through the back passenger window, he caught a glimpse of the fake Eiffel Tower that always made him roll his eyes—and the black sedan heading toward the curve to follow him, about thirty seconds behind. At least they had stopped shooting for now.

He roared under the canopy and glanced to his right, past the topiaries. A few idling taxies, a shuttle bus full of spent revelers leaving for the airport, and some members of the valet staff milling around.

The second the car came to a shuddering stop, they all jumped out and slammed the doors.

Sean threw the keys at a valet attendant and flashed his badge. "Emergency. I'll be back. Park it now!"

"Yes, sir," the young man answered.

He gripped Callie's hand as they ran toward the hotel, searching the line of taxis and praying that his instincts were right. *Bingo!* Away from the line of vehicles for hire he spotted a taxi with its light off and an older man napping in the front seat. He pounded on the window.

The man started and adjusted his ball cap with a glower. "Can't you read? I'm off duty."

"It's life or death. Please." Callie pressed her face to the glass and she might have thrust her breasts a bit closer to the window, too.

As Sean flashed his badge he wanted to gnash his teeth, but at least the guy wasn't scowling anymore.

"There's a thousand dollars in cash if you get us out of here in the next ten seconds." Thorpe reached into his pocket and pulled out a wad of bills. "And keep yourself off duty."

The driver straightened up and unlocked the doors. They all piled in as the cabbie peeled out.

"Where am I going?" he asked.

Sean looked at Callie, who crawled down to the floorboard. He didn't want to think about how filthy it was down there, but to her credit, she didn't blink once, just put their safety above possible germs. In order to conceal himself, he had to slink low in the seat and bow his head. Thorpe reclined, propping himself up on his elbow against the lumpy upholstery. Hopefully, they were hidden enough so that anyone driving by wouldn't notice them.

"Where's the nearest TV station?" she asked the driver.

"What?" Thorpe howled at her. "You're going to the press?"

"Oh, lovely," Sean began with a note of warning. "I don't think—"

"Hear me out. The egg can prove my identity. Because so few still exist, the owners of all the remaining pieces can be verified. What's on the SD card can prove that I'm not guilty of anything. It cuts through the red tape and BS. No going back into hiding."

"You're making yourself a bigger target," Sean protested.

"I'm not." She shook her head, her dark hair covering her shoulders and brushing her arms. "Whoever's been looking for me wants the part of the research that no longer exists. We go public with the fact that my father burned it. And whoever offed everyone else and is after me now wants to keep their dirty deeds a secret. By exposing it all, killing me doesn't bury anything anymore. It only draws attention to their misdeeds. Once the world knows I'm alive and what's happened . . ."

"There will be a media frenzy," Thorpe finished for her. "You'll have such a spotlight on you, they won't dare."

"Exactly."

"That's damn clever." Sean couldn't help but smile at her. "Lovely minx."

"So where's that TV station?" she asked the cabbie, who looked totally confused by their conversation.

"Less than a mile up the road. It's KSNV, the NBC affiliate. Will that do?"

"Perfect." Relief made her entire face glow. "The *Today* show should be on. It's got a great viewership."

"Word should travel fast," Thorpe agreed.

Sean wanted to pound the wistful expression off the other man's face and tell him that if he adored Callie so much, he should fucking stay. But no sense in arguing now. Sean had to focus on shielding her from the coming media storm. But he had no doubt he'd wish now and then that Thorpe had pulled his head out of his ass before it had come to good-bye.

"Um . . . that's great and all," the driver interjected, "but I think someone is following us. Black sedan?"

Sean resisted the urge to peek through the back windshield to verify. Damn it, how had these goons figured out their escape route so quickly? Why couldn't they shake these assholes?

"Act like there's nothing wrong. See if you can get him to pass us. Confuse him by taking a circular route to the TV station. Anything."

The car slowed for a moment, and the cabbie seemed to change lanes. He pulled out a smoke and fished around for his lighter. As soon as he found it, he dropped it and stomped on the gas pedal.

"What's going on?" Sean demanded.

"I don't think there's going to be any fooling the guys in the black sedan. They've got guns!"

And they were tenacious. A second later, a loud bang resounded, and the back window on the passenger's side shattered. Thorpe reacted quickly, covering Callie's body with his own.

Sean drew the Glock he'd been hiding in the waistband holster tucked inside his jeans and peeked out the open window. "Slow down so I can get a shot."

"What the fuck?" The man's gray brows slashed down in the rearview mirror. "I'm not aiding a murder, pal."

"I've got a badge, remember? I'm FBI, protecting a witness. Now slow down so I can get a damn shot. If you don't and we somehow manage to live, I'll arrest your ass."

"Fucking do what he said!" Thorpe barked.

Sean waited as the driver eased off the gas. The sedan roared up to their side again.

"As soon as I say so, take the next right and floor it. Got it?"

The cabdriver nodded excitedly. "I always wanted to do this. It looks cool in the movies."

Trying not to roll his eyes, Sean inched up and aimed his weapon out the window. He fired off a couple of shots, hitting the side of the car, but not the passenger or driver. That shit only happened in the movies. But even if they turned right suddenly, Sean didn't think it was going to be enough to prevent the attackers from pursuing. He needed to try again.

"Keep her on the floor and covered." He barked at Thorpe as he slammed back against the seat.

"I've got your back," Thorpe vowed.

Not always, but now wasn't the time to worry about tomorrow.

"Just a little farther," he told the old man at the steering wheel. "At the parking lot on the other side of the upcoming intersection, turn in. Don't signal, just do it."

"Got it."

"What's your name?" Sean asked.

"Bob." He gripped the steering wheel with white knuckles. "Maybe I'll get to be on the news?"

"Yeah, maybe." Sean nearly shook his head. "Ready?"

"Yep."

As they soared through the green light and just past the black car, he took another shot and hit the windshield. It splintered, caving in on the pair of mercenaries.

Bob jerked the car right, and it bounced into the parking lot. He dodged a hatchback swinging into the parking lot.

The sedan locked up its brakes and tried to turn right in front of the far lane of traffic. Tires screeched. A pickup truck hit the car's back panel on the passenger side with a cringeworthy metallic crunch. Sean twisted around to look through the back windshield. The sedan was almost backward in the intersection. The truck ground to a halt, along with several of the cars behind them, and blocked the intersection. The sedan was trapped.

A bystander got out to check on the people involved in the accident. The driver of the sedan, the older asswipe in uniform, rolled down his window and started shouting, gesturing wildly for everyone to get out of his way.

The back window on the driver's side of the car eased down. Out came the gun again. People screamed and dropped to the ground.

"Floor it!" Sean told Bob. "Get us to that fucking TV station now."

They made a right and left the scene of the accident—and their pursuers—behind. Sean breathed a sigh of relief.

"We did it!" Bob roared as he cruised down a side street.

"Is it safe now?" Callie asked under Thorpe.

"I think." Sean tapped Thorpe on the shoulder. "You, ease up. But be prepared, just in case."

Thorpe nodded and lifted away from Callie, but helped her up from the tight wedge of the floorboard, clutching her hand in his and drawing it closer to his chest. She looked so pale, it scared him.

Sean grabbed her chin. "Breathe, lovely. Don't pass out on me."

She shook her head and drew in a deep breath. "I'm good. I swear."

He wasn't convinced, but before he could question her further, Bob was pulling up into a parking lot, past a giant carport, heading for a nondescript off-white building with a big blue News 3 sign jutting from the flat roof. He brought the car to a grinding halt in a reserved spot with a big grin on his face.

Bouncing against the backseat, Thorpe thrust into his pocket and extracted Bob's money. Sean grabbed his wrist and counted out half, then gave it to Bob. "Stay here and idling for a few minutes. Once we know it's safe, one of us will give you the rest."

"Whew! You got it." Bob grinned. "That was a rush!"

Sean just hoped the station would talk to Callie, and he wouldn't be here for the cabbie's adrenaline crash. He opened the door and leapt out, reaching for Callie. She piled out, and Thorpe followed. All together, they ran for the doors. A security guard stopped them immediately inside the cool white linoleum lobby.

"Do you have an appointment?" the cop-in-a-box asked.

"We'd like to see whoever is in charge of the news," Callie said with her sweetest smile.

The thirtysomething guy looked at her like he'd rather ask her out than turn her down, but he still shook his head. "The news director is a busy man. You'll have to make an appointment and come back."

"We will give him the biggest news story of his career."

"He's heard that before and—"

"Put him on the phone with me," Callie pleaded earnestly. "I'll convince him."

"I've got strict orders not to disturb him."

Sean had reached his limit and fished out his badge. "FBI. He'll see us."

The security guard stepped back, looking from him, then to Callie, before scoping out Thorpe. Finally, his gaze settled on the glinting shield in Sean's hand.

"I'll call him," the guard said.

"Thank you for your cooperation." Sean wondered if the man heard the irony in his tone.

Less than a minute later, the news director appeared. A portly man with a shock of gray hair, he had a weathered look that said he'd not only seen decades' worth of news, but lived it.

"Roger Coachman." The man thrust out his hand at Sean. "What can I do for you?"

"It's what you can do for her." He gestured to Callie.

The news director turned his attention to her with a practiced smile, looking a bit impatient.

"I'm sure you're busy, so I'll get to the point. Is there somewhere we can talk privately? I think I have a story that will interest you."

"Sure. We can talk in my office."

As Coachman led them toward the secure area of the building, Sean turned back to the security guard. "You never saw us."

The man nodded, his expression a bit like a child denied a treat. Clearly, he was curious about Callie and her story. He'd find out soon enough if this went well.

The man escorted them down some halls. People in suits bustled about. An older blonde wearing a headset paced, brushed past them like she was on a mission. In the distance, a phone pealed with a loud ring.

As soon as the news director led them into his office, Callie sat in one of the chairs opposite his desk. Sean sat beside her, while Thorpe closed the door and lounged against the wall behind them.

"So, young lady, you have a story? I can't promise that I'll put it on the news, but I'll listen."

Only because Sean had flashed a badge, and that annoyed him. He understood the guy probably saw crackpots, but . . .

"No, you'll put me on in the next five minutes, or I'll be forced to take the story elsewhere."

Coachman laughed. "I can't do that. We're on network feed from New York for another few hours. We only get short breaks for local traffic and weather every so often."

Callie shook her head. "Call the network. They'll want this story, too. *Everyone* will."

"Does your dog talk or something?" he asked, his tone a bit patronizing. "Did the mold in your bathroom tub grow into the shape of the Virgin Mary, Miss . . ."

She stood. "If you're not even going to listen to me or try to take me seriously, I won't bother you anymore. Remember that I tried to give you a story that will put you on the map internationally as a hard-hitting journalist."

As Callie started for the door, Sean grabbed her wrist, wondering again if she was out of her mind. The street was too dangerous until this story broke.

She whirled on him and flashed him a sharp stare, but he couldn't mistake the calculating gleam in her eye. Thorpe grinned.

"No. Please sit," Coachman invited. "Sorry, but you have to understand how often I hear that someone has an important story, and it's usually nothing newsworthy."

Callie played reluctant before she settled back into her seat. "This should be a top headline across the country, maybe even the world. Promise me you'll call the network if I've sufficiently piqued your interest and get us on ASAP."

He shrugged his big, soft shoulders, rustling his navy coat. "Sure. If they'll take it."

She simply smiled. "Thank you. They will. Now let's get down to business, Mr. Coachman. I'm Callindra Howe and I can prove it. I can also prove that I didn't kill my father."

The news director's bushy gray brows rose and he leaned forward, elbow braced against his desk. His jaw looked like it might hit there as well. "You . . . You're . . . Wow. Okay, I'm listening."

Quite intently, too. Sean watched the man's reaction with satisfaction.

Flashing the older man a winning smile, Callie dug into her backpack and pulled out her mother's Fabergé egg.

*　*　*

LESS than ten minutes later, Callie shooed away the hair and makeup artist hovering around her. Predictably, the network had gobbled up her story. Coachman stared at her like she was a cross between a ghost and a mega celebrity. The local morning news anchor trembled and fumbled with his papers. His slightly terrified expression hinted that he might pee his pants.

She shared his nerves. The next ten minutes would determine if she could be herself again and finally start living. If everything went well during this interview, she'd get to share her tomorrows with a wonderful man she loved. As they did a last-minute camera check, Callie smiled at Sean. He gave her an encouraging nod. Thorpe stood beside Sean, looking both stony and proud.

Damn it all, she was going to miss him.

"Ms. Howe, can I get you anything?" Coachman's assistant asked, staring. "Coffee? Tea? Water?"

"No, thank you."

"So you've been on the run for almost ten years," the anchor said. "What was that like?"

Terrible. Scary. Frustrating. But in an odd way, a blessing. She would never have grown this much spine or met these two wonderful men otherwise. "As soon as we go on air, I'll tell you."

The station returned from commercial, and the network anchor in New York had been patched through, just waiting for them to go live with the breaking story. Callie drew in a deep breath as they finished the last of the audio checks. Finally, the director cued them on air.

And the questions began from the national anchor. She recounted being shot at, then betrayed by Holden, skipping towns, finding a safe haven in Dallas with Thorpe, then running from Agent Mackenzie, only for the two of them to find her again and help her discover the evidence she needed to go public.

"I owe them my life," she said softly. "I share a very special bond with them both."

Let everyone read between the lines. They'd dig and find out that she'd lived in a fet club and fallen for its Dungeon Master. They'd probably even uncover that she wore Sean's collar. Hell, she was wearing it now. Fingering it with a faint smile, she didn't care what anyone else thought. They'd judge, regardless of what she said or did. But she knew what was in her heart. The most important thing was exposing what the monsters had done to her family and clearing her name from anything criminal. Last time she checked, being in love with two men wasn't a crime.

"I wouldn't be standing here without the two of them," she elaborated. "I'll always be grateful."

Finally, they cut away. The news director was jumping up and down that every network in the country had just picked up the interview, along with a few overseas. The morning anchor sat, blinking in astonishment at her story. Now that she'd recounted everything, Callie couldn't believe that she had actually lived through it all.

It was over. The secret James Whitney and his mercenary brethren had fought to keep was out, along with the news that her father had burned all the research the criminals had sought. Hopefully, when the media circus died down, she could finally be herself and live.

Coachman approached her, still practically dancing a jig. "The network wants to fly you out to New York to continue the interview there with Matt Lauer tomorrow and—"

Thorpe cut the news director off with an intimidating stare. Coachman stepped back.

After working his way directly in front of her, Thorpe cupped her cheek, those gray eyes of his focused on her with such approval.

"You're a remarkably strong woman. You handled that perfectly. I'm so proud of you, pet."

His words warmed her. But his voice rang suspiciously with farewell.

"Mitchell—"

Sean appeared beside her next, then drew her tight against his chest. "You answered every question with such grace and poise, lovely. Brilliant plan. You're safe to be Callindra Howe again." Then he whispered in her ear. "But you'll always be my Callie."

When she looked up to smile at him, she noticed that Thorpe no longer occupied the room. She searched every corner with her frantic gaze. He was gone.

Before she could do more than open her mouth in disbelief and feel the tears prick her eyes, Coachman cut in again. "Ms. Howe, New York? The network needs to make arrangements. What time would you like to fly out today?"

"Um, sir," Coachman's assistant popped her head into the studio, looking somewhere between apologetic and worried. "The FBI is here to take Ms. Howe in for questioning."

Chapter Twenty-one

THORPE stared out the window overlooking Dominion's dungeon at the Friday night crowd diving into their play with gusto. With a critical eye, he surveyed the stations, the dungeon monitors making the rounds, the mood on the floor.

Satisfied everything was well under control, he locked up his observation room and headed downstairs into the secure area of the building. With a silent sigh, he returned to his apartment in the back and flipped on the TV, grabbing a fresh bottle of water. He should probably remove his suit, take a shower, and try to get some sleep.

Every time he closed his eyes, all he saw was Callie's face, her sparkling eyes, her lush mouth. Her "I love yous" echoed in his head.

Exhaustion weighed on him. He'd tried to resume a normal life since returning to Dominion. But the lump in his throat when he thought of her never quite went away. His eyes constantly stung. For the last three weeks, he'd been wracked with a vague but constant pain that debilitated his whole body.

Not surprising when he felt as if half of himself was missing.

Thorpe took a sip of water and tried to force the liquid down to drown the ache. That didn't work. That persistent tightness in his chest constricted even more. Why the fuck couldn't he take a deep breath?

Easing down into an overstuffed chair, he cued up his DVR. A mountain of news programs took up all the space on the device. He chose the most recent show, one he'd taped yesterday. The one that torqued his pain the most. Thorpe had never considered himself a masochist, but apparently he'd been wrong. He'd already watched this show half a dozen times.

The host introduced himself and vomited at the mouth about a bunch of political shit Thorpe couldn't care less about. He had several windbag guests he called pundits, each less significant than the last. They shouted at one another, full of self-importance. Thorpe stifled his impatience as he fast-forwarded past it all and finally arrived at the segment he sought.

"My next guest is all over the news. Her story of survival and vindication is the talk of the networks, water coolers, and Twitter-verse. She's gracing the cover of next week's *People* with her incredible tale. And I'm sure that's just the beginning for the beautiful Callindra Howe. Welcome."

The camera panned over to her. Thorpe hadn't thought it possible, but she looked even more beautiful than he remembered. Her eyes were magnetically blue. Her hair hung in touchable, inky waves. Her red lips curled up in a gracious smile. She almost looked happy. Someone who didn't know her would believe that she was. But Thorpe understood her too well not to see the sadness that haunted her eyes.

Fuck, his chest tightened again. He drank more water, but the feeling just wouldn't go away.

"Thank you for having me on the show." Callie's smile widened as she poised herself for the first question.

"The last few weeks have been insane for you."

"That's an understatement." She laughed softly. "It's been a whirlwind, but I'm satisfied now that most of the saga is finally over."

"Indeed." The geezer, who was a reputed letch, patted her hand, and Thorpe wanted to reach through the TV and rip his nuts off. "Let's take a look."

Footage rolled, showing a montage of the events—the murders, her years on the run. Next, the voiceover mentioned her time at Dominion. This was exactly why every time Thorpe left the building, he had to wade through a small sea of reporters. He'd called the police more than once to get them off his property because they were blocking members from entering the club's door. *Idiots.*

Then the clip went on to discuss him and Sean, crediting them with saving her from "dangerous mercenaries" the FBI was still trying to identify. Finally, they played a snippet of her first interview in Las Vegas. Callie looked tired and pale, but somehow glorious. No, complete. She didn't look like that now.

That had to be an illusion. Or wishful thinking on his part. She still wore Sean's collar because she loved him. The fed would always give her everything she needed and more.

In time, Thorpe knew he'd be an afterthought. If he wasn't already.

"Wow, that's an amazing decade," the host said. "You've survived a great deal. The FBI is still seeking the people who wanted you dead. Any update?"

"No, but I'm sure they're hard at work."

"What's it like to have so many people believe for years that you killed your family?"

Callie seemed to collect her words. "Crushing. I loved my family. I was prepared to leave them at sixteen, but I never anticipated not seeing them again. To have them gone so suddenly and violently, then hear that the police—along with public opinion—considered me a suspect was devastating. I had a lot of years when it felt like me against the world, but I'm happy that chapter of my life is over."

"And now you've been completely exonerated?"

"Thankfully, yes."

"I heard there's a book deal in the works. And a TV movie. What can you tell us?"

"Nothing is final yet. We'll see if it works out. In the meantime, I've been busy cleaning out my childhood home, deciding if I want to sell it. I'm also getting my affairs in order and moving on with my life."

"It's rumored you're giving several million dollars of the fortune you've inherited to charity," the host said.

"I am. I've actually started the Cecilia Howe Foundation for Cancer Research. All tests and experiments will be conducted according to the highest standards. No genetic trials will ever be performed. The foundation will be dedicated to curing cancer that affects women, especially ovarian cancer."

"Which your mother died of?"

"Yes."

"You're also continuing your father's scholarship and changing its name to the Daniel A. Howe Fund?"

She smiled. "The brightest young minds in American business should have the means to attend college. It's something my father was passionate about. I will always mourn his loss, and that of my sister, but I feel this is a good way to honor him and continue his legacy."

"You've also donated your mother's Imperial Fabergé egg to the Smithsonian."

"It's fitting. She loved to look at it. I know she'd be proud to have it seen by millions of enthralled people every year."

"Rumor has you romantically linked with Agent Mackenzie. Any comment?"

She blushed, unconsciously fingering the pretty bit of bling around her neck. "He's a wonderful man, and I'm very lucky."

"He'll be joining us shortly, and we'll get his side of the story. But Mitchell Thorpe is an enigma. He's declined all interviews and seemingly isn't interested in the spotlight."

The fondness shining in her eyes was apparent. That all-over mystery pain punched him again. "He's a very private man with a very big heart."

Thorpe's pectorals felt so damn taut. His heart stuttered. He struggled to breathe . . . but he feared how much it would hurt if he did.

"Have you spoken to him since you left Las Vegas?" the host asked.

Her smile faltered. "No, but he knows how grateful I am to him for all the years of protection and care he gave me. I love him and I always will."

He gripped the arm of his chair until his knuckles turned white. His chest seized up, constricting again. Thorpe wondered if he was having a heart attack.

Motherfucking son of a bitch.

He stopped playing the show, shut off the TV, and tossed the remote onto the nearby table. He glanced longingly at a bottle of scotch in the corner, then looked away. He'd gotten completely shit-faced his first night back at Dominion. Everything he'd been avoiding before the first sip was still there the following morning, along with a devil of a hangover.

He'd walked away from Callie and he knew the reasons why. But damn it, when she said she loved him for all the world to hear . . . How much more proof did he need that she wasn't like Nara? Or Melissa? And his father had been so fucking wrong. Perverts were capable of more than sex. He knew it now because he loved Callie more than life. How could he be worthy of her if he didn't try? He'd left her to avoid the pain of losing her, but it already hurt so bad he could barely breathe without aching.

Thorpe dragged in a lungful of air, and yes, there it was. The agony he'd been dodging, crushing him down like the weight of a steamroller. Every joint ached worse. Every muscle twinged in pain. He felt at least a hundred fucking years old. And hollow on the inside. He missed her so much.

Gulping water now, trying to wash away the thoughts, he wondered if he'd ever feel like smiling again. Or even like simply breathing. He didn't expect love or happiness. He'd given any hope of that away.

Fuck, that scotch really looked good.

A sharp rap sounded on the door, and he clambered to his feet. "Who the hell is it?"

"Axel."

Which meant there was a problem on the floor. He cursed. But wouldn't solving someone else's problem take his mind off his own? He'd operated that way for twenty years. And maybe, if he was really lucky, he'd get to help Axel crack some skulls.

Aggression sounded nice about now.

Thorpe yanked the door open. Axel plowed in—along with a host of other familiar faces. Logan and Hunter Edgington, Xander and Javier Santiago, Tyler Murphy, Deke Trenton, and his business partner, the infamous Jack Cole.

He knew exactly why they'd come. And it pissed him off.

"Is there some all-male gangbang I haven't heard about? You boys will have to play without me. I'm not interested."

Logan looked insulted. "We are *not* here to fuck your ass, dude."

"Just your mind," Jack quipped.

Self-controlled son of a bitch. Jack was happily married with a young son. What did he understand about this situation? Any of them, really? They were all settled. Well, except Axel, and that guy had layers of shit, so his head of security better not be up in his grill.

"Still not interested." Thorpe opened the door wider and gestured them all back into the hall.

Tyler scoffed. "Nice try. Avoidance didn't help me when I wanted to worm out of the intervention the wives all sprung on me before Delaney. Damn if they weren't right, too. So I think you should shut the fuck up and listen."

"Yeah," Deke piped in. "My cousin Luc had to give me some tough love before I was smart enough to get over myself and marry Kimber. It's a valuable mental ass kicking every guy should have. Good times . . ." He looked down the hall and frowned. "Speak of the devil."

Deke stepped aside for Luc Traverson to enter, who held a plate that on any other day would look and smell divine. Since returning to Dominion, everything had tasted like dog shit.

"Thank you, but I'm not hungry," Thorpe said politely.

As if he hadn't spoken, Luc shoved the plate in his hands and shut the door to Thorpe's living quarters behind him. "I hunted down what passes for a kitchen here and reheated a veritable masterpiece just for you. Axel said you haven't eaten a whole meal since you returned."

The platter under his nose held some sort of veal dish with a red wine sauce, roasted sweet potatoes, and glazed carrots. In a restaurant, this dish would be at least fifty bucks, probably more because Traverson made it.

Thorpe's stomach revolted. "I've already eaten."

"I hate it when people lie." Hunter stepped up and took the plate, carrying it to Thorpe's little bistro table in the corner. "Sit down and eat."

The older Edgington brother may have been a SEAL, but Thorpe didn't need for anyone to Dom the Dom. "I believe I've spoken. You don't come into my house and tell me what to do."

Logan gave him a shove toward his brother and the plate. "We will for your own good because we've all been there. Don't be a pussy. You said a lot of things I needed to hear before I won Tara back. Now you're going to listen."

Xander stood beside him with his arms crossed over his chest, his charcoal suit perfectly pressed. Javier had chosen something navy, but the pose was a dead ringer for his younger brother's. They both looked gravely serious.

"I'll have to echo Logan," Xander said. "Man up. Listening won't hurt. Much."

"I don't need advice. Thank you for the effort." Thorpe gritted his teeth. "I'm fine."

"You can dish out the good advice but you can't take it?" Javier challenged with a look that tried to shame him.

Thorpe snapped.

"I don't need advice about anything. I'm goddamn fine! I'm better than fucking fine. Never been happier. Leave me the hell alone!"

The moment he lost control, he wanted to kick his own ass. He had to get his shit under wraps or he'd give in to that nagging urge he'd been fighting to call Sean and ask if there was any way he could take back every fucking word of good-bye and join them. Callie deserved better than him.

Thorpe drew in a shuddering breath, forcing a lid back onto his temper.

Tyler shoved him in the chair. "What a bunch of BS. Fucking eat something."

Hunter held him down and shoved a fork in his hand. "As I said, I don't like liars. You're in love with Callie."

"She is Sean Mackenzie's collared submissive." Thorpe pressed his lips tightly together. And he was just waiting for the day he heard about their engagement. It was coming, he knew.

"Are you trying to bullshit me that you're not in love with her?" Logan scoffed.

"I'm simply stating that she no longer lives here and is no longer available." He didn't admit that it was killing him. They didn't need more ammunition when they were already so close to the bull's-eye.

"Don't give me that façade like everything is fine except for the stick up your ass and the ax in your heart," Axel complained. "You're so heavy these days, you're like a black hole, sucking the life out of yourself and everyone around you. I've seen you turn down no less than a dozen subs you've played with in the past. If you're not going to do something about the fact that you love Callie, at least get laid. Dena has been asking about you. I can call her to come release some of the pressure in your valve, man."

The thought of touching any of the women who had come to him and knelt and offered themselves . . . Thorpe hadn't thought it was possible, but the food smelled even worse. His stomach turned over. He pushed the plate away and stood.

"Callie loves you," Luc said. "She's stated that on TV repeatedly. If there's anyone who knows what it's like to be in denial about his feelings, it's me. I'm lucky Alyssa wanted me enough to put up with my shit. You want to look up tomorrow and find that Callie has moved on?"

She already had. How did these stupid fuckers not see it? "If you look in her room, you'll find she's not there. You will find her with Sean Mackenzie, where I'm sure he's making her very happy, which is what she deserves, so get off my fucking back!"

Thorpe winced. There he went, losing control again. Son of a bitch, he needed to get himself wired up tight enough to get them out of here. Then maybe he could gather the pieces of himself and move on. He held in a snort. *Like that's going to happen.*

"Here's the deal," Jack began, pacing up to him with a swagger that put Thorpe on edge. "Tell me you don't love this girl. Make me believe it, and we'll go."

Four words. All he had to do was say "I don't love her," and this goddamn torture would be over. It should be simple. Open his mouth, let shit come out, end the pain.

Thorpe quickly realized that if he couldn't admit out loud that he loved Callie, he also couldn't say that he didn't love her. It was a betrayal of everything he felt, and he refused to do it.

Logan was right. When had he become a pussy? These men told their wives that they loved them every single day. They were still standing and whole. Blissfully fucking happy even. If all he had to do to hold Callie again was tell her that he loved her, would that really be so hard? If love bettered a man, why couldn't it heal him enough to make him good for her?

He sat again and hung his head, feeling a shudder work up in his chest, the lump tighten in his throat. But now was the lightest it had felt since leaving Vegas . . . and Callie. "I love her and I sent her away."

"Do you regret it?" Deke asked.

"I'm too old for her. I'm too rough for her. I'm too . . ." *Bottled up for her.*

"She doesn't see it that way, I'm guessing," Logan said.

"And that isn't what Deke asked," Hunter reminded. "Do you regret it?"

"Yes." He scrubbed a hand through his hair. It was too long, but he just hadn't found the energy to have it cut. Or to give a shit about it. "I regretted it instantly."

The door to his apartment opened again. "That's all you had to say."

Thorpe whipped his head around at that familiar voice. Sean Mackenzie stood in the entry, then closed the door behind him with a soft snick.

Staggering to his feet, Thorpe approached the man on autopilot. His relief in seeing Sean was so strong, it felt physical. Suddenly, he didn't have an elephant sitting on his chest.

Instead, he had something far more dangerous: hope.

It occurred to him that when he'd said good-bye to Callie, he hadn't just lost the woman he loved, he'd also lost a partner . . . a friend. He'd come to like Sean. Rely on him.

He swallowed. "What brings you here?"

"Callie, of course." He looked around the room at the other men. "Can you give us a minute, guys?"

Most nodded. Deke looked disappointed.

Tyler sighed noisily. "I thought I was going to get to kick some ass."

But he grinned under that put-out expression.

Luc slapped him on the back. "You really are an asshole."

"Is that supposed to be news?" Tyler snapped back.

Collective male laughter filled the air as most of the guys filed out.

Logan hung back. "Listen, I owed you for helping me straighten my shit out. This was my way of repaying you. Someday, you'll thank me, and we'll be even. Now work it out with Sean, tell Callie how you feel, and fucking be happy. I want an invitation to the wedding."

With a wink, Logan shut the door.

The silence suffocated Thorpe. His palms began to sweat. A million words crowded his brain. He didn't know which one of them to speak first.

Swallowing, he sat at the bistro table, picking at Luc's plate and took a bite. He hoped that looking busy would cut through the awkwardness, but no. He still wasn't sure what to say. And damn, that veal was really good.

"How are you not horrifically pissed off at me?" Thorpe blurted.

Sean tried not to laugh, but it still slipped out. "Who's to say I'm not?" Then he sobered. "But Callie told me about your past. I can't imagine how devastating that was. A betrayal at every level. But you know it was a long time ago, right?"

"Yes," he agreed quickly.

"And you know Callie is nothing like the woman who took advantage of you as a kid."

"Absolutely. It's me. I just closed myself off and refused to care about anyone much. I've been a miserable son of a bitch." Thorpe drew in a shuddering breath. "I just didn't know how much until her. In over twenty years, I've never told a single person that I love them."

It had always terrified him, the fear of having his heart crushed again. Callie wouldn't hurt him on purpose; he knew that in his head. But he truly loved her in a way the boy he'd once been, blind with adolescent lust, couldn't possibly comprehend. In a way his own father had never been capable of. This was so much deeper. As vital as breathing.

It gave her so much power to hurt him.

So now he'd come to a fork in the road. He knew that safety came with loneliness, sharper now because he knew exactly how precious the woman he'd lost was to him. Callie had awakened something that just wouldn't rest again: his heart. But loving without risk was impossible.

He had to make a choice.

"I can't promise you that life will always be simple," Sean said. "We're three very different people trying to make something unconventional last. But I think we've got a few things in our favor. Our differences are our strengths. If you and I were the same, she wouldn't need us both. Would it be easier on my ego if she didn't love you? Yeah. I'm sure you feel the same."

Sean was absolutely right. But this had stopped being about Thorpe's ego and started being about his heart. And about Callie's. Clearly, Sean felt the same or he wouldn't be here.

"You're right," Thorpe said.

"We've already been through some really hard times. As long as we stood together, it made us stronger. No reason to think we couldn't grow with time."

"I don't think I know how to love." That realization made Thorpe feel inadequate—something both deeply unfamiliar and uncomfortable.

"I'm not an expert, either." Sean shrugged. "I've never really tried until Callie. But I think you've been loving her for the last four years. Maybe it doesn't look like a relationship in a movie, but I don't think it has to. It just has to be honest and make us all happy."

Thorpe grunted, but he couldn't look Sean in the eye. "You make love sound easy."

"Maybe you're overcomplicating it. Put her first. Be honest. Don't let fear stop you from getting what you want."

Sean was right. So simply right that he just stared. He'd been letting fear stop him for far too long.

"I don't deserve another chance, but I want one," Thorpe murmured, then finally met the other man's gaze. "If you'll give it to me."

"Can you tell her that you love her? Look her right in the eye and swear she's the most important woman in the world to you?"

Thorpe closed his eyes and focused on every emotion he'd been trying to dam behind a wall of numbness. He pictured releasing it and just feeling whatever came. And it did. God, it was a massive flood of biblical proportions—a wave bittersweet, poignant, and painful. It robbed his breath. He gasped. Then relief came.

And he was finally able to take a deep breath without agony for the first time in weeks.

He wasn't going to be the pussy Logan accused him of being any longer. And he refused to allow Nara's indifference or his father's contempt to break him. He was going to embrace life and love. He was going to settle down, grow old with Callie, be a good friend and partner to Sean, and enjoy every moment they had together.

"I don't think I could stop myself," he admitted.

Sean smiled. "Good. The rest is up to her."

"Yeah." He sucked in a breath. "Thank you. You've always been the bigger man when it came to Callie. If she'll have me, I'll at least meet you halfway from now on. That's a promise."

Sean held out his hand. "I'll hold you to it."

Thorpe shook it, then brought the man in for a brotherly hug. He still had so many thoughts pouring through his head that he couldn't process them all, but as Sean slapped his back, he felt certain this was right.

Finally, they backed away, and Thorpe had to work to keep it together. Another stiff breath, a long pause, then he was finally able to carry on. "What's next?"

"Let me catch you up on a few things. We've intentionally kept Callie in the spotlight so the mercenaries who tried to kill her will shy away from finishing the job. We can't say it on the air, and it's classified so don't make me shoot you, but the FBI is running down the identities of those assholes. James Whitney is part of a homegrown separatist group, run by ex-military malcontents, calling themselves LOSS, or the League of Secessionist Soldiers. We're trying to figure out who's funding them. The NSA is getting involved. It seems they've been working this case from another angle. But Whitney and some of his counterparts have slipped into Mexico. They'll be caught; it's just a matter of time. The most important thing now is that Callie no longer appears to be a target."

"That's good news. I think we'd be wise to remain cautious."

"Absolutely," Sean confirmed. "The bureau has kept me on the case, so I'm up on the latest. I also have some answers to the questions I didn't have when they first sent me to watch over her. According to my boss, the bureau knew about Aslanov's genetic research and knew the later findings had disappeared. Eventually, they figured out that Daniel Howe probably had them, but before they could reach him, LOSS did. Though the Chicago PD botched things by labeling her a suspect early on, everyone in the loop here hoped Callie had important information, even if it was something she knew unconsciously. These genetic experiments are still going on, and Uncle Sam isn't excited about the idea of an army of superior soldiers under the control of people who want to overthrow our government. Hence, all the secrecy. Since Callie had proven ridiculously slippery over the years to bring in, they sent me to her, hoping I could find out what she knew before she ran again. Of course, the bureau wishes Callie would have kept some of the details in her father's notes to herself, and if my boss had given me more information about my mission, I might have been able to facilitate that, but mission accomplished. Everyone is happy."

Well, almost. Thorpe nodded. "All the douche bags who've chased her over the years, who sent them?"

"The bureau is disavowing knowledge of any bounty hunters, but personally I think they're full of shit. It might have been the NSA or some other player of Uncle Sam's who hasn't shown his cards yet. Who knows? Either way, now that the secret about the research and Daniel Howe's murder is out, Callie knows nothing else of value to make anyone want to kill her. I'm guessing the assassins were sent by LOSS. We're still running that down." Sean shrugged. "There's not much else on that front."

"Well, then, we should talk about Callie. I'm making a huge assumption that she'll actually have me back." Thorpe held his breath.

If she wouldn't, he had no one to blame but himself.

"I can't speak for her, but I can say that she hasn't been the same without you."

"During her last interview, she looked . . . I don't know, sad. Not quite complete."

Sean nodded. "She was determined not to bother you if you didn't want her, no matter how much it was hurting her."

Thorpe grunted his disbelief. "I wish she had 'bothered' me. This is probably the only time I'll ever be tempted to turn her over my knee for following my directions."

"She'd like that." Sean grinned.

"I would, too." After he kissed her, held her tight, told her that he loved her and would never let her go. "This isn't a fling for me. It's the rest of my life."

"It better be."

"But . . . you know I'm getting old. Callie is still so young."

"What, are you Old Yeller now? You think I should take you out back and shoot you? Stop. It's going to work out if you let it. Don't think about anything except that we love her and she loves us."

"You're damn smart, Mackenzie." Thorpe shook his head wryly.

"I'll remind you of that next time you think about calling me a dumbass."

Despite the moment being cloaked with laughter, Thorpe knew that he and Sean had forged a friendship with respect.

"Where is she?" Thorpe asked. "I want to see her." *Desperately. Right now.*

"At home. I didn't want to bring her here or get her hopes up unless I knew that . . ."

"I'd pulled my head out of my ass?"

"Something like that," Sean admitted. "For now, we've rented a quiet little house near Highland Park. She's there now, probably in bed reading. She likes that."

"She always has." Thorpe smiled fondly. Then worry set in. "Where does she think you are?"

"Work. I rushed out the door after I got a few calls."

"From Axel?"

"The first one came from Logan to ask if I'd come. Axel rang next with details. Luc called to ask what you like to eat. Jack called to ask me a series of questions that told me he's a scary-smart bastard. You have some interesting friends."

Thorpe smiled. He did. He'd have to thank them, too. Eating crow would suck, but they'd been right.

Now that he was determined to be with Callie, a vital question stomped across his brain. "I have to know, have you already put a ring on her finger?"

"No. It's been a whirlwind for weeks, running from one interview to the next, dealing with her estate, moving into a new place. We're finally home for a few days, so . . ." Sean shrugged.

Which meant that Sean intended to propose.

"What if . . . I married her?" When Sean opened his mouth, Thorpe's stomach tightened. "Just hear me out." He paced for a silent moment, then turned back. "You've already collared her. That's sacred. I would never try to impede on that bond. But since you've got that claim on her, I have no other way to call her mine."

Sean said nothing for a very long minute. "Are you thinking of not sharing in her submission?"

The idea was like a stab in the gut. He would take Callie however he got her, but he was a Dominant through and through. Never having her kneel or call him her Sir, not really having the authority to punish or praise her except in the most vanilla ways . . . "I want her submission more than anything."

"That's what I suspected. Have you ever thought about claiming her before?"

Sean was so unflinchingly honest and unafraid. Thorpe knew he had to be the same. "A little more than two years ago, before I knew who she really was, I was mad for her. Completely smitten. I bought this."

He turned away to his bedroom, gesturing for Sean to follow. Inside his closet, he shoved clothes aside to reveal a safe. A few turns of the dial and he was holding a black velvet box. He handed it to Sean. "Open it."

The lid opened in soft silence. Sean's eyes fell to the contents and widened. "It's beautiful. It suits her."

"That's why I bought it. I have a jeweler friend, and when I told her I'd been looking for the right something for Callie, she showed this to me. I couldn't not buy it." He sighed. "I realized Callie's identity two weeks later and tried to tell myself it was for the best."

"Why didn't you return it?"

Thorpe had asked himself that question a million times. "I couldn't bring myself to. In my head, it was made for her."

"It had to have cost you a fortune."

He laughed. "It did. And at the time, I just didn't care. She was worth every penny."

"I understand completely. If you want to see Callie now, bring that with you and be prepared to use it. I've got an idea."

* * *

CALLIE looked at the clock again. After eleven. She frowned. If Sean wasn't assigned to another case, whatever happened tonight had to be about hers. Gawd, she hoped that Whitney and his cronies hadn't cut short their Mexican vacation to come back and finish murdering her for the hell of it.

Not that Sean had left her unprotected. She more than suspected that he'd hired bodyguards to watch the house day and night. Maybe it should bother the independent woman in her, but he cared about her safety. So even though she'd learned to take care of herself, his precautions made her a little warm and fuzzy.

She focused on her e-reader again, doing her best to lose herself in a cozy mystery. It was either that or wish Sean was home. And miss Thorpe some more.

Sighing, Callie looked out the massive French doors in the master bedroom, over the expansive backyard. Dominion was out there, only twelve point two miles away—she'd mapped it out—but the distance might as well be a whole universe. Thorpe was gone. He wasn't over his past and he wasn't coming back. Callie wanted to be angry, but she was mostly sad as hell.

Her saving grace had been Sean. His love, his reassurance, his laughter were all balms to her pain. Despite their travel and hectic schedule lately, he never missed an opportunity to make love to her. His touch—frequent and adoring—always made her feel like the center of the universe. Sometimes, she couldn't help but wonder if he was trying to fill the gap left by Thorpe's absence. How did she tell him that he already filled half of her so perfectly that just being next to him sometimes made her cry because she was so blessed? She didn't expect him to fill the other half of her left bleeding and empty when Thorpe had gone. Her former boss and protector couldn't fill Sean's half, either. Neither was a substitute for the other.

She simply loved them both.

Pointless thoughts. Callie tossed the e-reader down and rose, her short black nightie swishing around her thighs.

Across the house, she heard the sound of the garage door opening, the chime of the alarm, the door shutting, the rattle of keys, the sounds of footsteps. She smiled.

Sean appeared a few seconds later, his face unreadable. He crossed the floor directly to her, took her face in his hands, and pressed a rapt kiss on her mouth. With a moan, she melted into him. Now he would take her in his arms and strip off the scrap of silk covering her. He would show her his devotion and she would give it back, opening her heart even wider to him.

Instead, he stepped away. "Kneel for me, lovely."

Oh, he was in *that* mood. They hadn't engaged in any BDSM play since the houseboat. Now that the possibility was in front of her, she realized how badly she'd missed it. Itched for it. Needed to feel as if she could put herself in the hands of the man she loved, knowing he would push her to her limits, yet trusting him utterly not to break her.

"Yes, Sir." She fell to her knees at his feet, bowed her head, and waited breathlessly. Her body began to bloom with anticipation.

Without a word, he bent to her. She heard a little click, and the wire of white gold lifted from around her neck.

He had uncollared her?

Callie gasped and looked up at Sean with horror. "W-what have I done? How have I not made you happy?"

Sean crouched in front of her and smoothed a hand against her cheek. He held her heart in his hands. He was breaking her in two, and yet he looked so excited. If he left her . . . *No!* Her chest was already splitting open at the thought.

"You make me very happy. It's a different claim I want on you now." He pulled a little velvet box from his pants, and her crushing pain transformed into astonished joy. "Callindra Alexis Howe, will you marry me? God knows I've loved you from the beginning, and I can't imagine spending much longer without making you my wife. Please say yes."

As he stood and helped her to her feet, Callie teared up. She threw herself into his arms, gripping him so tightly, overwhelmed when he held her with the same intensity. Tears fell so swiftly as her heart overflowed. She pulled back and, through her watery gaze, stared into his eyes. She wanted him to know how much she meant this.

"I love you. I don't know if you'll ever understand how much, but I'll do my best to show you every day. Yes!"

Sean pulled her in and gripped her close again, and she clung for dear life, celebrating what would be now that they'd be husband and wife, what could be once they started a family. And mourning what could never be without Thorpe.

Callie dug her fingers into Sean. She had to stop that. Thorpe could not be the specter between them. He'd made it clear that he didn't want her, and she had to exorcise him. She'd ached for family, belonging, and happiness since her father and sister had been murdered. Eventually the people responsible would get their justice. But she wouldn't forfeit the love she shared with Sean now and forever to pine for a man who wouldn't share his heart.

Gently, Sean pulled back, peppering her face with soft, sweet kisses. Then he opened the box. Callie clapped a hand over her lips, overjoyed at the beauty of the ring—and the moment.

A lovely round center stone winked up at her, surrounded by a circle of smaller diamonds. The band was covered in the same delicate stones. It wasn't extravagant. It wasn't anything like the giant rock her father had given her mother—and she was glad. What Sean had given her was absolutely perfect and what she would have picked herself.

The poignant beauty of the event only felt more complete when he slipped the ring on her finger.

"I'm going to make you happy," she whispered, smiling through her tears.

"I know. I'll do everything I can to make you happy, too, lovely." He stole another soft kiss. "I always will."

She knew that. Her neck felt naked without his mark of possession there. That didn't make her happy at all. "I could still wear your collar too, you know."

He shook his head. "It's not how I wanted to make you mine. I first put it on you under false pretenses. You first accepted it for the wrong reasons. This"—he thumbed her engagement ring—"is for us. For the right reasons. I'm going to cherish you always. Besides, something else needs to go around your neck."

Sean caressed her cheek, then walked past her, settling himself in the big club chair in the corner. What the hell was he talking about?

"Pet?"

The deep voice that haunted her now rang in her head. She had to be hallucinating. But when she zipped around, Callie knew she wasn't hearing things.

"Thorpe?" He stood there, fatigued and distinctly nervous, but as commanding as ever with his feet spread, his hands behind his back. His gray eyes penetrated her, reaching all the way to her heart with one glance.

He raised a brow at her. "That address will do for now. Kneel for me."

She whipped her gaze over to Sean, who didn't say a word. He merely watched in silence.

"You brought him here?" she asked.

"We've talked. He asked to see you," her fiancé said.

To apologize? To make some stupid amends? For sex? She turned back to Thorpe, blinking in confusion.

"You're not kneeling yet, pet." He stared expectantly at the floor, then back to her. Everything about his demeanor said that he expected to be obeyed.

"I think you should do as he asks, lovely." Sean wore a faint smile.

Their byplay reminded her of Las Vegas. They were on the same page of some agenda she didn't quite grasp. But she'd loved the results then. Despite the danger surrounding her at the time, Callie had never been happier.

She sank to her knees, the plush carpet cushioning her. She risked a glance up at Thorpe's face. His expression softened.

He caressed the crown of her head, and the touch electrified her, radiating down her spine. She'd never imagined that she would ever see him again, much less be this close. The tears of joy that had assailed her during Sean's proposal returned. Her fiancé would never have brought Thorpe here if he intended to break her heart again.

Smiling, she bowed her head. "Sir?"

"That's closer to the form of address I'd like to hear, Callie. But I want you to call me something far more important." He cradled her chin in his hand and lifted it to him. "I want to be your Master. I desire you to be my one and only pet."

He brought his other hand in front of his body, gripping an oblong black box.

Callie blinked. His face was tempered with unmistakable affection and devotion. Her heart skittered, then began to pound.

Were all her dreams really coming true?

"I'm sure you have questions for me," he murmured. "And you have every right to them. Let me see if I can answer them for you."

"Please." She could barely choke the word out past the emotion constricting her throat.

"I was an ass for leaving you. Stupid. Logan called me something less complimentary, and he was right. I've never felt so complete as when I'm with you. You fulfill all my Dominant needs when you submit . . . and you're just bratty enough to be a challenge. I can't live without you anymore. Please don't make me try. If you say yes, I will treat your submission with the utmost care. I will push your limits and keep you safe, while giving you the discipline you need and the affection you deserve. There will never be another for me, and I will never leave you again. I hope you'll consent to wear my collar and call me Master with pride."

He opened the box, and Callie was in for the second jolt of amazement for the night. Nestled in velvet lay a glittering collar. A thick length of platinum would encircle her neck, unbreakable, symbolizing their bond. The glimmering metal met in the front and would be held together by one petite lock on each side of a massive dangling center stone. The stunning aquamarine was encircled with petite diamonds and would rest right in the hollow of her throat.

Callie raised astonished eyes to him. "Are you serious?"

"I think so. He bought it for you two years ago and has held on to it," Sean supplied.

"It was made for you, pet. I've always wanted you to wear it for me. Will you have me?"

"Will you really be here tomorrow?" The question sounded as scared as she felt. Callie bit her lip.

"Every day for the rest of my life."

Thorpe said everything right . . . except those three words that had been in their way. Still, were they important? She knew he loved her. Wasn't the commitment more important than the platitude? Yes, but she still yearned for him to hold her close, look into her eyes, and tell her what was in his heart.

"Isn't that what you want to hear, pet?" Thorpe prodded.

It was enough for now. But she'd also just committed her life to

Sean. He'd brought Thorpe here, so she imagined her fiancé approved, but . . . she looked his way in question.

"Thorpe and I have talked, lovely. We're reconciled. We both felt this arrangement works best because I've always wanted to marry you. I'm more traditional." He shrugged. "My ring on your finger means everything to me. The press already has us linked romantically. This will simply seem like the natural evolution of our relationship to the outside world. Because it is."

His ring on her finger meant the world to her, and she would be proud to be his wife.

"And I've always wanted you to be my submissive," Thorpe said, his voice thick. "I've had a wife. The marriage didn't give me that deep bond of trust and understanding I've been searching for my whole life. I entered into it for the wrong reasons. The union was easily broken, and I didn't mourn its loss. What we share feels nothing like that. The minute I left you, the pain nearly crushed me. I've never collared a submissive of my own to"—he turned to Sean with a nod—"'cherish' is the perfect word. Thanks for that."

Sean smiled faintly. "You're welcome."

"I want you to be the first and the last, Callie, to enter with me into the bond I hold most sacred." Thorpe stood before her, looking vulnerable but proud. Body tall, shoulders imposing, eyes all but begging.

She melted inside. For four years, she'd watched him with sub after sub, looking for something he'd never found. The discontent she'd always seen then was gone. Her fondest fantasy when she'd lived at Dominion was to become his collared one and only. She'd always suspected that if he let himself care and took one woman as his, he would do everything to make the bond as deep and real as a marriage.

"Now, that's not to say that he won't regard you like a husband," Sean added.

"Or that Sean won't praise or punish you like your Dom when you need it." Thorpe gave her a firm nod.

She expected nothing less.

"So you've heard what we want, but the choice is yours," Thorpe said softly.

The tears she'd managed to hold at bay fell in hot rivulets down her face. She shuddered in a breath, then looked up at Thorpe with her heart in her eyes. "I accept this collar as a symbol of your ownership. To you, I pledge my obedience and my love. I have every faith that you will give me both the affection and the discipline I need. In return, I offer to you the gift of myself and am proud to call you Master."

With a look of supreme pride and shaking hands, Thorpe fastened her new collar around her neck. Fleetingly, she noticed that it felt so right as he hauled her to her feet and brought her against him. "Thank fucking God."

"Amen," Sean said, rising from the chair in the corner.

As Thorpe layered his mouth over hers for a softly commanding kiss, Sean sidled in behind her and pressed his lips to her neck. "Now get ready to hear the words I suspect you'll hear often, lovely."

Thorpe cupped her face in his hands and fused their stares together, seeing right down into her soul. "I love you, Callie. You will hear it often. I hope you can get used to it."

The joy exploded inside her, and she was left gloriously bleeding with emotion, speechless, and so ready for the future.

"I love you, too, Mitchell." She turned in his arms to face Sean. "And I love you, Sean. My world is forever changed to the most beautiful existence possible because of you."

Sean kissed her forehead, her nose, then lingered at her lips. "I love you, and I'm sure you'll hear it from me often as well. But that wasn't what I was referring to."

"Oh?" She sent him a beguiling smile.

"I'm sure not, pet."

Callie cast Thorpe a glance over her shoulder. It warmed her to know that her acceptance of their bond put that contented look on his face.

"So what else did you mean to say?" She smiled coyly.

Thorpe drew in a deep breath. His shoulders rose, his chest widened. He wore his authority like a well-made suit as he gave her his first command as her Master. "Strip."

She flushed from head to toe. She'd been expecting it, and it still made her tingle, made her body burn with anticipation.

"Yes, Master."

Sean caressed her shoulder, and her gaze lifted to his face, the longing in his eyes. She answered back with a kiss.

"Now, lovely, if you please."

A smile broke out across her face. Her world was perfect. "My pleasure."

His to Take

Racing against time, NSA agent Joaquin Muñoz is searching for a little girl who vanished nearly twenty years ago with a dangerous secret. Since Bailey Benson fits the profile, Joaquin abducts the beauty and whisks her to the safety of Club Dominion—before anyone can silence her for good.

At first, Bailey is terrified, but when her kidnapper demands information about her past, she's stunned. Are her horrific visions actually distant memories that imperil all she holds dear? Confined with Joaquin in a place that echoes with moans and breathes passion, he proves himself a fierce protector as well as a sensual Master who's slowly crawling deeper into her head . . . and her heart. But giving in to him might be the most delicious danger of all.

Because Bailey soon learns that her past isn't the only mystery. Joaquin has a secret of his own—a burning vengeance in his soul. The exposed truth leaves her vulnerable and wondering how much about the man she loves is a lie, how much more is at risk than her heart. And if she can trust him to protect her long enough to learn the truth.

About the Author

Shayla Black is the *New York Times* and *USA Today* bestselling author of more than forty sizzling contemporary, erotic, paranormal, and historical romances produced via traditional, small press, independent, and audio publishing. She lives in Texas with her husband, munchkin, and one very spoiled cat. In her "free" time, she enjoys watching reality TV, reading, and listening to an eclectic blend of music.

Shayla's books have been translated in about a dozen languages. She has also received or been nominated for the Passionate Plume, the Holt Medallion, Colorado Romance Writers Award of Excellence, and the National Readers Choice Award. RT BOOKclub has twice nominated her for Best Erotic Romance of the Year, and also awarded her several Top Picks and a KISS Hero Award.

A writing risk-taker, Shayla enjoys tackling writing challenges with every new book. Find Shayla at ShaylaBlack.com or visit her Shayla Black Author Facebook page.